PAYBACK

PAYBACK

NANCY ALLEN

GRAND
CENTRAL

New York Boston

Copyright © 2023 by Assemble Content LLC

Cover design by Elizabeth Connor.
Cover images: running man on bridge © Silas Manhood; running woman © CollaborationJS / Trevillion; NYC skyline by Matteo Colombo / Getty. Cover copyright © 2023 by Hachette Book Group, Inc.

Grand Central Publishing
Hachette Book Group
1290 Avenue of the Americas, New York, NY 10104
grandcentralpublishing.com
twitter.com/grandcentralpub

First Edition: May 2023

Grand Central Publishing is a division of Hachette Book Group, Inc. The Grand Central Publishing name and logo is a trademark of Hachette Book Group, Inc.

The publisher is not responsible for websites (or their content) that are not owned by the publisher.

The Hachette Speakers Bureau provides a wide range of authors for speaking events. To find out more, go to www.hachettespeakersbureau.com or call (866) 376-6591.

Grand Central Publishing books may be purchased in bulk for business, educational, or promotional use. For information, please contact your local bookseller or the Hachette Book Group Special Markets Department at special.markets@hbgusa.com.

Print book interior design by Marie Mundaca.

Library of Congress Cataloging-in-Publication Data
Names: Allen, Nancy (Lawyer), author.
Title: Payback / Nancy Allen.
Description: First edition. | New York : GCP, 2023. | Series: Anonymous justice ; [2]
Identifiers: LCCN 2022057848 | ISBN 9781538719190 (trade paperback) | ISBN 9781538719206 (ebook)
Subjects: LCGFT: Detective and mystery fiction. | Novels.
Classification: LCC PS3601.L4333 P39 2023 | DDC 813/.6--dc23/eng/20221212
LC record available at https://lccn.loc.gov/2022057848

ISBNs: 978-1-5387-1919-0 (trade paperback), 978-1-5387-1920-6 (ebook)

Printed in the United States of America

LSC-C

Printing 1, 2023

To Randy

PROLOGUE

Whitney

ONLY TWO WEEKS prior, Whitney Novak had never seen the inside of a jail. She'd read about incarceration in the media and in fiction, of course. Watched news coverage on TV. From that exposure, she had assumed she understood the challenges a person might face in jail.

There was the essential loss of liberty, obviously, and the horror of being confined without the power to come and go at will. She knew inmates encountered violence, from fellow prisoners and guards. And she understood that incarceration robbed individuals of their dignity as well as their bodily autonomy.

What she hadn't anticipated, though, was the smell.

The dormitory where Whitney was housed at Rosie's—the Rose M. Singer Center for women on Rikers Island, New York—had a stink that was almost indescribable. In the lockup facility she shared, the mingled funk of forty-nine other unwashed inmates hit Whitney's senses like a blow from a truncheon. The dorm held women of all ages, sharing five

1

toilets and a couple of sinks, with limited access to basic toiletries or laundry. She still hadn't adjusted to the stench.

It was a price she had to pay for her decision to join the group.

As Whitney huddled on the narrow bed assigned to her, she reflected on the association that had landed her in Rosie's. She had lots of time to think about it. She wasn't going anywhere.

Months ago, she had been invited to join a group. A circle of talented misanthropes. Each one had his or her personal issues.

Not long ago, there had been nine of them. But she only knew where four of the others were right now.

As Whitney took shallow breaths through her mouth, she did a mental tabulation of the membership. Steven was a medical doctor who had stumbled into drug addiction. In recovery, or so he claimed. Rod battled PTSD, a product of his military service. That went with the territory. But in a fight, Rod was the man you'd want on your side. His girlfriend, Millie, was a drama queen who bitched about her anxiety disorder like it was a mark of pride.

Whitney had her own quirk. She was a gambling addict—bad enough to ruin a stellar career in finance. Before she landed at Rosie's, she'd been working hard to turn it around. Trying to stay out of casinos, to avoid scratching that itch.

The final member of the group was Kate Stone.

They had all been handpicked by a powerful figure, brought together for a worthy mutual goal: to deliver justice when the legal system slipped up. When the courts let people slip by without consequences for their actions, their group stepped in, wreaking swift, efficient payback. Sometimes it was personal, other times it was a matter of principle. It was a heady undertaking, a satisfying quest. The fellowship. The power. Whitney had sincerely enjoyed it. The group association had involved a gamble, and Whitney was drawn by the thrill of the game, the uncertainty of the outcome. And always, the possibility of a big payoff.

Until Kate had come along and screwed everything up. To fix the mess, the group had no choice but to resort to violence, and Whitney had been the only one brave enough to step up. It was all part of the group dynamic.

And she'd ended up behind bars. Facing felony charges that would be tough to beat.

In a bed nearby, one of her fellow inmates broke wind. When Whitney heard the audible warning, she buried her face in the fabric of her dirty jumpsuit and held her breath.

While she fought the urge to breathe, resentment created a ball in her chest that felt like it might explode. *I didn't sign on for this part, never agreed to this,* she thought.

Squeezing her eyes shut, she wished she'd never encountered any of the people in the circle of oddball vigilantes. Wished she'd never been lured into involvement by their dynamic leader. Fervently wished she could set back the clock, go many months into the past to unsee and undo everything she'd witnessed. Everything she'd done. Over the past year, she'd been exposed to ugly, vicious realities.

She'd also discovered a side to her nature she hadn't fully appreciated. And had tapped into a capacity for violence that until now had lain dormant.

All Whitney had wanted was a taste of justice. A righteous reckoning, on her own terms. If she had known the price she'd have to pay, she would never have ventured into the scheme and been ensnared in the trap.

A nagging voice whispered in her head: *You never know when to quit.* That was true enough. It wasn't a novel realization. She'd experienced the same compulsion many times, at craps tables, card tables, even the penny slots. She knew what gambler's remorse felt like. She was intimately acquainted with the phenomenon.

And Whitney had a bad case of gambler's remorse as she huddled on a jailhouse cot.

She had gambled with her life, and she'd lost. The absurdity almost made her laugh. And she'd thought she'd never laugh again.

A buzz followed by a grating metallic noise had become a familiar sound in lockup. She lifted her head to watch a guard enter the dorm. It was a woman, young enough to be Whitney's daughter—if she'd ever had a daughter. The officer kept one hand on the door as she called out, "Whitney Novak!"

It took Whitney a moment to react. She tried to think: Was she in some kind of trouble? She had tried to keep her head low, acquiring goods from the commissary to buy the goodwill of her fellow inmates. Maybe it was a visitor. But Whitney had received no visitors, to date. No one had traveled to Rikers Island to check on her—not even the attorney she hired had made the journey. She was bereft, totally on her own.

At the delay, a shade of irritation crossed the guard's face. "Novak! You deaf?"

"I'm here," Whitney said, dropping her feet to the floor and slipping them into flip-flops. She hurried over to the door where the guard stood. "Where am I going?"

The guard didn't offer an explanation. She cuffed Whitney's hands behind her back before leading her through a maze of hallways. Voices clamored all around, heightening Whitney's tension as she shuffled along.

"Am I going to court? Has a hearing been set?"

If so, she hadn't been notified. But communications in lockup were scant. She'd contacted her lawyer after she was arrested but had only had a brief meeting with him, over a week ago. It was a virtual conference, much of which concerned the retainer he required up front. When they finally discussed her case, the conversation hadn't been encouraging.

After a long walk, through barred doors and locked barriers, the guard delivered Whitney into a holding area where another corrections officer handed her a bundle. As she inspected it with shaking hands, Whitney was amazed to see that it was her own clothing, the pants and shirt she'd been wearing when she was arrested and taken into custody.

The guard didn't waste any words. "Get dressed."

Whitney clutched the bundle to her chest like a beloved infant. "For court? Am I going to court?"

"You're getting out. The bondsman's waiting. He's got the paperwork."

Whitney didn't argue. She stumbled as she stripped out of the jailhouse scrubs and stepped into the pants. She was trying to move fast before someone realized the mistake.

She shouldn't be leaving. Not Whitney. She was being held without bond.

For attempting to kill Kate Stone.

CHAPTER 1

Kate

THE LANDING AT LaGuardia was bumpy. We jostled in our seats as the plane hit the runway, and I inadvertently nailed the guy sitting next to me with my elbow.

"Sorry," I said.

He didn't respond. Maybe I didn't sound sufficiently apologetic. I brushed it off. It was LaGuardia.

The rain beat against the oval windowpanes as I waited to deplane. The stormy skies conveyed a moody welcome back to the city. That morning, I had made a hasty departure from my Florida vacation, where my mother and brother were still soaking up the sun. It looked like I'd be soaking up the rain as soon as I left the airport.

While I waited for the pilot to turn off the "fasten seatbelt" light, I pulled out my phone. I saw that my mom had called during the flight. She left a message. The transcript of her recorded voice jumped out of the screen at me, as if it was relayed in all capital letters, like she was shouting.

Do not get in touch with anyone from that support group when you return to the city. Do you hear me? It's a toxic circle. They're all suspect, every one of them. You don't know who you can trust.

Same old Mom. I deleted the message and hit my Twitter icon, just to kill some time. Scanning the home page, a post caught my eye. Someone I followed had retweeted a local headline: "Woman Jumps to Her Death in Midtown." I scrambled to turn off the phone and let the screen go dark. I couldn't read stories about jumpers. They triggered me, ever since my dad died.

Finally, we were allowed to deplane. As I wheeled my regulation-sized overhead compartment bag past the baggage claim carousels, a small cluster of limo drivers stood between me and the door, holding signs for passengers. I ignored them, even though a guy with dark hair slicked back in a ponytail held a handwritten card that read "Stone."

My surname is common. And I've never hired a private car in my twenty-eight years. So I was surprised when he followed me to the exit.

"Miss Stone?" he called.

Sure, I heard him. I kept walking. Like I said, I didn't hire the guy.

"Kate Stone?"

That stopped me. I whirled around, twisting my bag on one wheel. "Who are you?" I said.

He grinned, revealing a blinding smile marred by one crooked eye tooth. "Miss Stone, your mother ordered a limo. Well, a private car, technically. It's not a stretch. Don't want to get your hopes up."

I gave him a closer inspection. Sounding skeptical, I said, "I don't know what you're talking about."

He pulled out his cell phone and checked the screen. "You're Kate Stone, right? Your mother is Patricia Stone? She hired a ride to pick you up at LaGuardia and take you to your building in Morningside Heights. Said you were coming in on American flight one-eight-eight-six."

He held out the phone, adding, "It looks like you."

A screenshot on the phone displayed the photo my mother posted on her business website, stone&stonenjlaw.com. It was a fairly current headshot of me, dressed in business attire. The picture wasn't particularly flattering. I looked slightly angry—not an uncommon expression for me. Some people thought I had a bona fide anger management problem.

So the picture the driver held was undeniably me. Still, I hesitated. I'd just read a message from Mom. She didn't mention anything about a private car.

The driver nodded at my suitcase. "Can I take your bag, Kate?"

"No." I clutched the handle with a tight grasp. "Do you have any identification?"

I wasn't always paranoid, but I had experienced a recent brush with danger. After joining a support group that included deranged vigilantes who made attempts on my life, I didn't like surprise encounters.

One thing in the phone message from my mother had been spot-on. I didn't know who I could trust, not anymore.

He pulled out a plastic ID that identified him as an employee of Embassy Limousines of Bayside, Queens. The picture matched the guy, and even showed him with a grin that displayed his crooked tooth.

I pulled out my phone and hit my mother's cell number. "I'm just going to double-check."

While the phone hummed, a stranger gave me a shove. We were blocking the exit, apparently. I stepped out of the way, silently cursing my mother for failing to answer her phone. When it went to voice mail, I tapped the screen again.

"Is there a problem?" the driver asked. He didn't sound offended. When I glanced up from the phone, I observed he had nice eyes, with long eyelashes.

"Sorry about the delay, but I'm going to make another call." I hit my brother's number. Leo always had his phone at hand. He'd be able to run Mom down.

"Kate!" Leo sounded positively delighted to hear from me, even though he'd last seen me a few hours before, when I got into a taxi at the Fort Lauderdale resort. "How was your flight?"

"It was okay."

"How's everything in New York? Have you made it to your apartment?"

"Not yet. Leo, I'm at the airport and there's a driver here. He says Mom hired him to pick me up."

"Oh. That's nice."

"Did she mention anything about it?"

"No. But you know Mom. She doesn't generally seek my advice or approval."

That was true. I glanced at the driver. He smiled at me, with the same expression I'd seen on his ID.

"Let me talk to her."

"She's not here. She's at the resort spa, getting a massage."

"Shit."

"Yeah, sorry about that. She said she'd be back in a couple of hours. She's getting some treatments. The Swedish massage, then a facial and an eyebrow wax."

Well, so much for raising my mother. She didn't allow interruptions during spa treatments. I was familiar with that policy.

When I ended the call, the driver reached for the handle of my suitcase. "I can take this for you. Embassy Limousines likes our passengers to enjoy a red-carpet experience. We have a five-star rating."

"Great." I let him take the bag.

He wheeled it to the automatic sliding door. "We're in the parking garage. Do you mind walking? It's not far."

"Sure. No problem."

I felt awkward as I followed in the guy's footsteps. My mother loves five-star treatment, but it isn't my style. And as we tramped down the pavement and through the garage, it became apparent that he had fibbed to me. The car was parked at a pretty long distance.

We finally walked up to a shiny black Suburban. The driver popped the trunk of the vehicle and tossed my bag inside, then held the back passenger door open for me.

Before I slid across the seat, I thought to ask, "What did you say your name was?"

"Nick," he said, before pushing the door firmly shut.

Well, shit.

That was alarming. Because I was pretty sure his ID said his name was Christopher.

CHAPTER 2

"HEY, NICK, CAN I see your ID again?"

He didn't answer, just kept driving. While I waited, I started feeling decidedly edgy. As we neared an intersection, he hit the brakes. Shooting a glance into the rearview mirror, he said, "Sure. When we get to your apartment, I'll show it to you."

I didn't want to wait, I wanted to see it immediately. His power game sent my discomfort into the red zone. When we came to a full stop at a red light, I decided to bail out of the vehicle. I was uneasy with the guy, and I'd learned to trust my gut. I figured I could get my suitcase from the car service later.

But when I grabbed the door handle and tried to open the door, it remained firmly shut. I tried a second time, throwing my shoulder into it. Didn't budge.

I kept my tone good-natured. "Uh, Nick, the doors back here won't open. You got me locked in?"

The traffic light turned green, and he hit the accelerator a little too hard; the car bolted through the intersection, jerking me back against the seat.

"Yeah, that's company policy. We don't want kids falling out of the car and getting hurt."

Though the car was moving, I pulled on the handle again. "I'm no kid."

"Right. We don't want any customers falling out. Of any age."

This time, when I spoke, my voice had a definite edge. "Let's turn off the childproof lock, okay? It makes me feel claustrophobic."

"Just sit back and enjoy the ride, ma'am."

"I can't enjoy it if I feel trapped. It gives me the jitters."

"Ma'am, I promise, when you arrive at your destination, I'll pull the door open for you with my own hands."

That wasn't the response I wanted to hear. His refusal made me genuinely agitated. I started to get hot, felt like I couldn't breathe. I pushed the button to roll down the window, to get a breath of the murky air of Queens.

No luck. He'd childproofed the windows.

I pulled my phone from my pocket. If the driver wouldn't listen to me, I needed to go over his head, like a middle-aged woman demanding to speak to the manager.

"What's the phone number for Embassy Limo?"

"Why do you need it?"

"So I can tell your employer they need to revise this practice of locking the customers in. It's bad business, you know why? Because there's liability under state law for false imprisonment. It's illegal, an intentional tort." I started rubbing the web of skin between my thumb and finger. It was an old habit. Since I was a kid, I unconsciously did the move whenever I was tense.

Without taking his eyes from the road, he tossed his ID into the back. It fell on the floorboard, by my feet. When I picked it up, I studied the photo again. It was a good match, definitely the man behind the wheel. And my recollection was accurate. The card identified him as Christopher Romano.

A phone number was listed for the business. When I tapped it onto my phone, I waited for someone to pick up. My call went straight to voice mail. No business recording, just an instruction to leave a message.

I did, a brief message giving my name and stating my business, asking for a return call. When I ended the call, I hit the camera app on my iPhone. Just as I held my phone up to take a photo of the guy's ID, he reached into the back and grabbed the laminated card out of my hand.

Trying to keep my voice casual, I said, "So why'd your employer mess up your name on the ID?"

"Small mistake."

"Getting your name wrong? That's a big mistake. What about payroll?"

"They didn't get it wrong. My name's Christopher, my friends call me Nick. It's a nickname."

I wanted to argue with him, to tell him that Nick isn't a nickname for Christopher, never has been. You don't have to be born Italian to know that.

He was driving fast, tearing through neighborhood streets of Queens like he was running late to something. And he was taking a weird route, one I'd never traveled in my life.

"Why'd you get off the BQE? Aren't you taking the Triborough Bridge?"

"What?"

"The Triborough Bridge, Robert F. Kennedy Bridge. That's

the best route to my neighborhood. Are you getting paid by the mile? That's kind of a scam."

"Why do you bitch so much? Why don't you shut your mouth?"

Something was definitely off. A young guy might get away with saying that to me, if he used the right tone—joking, like he was just messing with me. But this driver wasn't trying to be funny. His voice was gruff. He genuinely wanted to shut me up. The affable limo driver had disappeared, and I was nervous to be in the power of the persona he was sharing with me now.

His eyes were reflected in the rearview mirror, the dark eyes with long lashes. They didn't look so nice anymore. They were hard, cold.

Leaning to the side, I could see his hands clenching the steering wheel with a compulsive grip. My fight-or-flight reaction kicked into high gear. As we approached another intersection, I said, "Pull over by that pharmacy. I'm getting out."

Instead of applying the brakes, he hit the accelerator and sped through a red light. We narrowly avoided a collision with a silver minivan. I heard the screech of the van's tires and the wail of the horn.

I tossed the phone on the seat next to me and unbuckled my seat belt. Reaching over the driver's shoulder, I tried to hit the lock controls on the armrest of his car door.

He hit my hand with his fist, yelling, "Get back! Sit down and buckle up."

Yeah, that wasn't happening. I pushed my upper body past his headrest and had just managed to hit the lock control when he elbowed me squarely in the nose with his left arm.

The blow dazed me. I backed off, falling into the back seat with my hands over my nose. Blood gushed from both my nostrils, making my fingers sticky. I rubbed my hands on the upholstery to dry them and then lunged back over the driver's seat and grabbed his ponytail.

"Stop the damn car," I yelled, giving his hair a vicious twist and jerking his head back.

He kept driving, gunning the engine. Panicking, I looked through the windshield, watching the car speed close to a deserted green space. I didn't see any bystanders or pedestrians in sight. Reaching around his headrest, I got the driver in a choke hold with my right arm, trying to grab the steering wheel with my left hand.

His hands left the steering wheel to grasp my arm, and the car veered out of control, spinning off the roadway and onto the grass. When the Suburban rolled, I shut my eyes and hung on to the driver's neck with both arms. His seat belt held him in place, but I was thrown around the vehicle like a kernel of corn in a popper.

When the car landed upside down, the driver was still buckled in, wrestling with the deployed airbag. I tried to open the door, but it remained firmly shut. While he punched the airbag, cursing, I used both feet to kick out the back passenger window. It took three tries, but I busted it out just as the driver unbuckled himself. As I escaped the vehicle, there was a thump when he fell to the roof of the overturned car. It must have hurt, I heard him howl. He was cursing as I crawled through the window and struggled to stand.

Looking around, I had no problem getting my bearings. I stood in Gantry Plaza State Park. The East River was behind me. The Suburban had landed in direct sight of the iconic four-story Pepsi-Cola sign in Long Island City, Queens.

CHAPTER 3

I MOVED AWAY from the vehicle as fast as my battered knee let me. My nose throbbed with pain. The blood had flowed all the way down my chin, dripping onto my shirt and staining it.

A crowd of curious onlookers assembled on the sidewalks outside the park. I was glad to see them, especially a couple of young guys holding up their cell phones to record the crash. I hobbled directly into their midst, because I figured there was safety in numbers. The Suburban driver wouldn't be inclined to follow me or attempt to grab me in the presence of witnesses. I hoped not, anyway.

Curious stares met me as I limped down the sidewalk. One woman said, "Hey! You okay?"

I ignored the question. She didn't need to be entangled in my drama. On a street corner in the distance, a neon sign blinked at me. I headed for that.

Inside the pub, I walked up to the bar and called out to the bartender. "You got a phone I can use?"

He gave me an uneasy glance and scooted several steps away from me. I couldn't fault his reaction. In the mirror behind the bottles of liquor at the bar, I saw the reflection of a woman who'd been in a brawl. My hair was wild, my shirt spattered with the blood that still ran from my nose and was smeared across my face.

I tried again. "I've been in a wreck. Did you see that car go out of control? Black Suburban? It's sitting upside down by the Pepsi sign."

"Yeah, I heard it. Somebody was driving batshit crazy." He looked impressed, actually.

"Right, the driver was dangerous, that's why I had to get away. But my phone is somewhere in that car. And I need to call 911."

"To report the collision. Okay, sure. You need an ambulance?"

"No, I'm all right. Pretty much." I studied my reflection again. A knot on my forehead had already started to swell, and I was afraid he'd broken my nose with the elbow jab. I felt like I'd been on the losing end of a boxing match, but I didn't need an EMT. I could get a better level of care for free, if someone would just hand me a damned phone.

The bartender pulled a cell phone from his pocket. I could see him hesitate. He really didn't want to hand it over to a blood-spattered stranger. I had to wonder—what did he think I was gonna do? Grab it and run off? He could easily overtake me with my bum knee. After a minute, he looked down at the phone and tapped the screen. "I'll call 911 for you. We're really not supposed to let customers use our phones. It's a privacy issue."

I knew what the problem was. My hands were sticky with blood. No one in his right mind would want to hand me his cell phone.

There was nothing to do but wait. I hobbled up to the bar and took a seat. After twenty minutes, a uniformed NYPD officer finally walked in. I was still sitting on the barstool, sipping my second gin and tonic. Thank God I carried my wallet and ID in my pocket. The bartender wasn't giving away any pity cocktails.

The cop, a woman named Anita Gomez, took my report. When she asked, I gave her a detailed recitation of the facts. Nevertheless, she didn't look particularly convinced when I informed her I'd been the victim of an attempted abduction. She cut her eyes at my highball glass, as if calculating the odds that I was manufacturing facts to cover up my own wrongdoing.

"We've been to the scene at the collision. We didn't find another party over there," she said. "The driver you described has disappeared, I guess. You sure you're remembering everything clearly?"

Oh. Great, I thought. She didn't believe me. Apparently, Officer Gomez thought I was a flake, or something worse. Maybe she thought I was behind the wheel. If I wasn't careful, she'd be subjecting me to a series of sobriety tests, and I didn't feel up to standing on one leg or touching my fingers to my sore nose.

I put on my best, no-nonsense attorney voice. "I'm absolutely certain. Did you talk to any of the bystanders? There were a bunch of people gathered around when I crawled out of the car."

"We asked around. But I didn't find any witnesses to the actual event."

"Officer, there were multiple witnesses to the collision," I insisted. "They were taking video. I saw them."

In a flat voice, the cop said, "If you say so. Too bad you didn't stick around and get their names. Um, you got any idea why someone would pick you up at the airport and try to abduct you?"

I wondered whether she'd be familiar with my story. She was a Queens cop, but it would have made the rounds in law enforcement circles, due to my father's longtime career at the NYPD.

"A couple of weeks ago, I was the victim of two separate attacks on my life."

She'd been taking notes, but at that point she paused and made eye contact. Her expression was skeptical. She thought I was a nut.

"I'm a former assistant DA in Rubenstein's office, just resigned this year. His office has charged Whitney Novak with multiple counts after she attacked me and my brother at Bellevue. Another patient was murdered. Maybe you read about it."

I saw the moment she made the connection. "You're Morris Stone's daughter."

"Yep."

Her demeanor changed. She gave me a sympathetic look. "That was a real tragedy, your dad's suicide. Some of the older guys in my precinct knew him. They were real torn up when he jumped out of the window a few years back."

The topic made me tear up; I could feel it in my nose, which already hurt like hell. "He didn't jump."

I knew that most people believed my father committed suicide to avoid testifying against his fellow cops in a manslaughter trial, but I would never believe it. Someday, I was determined I would clear his name.

She blinked, then switched the topic. "Your case was big news. You were shoved onto the subway tracks in Midtown, weren't you? Close to Times Square."

I nodded, glad to get away from the dicey subject of my father's demise. "That's me."

"They were talking about it at the station, and I read it in the *Post*. They had a picture of you strapped onto the gurney when they put you in the ambulance."

When I'd seen the picture, I didn't recognize myself. That was a weird feeling. *Scary.*

"I don't remember being in the ambulance, actually. I don't remember anything after I landed on the tracks."

She gave a shrill whistle, and said, "You were damned lucky."

"True that." Cautiously, I dabbed at the drying blood circling my nose. "I'm starting to wonder how long my luck can hold out."

Shaking her head, the officer muttered something under her breath. It sounded like she said my luck might have run out already. I took that as a discouraging sign. I tend to be superstitious. Though I try to fight it, I pick up on omens. At least, I think I do.

She said, "Why are these people messing with you? What have you got on them? You were in the DA's office for a while, isn't that right?"

"I don't know why they're messing with me. If I could figure that out, I'd be in a lot more comfortable position."

She put her notes away. Speaking briskly, she said, "Okay, Ms. Stone, they tell me you have refused medical aid. You sure?"

"I'm sure. I know a doctor. He's a personal friend."

"Is someone coming to help you get home? You look pretty beat up. I'd hate to see you on public transit with that face. The more vulnerable a woman looks, the more likely she is to become a target."

I sighed, hoping she'd lend a hand. "I made a speedy exit from the Suburban, left my phone behind. Did you locate my cell phone at the accident scene? My suitcase was in the back of the vehicle, too."

"We found a phone in the vehicle." She pulled a cell from her pocket. I groaned with relief. It was mine; I recognized the case. I extended my hand to take the phone but she held it out of reach.

"What's the password? Not that I think you're lying. I just have to take the precaution."

I recited the number. She tapped it in, and the screen-shot appeared. Handing the phone over, she sounded contrite. "Nice picture of you and your dad."

"Thanks." It was a good picture, a selfie I'd taken of the two of us, the day I was sworn into the New York Bar Association. I hit the phone icon and started to enter a number. Then I paused.

My mother's warning popped into my head, unbidden. I could hear her voice in my ear. *Do not get in touch with anyone from that support group.*

As I tapped the screen to call Steven Salinas, her voice shouted inside my head. *Toxic! Do you hear me?*

The officer said, "So who's coming for you? Boyfriend?"

The question gave me pause. How would I describe my relationship with Steven? We met months ago at an anger management support group in Midtown. He'd followed me afterward and asked me to join a different session, a group of individuals who tried to correct injustice when the legal system failed.

Steven and I forged a definite connection. We certainly enjoyed a sexual chemistry. But I didn't want to overstate our relationship. Also, the term "boyfriend" had a juvenile ring. He wasn't a boy, he was all grown up. We weren't a couple of teenagers, going steady.

I tried to sound totally cool as I said, "Steven is just a guy I've been seeing."

She laughed at that. "Easy to tell you're a lawyer, you don't want to give a straight answer."

Steven's cell phone was ringing. When he picked up, a wave of relief rolled over me. "Steven! Hey, I'm back in the city, but I was in a car wreck, and I'm stuck in Queens. And I've got some injuries. Nothing critical, but I'd really appreciate you taking a look. Can you come?"

I gave him the address, and when I ended the call, Officer Gomez was still standing beside me. "Is he coming?"

"Yeah. He said he'll be here as soon as he can."

"Where is he now?"

"He's at work. In Harlem."

She gave a thoughtful nod. "Okay then, it's a test. You

know how long it takes to get from Harlem to Queens. How motivated is he to come to the rescue?"

"What are you talking about?"

"If he's here in less than thirty minutes, he's your boyfriend."

Steven walked through the door of the bar in Queens in exactly twenty-eight minutes.

CHAPTER 4

TWENTY-EIGHT MINUTES made it official.

Having an unlicensed medical doctor as a boyfriend carries distinct benefits. Steven cleaned up my bloody nose and then examined it as I sat at the bar. The bartender obligingly provided a bag of ice when Steven requested it. I held the ice to my face while Steven checked a bump on my head and tended the injured knee. He recommended RICE: rest, ice, compression, and elevation.

He even ran to the scene with Officer Gomez and rescued my suitcase before the car was towed away. When he returned, he checked my nose a second time.

"We need bags of frozen peas," he said, as he tilted my head back and peered up into my nostrils.

"Frozen peas?"

"They cover the injury better than ice cubes. Any chance we can find them in your apartment?"

The question made me laugh despite my aches. "Peas? Steven, what do you think?"

He met my eye, grinning. He knew the answer. Not much cooking goes on in my studio apartment on 124th Street. "After I get you settled in, I'll go pick some up. Do you think your neighborhood bodega carries them?"

"I can't say for sure. I know they carry beer in six-packs and twelve-packs."

"Beer cans won't keep the swelling down," he said, pulling out his phone. Steven called for an Uber, and we went outside to wait for them by the curb. I was grateful for the driver, this time. I wasn't up for a forty-minute train ride, and Steven thought I needed to get home as soon as possible.

When we arrived at my six-story brick apartment building in Morningside Heights, I pulled the front door open and walked straight into the lobby.

Steven said, "The landlord needs to fix that, Kate. Anyone can come in off the street and walk straight into your building. It's a dangerous security lapse for a building in the city. And especially risky for you."

I shrugged. "I mention it to the super whenever I see him, I'm like a broken record. And I complain to the landlord every month when I pay the rent. They're not too interested."

The ancient elevator rumbled and the door slowly opened. An old lady emerged, pulling her portable shopping cart behind her. When she saw us, her wrinkled face lit up.

"Hey, Kate! Look, the elevator's working today!"

Limping toward it, I said, "Edie, that's really good timing. I've got a messed-up knee."

Squinting, she tottered up to me and inspected my face through her cat-eye glasses. "Looks like your nose is messed up, too. And you've got a nasty knot on your head. Did your boyfriend take a swing at you?" Her eyes shifted to Steven with a suspicious glare.

"Edie, I was in a wreck, got thrown around the car. Don't blame Steven, he's an innocent party. He helped to patch me up."

The explanation appeared to satisfy her. She toddled off with her shopping cart. "Fasten your seat belt next time, honey."

When we got into the tiny elevator car with my suitcase, I pushed the button for the sixth floor, thankful that I wouldn't have to flex my knee up all of those flights of stairs.

As the elevator door was closing, Edie called out to me, "Bad news, Kate! Someone on the sixth floor let their garbage rot! You gonna have to hold your nose."

Her message made me nervous. As the rumbling elevator slowly ascended, I tried to remember. Had I thrown all of the food out before I left for my Florida vacation? It seemed like I had cleared everything out of the fridge and tossed it in a trash can. But I didn't specifically recall whether I'd taken the trash bag to the garbage chute.

My guilty suspicion ballooned when the elevator ground to a stop on the sixth floor. My apartment was located at the end of the hallway. When Steven and I got off, I detected a distinctly unpleasant odor which grew stronger as we neared my place. I unlocked the door to apartment 6E. Stepping over the threshold, I gagged at the fetid stench that assaulted me.

My arm automatically jerked up to cover my nose, jarring the injured cartilage. "Ouch! Shit, that hurts."

Steven sidestepped me and strode over to the window. Unlocking it, he pulled up the sash. The air from the street wafted in, but it didn't provide any relief from the disgusting stink. A ball of dread squeezed my chest as I bypassed my bed to walk over to the kitchenette. The garbage can was empty. When I checked inside the refrigerator, I only found a bottle of ketchup and some packets of horseradish sauce.

As I stood looking inside the refrigerator, three bloated houseflies buzzed me, attacking my face. I slapped them away, swearing, before I called to Steven in the next room. "Steven, there's no garbage in here, no food. I don't know what I left to rot that went bad and make this wretched funk."

"It's not rotten food causing this, Kate. Smells like something died, I'm afraid. Hope it wasn't trapped inside the wall." He opened the door to my tiny bathroom and stepped inside. I saw him check the toilet. "No problems here. Your bathroom's okay."

More flies were circling my Murphy bed. The bed was down, resting on the floor; it had been pulled from its storage place in the wall. A cloud of flies buzzed around the sheets and over the covers. When I studied it, I experienced a sinking feeling. Because I wouldn't have left the unmade bed out on the floor before going to the airport two weeks earlier. My apartment was a one-room studio, and the bed took up a lot of space, didn't leave any room to walk around. So I always pushed it back into the wall when I got out of bed in the morning.

Tentatively, I stepped up to the bed. Though I kept my hand cupped over my nose, I couldn't block the stench, it was unbearable. Looking down at the rumpled blankets, there was a lump under the covers, too small to be a pillow. I grabbed the sheet and jerked it down.

And then I shrieked when I beheld it, a huge rat decomposing in my bed. Its body crawled with maggots. The white larva squirmed and wriggled in the rat's decaying flesh.

I gagged again, covering my mouth as I ran to the kitchenette. I gripped the kitchen counter and retched over the kitchen sink. The flies followed me again, buzzing around my head as I puked.

I heard Steven shout when he saw it. "Jesus! Shit!"

He had more intestinal fortitude than I possessed. While I heaved into the sink, he rolled the rat up in my bedsheet and ran for the stairway.

When my dry heaves subsided, I turned on the kitchen tap and ran cold water, cupping my hands together and splashing it onto my face. Almost ten minutes passed before I heard Steven return to the apartment, slamming the door shut behind him. He headed directly for the bathroom, turned the faucet full blast and scrubbed his hands in the bathroom sink. While he soaped up, I stumbled over to the window and hung my head out to breathe the city air. Even with my head stuck outside, I had to breathe through my mouth. It seemed that the stench was branded into my nasal passages, stuck inside my aching nose.

After a few minutes, Steven came and stood beside me. Water dripped from his hands. I didn't know whether I failed to leave a towel hanging in the bathroom, or whether he was hesitant to touch anything in the reeking apartment.

He said, "You can't stay here tonight."

I groaned in agreement. "That's the damn truth."

He wiped his hands on his shirttail. "Before we get out of here, we should check and see if there's any sign of forced entry."

Though I was eager to leave, I knew Steven was right about that. I pulled my head back inside the room and did a quick check of the space. It appeared that nothing else had been disturbed. No one had bothered to rummage through my meager belongings or steal any of my possessions. And the lock on the apartment door hadn't been forced. The door itself wasn't damaged, nor were the windows. So no one entered by kicking in my door, or breaking a windowpane.

But Steven and I had friends who knew how to gain access to locked spaces. We had enemies who possessed special skills, too.

As Steven double-checked the dead bolts on the door, I said, "I can't deal with this, Steven. Not today. We've got to get out of here, I can't stay in this room for another minute."

I didn't even grab a change of clothing. Aside from the suitcase I'd brought back from vacation, everything I owned was infested with the odor of the rat.

Steven followed me out of the apartment. After I locked it up, I clutched the handle of my suitcase, which still bore the airline baggage sticker. I hobbled down the hallway toward the elevator as fast as my injured knee permitted.

Steven pushed the button. While we waited for the elevator to reach the fifth floor, he said, "I can take you to the shelter on Amsterdam. You can stay with me in my room tonight."

Steven worked with the homeless in a shelter in Harlem and lived in a room over the facility. His living conditions were even more humble than my own, and I set a low standard.

I searched through my bag, intending to call an Uber. When I spotted my wallet, I thought of a better plan. Opening it, I pulled out a card that I swore I would never use. It was an American Express card in my name that my mother had provided after I graduated from law school. When she handed the card to me three years ago, I'd reacted with righteous indignation, tried to give it back to her. She'd brushed off my reaction. "Don't be so dramatic. Keep it for an emergency," she advised.

I held it in my hand, considering. It was shiny, like new, though it was nearing its expiration date. None of the numbers had been rubbed off with use.

To Steven, I said, "We're getting a hotel room tonight."

His brows raised. "We are?"

"Yeah." My head space was dark and gloomy. In my mind's eye, I could still envision the maggoty rodent in my bed.

I needed to look at something stunning. "We're getting a room with a view. On Central Park."

CHAPTER 5

THE SOUND OF a door opening roused me from sleep. With a jolt, I sat up in bed, my defenses on high alert. A woman living alone in a city with one and a half million other people has to hone her survival skills.

Steven walked into the room carrying a white paper bag. The door swung closed behind him. "Sorry, I was trying to be quiet. I wanted you to sleep in."

He set the bag down on the dresser and then stepped over to the drapes and pulled the cord. A wide window let the sun in, illuminating the hotel room. From my vantage point in the bed, I could see the glorious green view of Central Park and the buildings rising over the tree line on the East and West Side. The nineteenth-floor room at the front of the Essex House commanded a magnificent view.

"Good Lord, just look at that." I was so overawed that I spoke in a reverent whisper.

Gazing out, I wondered, what would it be like to wake up to that view every day? The window in my studio apartment on

31

124th Street didn't even provide a piece of sky. When I looked out, I could only see the red brick wall of the adjacent building five feet away. That, and the window air-conditioning unit of my neighbor across the way. He didn't take it out in the cold weather. It stuck out his window like a wart fifty-two weeks a year.

Looking out at the sunlit trees, I wondered whether a magnificent view could change a person's perspective. Make them happier, kinder. More generous and upbeat.

But probably not. The names of some rich New Yorkers popped into my head, people who lived on the Upper East Side. Ian Templeton, for example. The late Max James. They didn't have a generous bone between them, and those types could afford a view like this one from every room of their showy apartments.

Steven was pulling steaming cups and paper-wrapped bagels from the bag. My stomach rumbled in anticipation.

He said, "I want to make sure you eat something before I go." He delivered coffee and a bagel to me. It was a lovely prospect. I unwrapped the bagel, happy as a kid on a snow day. Breakfast in bed was an uncommon luxury. Taking a sip of coffee, I gave an appreciative groan. It was far superior to the brew that dribbled out of the old coffee maker at my apartment.

He winked and said, "Eat. Doctor's orders."

Glad to oblige, I bit into the bagel. It was my favorite, a fresh everything bagel with a smear of cream cheese. Talking with my mouth full, I said, "So. Good."

Steven pulled an upholstered chair up to the window and sat, looking out at the view as he sipped his coffee. "What's your plan for the day? Going back to your place?"

The suggestion that I return to my studio apartment brought the memory of the dead rat into sharp focus in my head. With an effort, I banished it. "I need to go to the court-house, to talk to Bill. I'll try to run him down at the Criminal Courts building this morning."

"Have you talked to Millie lately?"

I stopped to think: when had we spoken last? Millie was a friend, one of the cohorts in our circle of renegades who hadn't turned on me. With my rush to leave Florida, I couldn't remember our last contact. I'd have to check my text messages.

"We talked on the phone when I was in the hospital, I think. I was pretty out of it. But we texted while I was on vacation. Why? Is something the matter?"

"She wants to see us. I think we need to be on our guard." He looked somber, like he had bad news to share. Again, I recalled my mother's adamant message, warning me to stay away from the members of the group. I started rubbing the web of skin near my thumb.

I'd missed seeing Millie, but Steven's demeanor made me sense that our reunion wouldn't be a happy event. "What's up? Has something happened, are you holding out on me?"

"Of course I'm not."

"What have you heard since I've been gone? About all of them, any of them."

"I haven't received any official contacts, none of those encrypted texts I used to get when we were all working together. We know Whitney's in jail because you heard about that from the police."

But the other two members I wanted to see punished were

Larry, an alcoholic engineer who lured me to the subway station at Times Square, and Edgar, the antisocial artist who pushed me off the subway platform and onto the tracks. Edgar had shoved me in front of an oncoming train, but I landed between the row bed and the rails. That's how I'd survived when the train passed over me. The two men who tried to orchestrate my death on the tracks were still out there somewhere.

"As far as I know, Edgar's never been picked up for the subway shove. And didn't you tell me that Larry led you to the subway and set you up for Edgar's attack?" Steven asked.

The memories came rushing back, making my ears ring with the recollection. I could hear the oncoming train and the shrill screech of the whistle. When I'd been in Florida with my mother and brother, it had been easier to suppress it.

Steven said, "Have you heard any new information on him? Are the police looking for Larry?"

My hands felt cold. I wrapped them around the coffee, hoping to warm them up. "I should probably check in with the detective at NYPD this week. See how the investigation is going."

"You should." He frowned at the uneaten bagel. Looked like he had more on his mind.

And I needed to hear it. "So? What are you thinking?"

He shook his head. "Just that we can't assume it's all over, that the group has disbanded and we'll never see them again. I've been wondering whether I should call Devon, or Diane. See what they have to say."

"No."

He gave me a curious look. "Why? Neither of them was involved in the attack on you."

He was right about that. Of the nine original group members, three had attacked me. And three were friends. That left Devon, a rising star in the tech industry, and the last was Diane. Their status was unknown; I hadn't seen either of them at the subway or in the hospital afterward. Still, I didn't like his suggestion. Diane and I never saw eye to eye, even when we were all united in our cause. And Devon was a kid, obsessed with his gaming addiction. We didn't share a bond.

In hindsight, it seemed like such a stupid enterprise to join up, becoming the ninth member of a group of malcontents who were disenchanted with the justice system. I never anticipated all that would transpire. I thought we were going to right some wrongs, correct a few injustices the courts had overlooked. I didn't intend to hook up with a bunch of crazies.

And I certainly never wanted to become a puppet for an invisible leader who called the shots.

I was relieved when he dropped the subject. After a quiet moment, he came and sat beside me, on the edge of the bed. He said, "I want to examine you before I go."

The idea of his departure left me feeling bereft. I'd hoped we would put the hotel bed to good use before checking out. "Where are you going so early?"

"It's the weekly clinic day," he said, as his hands gently pressed the cartilage of my nose. The pressure hurt, but I locked my jaw and didn't complain. As he lifted my chin, he said, "City Clinic sends a visiting nurse once a week. We'll have a long line of patients, all the way out the door and down the sidewalk. Rueben—he's my coworker. You met him once, right?"

"Yeah."

"He usually supervises the lobby while I assist the nurse or the PA, whoever they send over to run the clinic at the shelter."

Which was ridiculous. Steven would perform the lion's share of medical assistance for the homeless residents; he was a trained physician, regardless of the judgment of the state medical society. I frowned, wanting to weigh in on the issue.

But he was pretty good at reading my mind. Before I could frame my protest, he said, "I wasn't going to tell you until I got some feedback, but I finally took your advice. I've applied to have my license reinstated." He turned his attention to my knee, maybe so he wouldn't have to meet my eye. "One of the sponsors of the shelter is backing me."

I gave an enthusiastic whoop of encouragement. "Thank God. You're the best doctor in this city, best I've ever known. When will you find out?"

He shrugged, shaking his head. "Who knows? It's a long process. No guarantee of the outcome."

I didn't want to drop the topic. I was too excited. "We'll talk to my mother about it as soon as she gets back from Florida. Mom is such a junkyard dog. She'll help, I promise. And I will, too, obviously."

He looked a shade unconvinced. Whether he lacked faith in his chances or in the counsel of Stone & Stone, I couldn't guess. I wanted to discuss it further, to build his confidence, but at that moment, my phone hummed. It was a text from Bill, my friend and former coworker at the DA's office. He was responding to the message I'd sent to him the night before, after we checked into our room at the Essex House.

Bill's text read: I'm assisting in a jury trial today but if it's really urgent, I can see you at the lunch break. Meet you by the halal cart.

I typed a hasty reply, agreeing to meet. Steven had returned to his cup of coffee, swigging it as he put his medical equipment away. He looked like he was preparing to depart.

"You're not leaving?" I sounded petulant, like a disappointed kid.

He looked up, a question in his eyes. "Yeah. Don't we both have somewhere we need to be?"

I tossed the duvet to the side, hoping to entice him with a glamorous nude reveal. Arguably, the sight was not entirely alluring. Purple splotches of bruises and red scrapes bloomed down my hips and legs.

But I persevered. "Checkout isn't until eleven o'clock."

He smiled and put down the bag.

Men are so easy to tempt.

CHAPTER 6

IN THE SMALL park across the street from the Criminal Courts building, I hovered by the food wagons, waiting for Bill to appear. When he didn't show, I obsessively checked my phone for messages. Ten minutes stretched to twenty-five as I paced in front of the carts by the park benches, dodging the government employees on break and keeping my eyes on the courthouse. I anticipated that he would surely exit through the main doors and come down the stone stairs.

Finally, I spotted Bill, hurrying down the steps of the grim limestone fortress and making his way toward me. I was surprised to notice he'd cut his hair short since I'd seen him. It was a new style, parted neatly on the side. He was wearing his best suit with a new tie. We had shared an office in the Manhattan DA's office for three years. I knew Bill's wardrobe by heart, could recite his ensembles from memory.

I hobbled up to meet him, wearing a smile. I didn't even have to fake it. I had missed my coworker. It still felt strange to start a workday without the odor of smoked salmon garnishing a morning bagel, Bill's go-to breakfast.

"Kate, how are you doing? Are you all recovered from the subway attack?"

The reminder of the recent push that had landed me on the train tracks gave my head an involuntary twinge. I shook it off. "I'm good. Thanks for asking."

He edged closer, studying my face through his horn-rimmed glasses. In a hesitant voice, he asked, "Did you get hurt kickboxing? Or did somebody punch you in the nose lately?"

I groaned. "Long story."

He bypassed me, stepping up to stand in line at the food cart. "Glad to hear you're okay. Wish I had more time to catch up, to hear what's been going on with you. But we'll have to make this short. I have to get back inside in a few minutes."

"No problem. Look," I said, lifting up a plastic bag I'd been gripping in my right hand. "Let's go find a seat. I got your favorite, a gyro with white cucumber sauce. I haven't forgotten your preferences, Bill."

He checked his wristwatch, an accessory that he broke out as part of his trial wardrobe. "I've got to take lunch back to Maya. She wants the chicken curry."

His cocounsel's curry was messing with my plans. "Why are you the errand boy? Can't she get her own lunch? Bill, don't let her order you around."

He looked over his shoulder, undoubtedly worried that someone from the office might overhear. My outspoken tendencies had always made him uncomfortable.

Dropping his voice, he said, "This jury trial is a great

opportunity for me. I wish you'd respect that, Kate. I don't mind making the lunch run. I'm second chair."

"Okay, fine. Sorry I said anything. Tell me about the case. What's the charge? Who are you prosecuting?"

He paused for a beat before he answered. "Embezzlement."

"Aha." He sneaked a look at me. He knew what I was thinking. We'd gone around on this issue before. "Who's on trial? A low-level employee, perhaps?"

"A Macy's employee. Stealing merchandise."

I pretended to look impressed. "Really? Taking it for resale?"

He gave me a resentful frown, like I was dragging information from him. "No. For her personal use."

"I see," I said. I made no attempt to suppress my disapproval. Bill gave me a warning glance over the top of his eyeglasses, but it didn't shut me up. "So the DA's office has a white-collar crime department with eighty attorneys, and Frank Rubenstein is using these resources to prosecute a shopgirl from a retail giant for snatching a pair of shoes. Sounds very Dickensian."

"You know our office policy on white-collar crime. We prosecute all cases, big and small."

I digested the statement while Bill stepped up to the window and rattled off the lunch order for his cocounsel, Maya. After he paid and received her bag of chicken curry, we broke away from the crowd lined up for the lunch trade.

"Come on, Bill, spill your guts. You know what I want to hear about. Is your department doing anything about Ian Templeton? That would be a big case, a better use of the resources then some girl wearing a pair of shoes from Macy's.

Ian Templeton is big time, and I still think he's rotten to the core. I happen to know that the white-collar division received a ton of evidence about a Ponzi scheme he was operating."

Templeton was a Wall Street magnate whose enormous wealth had been obtained illegally. In the past year, I'd tried to provide proof of his rackets to the DA's office. They hadn't taken any action against him as yet. Apparently, their focus was on prosecution of retail shoe thefts.

Bill started walking back to the courthouse, with me struggling to match his pace. When he spoke, his face wore a dogged look. "Kate, you know I can't share that information with you. You're not working on the law enforcement side anymore. You joined your mom's defense firm in New Jersey. We can't speak freely about things in the office, not these days. You understand; you're not wearing the white hat."

That last comment stung. Because actually, I believed that I was. It seemed like there should be room for heroics outside of Frank Rubenstein's office. I was still dedicated to seeing justice done. I just wasn't working as a prosecutor anymore, wasn't wearing the ADA's hat.

We were moving so fast I thought that Bill might break into a run at any moment, and I'd lose him. My knee still didn't permit me to move with much speed. "Bill, when can we get together for a serious conversation?"

"Conversation about what? I thought you were going to be in Florida until next week. Did something happen?"

I had returned earlier than planned because I'd wanted to check in with Bill. But now that we were face-to-face, it seemed like a foolish impulse. Feeling defensive, I said, "I'm not comfortable with your situation in the office. Those white-collar ADAs aren't our kind of cat. They have a different perspective on the prosecution role. And Rubenstein? He gives me a bad vibe."

"That's not fair, Kate. You never really knew him."

Of course I didn't. Rubenstein was a public figure. When I worked for him, I was a low-level assistant DA. That's why it was jarring to hear Bill's next statement. "Ruby is genuinely concerned with the welfare of his staff. He's invested in all of us. That's a quote, by the way."

"Ruby?" Ruby was a nickname reserved for the DA's close friends. "Since when did you start calling him Ruby?"

Bill's face flushed—and not from the walk up the stairs that led to the courthouse entrance. "Since he's been counseling me. We've been chatting on a pretty regular basis. About my therapy."

"Whose idea was that? Don't let Frank Rubenstein push you into therapy. It's overreaching. You know he coerced me into it. He's not a doctor, for God's sake."

Bill came to an abrupt halt. "Really, Kate? 'Pushed into therapy'—like it's a punishment? That's an incredibly dated reaction. That attitude is the reason there's still a stigma to mental illness."

He was right. Maybe I was out of line. But I didn't drop it. "I'm just saying."

"You've got to stop this. Ruby is advancing my legal career. The white-collar division is incredible. Have you heard about the cyber lab?"

"Nope." That was a lie, actually. I heard Rubenstein give a press conference, bragging about his state-of-the-art cyber lab that was battling cybercrime on the dark web. "What about Templeton? I think maybe Rubenstein won't charge him because he's covering for the guy."

"God, Kate. You don't understand him at all."

He reached out and squeezed my shoulder. I tried not to wince, because he grasped a spot that had been banged up in the Suburban the day before. "Maybe instead of projecting your doubts on Ruby and Templeton, you should look inward."

"Huh?"

"You tend to be paranoid. And everybody knows about your anger problem. Ruby tried to help you with that. Personally, I think you should go back and get therapy, find a support group. Give it a real effort this time."

I snorted. Because the last time I joined a support group, I had connected with some dangerous characters. My support group involvement had damn near killed me.

My face must have revealed my honest reaction to his suggestion. Because Bill pulled me in for a hug, bumping the bag of chicken curry against my back.

His whisper tickled my ear. "I worry about you, Kate. You're one of my best friends. I don't want to lose you. Promise me you'll get help."

"I promise," I said. And then he squeezed me tightly. *Damn*, it hurt.

After he released me, I watched him scurry through the courthouse door with his lunch bags. And I thought about the promise I had just made to him.

I did intend to get help. Probably not the kind of help Bill envisioned.

As I limped away, I felt foolish. Bill didn't share my reservations about his switch to the new division, and he turned a deaf ear to my accusations against Ian Templeton. I'd achieved nothing by rushing back to the city.

If I could have a do-over, I'd be lounging on the beach in Florida.

CHAPTER 7

RIDING THE SUBWAY that day posed a challenge. It was the first time I'd walked onto the subway platform since my brush with death. As I heard the sounds of the underground cars speeding by, a wave of anxiety swept over me, making my stomach knot up. And my brain played a flashback of the moment I felt the powerful shove at my back and plunged onto the tracks.

It was essential that I overcome the trauma. I had to toughen up, conquer my newly developed reaction. I was a New Yorker. I relied on the train.

When the doors to the 1 train opened, I steeled myself and boarded the subway to ride back to upper Manhattan. Luck was with me that day, because I didn't have to fight for a seat. An earlier customer had left his copy of the morning *New York Times* behind; the paper was strewn across the floor of the car. The business section was under my left foot. I bent down to check it out when I spotted Templeton's name in the headline.

The bold headline said: "Templeton's Cryptocurrency Is the Top ICO to Watch." I wasn't certain what it signified, but if Templeton was pitching it, it was sure to be a rip-off. The article looked like something I ought to read, but I wasn't tempted to pick the newspaper off the grimy floor with my bare hands. It could wait until I was out of the subway and my Internet connection was restored.

When the subway slowed and ground to a stop, it was a relief. I'd survived the first train ride, and it would be easier the next time. I had my phone in hand as I mounted the concrete steps, eager to check out the press on Templeton's new scam. As I emerged onto the street, I googled the article but didn't have the chance to read it before my phone pinged with a FaceTime call.

Leo and Mom were calling in. I tapped the screen, and two faces appeared. One of them was smiling.

"Hey, Kate!" my brother said. "We're missing you down here in Florida. Think you can fly back and join us? The weather down here is great, and the water—"

My mother broke in. "What the hell happened to your face?" she snapped.

I said, "Didn't you get my message yesterday? I texted you. Leo, did you tell Mom about my call?"

His face fell. And then, he got the nervous expression he wears when he thinks trouble is brewing.

My mother said, "What phone call? Kate, you know I don't pay attention to texts. That's not how I communicate. I'm not a teenager."

A bolt of irritation flashed through my brain. I had hoped that my mother and I might enjoy a new and more agreeable

46

stage in our relationship since we'd survived the peril I'd encountered recently. Clearly, it was a false hope. Why would I think she would magically change after knowing her for twenty-eight years? I was fooling myself.

My voice sounded snippy when I replied, "So why did you call? I assume it wasn't to give me the Fort Lauderdale weather report."

"You're right," she said. On the FaceTime video, I could see her eyes narrow as she prepared her cross-examination of me. "What are you doing up there in the city? What's going on with you? I got a notification on my American Express account. Someone put a room charge on one of my cards. A deluxe king at Essex House, Central Park view. I thought you were living in your humble flat in Morningside Heights. Has your card been stolen by one of the miscreants in your dismal part of the city?"

"No." She could always make me feel like an unruly kid. I steeled myself, trying not to take the bait. *Don't sound defensive*, I thought.

"I see. Then it was you. Dear God! What on earth are you up to? I thought you had to go back to the city to address some emergency with that coworker of yours."

I tried to break in. "I did, I just left him."

She talked over me. "And here's something we need to clear up. Why do you need a hotel room? If you are sleeping with your coworker, why in God's name didn't he pay? Doesn't the man pay for accommodations anymore?"

During the tirade, her voice had grown shrill. Everyone on the sidewalk could probably hear her. Fortunately, no one displayed any interest. I held the phone farther away to spare my ears. "Mother. I'm not sleeping with Bill."

"Well, he would be a better choice than that doctor who lost his license. That doctor sounds like a complete waste of your time. What did you say that guy's problem is? Was it drug addiction, do I remember that correctly?"

"No." *Why was I lying?* I wondered. The product of a lifetime habit, I guessed. It was easier to shut her up if I avoided uncomfortable truths. "Do you want to hear what happened yesterday? Can you stop talking for a minute and give me the opportunity to speak?"

She let out a long-suffering sigh. "Fine. Go ahead."

Someone was walking directly beside me. I gave him the side-eye. I didn't mind strangers hearing my mother's rant, but I wasn't keen to broadcast the story of my mishap the day before in Queens. He didn't look like he'd be interested in my conversation, but you never know. Slowing down, I let him pass before I said, "I was the target of an abduction attempt yesterday."

As I spoke, an ambulance passed, its siren blaring. Leo said, "What? Couldn't hear you."

So I repeated it and braced for a reaction.

Mom's face was blank. "Are you serious? Abduction attempt—is that a metaphor for something else? Or is it some kind of joke?"

"Yeah, I'm serious. A guy met me at the airport, and said you'd hired a limo ride to take me into town."

"That's ridiculous. Why would you believe that? It's totally unlikely. I know you are capable of getting yourself from LaGuardia back to your place in Morningside Heights."

Mom's words were sharp, but her tone had changed. I saw the lines furrow in her brow. She must have skipped her Botox appointment this month, with all the crazy stuff that had happened.

I said, "I know that. So I called you to check it out, but you were at the spa. And the driver was really persistent. I ended up just going along, getting in the car with him."

"Why on earth would you do that? Kate, you just got out of the hospital. A woman has been charged with felony assault and attempted murder, and the police are still searching for the man who pushed you onto the subway tracks. He hasn't been apprehended yet."

When she put it that way, it made me feel foolish. My instincts must be off for me to have let my guard down at LaGuardia the day before.

Someone bumped into me, throwing me off-balance. I needed to end the call. "Hey, I'm getting off now. I gotta go."

"Where are you headed? Kate, I want more information. Are those freaks following you again?"

Her questions made me uneasy. I looked over my shoulder.

"I'm going to meet Steven, at the shelter."

"What shelter?"

"The shelter on Amsterdam. The homeless shelter."

"Why meet him at a homeless shelter?"

"Because that's where he lives, Mom."

At that, she shrieked something unintelligible. I could only make out some of the curse words. I ended the call and glanced behind me to check out the pedestrians on my side of the street. No one was tailing me.

I didn't think so, anyway.

CHAPTER 8

I STOPPED AT the corner, waiting for the light to change. The shelter where Steven worked was a short distance away, just a brisk walk for a person whose knees were working right. After a couple of blocks, I turned a corner and spotted the century-old sign for the Bohemian Hotel.

The shelter was housed in an old hotel on Amsterdam. Like its occupants, the once distinguished property had fallen on hard times. The exterior had suffered sad neglect. The brick facade had crumbled, and the stone foundation was defaced with graffiti that no one took the trouble to remove. Even the name of the establishment had undergone a change. In recent times, the Bohemian Hotel was commonly referred to by a nickname: the BoHo.

As I approached the BoHo, I saw a couple of men lingering out front, sharing a cigarette. When I neared the entrance, they gave me a curious glance.

I paused and said, "I'm here to see Steven Salinas. He works here."

Without comment, they turned away, passed off the cigarette again. I felt a little ridiculous as I walked on. What had I been thinking? They didn't care what I was doing there, didn't need me to justify my presence.

I pulled the front door open and stepped inside. A huge counter of carved walnut sat in the back of the lobby, the old registration desk from the hotel's glory days. Rueben, Steven's coworker, stood behind it. He gave me a speculative glance as I walked up. Steven had introduced us before, but maybe he didn't remember me.

Or maybe he did. I don't always make a great first impression.

I tried to remedy that. Pasted on a wide smile. "Hi, Rueben. I'm Steven's friend, Kate Stone. Is he around?"

He leaned on the counter. The surface was marred by ancient water rings and cigarette burns. After he studied me for a moment, he said, "He's working. City Clinic is here. They should be done, but they're running late. Probably wrap up at one."

I figured I'd stick around. I had no pressing appointments. There was a clock behind the reception desk. I checked the time. It read eight thirty.

Not a reliable timepiece, apparently.

"I'll wait," I said. "Can you let him know I'm here?"

He didn't comment, just turned his attention to a laptop that sat on the battered countertop.

Okay, I thought. The reception guy didn't need to deliver my message, I'd do it myself. I'd shoot Steven a text, and then I could stick around for him to finish his medical duties. I found an unoccupied chair in the lobby. The seat was rickety, listing to the side when I sat, but it would suffice while I waited.

When I pulled out my phone, I had a message waiting for me—from Millie. I was happy to hear from her. We had grown really close that year. She and her boyfriend Rod were the people in the support circle I could actually trust. Aside from Steven, of course.

Her text was brief. Just three words, in all caps.

CALL ME

URGENT

That shook me. I hit the call button. She picked up on the fourth ring. Her voice was a bare whisper as she said, "Kate?"

"Hey, Millie, it's me. What's up? How are you doing?"

"Oh my God." She was still whispering; I had to cover my other ear, to hear her over the buzz of conversation in the shelter lobby. "Where are you?"

"I'm back in town. Hey, can you speak up? I'm having trouble hearing you."

I'd never spoken these words to Millie before. It was sometimes necessary to ask her to tone down, never to speak up. Theater people don't tend to be soft-spoken.

"You're back? Thank God. Kate, I'm going crazy."

She sounded distraught. "What can I do for you, Millie?"

"We need to talk. When can we meet?"

Her whispery voice had quickly grown shrill. I wanted to help, because I was genuinely concerned. "Hey, I'm free right now. Tell me what's going on."

"No, I don't want to talk on the phone. We need to meet in person."

"Okay." I made the mistake of checking the wall clock again. Still eight thirty. *Duh*—the time was right there, on my phone. "Want to get lunch? Or we can meet for a drink. Is there a bar near the conservatory?"

Millie studied classical voice in the city. She was an anomaly, a country kid trying to sing opera in New York, not Opry in Nashville. "I'm not at school. They'll look for me there." Her voice hushed again. "Can you come out to Brooklyn? I've been staying over here, hiding out at Rod's apartment in Gravesend."

Hiding out? That was a troubling word choice. Whatever the problem was, I hoped I could help. "Sure. What's a good meeting spot for you?"

"It should be a public place, lots of people. Coney Island. It's not too far from Rod's place. The Boardwalk. Tomorrow at two o'clock."

I calculated the distance to Coney Island from Manhattan.

"You sure? It's going to take an hour to get there. I'm okay with that if you're set on it, but maybe we could meet somewhere midway. Want to get lunch in Brooklyn Heights?"

No answer. I checked my phone. The call had ended.

Slipping the phone into my pocket, I decided that the Coney Island destination wasn't such a bad plan after all. With my mother still in Florida, I was on vacation. Her office was closed, no cases were set.

Steven called out to me. "Kate! What are you doing here?"

He was walking down a curved stairway, headed to the lobby floor. And he was smiling. That was a good sign. I hadn't let him know I was coming.

I jumped up, headed his way and met him at the bottom of

the stairs. "I had an idea," I said. "I'm thinking about having a staycation."

He tilted his head, like he hadn't heard me right. Maybe it sounded stupid. I rushed to explain.

"I came back early because I wanted to chase Bill down. I was worried about him when I was in Florida, I thought he was in trouble."

"I know. That was really considerate of you." He reached for my shoulder and rubbed the back of my neck. It felt good, making me relax. "Very thoughtful. How'd it go? Did you talk to him?"

"Yeah, I saw him on his break. When we had the chance to talk, he wouldn't listen to me. Thought I was nuts for worrying. Says everything is great. Apparently, he doesn't think he's being manipulated. Obviously, he doesn't know what he's gotten himself into. But I'm not going to convince him. I'll have to find a way to help without him knowing."

Rueben called out from his spot behind the counter. "Steven! They're serving lunch in ten minutes."

He looked down at me, giving me a rueful smile. "Duty calls. I'm working the cafeteria line."

He leaned in and kissed me on the forehead.

When he started to walk away, I grabbed his hand. "I left my suitcase at the hotel. In baggage claim."

He gave me a quizzical look. "You didn't go back to your apartment?"

"No! I can't face it, not yet. Besides, I'm officially supposed to be on vacation, right? So I'm continuing my vacation here. In town."

He laughed and said, "That sounds like a great plan. Enjoy." He walked off, heading back to work.

I called after him, "You're welcome to join me. You're officially invited."

When he didn't respond immediately, I added, "We can watch some porn on the in-room movies."

The BoHo lobby had great acoustics. My voice carried. All the conversation stopped. Someone shouted, "I'll come over!"

Steven wheeled around and gave me a look. I didn't wait for his answer, though. A woman's got to have her pride. I turned on my heel and left.

Figured I'd let him think it over.

CHAPTER 9

GRAY SKIES STRETCHED over the beach. The churning water of the Atlantic was black and foamy as it crashed on the shore in South Brooklyn. No swimmers braved the surf that day, and the brown sand was dotted with a bare handful of hardy souls huddled on beach towels. Even the seagulls sounded disgruntled, screaming overhead as if they meant to voice complaints about the weather.

But the boardwalk at Coney Island was hopping. The usual suspects were putting on a show, either in a bid to collect spare change, or simply for their own entertainment. A shirtless man with a grizzled beard roared as he attempted a hand flip, landing hard on his back. Recovering with incredible speed, he jumped to his feet and shouted, "Bing, bong! Who wants to see me do that again?"

Steven and I kept walking. Under my breath, I said, "Jesus, that guy is high as a kite. He needs help, and he's not going to find it on Coney Island."

Steven shook his head but didn't comment.

I tugged his arm. "Come on, what do you think? You work with people like that all day. Is that guy a hopeless case?"

"I don't think anyone's hopeless." He pointed at a food stand down the boardwalk. "Is that the place? Didn't you say we're meeting her at Paul's Daughter?"

I picked up my pace when I saw the famous figure on top of the roof at our destination: a man holding up a huge hamburger. We dodged under the blue-and-white striped awnings and stepped up to the counter.

As we waited to order, Steven nudged me. "What are you in the mood for?"

A dizzying array of choices confronted me. Signs depicting fried clam strips, lobster rolls, hot Italian sausage with peppers and onions.

When it was my turn, a kid wearing a white T-shirt with a blue ballcap pushed back on his head asked, "What you want?"

I didn't hesitate. "Clam strips and fries. I need tartar sauce with that. And a Blue Moon."

"Draft?"

"Yeah." I looked up at Steven. "Do you see anything on the menu, or do you need to go someplace else? There aren't a lot of vegan choices, you probably noticed."

Steven looked thoughtful. To the kid behind the counter, he said, "Do you have any menu items that don't contain meat?"

Pulling down the bill of his ballcap, the kid smirked. "Sure. We got cotton candy."

Steven laughed. "I'll take it."

We sat at a white picnic table under an awning. While I

ate, I kept an eye out for Millie. I had just checked the time on my phone, wondering whether she had changed her mind. That's when she appeared, moving through the crowd at a quick pace. I almost had to do a double take when I spotted her, to be certain it was Millie.

Millie was a transplant, a kid from the rural Midwest who'd come to New York with a dream of making a career on the stage. She customarily wore a full face of makeup, displayed high spirits, and spoke at an earsplitting volume.

She dropped on to the bench beside me, breathing hard. "I'm so glad to see you, Kate. Really, really glad."

She had undergone a change in the past two weeks. Her face was pale, her mane of long blond hair looked limp and straggly. The shirt she wore was wrinkled and soiled, like she'd picked up dirty clothes off the floor and pulled them on. If I didn't know her so well, I might not have recognized her.

Steven said, "Millie? Are you okay?"

She checked over both shoulders, scrutinizing the people sitting nearby, before she replied, "Oh, please. Good God. I haven't been okay in ages." She stared down at the plastic bag of pink and blue cotton candy resting on the table. "Can I have some of that?"

"Sure." Steven handed it to her.

Millie pulled a thick blue wad of the candy from the bag. Before she poked it into her mouth, she said, "I haven't eaten anything today. Maybe not yesterday, either. It's hard to remember. Everything's so crazy."

"Millie! Sorry to hear that." I stood, determined to feed her. I was afraid she'd get sick if she didn't start taking care of herself. "I'll get you something. What sounds good? You want a burger?"

She halted me, grasping my arm with a sticky hand. Her lips were turning blue from the dyed sugar. "We don't have time. I need to talk to you, it can't wait." Her voice dropped to a whisper. "It's urgent. I'm desperate."

Alarmed, I exchanged a look with Steven. Millie tended to be dramatic, but this was over the top, even for her. "Okay," I said, sitting back down on the bench. "You didn't give me any details on the phone, but I could tell you were upset. We've been worried about you. What's got you so scared?"

"We can't talk here. Someone could be listening." She picked up my plastic cup of beer. "God, I'm thirsty." After she drained it, she slammed the empty cup on the table and said, "We need privacy."

Steven gave her a bemused look. Nodding his head toward the crowd on the boardwalk, he said, "Millie, you chose this place. You wanted to meet on the Coney Island Boardwalk. It's pretty much impossible to find a private spot around here."

She looked haunted. "I feel safer in crowds. But I don't want anyone listening to us."

I wadded up my paper napkins and stuffed them with my trash. "No problem. I know where we can go."

Millie clutched the bag of cotton candy. In a hushed voice, she said, "Where?"

Before I replied, I scooted around in my seat and looked up at it, towering fifteen stories overhead. It was a comfort to know that some things didn't change. This vision was one of them.

"The Wonder Wheel."

CHAPTER 10

AS WE APPROACHED the Wonder Wheel, Millie looked up, staring at it with apprehension. "I've got a thing about heights," she said.

The old Ferris wheel is tall, one hundred and fifty feet high. But it's not a wild, adrenaline-spiking carnival experience. Passengers ride in old-fashioned enclosed cabins, rather than a conventional open seat. Even with Millie's tendency for the dramatic, there was nothing very scary about it.

"You wanted privacy," I said, heading into the ticket queue. "We'll have a car to ourselves."

Steven tapped my shoulder. I paused. "What?"

"You're in line for the moving cars, the ones that slide around," he said. "I'd prefer the other experience."

"Good God," I said. "Really?"

They were seriously interfering with my fun. The old Wonder Wheel is what they call an "eccentric" Ferris wheel. There are two different ways to ride it.

Millie pointed up as the wheel rotated high over our heads. "Why are some of the cars rolling around?"

"They're not fixed to the rim," Steven said. "They slide back and forth along the rails while the wheel turns."

Millie turned to him, her eyes frantic. "Is that why I hear people screaming?"

"Yeah." When Steven reiterated his preference, his voice wasn't remotely apologetic, to my consternation. "Millie and I vote to ride in the stationary cars. If you're okay with that."

Actually, I wasn't down with that. Nobody except old people and infants would choose the stationary cars. I was chagrined as I followed them to the queue for the senior citizen–style cabins, embarrassed to be associated with the tame customer option. Making sure they could hear me, I grumbled. "This is a first for me, and I've been coming here for years. My dad wouldn't be caught dead in one of these white cars."

The sixteen moving cabins were brightly painted in red, blue, and yellow. They carried the passengers who were squealing with fun. We would be assigned one of the white cars, inexorably fixed directly to the rim of the wheel. The ride Steven chose was *not* where the action was.

As we boarded the white cabin, the carny who shut the door said, "Enjoy the ride!" I thought I detected a note of sarcasm, and avoided making eye contact with him, out of shame.

The wheel began to turn. Millie rubbed her nose and said, "I can't believe I'm even saying this. They picked Rod up at work. He's at Rikers."

My discontent forgotten, I said, "Millie, no! Oh my God, that's terrible."

Steven said, "What did they arrest him for?"

"Something about his bond on an assault charge. A bondsman changed his mind, withdrew it?" Her face crumpled. "Remember when he got busted at that yacht party? We thought Gatsby fixed it, liked he always used to do."

"Gatsby" was the name Millie had always used to refer to our anonymous benefactor, the leader of the pack who had supported and funded our various schemes to balance the scales of justice.

She said, "He got Rod bailed out right after his arrest that night, and we assumed that the problem just went away. Gatsby had done it for us before, just hired a lawyer who took care of it, and we didn't have to worry. Rod didn't figure anyone was pursuing the charges. But the cops came to the nightclub with a warrant. They put him in cuffs and took him away. I didn't even know about it until he never made it home from work. I called the manager at the club, and she told me. And now, I don't know what to do."

She ducked her head as she started to cry. I slid off the bench I shared with Steven and sat beside her. Pulling her into a hug, I watched the red and blue cars slide inward on their tracks while Millie sobbed.

When we were high in the air, the wheel paused to admit passengers down below. Millie wiped her eyes and looked up at me. With blue sugar still clinging to her face, she looked so young, it stirred a protective impulse. Her voice broke when she said, "You're a lawyer, Kate. Tell me what to do."

Though I was seriously rattled by the news of Rod's incarceration, I made an effort to sound chill. Millie needed a rock, not a sob sister to cry with. "Have you talked to him?"

"Yeah, he used his one phone call to get in touch with me.

But I wanted to talk to him in person. So the very next day, I went to Rikers. But when I got there, they wouldn't let me see him. They said that there are rules about visiting, and I didn't follow them. But I don't know what the rules are, I've never been in this situation before. I needed help, but I didn't know who to ask. I'm afraid to talk to anyone else in the group. And I don't know how to contact Gatsby."

"Don't do that." I could see my mother shaking her head, with that look of warning she often wore.

"I don't have his number, couldn't do it if I wanted to. I figured I needed legal advice. But you're the only lawyer I know, and when it happened, you were in Florida."

"I'm back. And I'm on it, Millie. I'll go to Rikers tomorrow."

"Will they let you see him?"

"I'd like to see them try to stop me." I gave her another hug, and she let out a sigh of relief.

"Tell him, when you talk to him, that I want to visit him. I just have to. I can't stand it. It's making me crazy with Rod away, locked up in jail. I miss him so much. Will you tell him that?"

"Sure thing, I'll let him know exactly what you said."

The wheel started moving with a jolt. As we commenced our downward turn, I tried to redirect Millie's thoughts. "Check out the view. It's beautiful Coney Island down there."

She didn't even look out the window. "There's something else. But I'm afraid you're going to say it's my imagination."

Steven reached out and took her hand. "Tell us what you're worried about, Millie."

"They're still following me."

Steven and I exchanged a glance. "Who?" he said.

"Who do you think? The people in our group, our old justice group. The bad guys."

On instinct, I looked around, even though we were riding alone in the stationary car of the Ferris wheel. Careful to lower my voice, I could barely be heard over the shrieks coming from the nearest sliding car as I said, "Who have you seen? Which one is it?"

"I haven't seen anyone, not exactly. But I can feel it." She peered through the window, looking down over the carnival scene below. "I think Whitney's here."

I shook my head. If she'd seen a dark-haired kid with a ponytail following her, that would be cause for concern. But we didn't need to worry about Whitney. "Millie, you're wrong. You're imagining things. It's probably just the shock."

"No, it's not. I can feel her negative energy. I always could pick up Whitney's vibe, even before she walked into a room."

Her crazy talk was making me wired. I wanted to argue her down, dispute her judgment. But when Steven spoke, his voice was gentle. "We've all been through a lot, Millie. And with Rod's arrest, it makes sense that you're on edge. With all that's happened, it's natural to feel paranoid."

Millie scooted away from me, pressing back into the corner of the cabin. "I knew it. Knew it would happen. You're not taking me seriously. This isn't helping."

Steven went on, using his doctor's voice. He sounded reasonable and soothing, like he was reassuring an agitated patient. "I hear everything you're saying. But I don't want you worrying about invisible enemies. That's just gonna make you crazy. You need to focus on the concrete issues you are facing. Right?"

She didn't respond.

He continued. "You need to get help for Rod. He needs legal assistance. But you're already making progress. Kate's stepping in; she'll find out what's going on. And you've got to take care of yourself, too. Remember to eat, try to sleep through the night."

"I forget to eat. And I can't sleep, I'm too worried about Rod."

"Get back into a normal routine. Concentrate on making it through the day, and giving Rod the support he needs. Don't imagine any additional problems. You have your hands full, as it is."

What Steven told Millie made perfect sense. I really wanted to chime in, to echo what he said. A real friend would offer reassurance.

But my head kept returning to the suspicion she'd confided. If Millie really thought she was being followed, maybe I shouldn't be so quick to discount it. I'd been taken on an involuntary joyride in a Suburban at LaGuardia that week. And I'd arrived home to find a dead rat stinking up my bed. Someone planted it there, to give me a scare. Maybe I should reserve judgment.

So I didn't tell her that everything was fine, that she wasn't at risk. I can't kick my superstitious tendency. Suppose I said, "No one is following you, Millie," and some psychic force overheard. I might be tempting fate.

CHAPTER 11

THE WONDER WHEEL completed its circuit, and Millie, Steven, and I disembarked. She was still shaken as we exited our tame white cabin. We had barely reached the sidewalk when Millie announced she wanted to leave. I tried to convince her to stick around.

"Really?" I said. "But it's early. You don't want to get a drink? Something to eat, maybe a hot dog at Nathan's?"

As we walked along the pavement, I could smell hot grease wafting from the food stands, whetting my appetite for more carnival food. "Or a corn dog, dipped in yellow mustard."

"No." Millie tossed the crumpled bag holding the remains of pink and blue cotton candy into a trash can.

I didn't want to see her go. She still had remnants of cotton candy on her hands. I thought I could tempt her with another round of sugar. "Maybe something sweet? We can find a place that sells funnel cakes. I'll split one with you."

"Really not in the mood. I'm not feeling too great. I walked here, but I think I'll take the train. The subway station is on Stillwell, right? Can you point me in that direction?"

She wheeled around, searching the area with an anxious face. I suspected she wasn't hunting for the Stillwell Avenue station. She was keeping an eye out for Whitney.

"We'll walk with you," Steven said. Millie leaned against him, grasping his arm with her free hand, as if she needed help to walk the short distance. I followed a pace behind them, watching her with concern. Millie always tended to be theatrical, that was her standard behavior. She was a classic diva, but on this afternoon she was acting unhinged.

We passed a cluster of carnival games on the boardwalk. The barker tried to engage Steven.

"Come on, big guy! Win your girlfriend a cute stuffed Elmo! One basketball in is all it takes to win!"

The carny reached into the rack behind him and pulled an Elmo toy from the shelf. He waved it under Millie's nose. She flipped, hiding behind Steven and crying out in fear.

The carny backed off. As I passed by, he said to me, "That woman is *wack*."

I wanted to refute his accusation, but what could I say? Even by Coney Island standards, she was acting kinda nutty.

Steven and Millie walked so fast, I had to trot to keep pace. I caught up with them near the subway entrance. When I came within earshot, I heard Steven speaking earnestly to her. He was holding her hand.

He said, "Are you sure? Maybe you shouldn't be alone right now."

"I'm okay, I think. I'll feel better when I get to Rod's apartment and lock the door."

Steven hesitated. "I don't know. Maybe Kate and I should ride home with you, make sure you get there safely." He shot me an inquiring glance.

"Absolutely," I said. "We'll deliver you to Rod's apartment. We can come inside and stay until you feel better."

"Not necessary, honestly. I don't need a babysitter, I just need to get Rod back." She looked forlorn as she turned to enter the subway.

I followed her to the entrance. "Steven's right, we can keep you company. You sure you don't want that?"

"Absolutely sure." Her voice held a pleading note as she clasped my arm and added, "I can't reach him by phone, I've tried. Call me tomorrow, right after you talk to him. Tell me whether he's all right, when he's getting out of there. I'll have my phone with me all day, waiting to hear."

Standing close beside Steven, I watched her go. As she disappeared, he said, "Hope she eats something, gets some rest."

"Yeah." Personally, I had my doubts.

He glanced around at the carnival chaos. "What do you want to do? Are you ready to head back to the city?"

"Hell no. We haven't taken in all the sights." I jabbed him with my elbow, just a teasing nudge.

With a sigh of resignation, he said, "Okay, we can hang around for a while, I guess. What do you want to ride next? The carousel?"

Over the voices in the crowd, I could hear the notes of tinny organ music floating through the air. The melody didn't lure me. Heading back to the rides, I didn't spare a glance for the flying horses. "No way. Carousels are for little kids. But I'll let you choose the next adventure. Spook-A-Rama? Or the Cyclone?"

With a wry smile, he just shook his head. I chose to ignore his lack of enthusiasm. Clearly, he was unmoved by the spectacle, but carnival rides still held a charm for me. My dad would take me and my brother, Leo, out to Coney Island at least once every year, when he had us for a month of summer visitation. We would ride everything on the park grounds twice, screaming our heads off, even when we were too old to be scared anymore.

Steven opted for the Cyclone. I cast a longing glance at the familiar skeletons of Spook-A-Rama as we passed. *I'll be back*, I thought, though I didn't know when the occasion would arise.

The line to board the Cyclone was long. When we finally slid into a seat and the carnival worker pulled the hand bar down on our roller-coaster car, he winked at me. "Hang on tight! You promise?"

"Cross my heart," I said, giving him a saucy grin. For a moment, I was fifteen again. Coney Island can do that for you.

Of course, I was lying to the guy. When the Cyclone cars crested the steepest part of the track and started to plunge, I raised both arms high into the air and screamed my head off. Steven, by contrast, gripped the grimy metal bar in front of him, hanging on like his survival depended on it.

When the ride ended and our car rolled to a stop on the track, I waited impatiently for the Cyclone worker to set me free. As the guy made his way to our car, I said to Steven, "That was fun. Right?"

Steven gave me a baffled look. "Not my definition of fun. I'm not into the adrenaline rush."

I scoffed. "Steven, I worry about you. Sometimes you sound like a guy who doesn't know how to have a good time."

As a rule, I was drawn to guys who liked to have fun. I was also partial to carnivores. With Steven, I was entering unknown territory.

The carny reached us, lifted the bar and let me scoot out. After Steven climbed out, I asked him, "Time for a funnel cake? Or a cold drink? I'm ready for a beer."

"Wish I could have a beer. I need one after that experience."

I just laughed as I headed off. Steven called out after me. "Hey, where are you going? The beer is in the other direction."

"I have to buy a souvenir photo."

He followed me. "What the hell do you want a photo for?"

"It's a tradition." Actually, it was. Dad always got a photo when we came for our summer holiday. Then we'd argue over who looked the funniest in the picture.

When the vendor handed me my purchase, I tucked it away, refusing to let Steven see it.

"We have to have a beer, and a place to sit down. There is a process to this. You can't just grab the souvenir photo and give it a quick glance."

He went along with me, was a pretty good sport about it. Steven waited at the picnic table while I bought a beer and a lemonade in plastic cups. I was glad to see that the weather had undergone a dramatic change during our time on Coney Island. The clouds broke up, and the sun had finally come out. It cast a glow on the beach and changed the color of the ocean to blue. The sunshine gave me a boost, too. It warmed my shoulders as I stepped over the wooden bench to join Steven.

I said, "We ought to stay here all afternoon. Play the games, ride some more rides."

"How about skipping the games and the rides, and just sit on the sand. We could watch the water."

I laughed at him. "Probably better for your nerves, right? I didn't know you were such a baby, Steven. Scared to pieces by a roller coaster."

"That's an overstatement. I wouldn't admit to being scared to pieces."

I held up the souvenir photo. "This is photographic evidence. It will show your true, unvarnished reaction."

I set the picture on the table between us, so we could both take a look. Steven started laughing uproariously.

"Kate, you're right. Not gonna lie. It's pretty damned funny."

I stared at it. Not so funny. Not to me.

The photo caught a partial shot of the roller coaster, a section of four cars, holding a total of seven people. Steven and I were in the first car in the shot, with our mouths wide open.

Three rows back, a woman sat alone in the middle of her seat. Like me, she raised her arms, and they partially blocked her face.

Still, she looked a lot like Whitney. Exactly like Whitney, in fact.

But that was impossible. Whitney was in jail, awaiting trial. For attempted murder.

Of me.

CHAPTER 12

I HAD THE contact information for the detective who was investigating the cases in which I'd been the victim of attempted murder and felonious assault. I intended to give him an update, inform him I thought I might have spied Whitney. When I made the call, I hoped he'd tell me that it was impossible, that she was locked up tight. Though I called twice, I couldn't reach him. I was tempted to go to his office the next day, to tell him in person.

But Rod was in custody. That rearranged my priorities. I needed to keep my promise to Millie.

In fact, I was determined to do it. In the past year, I'd forged a tight bond with Millie and Rod. We had rallied together to fight some formidable enemies. I had unwittingly set the events in motion that led to Rod's current incarceration. The three of us had pulled off a tremendous coup when we gate-crashed a party on Ian Templeton's yacht, seeking evidence of his criminal activities. Rod and Millie had participated because we all wanted to bring down a man the criminal justice system wouldn't touch. The DA's office might be intimidated by Templeton's wealth, but we weren't.

Rod was a fighter, a standup guy, the kind of person I admired. He'd fought on my side before, and I was ready to return the favor.

But when the bus took me over the bridge onto Rikers Island, stopping at the visitors center, I figured out pretty quickly that it wasn't going to be easy.

Before we could exit the bus, a uniformed New York City corrections officer boarded. He said, "When you get off the bus, you're going to line up single file. Got that? And all contraband must be left on the bus. You listening? I'm telling you to leave any and all illegal items behind."

We got off the bus and shuffled into line, following his instructions. As I stood in line behind a woman holding a child by each hand I said, "We haven't even made it to the building yet. Why are we standing here? What for?"

She didn't turn around to look at me. But I heard her say, "Search."

"Oh. Okay."

I looked overhead, checking the clouds. "Hope it doesn't rain."

She didn't comment. But the child on her right hand tugged at her shirt and said, "How many searches today, Mommy?"

"Hush."

That was unsettling. Not because I had contraband, obviously. I didn't worry about the results of a search; I certainly hadn't stashed any illegal substances on my person before I came to Rikers. And it wasn't a shock that we'd be subjected to a search to gain access to the facility. But I was impatient to get inside and check on Rod. Again, I spoke to the woman standing ahead of me. "Multiple searches? How long does the whole process take? When do we get inside the facility and have the chance to sit down and talk with the people we've come to see?"

This time, she did turn her head and looked me up and down. I hadn't worn a suit that day. I didn't bother donning business attire for a trip inside Rikers because I wasn't representing Rod. I was there as a friend. And it was common knowledge that conditions at the corrections facility were notoriously bad.

So she probably didn't peg me as a lawyer. However, she undoubtedly realized I was a novice.

Her eyes were already tired, and we'd barely begun. "You better not have anything else going on today. Because you ain't gonna make it."

When she turned away from me, I muttered, "Well, *shit*."

The tot directly in front of me had sharp ears. He parroted my inflection perfectly as he repeated it. "Well, *shit*."

His mother smacked the back of his head. "Stop that."

When the kid started to cry, I edged away, wishing I had kept my mouth shut.

We'd been in line for twenty-three minutes before I made it into the Perry Center. Once inside, we were ordered to stand in a circle. The corrections officer said to us, "Hats off! Hold your bags to your sides! If you don't follow instructions, we'll pull you out of line and do it again."

And then, they brought out the dogs.

I'd heard that Rikers subjected visitors to passive canine searches, but never gave it much thought. As the corrections officers led the drug-detection dogs twice around the circle of bedraggled women and children, it made me significantly uneasy. One of the canines was a huge German shepherd that looked like it could rip my throat out. And the dog's handler gave off an overeager vibe, like he was hoping the dog would maim somebody.

When the German shepherd drew close to us, the kid standing beside me started crying again. I couldn't blame him. His mother snatched him out of range, placing her body between the child and the dog. Maybe her mothering instincts were spot on.

Come to think of it, she kind of reminded me of my own mother. Including the smack to the back of the head.

The noise the child made drew attention to us. The corrections officer came closer. So did the dog.

I couldn't remain quiet. "You're using that dog to scare a little kid," I said. "I don't think that's what the New York City Department of Corrections has in mind when they train these dogs."

The guy didn't like my commentary. It shouldn't have come as a surprise when he pulled me out of the circle. What did I expect?

First, he set the dog on me. Then he emptied my bag onto the floor and ordered the dog to search the contents. Turns out, the dog was more ethical than the handler. Fido gave me a pass.

After my individual search, I had to move fast to catch up with my group. I found them outside the Central Visit House, leaving their personal belongings in lockers. I tried to follow suit, but was stymied when I figured out that I needed a quarter to operate the locker. After a frantic search, a miracle occurred. I happened to have one coin in the bottom of my bag. The requirement, though, was frustrating. Normally, I don't carry change. Who uses coins these days?

After that, I presented my ID and then made it through a metal detector. And then I was directed to a waiting area. It had been an exhausting process, but I figured that would be the extent of it. Painful, inconvenient. And humiliating, particularly the game they'd played with the dogs. But not illegal. No one had violated my civil rights.

At the visitors' waiting area, I bided my time in another line. When it was finally my turn, I showed my ID again, to yet another corrections officer.

He said, "Who are you here to visit?"

My tone was curt. I was pretty worn out with the process. "Rodney Lamar Bryant."

I hadn't known Rod's full name when we originally met. Our circle was anonymous, that was the policy. Those of us who rebelled against the constraints of the group's rulebook had dispensed with the whole anonymity ruse. Rod, Steven, Millie, and I had come a long way together.

"Book and case number?"

That shook my attitude. Millie hadn't mentioned anything about it, and I hadn't anticipated that requirement. As an ADA, I'd never visited Rikers, and I was new to criminal defense. "I don't have that information. Can you look it up for me?"

He gave me a *WTF?* expression. "You're supposed to look it up. Before you get here."

"I didn't know. No one told me."

"Well, now you know. So next time, have the correct information and you'll get to see your inmate."

"Oh come on." I could feel the heat rise in my face. "This isn't fair."

"Next!"

A woman tried to shove past me and gain my spot. I grabbed the counter of the table and broadened my stance. I wasn't moving, no way.

"I'm Rodney Bryant's attorney. He's entitled to see me." It wasn't strictly accurate because Rod hadn't engaged me as counsel. But without playing the lawyer card, I was starting to suspect I might not get access to him. "Right to counsel is guaranteed by the Sixth Amendment. So look up his book number and his case number, if you need that. Then let me through this goddamned line and give me a private space to conduct attorney-client communications."

The CO looked up, like he was thinking. Maybe he was plotting his next step to confound me. When he broke into a smile, it sent a shiver down my back.

"How come you were standing in the tramp line if you're really a lawyer?" His voice was loud enough to be overheard.

"Hey!" The woman behind me sounded hurt.

She was right to be offended. I was also bothered by his choice of words. Most of the visitors waiting to see inmates were female: wives, children, girlfriends were suffering the obstacles of Rikers visitation hell. Apparently, it was an insult borne by the female sex. Like the pangs of childbearing. Or menstrual cramps.

The CO leaned back in his chair. "You got a New York Bar Association ID?"

I did. After I handed it to him, he held it up for close scrutiny. He scoured it with his eyes like he thought it might be counterfeit. My hands curled into fists. He was goading me, and I was itching for a fight. But I kept my hands to myself and my mouth shut. I needed to get inside.

Finally, he handed the card back to me. "So your attorney-client meeting—it was prescheduled, right?"

It wasn't. I should've thought of that before I made my representation claim because I dimly recalled that prescheduling was a thing. One lesson I'd learned that day: as a defense attorney, I was clueless, completely naïve. As I stood in that miserable line, I fervently wished I'd done more homework in advance. My time in the DA's office hadn't prepared me to maneuver Rikers.

I considered lying. Telling him I had, in fact, prescheduled. But I decided that the way my luck was going, they'd incarcerate me for intentional misrepresentation to a corrections employee. I didn't think that was a violation of city or state statute, but I couldn't swear to it. And then they might lock me up in a room with the angry drug-sniffing canines.

So I told the truth. "No. I didn't schedule it in advance."

"That's too bad." He leaned to the side, checking the time on a clock that hung on the far side of the wall. "It's past three. Too late for an unscheduled attorney visit."

There was a three o'clock cutoff? Didn't know that, either.

My fists clenched. I wanted to punch the smirk off his snide face. My eyes narrowed in focus as I glared at him. I could see the precise place where I would land the blow. I imagined the surprise in his eyes right before the pain registered and blood spurted from his mouth.

Maybe he read my mind. His voice was loud as he said, "Step aside! Now!"

As I turned away and walked back through the visitor center, my shoulders sagged with defeat.

How on earth would I explain this to Millie?

As I slumped in my seat on the bus for the bumpy ride back to the city, the sense of failure weighed me down. I pulled out my phone, intending to do some in-depth research on the proper way to navigate the perils of the inmate visitation process. But I had an email in my inbox from NYPD. The sender was a cop named Brennan from the 108th precinct in Queens.

He had encouraging news to report. They had a lead on the Suburban driver. He wanted me to come to the station house the next day.

That was progress. At least one thing was going right. I perked up, experiencing a rise in my energy level. As I jounced in the bus seat, I briefly considered spending the remainder of the day at my apartment. Maybe it was time to tackle the cleanup.

And decided against it. I was really liking that hotel living. A person could get used to that.

And then a new text appeared, from Bill.

Jury verdict in

Guilty on all 3 counts

Victory drinks @ Twilight 5:00

I tucked the phone away. Looked like I wouldn't be going straight to the hotel after all. I had a new destination in mind.

CHAPTER 13

Bill

BILL PARKER WAS living his best life.

It was as if he'd visualized what his future could be, and the vision had materialized. He had been transferred to the white-collar crime division in the upper echelon of the Manhattan DA's office. The workload was easier because there were fewer cases than he'd juggled in violent crime. The pay was better. And though he was ashamed to admit it, the white-collar ADA's dealt with a better class of victim—no more hysterics in the courthouse hallways from disgruntled state's witnesses who were unhappy with the system.

He was working with a different set of lawyers, too, on both sides. No more inexperienced and overworked public defenders. And his coworkers were handpicked for their talent and skill, the crème de la crème of the DA's staff.

He'd become a member of the club.

As he stood in the midst of a cluster of well-dressed attorneys sipping cocktails near the bar, Bill felt like he'd finally arrived. After years of striving, he'd been invited to join the DA's A-listers at Twilight, the place that was frequented by the chosen ones of the DA's office. He'd never walked into Twilight before, though he frequently passed it on his way to the Criminal Courts building. In the past, he would've felt like an interloper, a gate-crasher, a pretender.

But on that night, he was where he belonged.

Maya tugged at his sleeve. "Can you get the bartender's attention? Cam needs a lager."

Bill immediately obliged, murmuring apologies as he worked his way to the front of the long bar. He had to wait to catch the bartender's eye. Bill had never been the guy who got picked first. But he was accustomed to that.

"Bill!"

He turned when he heard Kate's voice. She was shouldering her way toward him, a force of nature as she fought through the tight cluster of bodies. She didn't apologize when the bar's patrons had to make way for her to pass.

Kate reached him at the bar, grabbed him, and gave him a squeeze.

"Congrats on the win," she said. "What are you drinking? I'll buy."

She rose on tiptoe and leaned over the wooden bar. "Hey! Can we have service down here? I'm dying!"

It was like she'd waved a wand. The bartender turned his head and called out, "What do you need?"

"Tanqueray and tonic, two limes!" She gave Bill a look. Hastily, he said, "A lager."

"And a lager!" Bill watched her pull the credit card from her wallet. She paid for both drinks before he could stop her. As a rule, Bill and Kate split the tab.

After the drinks were served and they had picked up the glasses, Kate raised hers and said, "Here's to justice."

She drank. Bill didn't.

Kate frowned. "You're not an advocate of justice? You're not drinking. Were you unhappy with the verdict?"

Bill made an apologetic grimace. "It's not for me. Maya asked me to get her a drink."

Kate rolled her eyes. "I'm buying Maya's drinks? Fuck that shit."

As if Kate had conjured Bill's cocounsel by speaking her name, Maya appeared at Bill's elbow. "Is that for Cam?"

He nodded and handed it off, hoping that Maya would turn and go because Kate was putting off that edgy vibe of hers. He'd observed it before, many times.

But Maya remained rooted to the spot. The women regarded each other in an unfriendly fashion.

Kate broke the silence. "I'm Kate Stone. Used to share an office with Bill when we worked in the domestic violence division."

"I've heard of you." Maya's voice was frosty. "Maya Wilhoit. White-collar."

Bill could feel perspiration bead on his upper lip as his anxiety level ratcheted up. His hand slipped inside the pocket of his jacket to grasp the pen. He needed to vape his medical marijuana, to get a prophylactic dose of THC before the panic spiked.

Cam, the chief assistant of their division, pushed his way through. "Is that mine?" he asked, looking pointedly at the foamy beer Maya held. When she nodded, Cam grabbed the mug from Maya and took a gulp.

"Thank God," he said. "I was just wondering who you have to fuck to get a drink around here."

"That would be me," Kate said. When Maya and Cam gave her startled looks, she added, "I bought your beer."

"Oh. Thanks." Cam extended a hand. "Cam Leong. Manhattan DA's office."

Bill was relieved to see Kate shake his hand. You never could tell what she might do when her temper flared.

Kate said, "White-collar crime division, right?"

"Right." Cam took another swallow of the beer.

Bill tried to figure out a way to compensate Kate for purchasing it but figured it would make the situation even more awkward. He watched uneasily as she sipped her gin. Bill knew that gin could make Kate's mood brighter. But it could as easily have the opposite effect. He kept a worried eye on her, waiting to hear what she'd say next.

Kate glanced at Bill before she focused on Cam. "What are you doing about Templeton?"

Cam set the mug on the bar. He gave her a look that clearly showed his confusion. "Excuse me?"

"Templeton. The finance guy. When are you filing charges?"

Cam burst into laughter. After a moment, Maya joined him. Kate's face grew stony as the laughter echoed in Bill's ears.

When Cam recovered, he said, "Sorry, I assumed you were joking."

"Nope. Not a joke. Just wondering when you'll prosecute that Ponzi scheme he was operating last year."

Bill wasn't a religious man, but if he'd been a believer, he would have prayed for the floor to open up and swallow him. So that he could disappear and not have to witness what would happen next.

Maya said, "Templeton is a finance king. Like Midas." She turned her back on Kate, cutting her out and directing her question to Bill. "Have you heard about his new crypto-currency offering?"

Bill shot a nervous glance at Kate before he answered. "Yeah. I think so."

"It's Zagcoin. It's going to be huge."

Cam said, "I'm putting everything I can spare into it. The value is going through the roof."

"You don't think that's unethical? For an ADA to invest with a guy who's been ripping people off?" Kate's voice was so loud when she spoke up that it made Bill wince.

But they weren't listening. They had cut her out of the conversation. Bill felt bad for Kate. He knew what it was like to be a fifth wheel. He'd been in that position count-less times.

Maya put an arm around Bill's shoulder, effectively remov-ing Kate from the circle. "Cam, just so you know, Bill was my right arm this week during trial. I couldn't ask for a better second chair. I hope you'll let us team up again."

Cam punched Bill in the shoulder. It hurt, but he didn't let on.

"Bill, you should be proud of those embezzlement con-victions. Because of you and Maya, that woman is currently residing at Rosie's. We'll drink to that!"

Bill didn't have a glass to raise, but it wouldn't have made any difference because Kate's voice cut into the celebration.

"Have you seen Rikers lately? Ever been over there? The

conditions are horrible. It's nothing to celebrate, I promise you that. I just got back from Rikers, and here's my experience."

Bill broke away from Maya's hold. As Kate stepped into the space he'd vacated and launched into her tirade, Bill pulled the vape from his pocket and stuck it into his mouth.

If they kicked him out of the bar for vaping, it might be for the best.

CHAPTER 14

Kate

THE SUN WAS shining as I walked up to the 108th Precinct station house on Fiftieth Avenue in Long Island City, Queens. The sky over the three-story, brick-and-stone building was a brilliant shade of blue. I trotted up the old stone steps at a brisk pace. I had someone to meet, and I didn't want to be late.

I was pumped to know that the police in Queens had a suspect for the LaGuardia abduction. Sounded like they were taking it seriously.

The lobby was crowded, the usual crush of people bustling around a police precinct. I was ushered through the bedlam into the offices occupied by the detective squad. In that congested space, plainclothes officers occupied battered metal desks placed back-to-back upon the tiled floor. Window air conditioners labored without success to cool the space.

The uniformed officer serving as my escort shouted across the room. "Hey! Brennan!"

A stocky gray-haired guy sporting a bristly mustache looked up. I strode up to him, extending my right hand.

"Detective Brennan, I'm Kate Stone. I got your email yesterday, thanks for getting in touch. I'm relieved to hear that you already have a suspect in my abduction from LaGuardia. That's fast work."

"Yeah, we got a lead on our social media post. Happens sometimes. We got lucky."

He was eating a glazed donut. At the sight, I struggled to hide a grin. Some stereotypes are based on reality. My dad loved a donut, too, when he served with the NYPD.

Brennan used a paper towel to wipe icing from his hands before unearthing a file folder from the pile of paperwork on his desk.

"You ready to do a photo lineup for me, ma'am?"

"Sure. I'm ready."

"I've got twelve pictures here. Tell me if you recognize anyone. Look at each one carefully. Take all the time you need."

He handed me the file. I opened it, flipping through mug shots on each page. When I didn't find him, I started over at the beginning, thumbing carefully through the pages. Same result.

Disappointed, I slid the file back to the detective. "He's not in there."

His brow furrowed. "You certain?"

"Yeah." I sounded discouraged. I'd hoped they had the dude in their sights. Opening the file, I skimmed through again until I saw the face on the ninth page. Handing the photo to the detective, I said, "This guy looks like him. There's a resemblance. But it's not the guy who met me at LaGuardia, who drove the Suburban. I don't have to guess. I had plenty of opportunity to look at him."

"There's more to the file. You sure you don't want to look through all of them?"

"I'm sure. Most of the others don't even match the description I gave to the officer. Caucasian male in his mid- to early twenties, five feet nine inches, approximately one hundred eighty-five pounds. Straight dark hair, pulled back in a long ponytail. He gave his name as Christopher, also Nick, possibly an alias. He spoke with an accent that sounded like New Jersey." I bared my teeth, touched my incisor, and then tapped the image. "If he'd smiled for the camera, you'd see a crooked eyetooth right there."

The detective nodded with approval. "You've got good recall. Most victims we deal with, well. You know. Not so specific." He didn't elaborate. But he tapped his temple with an index finger and rolled his eyes.

I didn't comment. But I detected signs of burnout. Sometimes, cops have been on the job so long they lose their compassion for crime victims. It didn't happen to my dad. But I've seen it in other police officers. Prosecutors, too. When I was at the DA's office, some of the attorneys soured on the job when they wearied of the state's witnesses.

Brennan closed the folder and tossed it into an accordion file. "We'll keep looking. We received some recent information, could help out. That car he crashed, the Suburban. It was reported as stolen."

That was news to me. "Who owned it?"

"It was a business vehicle."

"Can you tell me who it was registered to?" The guy had told me he worked for Embassy Limousines, kept talking about the red-carpet experience. Some red carpet—an elbow to the nose and a ride that could break your neck.

So if Embassy Limos had reported their own vehicle as stolen, I intended to call bullshit.

"Let me look." He sorted through the accordion file and pulled out a sheet of paper. "Says here, Pyramid Investments, LLC."

That didn't ring a bell. I made a mental note to check it out.

"We'll keep looking for the guy. Maybe there was some camera footage from the place he broke into the car. I'll find out. Hey, thanks for coming by today. We can eliminate the suspect in the lineup, start over. Your description will help out."

I said, "I ought to be able to provide a decent description. I was in the DA's office for three years, and my dad was a cop."

"That so?" His mustache twitched, maybe hiding a smile of his own. "Then it makes sense. You should know what goes into a police report."

"Oh hell yeah. I had a lot of exposure to the particulars growing up, and on the job. And I've had personal experience lately, just within the past month."

Brennan hadn't indicated whether he knew of my recent experience, but glancing at the computer on his desk, it occurred to me that he might be privy to some inside information. "Hey, while I'm here, can you do a quick check for me? I was the victim of a subway push a few weeks back, and no one has told me whether they ever got the guy in custody."

"Well, damn! You're *that* former ADA. You had a big fight on the subway platform, ended up on the tracks, am I right?"

"Yep."

He squinted at me, like he was thinking. "Are you that Stone? Morris Stone's daughter was a victim of an attack recently. Or am I mixing it up with another case?"

"Not mixing it up. That's me." The longtime connections my dad had forged never failed to amaze me. But law enforcement is tight.

"We went through training together, years ago. Morris and Victor Odom were partners."

"Right."

"Victor was a character." He shook his head. "He never could keep his hands clean. But Morris, he was solid. A good cop. Sad to hear how he died."

The response surged automatically, and I wanted to voice it. *He didn't kill himself. He would never make that jump.* But there was no point in arguing. In the past year, I'd tried to investigate his death myself, to prove it. I never got to the bottom of it.

"That subway push! Damn, you're lucky. I saw the video. It was—"

I finished his sentence. "On the website of the *New York Post.* Yeah, I know. So, can you check it out? See if there's any updated activity in that investigation? It would be a tremendous relief to know whether they've picked up the guy who attacked me. I'd love to hear that the guy isn't walking around Manhattan. I don't particularly want to bump into him."

Obliging, Brennan hit the mouse and studied the monitor. As he searched for information, I waited. I could feel tension building. The muscles in my back tightened. I started to rub the skin between my thumb and finger.

When he frowned, I pinched my skin so hard that it hurt. He said, "Yeah, I'm seeing that they picked someone up.

A thirty-eight-year-old male is being held on suspicion of the subway attack. Name is Phillip Edgar Hoffmann. Does that sound right?"

Hearing that the police had apprehended Edgar made a wave of relief wash over me. "Yes! I knew the guy as Edgar. Is there a mug shot?"

He showed me the picture on the screen. It was Edgar, for certain. But the photo was shocking. He looked terrible, gawking into the camera with an expression of horror.

Looking at his face and profile, I shuddered. Brennan gave me a sympathetic glance as he said, "Hoffmann is the only recent arrest. The other suspect named is a woman, Whitney Novak."

I wasn't yet accustomed to hearing Whitney's last name. It wasn't the first occasion in recent days that I wished our old vigilante group hadn't embraced anonymity, insisting on first names only. If I'd known Edgar's full name, the cops could have picked him up faster. And the police hadn't yet apprehended Larry, who lured me to the subway that day. I'd still have to watch out for him.

To Brennan, I said, "Glad they got Edgar in custody. I'm really relieved that I don't have to worry about Whitney, either. That's some comfort. She's charged with attempted murder."

He stared at the screen. "Assault."

"No, it's an attempted homicide charge. Attempted murder at Bellevue."

"That's not what I'm seeing."

"Maybe you've got a glitch in your system, or you're looking at an old report? NYPD contacted me when she was charged. I was in Florida on vacation, but I was told she'd been picked up and was being held without bond."

The cop's hands returned to the keyboard. For someone who only used a few of his fingers to type, his hands moved pretty fast. He squinted at the screen and then nudged the monitor so that I could see it from my seat.

He said, "There's the docket sheet. Charges were amended after her first appearance, and they had a bond hearing. The judge found that the assault didn't involve a firearm or deadly weapon. Does that sound right? How did it go down?"

I was so shocked that I stammered in response, unable to articulate a rational answer.

Whitney hadn't attacked me with a gun or knife, but she had come for me in my hospital bed, messing with my pain-killers and trying to shoot an air bubble up my arm with a hypodermic needle. It was, without doubt, an attempt to kill me; the facts were clear. Staring at the docket sheet on the computer screen, I shook my head in disbelief. Brennan was right. With my own eyes, I saw that the detective's statement was correct.

A hearing was held in Judge Callahan's court. He set a cash bail amount at ten thousand dollars. Whitney had bonded out a week ago, while I was still in Florida.

A red-hot surge of fury rolled through my head, deafening me. I thought of the trip out to Coney Island, of Millie's fears that Whitney was trailing her. I recalled the picture from the roller coaster, the partial shot of the woman sitting three rows behind me.

Caught up in my dark mental rumination, I almost missed the detective's next observation.

"This would never happen in Queens. Our DA is a believer in law and order. But that guy you've got in Manhattan, he's soft on crime. That candy-ass just goes whichever way the wind blows. The legislature in Albany decides that 'no bail and low bail' is the fashion—because that's the trend right now. Rubenstein chases it, he throws open the jailhouse door."

As Brennan gave me a sympathetic look, his mustache twitched again. "I can't believe the guy would do this to a former ADA. You were on his staff, right? That's a poke in the eye with a sharp stick."

Brennan was absolutely right. This was no coincidence. My eyes watered as I absorbed the information, like they'd literally been poked.

And I knew who held the stick.

Rubenstein.

My old boss was going soft on the woman who tried to kill me. Whitney was out, and she was following me around.

My gut said she was coming after me. Whitney was going to try it again.

CHAPTER 15

THE SECOND TIME I appeared at Rikers, my path was less rocky. The corrections officer acknowledged that my pre-scheduled meeting with Rod appeared on his log. I only had to go through two metal detectors. They made me stow my belongings in a locker, but at that point, I knew the ropes. I had a quarter in my pocket. And this time, they didn't throw me to the dogs.

Still, as I sat alone and waited in a dank cinder-block cubicle, I kept waiting for disaster to strike. Maybe they'd appear to say that my meeting was canceled, due to unforeseen circumstances. They might announce that they'd done a random search of my locker and found contraband. Or they'd throw me with a rule change, one that they had arbitrarily and capriciously determined. Maybe they'd claim that lawyers whose names began with the letter "S" could only meet with clients on Sundays and Wednesdays, every third week.

Anything was possible.

I heard the door open on the other side of the cubicle and

I tensed up, bracing myself for disappointment. I thought I'd be relieved, grateful, to actually see him come into the room. I was wrong. It was deeply unsettling when Rod walked through the door, dressed in jailhouse scrubs, with his hands cuffed behind him.

The sight of my friend restrained in handcuffs sent my fight reaction into overdrive. I could feel the adrenaline bounce in my brain. It required a huge effort to keep my demeanor cool and professional.

Before the corrections officer left, he glanced at me through the prisoner partition and said, "You got forty-six minutes."

That shook me. "Hey! He gets an hour for attorney visits. The website says so."

Without giving me another look, the guard said, "Took seven minutes to walk him over here from his cell. And it will take seven minutes to get him back."

And then he disappeared, with the door swinging shut behind him.

I scooted close to the window, and said, "Rod, I'm sorry it took so long—"

He interrupted me. "How's Millie? Is she doing okay?"

"She's all right. Mostly worried about you. She really wants to see you, Rod. She misses you like crazy. The first time she came out here, they wouldn't let her in. But she's coming back, guaranteed."

"No." Through the grimy partition, his eyes pinned me to the wall; he wasn't messing around. "I don't want her here."

"Rod, I don't think you can keep her away. I told her I'd come first, to clear the path, because they didn't let her in when she tried to visit. But she's desperate to see you."

"No," he repeated, louder that time. "You hear me? I don't want her anywhere near Rikers. It's too dangerous. This place is a hellhole. God, if something happened to Millie, I don't know what I'd do. Anyone who laid a hand on her, I'd kill him."

"Stop! Jesus, Rod, don't even think like that." I glanced around the small room, worried that someone in the Department of Correction could be eavesdropping. Sadly, I couldn't tell Rod his fears were groundless. I had seen horror stories in the media and heard tales from other lawyers. Plus I had firsthand experience with the "tramp line."

He leaned forward, folding his arms on the counter behind the window. "I didn't expect to see you, to be honest. Good surprise. But they told me I'd be getting a public defender."

"Who told you?" I wasn't shocked to hear that no one informed Rod in advance of my attorney visit. Rikers didn't run a tight ship.

"The judge. At the arraignment."

"They took you over to the courthouse? When?"

"No. I haven't been out of this shithole since the cops picked me up a week ago. The arraignment was virtual, on video. The judge read the charge to me and asked if I had money to hire a lawyer. I actually thought I had representation because Gatsby always had a guy on retainer if we ran into trouble. But the judge said there was no record of a lawyer entering an appearance. I don't have any money set aside, neither does Millie. So the judge said he'd appoint the public defender. But no one has been by to see me. I think that's pretty standard. That's what I'm hearing in my cellblock."

He was right about that. The public defender system was

shamefully understaffed. A lot of inmates didn't have the opportunity to consult with their lawyers until it was time for trial.

"Jesus, Rod. Why didn't you call me?"

"Last I heard, you were in the hospital, flat on your back. I didn't figure I could ask you to wheel into court on a stretcher."

"Do I look like I need a stretcher?" I asked, pretending to be offended. "I was in Florida when they picked you up. But if you'll have me, I'd be glad to enter my appearance on your behalf."

As he nodded, a ghost of a smile crossed his face. He looked weary, like he hadn't slept in days. And even in the dim light, I could see marks of a battle: the discolored skin around one eye and an abrasion on his cheekbone.

I needed to address that. "Who's been knocking you around?"

"I could ask you the same question."

His statement caught me off guard; I kept forgetting about the bruising from the Suburban ride. But that wasn't Rod's problem. "I was in a wreck, coming home from the airport. What about you? I'm your advocate, you gotta keep me advised."

I expected to hear him attribute it to a prison guard. But if I had bet on that, I'd have lost my money. He said, "Two guys jumped me in the cell yesterday. A couple of skinheads."

I experienced another wave of righteous anger on Rod's behalf. My muscles tensed involuntarily, as if preparing to join a fight. "Two guys? How many men to a cell?"

"It's unreal. A cell with two beds, they're squeezing three or four of us in there at a time."

Had I heard about that extent of overcrowding? The DA's office never spent much time discussing jailhouse conditions. When I tried to describe my Rikers experience to Bill's co-workers at the bar the night before, they'd shrugged it off.

"Why'd they do it?"

"Do skinheads need a reason to jump a Black man?"

The words made my stomach turn. Rod looked down at his hands. The skin on his knuckles was raw. He made a fist with his right hand, rubbing his knuckles with his left.

"I didn't have any trouble fighting them off. There were only two of them, for fuck's sake."

When our eyes met, we both grinned. Before working in lower Manhattan as a bouncer, Rod had done two tours of duty in Afghanistan. Those skinheads at Rikers had picked the wrong guy to mess with.

"But it was weird, I'll tell you that much. There were two guards there, right down the hall on the cellblock. They just turned a blind eye."

"What about when it was all over? There wasn't any trouble from the guards? They didn't try to blame it on you?"

"Didn't do shit about it. But last night, they moved the skinheads out. No explanation, even though they kept asking them what was going on. I thought maybe they was being released. But I saw them in the mess hall this morning."

I shook my head. Didn't know what to make of it. "So how many in the cell now?"

"Three. They moved two new guys in. Russians."

"How's that working out?"

"Don't know yet."

It worried me. The DA's office had referred cases to the US

Attorney, allegations concerning the expansion of organized crime into the city from a "Russian mafia." "We need to get you out. What bond amount has been set for you?"

I hoped it was a reasonable sum, that I would have enough borrowing power to post it, or to pay a percentage to a bail bondsman. I was willing to lean on Mom's credit. Funny to think I'd sworn I'd never use it.

"That's another weird thing. I'm being held without bond."

"You're fucking kidding me. For a misdemeanor assault? Who's your judge?"

"I wrote down the name, so I'd remember it." He reached into the pocket of his scrubs and pulled out a scrap of paper. "It's Callahan."

I squeezed my eyes shut as a bolt of pain drilled my left eye socket and rebounded across my forehead.

Judge Callahan? Again? It couldn't be a coincidence.

Someone was coming for us. And they were using the courts to do it.

CHAPTER 16

I DIDN'T BURDEN Rod with my personal fears. And I didn't share my doubts about Judge Callahan's ethics. If Rod knew he was in purgatory while Callahan set a ten-thousand-dollar bond on Whitney and let her go, he'd flip out.

I tried to project confidence as I said, "I'm going to get on top of this. I'll enter my appearance and go to the Criminal Courts building tomorrow, run down the assistant DA who's handling it. Maybe there's been a mistake. That's the only reasonable explanation."

He let out a long sigh, and his body seemed to relax. "I appreciate it. How are you doing? Have you recovered, pretty much? We were worried about you. Jesus Christ—who gets run over by a train?"

"I'm on the mend. But I'm getting out of shape, Rod. I look forward to bouncing you out of lockup, so we can meet at the gym again. I need a sparring partner."

He cracked a smile at that. "What about Steven? Can't he fill that role?"

"Steven? Oh, please."

"Really? I thought you two had a thing going on."

I tried to sound casual. "Well, that doesn't mean he can take me down in a fight."

I was trying to be funny. Rod didn't laugh. "I'm serious. Are you and Steven together?"

It didn't sound like idle curiosity. Rod was getting at something, I could tell. "Yeah, I guess we are. Looks like it."

"So you've seen him, since you got back to town."

"Yeah."

"Have y'all had any trouble? Since you've been back?"

"How do you mean?"

His eyes shifted, and he dropped his voice. I had to lean up to the partition to hear him. "I mean, with any of those assholes we used to hang with. I'm not talking about Whitney. She's locked up at Rosie's, I heard that. But Edgar's still out there, right? He didn't get picked up, did he?"

I almost told him then, almost said it. *Whitney's out.* But I couldn't offer any reasonable justification, couldn't explain why the system cut her loose and incarcerated him. Until I figured it out, I'd keep it close to the chest. So I just shared the good news. "I heard yesterday, from a cop in Queens. They picked Edgar up. Phillip Edgar Hoffmann. I saw the mug shot, and it's definitely him."

"Really? I'm glad to hear that, after what he did to you. Where's he being held?"

"In here, I guess. Think you'll run into him?"

"No telling. But it's not likely. They got over five thousand inmates on this island. What about the others? Diane, Devon, Larry. Anybody heard from them?"

Rod may not have known about Larry, that he had led me to the subway where I almost died on the tracks. I saved that story for another day—but not because I was trying to withhold information from him. I mean, Rod was locked up. Larry was my problem, not his.

"Nobody has seen them. Not that I know of."

"Last time I saw Larry, he was drinking again. Somebody's gonna pop up. I worry about Millie. She can't fight them off, not with me locked up on Rikers Island."

I tried to sound unconcerned, to allay his fears. "Why would anyone bother Millie?"

"She's a loose end. We all are. They've put me in jail. They came for you. We've all got targets on our backs, all of us."

I started to argue the point, just to offer reassurance, to ease his mind. But the words died before I could articulate them.

He was right. It wasn't over. He'd figured it out before I had. There was nothing to be gained by denying it.

Rod went on. "Someone was calling the shots when we were all in it together. We thought we were justice fighters, remember? It was bullshit. We were pawns."

A shiver danced down my back. "But we're not a threat to anyone. Makes sense they'd want to move on, leave us in peace."

I was lying. Lying to Rod and lying to myself. Someone was still motivated to shut me down. My ride from LaGuardia demonstrated that.

And that raised another troubling issue. The man behind the wheel of the Suburban hadn't been a member of our group. There were new players, people I'd never before encountered.

And I still didn't know who was in charge. Somebody provided the money. Someone had been able to keep us out of trouble, grease the wheel in an arrest. That person had turned on us. And I didn't have a clue who it was. "Gatsby" wasn't a real name, it was a catchphrase we used to refer to the anonymous, unseen benefactor.

As if Rod could read my mind, he said, "That person is still out there. Someone's calling the shots. You know what I think?"

"What?"

"I think it's the rich dude. That billionaire, Templeton."

"Ian Templeton? You think? But he was never a part of our group, he was one of our targets. Why would the group organize an attack on Templeton if he's in charge?"

"He's loaded, he has the power to pull those strings. Maybe the whole thing that went down on his yacht, finding that evidence, could have been phony, a farce. We were duped. And we only found what he wanted us to find."

"But you're speculating, right? Really, how do you know anything for sure?"

Rod laughed at that, but the sound was eerie, devoid of humor. "How do I know? Because we uncovered all those files of his white-collar crime. And we sent it to the government. But he's not sitting in jail. I am."

It was hard to argue with that.

He said, "So he could initiate hits on people like us. We've got to be careful. You and Steven, Millie and me. Because of what we know."

I grimaced, shaking my head. I wished I could solve the

riddle. It would make me feel safer, not so vulnerable. "What exactly is it that we know? That's so fucking dangerous? Because I'm still in the dark."

He shrugged. "Something huge. Big enough to get you killed."

I felt like time had taken a backward turn. Suddenly, I was in the same situation I'd escaped just a few weeks ago. That feeling was back, that I was the prey, and the predator was lurking, waiting for the right opportunity to pounce.

I heard footsteps outside the interview room, the booted feet of a corrections officer. My head turned toward the sound. "Is our time up already?"

"Yeah, probably. Kate, you gotta promise me."

I heard the key jangle in the lock on Rod's side of the partition. "What?" I said.

"Millie. She can't come out here to see me."

"I'll tell her."

"Another thing. I don't want her living alone, in my place in Brooklyn. They know the address. What if they come for her? Tell me you'll keep her with you."

The door swung open. "Meeting time's over. Wrap it up."

Rod pushed his chair back. "We're done."

The corrections officer pulled the handcuffs from his belt. "Stand up, hands behind your back."

Rod's jaw was tight as the corrections officer jerked his wrists into the cuffs and tightened them. Giving me the side-eye, Rod said, "I'm counting on you, Kate."

"I know. It's a promise."

As Rod left the room, I slumped down in the chair, thinking. I was making a whole lot of promises lately.

I wasn't completely sure what Millie would think of the commitments I'd made on her behalf. It was hard to predict how she'd react to the new living arrangement Rod had devised for her.

Making a promise is easy. Keeping it is hard.

CHAPTER 17

Bill

BILL PARKER HAD just turned the corner onto Ninth Avenue when fat drops of rain began to fall. He looked up at the dark clouds overhead and picked up his pace.

The downpour held off long enough for him to reach his destination, an undistinguished ten-story building of red brick. He paused in the doorway to remove his houndstooth sport jacket and shake off the drops of water clinging to the fabric. The brand-new coat was a prized possession. As the skies opened up and rain pelted the sidewalk outside, he slipped the jacket back on, grateful for his reprieve from the elements.

He walked down the tiled hallway to the room where his therapy group met. At the door, someone had tacked up a sign: "Anxiety Support 7:00 Tonight."

Bill was early, but in hindsight, it was a lucky circumstance. If he'd been on time, his sport coat would be soaked, and he wanted to keep it looking fresh as long as possible.

Stepping inside, he saw the meeting room was deserted and the floor bare. His support group always sat in a circle in the middle of the room. A cluster of metal folding chairs leaned up against a cinder-block wall. The room wasn't set up.

Since Bill was the first person to arrive, he figured he should get the room ready, so that they'd be able to jump right in at seven o'clock. He'd been looking forward to the meeting.

He grabbed two of the chairs, carried them across the floor, and set them up. When he returned to pull the next pair of chairs from the wall, he must have disturbed their tenuous balance. The stack of chairs slid from the wall, giving him a nasty jab in the ankle as they fell to the floor.

"Shit," he whispered, hopping on one foot while he clutched the injured ankle. He was starting to regret his helpful impulse.

Doggedly, he bent over the jumble of chairs, grabbed two more, dragged them to the center of the room, and unfolded them. After four trips, he'd set up an untidy circle of ten seats. That might be enough.

As he straightened the rickety chairs into a more cohesive circle, Bill considered how he might introduce the subject of his courtroom triumph. He was ready to speak up in group tonight to confide the progress he'd recently made. Bill wanted to tell the group about his role in the jury trial and securing convictions for white-collar crime. He'd describe how it felt to sit at the counsel table with his stomach in knots and hear the jury pronounce the verdicts in the DA's favor.

But wouldn't that be bragging? The thought gave him pause as he returned to the pile of chairs still scattered on the floor. When he bent down to straighten them, he thought he felt the seam strain in the shoulder of his coat. His brand-new sport coat.

With a pang of guilt, he left the jumbled seats where they lay. Bill checked the time and saw he still had ten minutes before seven.

The prospect of speaking up in the group had him feeling kind of anxious. He decided to go to the restroom.

In the bathroom, he bypassed the urinals and locked himself in a stall. He pulled out a vape pen, sucked on the mouthpiece, and inhaled. After the first hit, he almost put it away. Then he changed his mind and took another draw. He wasn't looking to get high. He just needed to relax before facing the group.

While he took a third hit, Bill heard the door creak open. Someone walked into the restroom and entered the stall next to his. He heard the rustle of fabric, followed by an exclamation as an object smacked against the floor. Curious, he squatted and peered under the stall. A pint bottle of off-brand vodka lay on the dirty tile. By some miracle, it hadn't busted. He saw a shaking hand reach down to retrieve it.

The sight of the palsied hand sent a jolt of remorse through him. Bill stood, ashamed to have intruded on the guy's privacy. He hurried out of the restroom and back into room 113, where another person had arrived. Bill paused in the doorway, trying to place her.

She was a middle-aged woman with frizzy hair. The trench coat she wore had seen better days, and the buttons strained across her abdomen. But she carried herself with an attitude that made him step back. When she met his eye, he smiled at her. "Hi. I'm Bill."

She didn't return the smile. "Good to see you," she said.

Bill noticed that the woman didn't offer her name. But, hey—it was anonymous. She wasn't required to introduce herself, and that didn't mean she was putting anything un-friendly out there. The anonymity took a while to get used to. Bill was still adjusting.

Determined to give her some space, he sat in one of the chairs and pulled out his phone. While he checked his email, he decided that the woman was a new arrival because he was certain he hadn't seen her before. He was surprised she seemed so at ease in the room. No first-time jitters.

Two more people came in—women he'd met from a prior meeting. They waved at Bill as they took seats across the circle. And then a man appeared in the doorway, pausing at the threshold. From a glance, it would appear that a homeless guy had wandered in off the street, seeking shelter from the elements. His ill-fitting, mismatched clothing was soaked from the rain, and his shoes squelched with water when he stepped into the room.

But Bill knew the guy because he'd been to meetings before. One glance at the sodden shoes confirmed that he was the vodka drinker in the adjoining restroom stall. Bill glanced swiftly away from the shoes, chagrined to think that he had peeked under the stall while the guy battled his demons. A support group was supposed to be about offering support. Bill wanted to reach out to make the man feel comfortable. "Hi, Larry," he called to him. "Good to see you again."

Larry didn't respond. He didn't even look Bill's way. He was focused on the woman—the newcomer.

Other people were arriving, but over the buzz of voices, Bill heard Larry address the woman, saying, "What are you doing here?"

She gave him a bland look. "It's a group meeting. Right? I'm in the group."

Bill didn't want to intrude and certainly didn't intend to be an eavesdropper. He rose from his seat and walked back to the untidy heap of chairs he'd left scattered on the floor. Picking them up one by one, he stacked them back against the cinder-block wall.

As he finished, the group leader arrived. Curtis was the therapist who conducted the meetings. "Bill! Thanks for stepping up, man. I'm running late. I was afraid nobody would have a place to sit."

Bill smiled, watching as the therapist set his saxophone case carefully in the corner. Curt was a musician, one of the people in the city who juggled a job and an artistic passion. He was fast becoming Bill's idol.

Most of the chairs had filled by the time Curt sat down in the circle. The leader shook his long hair back and said, "Okay! Good evening! Let's get right to it. Who has something to share? Anyone able to use the techniques we learned last week?"

Bill was ready. He lifted his hand. Curt gave him an encouraging nod.

"I had a jury trial last week. My first one in the new division."

He was tempted to elaborate, to hint at the importance of the position, for the leader's benefit. "I was assigned opening statement—there were two of us, cocounsel. And I was pretty anxious. You all can understand."

Several heads nodded. All eyes were on Bill. He was glad he'd had a couple of pulls on his pen before the meeting.

"So when I was at the counsel table, I knew I needed help. So I remembered the grounding exercises Curtis talked about for anxiety. And I used one."

Curtis appeared to be enthralled. "Which technique?"

Bill was proud to have his attention. "The five senses method, five-four-three-two-one. I looked around the courtroom. Noticed five things I could see. Four things I could feel. Three things I could hear, two I could smell. And one I could taste. And when I gave my opening, I felt in control."

Bill paused, breathing out in satisfaction. The people in the circle were nodding and smiling.

Most of them were.

Bill's version of the story wasn't entirely accurate. It was true that he'd suffered anxiety in court at the prospect of delivering the opening statement. At the counsel table that morning, he'd felt the panic mount, the perspiration dampening his hairline, adrenaline heating his neck. Also, it was true that he'd tried the senses method.

But the exercise hadn't worked the necessary magic. Maybe the environment was partly to blame. A courtroom isn't an ideal sensory environment. Try as he might, he couldn't hear three things, only two. And the only smell was Maya's cologne. And he couldn't taste anything at all.

So he had dry-swallowed a Xanax he'd secreted in his pocket, just in case. That took care of the sense of taste. The drug was bitter, leaving a nasty aftertaste on his tongue.

Fortunately, it did the trick. The judge ran late, and then the defense attorney argued at the bench with Maya for a while. Then there were instructions read aloud by the judge. By the time Bill stood before the jury box, the medication had kicked in, and the calm he exhibited in his presentation was genuine.

But in his support group, he left out the part about the Xanax. He also omitted the fact that he'd hit the vape on the morning of trial, too.

One of the women in the circle said, "So it really works? The five-four-three-two-one turned off your anxiety, Bill?"

"It sure did, Chloe. Just like we learned in this room. It worked like a charm."

The group gave him a soft round of applause while Curt smiled and nodded his approval. Bill received the reaction he'd desired, but it wasn't as satisfying as he'd hoped.

As he looked around the circle, Bill had the weirdest feeling. Though they didn't say a word, he thought that Larry and the new woman knew he was lying.

CHAPTER 18

Kate

WALKING UP THE steps of the Criminal Courts building, I focused on remaining positive. I thought it might be nostalgic to visit the Manhattan DA's office. After all, I'd worked there for three years. Learned how to try a case and do my best to sway a jury of twelve. And when I was in trial, I'd spent long hours in that building. In some ways, it had been more like home than my studio apartment in Morningside Heights. So I looked forward to walking those hallways again, assuming that it might have a warm, welcoming appeal. Like a homecoming.

Yeah, I was wrong about that. Dead wrong.

I did manage to make it past security without incident. My recent tenure in the prosecutorial ranks accomplished that much. They let me through without much resistance.

But once inside, I discovered that I was in fact an outsider. Already, there were new hires, unfamiliar faces walking the building, people with whom I had no shared history. And the familiar figures, the former coworkers I encountered, didn't treat me like a long-lost friend. I got a couple of nods of recognition. One woman said hello to me as she hurried past. The rest of the DA's staff regarded me with curiosity, or worse, suspicion. They acted as if they wondered what the hell I was doing back there. Because I was no longer one of them.

I shouldn't have been surprised, really. Law enforcement is like that. My dad was a career cop, and police are notorious for their insider-outsider perspective. To a certain extent, prosecutors share that quality.

My first goal was to run down the assistant DA who'd appeared for Rod's virtual arraignment. His office was just down the hall from my old digs. I figured he'd give me some inside information, or at least some background.

When I knocked on the door and stuck my head inside, his desk was empty. His office mate, a woman whose name didn't immediately come to mind, sat at her desk, deep in conversation on her cell phone.

I was polite, didn't intrude into her space. I waited for her to look up. When she did, she wasn't happy.

"This is private," she said. "What do you want?"

"I'm looking for Marcus. We need to talk about a case, a guy who's being held at Rikers."

She pointed at his empty chair. "He isn't here."

"Yeah, I can see that. Can you tell me where to find him?"

She pulled a face, to make it clear that I was bothering her. "I'm not in charge of his schedule."

And then it came to me. Her name was Moira. Moira Schwartz. "Moira, I know you don't want me hanging around, waiting for him to get back. Are you sure you don't have any idea what he's doing this morning?"

She relented. Maybe she had belatedly remembered me, too. "Callahan's got a docket call. Marcus might be down there."

Judge Callahan. My least favorite jurist in the building. *Great.* "Thanks," I said, before I pulled the door shut.

Since I was there, I tried to nail down additional pieces of information. My next attempts were even less successful. The lawyer who had appeared on Whitney's bond hearing wasn't around, and no one could tell me where she might be found. And when I tried to locate Bill's new office in the white-collar division, I hit a brick wall. They wouldn't give me any information whatsoever about my good friend. I tried to explain who I was, the longtime connection Bill and I shared. They didn't listen. It made no impact. I couldn't get a foot in the door. It was eerie. Like white collar operated behind an iron curtain.

I shot Bill a text, telling him that I was in the building and wanted to chat. While I waited to hear back, I was confident I'd get a speedy response. Bill wouldn't ghost me. We were tight. Genuine friends.

My phone pinged with a quick response, so I was correct on that score. But I wasn't happy with the message.

In a meeting with Maya

Maybe later?

So I was pretty discouraged when I left the DA's office and walked back to the elevator. I had assumed I would get all my business done that morning. So far, I had struck out altogether.

I took the elevator up to the floor where Callahan's courtroom was located. People milled around in the hallway, mostly staring at their cell phones. Bailiffs in dark navy uniforms paced up and down the hall. I watched a defense attorney chase down a prosecutor, begging for a better plea bargain.

When I approached the door to Callahan's court, I pulled it open and peeked inside, hoping to see Marcus. In my head, I had my pitch, ready to advocate on Rod's behalf. I wanted to spring him from Rikers.

But I didn't spot Marcus as I looked around the room. In fact, court wasn't in session. The bench was empty, so I figured Judge Callahan must have declared a recess. A couple of lawyers sat on the wooden benches at the front of the room, laughing together about something. But they weren't the people I sought.

I shut the door and stepped away, thinking I had planned my morning poorly. I should have made contact ahead of time, to nail down meetings, instead of running down to court first thing on a weekday morning. As a defense attorney in private practice, I had a lot to learn.

I pulled out my phone, ready to make some calls. That's when I saw him. Callahan was striding down the hallway dressed in a shirt and tie. He must have left his black robe in chambers. His clerk walked beside him, her head nodding energetically as the judge spoke. Apparently, providing constant reinforcement was part of her job description. I didn't envy her the post.

I stood my ground, watching him approach. He continued talking, a stream of commentary directed at the clerk. I figured he might not notice me. He could have forgotten who I was. Hundreds of lawyers go through the DA's office.

And then he glanced over at me, where I stood beside

his courtroom door. Our eyes met. I saw it, the moment that recognition struck and he made the connection. I fancied that I could read his mind. *Oh my God, it's her.*

And when it registered, he stumbled on the tiled floor. Even though there was nothing under his feet to trip him up.

"Judge Callahan!" His clerk grabbed his elbow, to steady him. "Are you all right?"

He snatched his arm away from her as he walked past me. He didn't give me another look, but it wasn't necessary. I'd seen his mask slip.

Asshole. He knew what he had done to me.

The question, of course, was why he'd done it. As I watched him go, it occurred to me. I should ask him. He was available, right at that moment. I wouldn't need to hunt him down.

I turned to follow, walking fast down the hall, so I could catch up.

That's when I heard it.

"Kate Stone! Hold up!"

I knew that voice.

It was my old boss, the district attorney of Manhattan. Frank Rubenstein.

CHAPTER 19

I PAUSED, UNCERTAIN which way to go. I was unwilling to lose my prey, and Callahan was making a getaway while I dawdled.

But Frank Rubenstein had caught up to me. Extending his hand, he said, "Kate! How are you?"

Wary, I accepted his handshake. Historically, Rubenstein and I hadn't been chummy. When I was on his staff, I worked my tail off, racking up jury verdicts, taking cases that scared other ADAs away. But back then, he only took note of my existence when he wanted to criticize my performance.

Or, to offer unwelcome personal advice. Rubenstein had required me to join a support group to address what he designated as my anger problem. Since I don't believe I have a problem with anger—and I acknowledge that reasonable minds could differ on the issue—I resisted his suggestion. So he made anger management therapy a condition of my continued employment in his office. I'd followed through with his mandate, since I had no choice.

It hadn't ended well. My support group tried to kill me. Living with my unrestrained anger was the safer choice, in my case.

I could've shared those thoughts with him, but I didn't see much point. I managed a tight smile. "I'm doing all right, Frank. Thanks for asking."

I glanced down the hall, hoping it wasn't too late to catch up with Callahan. I spotted the judge as he stepped into an elevator and the doors closed.

Meanwhile, Frank Rubenstein still had my right hand in his grip. The extended hold made me uncomfortable. I was pretty sure it was the first time we'd ever made physical contact. I wanted to jerk my hand away.

And when he clasped it between both of his hands, my jaw almost dropped.

He said, "We need to talk, Kate. I want to catch up. Do you know how worried I've been about you?"

In fact, I didn't know. Frank and I had never had the kind of relationship that fostered any belief in his genuine concern for my welfare. He was often concerned, however, about his own welfare. He sometimes expressed concern that my antics would make him look bad.

"What are you doing up here? Do you have time for us to catch up, chat? We could go down to my office. I'll order in coffee for us."

Rubenstein was offering me a cup of coffee? Inside his private sanctuary? That was a first. I found myself incapable of turning down the invitation. The novelty of the scenario was irresistible.

Five minutes later, I sat in the chair near his desk—the

same spot I used to occupy when I was called on the carpet and taken to task. A steaming white mug of coffee, emblazoned with the words "El Met," was placed on a table next to me by an administrative assistant.

"Thank you, Sonja," Frank said, as she slipped through the door.

When the door shut behind her, Frank said, "Miguel Lucian is an artist in residence at the Met."

He smiled, like he expected me to follow the thread of his statement. I didn't want to look stupid, so I took a stab at it. "The opera? Or the art museum?"

"The Met. Metropolitan Museum of Art."

"Oh. Right," I said. "I'm a fan." My mom would occasionally drag Leo and me to the Met when we were younger, when she thought we needed a dose of culture. Leo exhibited more enthusiasm than I possessed at that time. He'd roam around the suits of armor, asking questions Mom couldn't answer. She was more interested in the Impressionist paintings. Mom would rhapsodize over Renoir while I sat on a bench nearby and sulked.

"'El Met' is how they say 'the Met' in Spanglish. Latinx people in New York call it that. The museum is marketing merchandise to support the acquisition of Latinx art for their collection."

I lifted the mug with new respect. "So this mug is actual merch from the Met? What did it cost?"

"Twenty dollars."

I snorted, setting the mug down like it had burned my fingers. I'd paid less than twenty bucks for a whole set of "I Heart NY" mugs.

Frank stared at me with his hands folded on the desktop. The scrutiny made me uncomfortable. For a long moment, we just sat there in silence.

Finally, he nodded and said, "From outward appearances, it seems you've recovered."

I wanted to make sure we were on the same page. Frank and I don't always connect, and I wanted to make sure I knew which recovery he was referring to. "You're talking about the subway, right?"

"Yes, of course. I know you sustained injuries and had to be hospitalized. I kept up to date on all of it. Viewed the coverage. Had the police reports delivered directly to my desk."

"Wow," I said, genuinely surprised.

He shuddered. "I can't imagine what you experienced. Can't even imagine what it was like."

That was probably true. Rubenstein didn't take the train. He had a private car, with a driver. I'd seen it, pulled to the curb on Centre Street. When Rubenstein emerged from the building, the driver hopped out to hold the door open for him. It's a wonder he didn't make the driver wear a chauffeur's cap.

"I'm back to normal. Pretty much," I hedged. The doctor still hadn't released me to resume all my usual activities. No kickboxing yet, no karate. He didn't want me to risk a blow to the head. That's when it occurred to me I should probably call the physician's office to tell him about my recent misadventure. My face was banged up, and I was still stiff from the roll in the Suburban.

Maybe Frank was picking up brain waves. He gestured in front of his face. "I assume that you sustained that recent bruising from the incident at LaGuardia. I'm staying up to date on that, too. I'm in touch with the DA in Queens. She says they haven't located the driver of the Suburban yet, but they're working on it. They got footage from a traffic camera."

"Really?" Detective Brennan hadn't mentioned it, so it must have been a recent breakthrough.

"Yes, they got tape from surveillance cameras at the two nearest intersections. They're trying to track the driver using facial recognition."

"That's fantastic." I was seriously impressed.

"Don't worry. We'll leave no stone unturned. That's a promise."

I was liking Frank better, until he winked at me.

That was creepy.

I scooted back in the chair, creating some distance between us. "So about that. I'm encouraged, honestly, that the precinct in Queens is working so hard on the investigation. And it's gratifying to hear you're interested in it."

"I'm invested. Obviously. And proud that NYPD apprehended the two primary perpetrators of the attacks on you in Manhattan, Hoffmann and Novak."

"Right. I appreciate that, really. So how come you released Whitney Novak?"

His face froze. "What?"

"Whitney, the woman who attacked me in my hospital room at Bellevue. She's the woman who has been accused of killing another patient on the same day."

"She's at Rosie's. I'm certain."

I was certain Whitney *wasn't* there. Just two days prior, I'd been sitting with Detective Brennan in the precinct house in

Queens when he dropped the bomb about Whitney Novak's release.

Frank swiveled in his chair, and his hands started moving across the keyboard. "I personally intervened, gave an instruction in the case. I said that she should be held without bond."

He covered his mouth with his hand as he studied the computer monitor. I sipped from the El Met mug as I waited to hear what he'd say. It would be interesting to see how he'd react when he realized what his office had done.

I saw him toy with the mouse, squint at the screen and lean forward. If Frank was faking his surprise, he was a good actor.

He pushed away from the desk and sighed, shaking his head. "Sign of the times. I'm sorry, Kate. You're right, she's out." In an apologetic voice, he added, "It's a supervised release. So there's that."

"Come on, Frank. You know that doesn't mean shit. Nobody's watching her."

This was as good a chance as any to segue to my mission at the courthouse. "Meanwhile, I have a client who's being held at Rikers on a less serious offense—way less serious. And he's locked up tight."

Frank eyed me with surprise. "You're doing criminal defense?"

"Sure. I'm not an ADA anymore. And criminal law is what I know."

I pushed out of the chair and stepped up to his desk. "While you've got the website up, look up Rodney Lamar Bryant. I need to know who's got bargaining authority over his case in your office, so I can pitch it for an ROR. Rod doesn't belong at Rikers. He's a vet, honorably discharged. Served in Afghanistan."

Frank's hands obligingly tapped the keyboard, then suddenly went still. Looking up at me, he said, "You're perfect."

Those were words he'd never spoken to me before. "Huh?"

"I'm creating an advisory board. We're going to give oversight to the New York City judges on bail reform, how far it should go, what the boundaries should be."

"Really?"

He dropped his voice, as if we might be overheard, though we were alone in the office. "You wouldn't believe the pressure I'm under. They're pushing me from both sides. The progressives demand an end to cash bail, alternatives to incarceration. But with this recent crime surge, there's been a lot of pushback on that. You've read about it, I'm sure."

"I have." I read the *Post* and the *New York Times*, almost every day. They'd drawn opposing battle lines.

"We're creating a representative body to reflect all perspectives. And you would fit right in."

"You think?"

I was extremely flattered, but it seemed incomprehensible. Would Rubenstein actually grant such a plum appointment to me?

"I do. You know the criminal law, you're a former ADA You've also been a victim of crime, but you represent individuals charged with criminal offenses. And your background has an interesting degree of balance. Your mother is a defense attorney, your father was an officer with the NYPD."

He smiled, pleased with himself, like he'd solved the riddle of the sphinx. "It's the perfect combination. Are you in a position to accept the appointment? There's no compensation, but reasonable expenses will be covered. And there's lots of positive exposure. A feather in your cap, right? Every young attorney can use that kind of publicity."

"That's true. Yeah, I've got the time."

"Perfect. I'm plugging you in. Do we have your new contact information? I'm adding you on right now."

I gave it to him, gladly. His hands flew across the keyboard. "We'll try to avoid making undue demands on your time. Don't want to burn out our board members."

And then he stood, offering his hand for another shake. "Congratulations, Kate."

"Thanks, Frank. Appreciate it."

He was walking me to the door. Clearly, our meeting was over. Before he could push me into the hallway, I said, "Before I leave, tell me again, who do I speak with about my client Rodney? We need to talk about an ROR, about a hearing in court, a possible plea bargain."

"Oh, that. Take it to Donald Rudd. He's head of the division handling lower-level violent crime. No weapon involved in your client's case?"

"None." I pulled out my phone to look up Donald's office number in the building. He'd be my next stop.

"Great. Perfect. Donald can help you out. He's out of town right now, making a presentation at a state criminal conference. But you should contact him when he gets back."

Deflated, I realized I wouldn't be able to help Rod until Rudd returned.

Frank Rubenstein beamed at me as he stood in the doorway. "I'm so glad I ran into you today."

The funny thing was, he actually sounded glad.

Then his face sobered. He said, "Before you go, tell me. How's your anger management therapy coming along?"

Well, shit.

Some things don't change.

CHAPTER 20

I DODGED FRANK'S therapy probe. Frank Rubenstein wasn't the boss of me, not anymore. I wasn't required to take his advice or answer nosy questions.

On the other hand, Rubenstein's invitation to participate in the bail reform was tempting. Beyond tempting, in fact. I was pleasantly intoxicated by the notion. The opportunity to shape policy appealed to my desire for control in the criminal justice system. I had strong opinions on the state of preconviction procedures, and it would be exciting to mold and affect new practices.

Also, as Frank suggested, it would get my face out there. I'd make contacts in the profession, connections that could lead to employment in the city. I really needed to dig up a job offer in New York. I didn't know how long I could work at my mother's firm in New Jersey before one of us killed the other.

My head buzzed with ideas as I crossed Centre Street and bought a can of Diet Coke from a food cart. While I sat on a bench at the small park across the street from the courthouse, I sipped the soda and tapped notes on my cell phone as I recorded my thoughts.

My phone buzzed as I worked. The screen showed Millie's name. I winced, dreading the sorry news I was obliged to pass along.

I answered. "Hi, Millie."

"Kate! Did you go to the courthouse? Is Rod getting out?"

"I did go, first thing. And I went to the DA's office. I just left a few minutes ago." I paused for a fraction of a second, prepared to break the bad news.

Millie didn't give me the chance. "Did you talk to anybody? Who?"

"Actually, I talked to Rubenstein himself, if you can believe that. He gave me the name of a guy to deal with on Rod's case. But that ADA is out of pocket today."

"No!" Millie's voice was a powerful instrument. It boomed out of my cell phone speaker, making people who sat on a bench nearby shoot me resentful looks. "You said you'd do it today, Kate."

Her dismay made me feel genuinely guilty. What kind of defense attorney was I, if I couldn't get a man released without bond on a misdemeanor, in this town?

"I tried. Really, I'll track the guy down, Millie, but he's at a conference out of town. Don't lose it, okay?"

The phone crackled when she spoke again. I hastily pushed the button to reduce the volume.

She said, "What about the judge? Did you go to court to ask the judge about Rod's bail? What did the judge say? Was it a mistake?"

My brain painted a mental image of Callahan, dodging me in the hallway of the Criminal Courts building. "I didn't catch him on the bench. I need to work on this internally, with the assistant DA. He'll see that the hold on Rod is all a big mistake. Then we'll present a united front before the judge, and the judge will follow our recommendation. That's how it works."

I could hear tears in her voice as she said, "Kate, you've got to get him out of there."

"I'm trying." More courthouse workers were gathering in the park. One guy sat so close to me that he almost knocked my Diet Coke can off the bench. I scooted away from him. "I'm doing everything I can. I'm sure he'll be out, just as soon as I touch base with the ADA."

"I can't wait around for that. I've just got to see Rod, to make sure he's all right."

She sounded determined. I was unhappy to hear it. I decided to take the conversation out of the park, where I was surrounded by government employees. I headed for the subway, still talking into the phone.

"Rod doesn't want you there, Millie. He was very definite about that."

When she didn't answer, I talked louder. "Let me handle this."

Still no response. I said, "Have you started packing? You know Rod thinks you should stay with me."

Silence. I checked the screen.

She'd hung up on me. Again.

"Damn," I muttered, pocketing my phone. The prospect of Millie being subjected to the visitation obstacles at Rikers was unsettling. Millie was capable of inciting a scene in far less challenging circumstances.

It would be a shitshow, that was certain. And I'd made a pledge to Rod to keep it from happening.

My mood plummeted as I descended into the subway and took the train uptown. While I clung to a metal pole, I ruminated about Millie's response. Rod wouldn't be happy if she turned up at Rikers.

I got off the subway and climbed the stairs, emerging on the city streets. I wasn't far from the Bohemian Hotel. I hoped I could catch Steven at work. He would know what to do. He always kept a cool head.

As I approached the building, a handful of residents had gathered near the entrance. A circle of three men passed around a cigarette. As I walked by them, one of the men called out to me, "Hey! Spare a dollar, spare a dime?" He held out a battered foam cup. "I need money for a bus ticket, my mother is sick and I want to see her before she dies."

People generally say you shouldn't engage. My dad always told me I should keep moving. He'd seen the homeless all his life in New York, had dealt with them in the precinct. Nine times out of ten, he said, the money they received went to drugs. People think they are helping them, but they enabled the addiction. That's what he told me. Also, he said, most of the hard luck stories are bullshit.

But what my dad said and what he did were two different things. He kept loose change in the left front pocket of his pants, and deposited it freely, making conversation while he did it. When I was younger, I would ask why he was doing what he had told me to avoid. He just shrugged it off, with that line about a foolish consistency, that famous quote that uses the word "hobgoblin."

Ultimately, I followed his example rather than his advice.

On that day, I didn't have coins in my pocket, so I pulled a one from my wallet. The guy was jovial. "You have a good day!"

"Thanks. It hasn't been great so far."

I continued toward the entrance. He fell in beside me. "That's too bad. You got a cigarette?"

"Nope. If I had a cigarette, I'd be smoking it."

The very mention of tobacco tickled something in my brain, and I suddenly wished I did have a smoke. I hadn't bummed one in weeks, but I felt that urge, a longing for a soothing hit of nicotine.

It was just as well I couldn't indulge, because I would have been busted. Steven came out through the front door at that moment, and he liked to give me a hard time when I smoked.

When he saw me, he broke into a smile. "Kate! You didn't tell me you were coming over here."

"Is that all right with you? Am I interrupting something?"

"We're about to serve lunch." To the men standing nearby, he called, "They've got everything ready for you inside. Looks good today, we got food donations from a deli."

The information was received with enthusiasm. The man who stood beside me said, "Did they send over potato salad? I could go for that."

"Then you're in luck," Steven said. "They've got two kinds of potato salad."

Most of the men moved from the sidewalk and entered

the building. But the man holding the foam cup lingered. He emptied the coins and bills from the cup and slipped the money in his pocket.

"Is this your lady, Doctor?" he asked Steven.

"She's a friend of mine," he said.

Turning back to me, Steven said, "You won't believe who got in touch this morning."

We didn't have that many common acquaintances. Still I couldn't guess. "Who?"

"Devon. He wants to get together, to talk."

"Really?" I didn't know how I felt about that. Devon and I weren't particularly tight. But it wouldn't hurt to see how he was getting along. Rod had speculated that we were all in trouble.

I said, "Maybe we should meet up. Couldn't hurt, the way things are going."

"Good. Because he's coming by in an hour. We're meeting for coffee at the deli around the corner." Steven bent his head down close to mine and gave me an inquiring look. "Kate, did you go to the courthouse?"

"Yeah. I just came from there."

"And? Any luck, any progress on Rod?"

"Not exactly. I'm still working on it. When I told Millie, she flipped. She said she's going to Rikers."

The panhandler let out an ear-piercing whistle. "Rikers? Who you got locked up in that shithole?"

I didn't share the details with my new acquaintance. To Steven, I said, "I actually talked it over with Rubenstein. He made me a proposition. He says he's putting together an advisory board on bail reform, and he asked me to serve on it."

Steven pulled a disbelieving face. "You're kidding."

"I know! Isn't that incredible? I'm interested, frankly."

"I don't understand you. Why would you agree to have anything to do with Rubenstein?"

The panhandler had joined us, standing directly beside me. "Yeah! Rubenstein's a dick!"

I ignored the guy. My face heated as I said to Steven, "Because it's an incredible opportunity. And an important job."

"Where you will have to associate with Rubenstein. Didn't you tell me you despised him? I seem to recall that you suspected him of covering for Ian Templeton when his office didn't charge him with fraud."

"Yeah!" our third wheel interjected. "He's a bad dude."

"That was conjecture," I said.

Steven's eyes narrowed, and he frowned with disapproval. The expression kicked off a defensive response in me.

I said, "I can still look into Templeton. That won't change, whether I serve on the board or not."

He took a step away from me and nodded toward the door. "I have to help serve the meal. You want to come in? You could help out. We can always use another pair of hands. And we've got an hour to kill."

Ordinarily, I would've been glad to help. But he'd made me mad. I shrugged, kept my voice cool. "I should go back to the hotel, see if I can get in touch with Rod. I need to let him know what's up."

"You don't want to see Devon?"

I hesitated. Did I? After my brush with death, Devon hadn't checked in on me. He'd pretty much dropped out of sight.

And my mother's voice shouted in my head again, telling me to steer clear.

"I've got some things to do."

Steven shrugged. "Later," he said. He disappeared inside the building.

But the panhandler lingered. As I started to walk off, he followed me. In a singsong voice, he said, "Someone's looking for you."

I stopped abruptly. Facing him, I said, "What do you mean?"

His hand was in his pocket, jingling the change he carried. "You're the one they're looking for. Kay-tee! He's after you!"

His eyes had a sly look, like he knew a dark secret. About me.

The guy crooned, "He's sniffing around! Boozing to get his nerve up, just waiting to get you."

I was crazy to stand there. What had my father taught me, since I was a kid? *Don't engage.*

But my feet were rooted to the sidewalk. "Who are you talking about? Why would anyone be looking for me?"

The panhandler started backing away from me. He pulled his hand from his pocket, and I saw him make a hand gesture, the sign of the horns. He extended his index finger and pinky, holding the middle and ring finger down with his thumb.

"The devil's after you," the panhandler said. "He'll smash you like a bug, set his demons on you."

"What the hell?" He obviously suffered from mental illness, his display was too bizarre to take seriously. But there was something about the look on the man's face that held my attention. I couldn't walk away.

The panhandler turned abruptly away, muttering under

his breath. Instead of entering the shelter, he hurried down the street with his head bowed. As he walked away, I saw that he held one hand behind his back, still making the sign of the horns.

He was warding off the evil eye. Crazy.

So why did it scare me so much?

CHAPTER 21

ONE HOUR LATER, I sat next to Steven in the deli around the corner. My coffee was growing cold as we waited for Devon to arrive.

Steven scooted closer in the booth. "You feeling better?"

"Yeah. Sorry I was kind of a jerk earlier."

I couldn't stay mad at Steven. After the panhandler freaked me out with his talk about people looking for me and the devil following me around, Steven was the person I turned to. I ran into the BoHo and found him in the dining room. He talked me down.

"And you're not letting that guy on the sidewalk get inside your head?" he said.

"No. I got past that, thanks to you."

He lifted his empty cup. "You want more coffee?"

"I'm good," I said.

After he paid for a refill, he slid back onto the seat beside me. "I'm glad you changed your mind about seeing Devon."

"Yeah, it's best to stay in touch, considering. And Devon's a good person to know. Very smart."

Devon *was* smart, a whiz kid in the tech industry. He was a brilliant computer geek and knew more about electronics and programming and network systems than I could imagine. He knew about security, too, and how to hack around it.

I saw Devon outside as he passed the glass window and pulled open the door. He acknowledged us with a wave before grabbing a bottle of sparkling water from the refrigerator case and carrying it to the counter. Unlike Rod and Millie and me, Devon looked untouched by the drama that had transpired since we last met. He still wore his clothes with careless grace, and his short locs hairstyle hadn't changed. No one had ever divulged his age. I knew he was out of college and working in tech, but he could still easily pass for a kid in his late teens. And like any teenager, his head was bent over his cell phone as he waited for the cashier.

When he joined us, he said, "This is weird, right? Steven, I didn't even know whether I could reach you at that cell number anymore when I gave you a call this morning. Now that the group's dead."

I wasn't sure I was comfortable with the description. "Not dead, exactly."

"That's why I got in touch, just to make sure it's dead. Hope so, for my sake. It's splintered up, kaput. Right? Everyone scattered, so we're done."

His breezy dismissal made me indignant. "We're done? Everyone scattered? Where the hell is that coming from?"

Devon regarded me like I'd lost my mind. "What's your problem? Did I say something that pissed you off?"

Steven interjected. "Kate's been through a lot, Devon."

I cut him off. No one needed to apologize for my reaction. "We're not done."

Devon sighed, "Shittttt. Really?"

"Yeah. And everyone hasn't scattered. Millie's around. I'm looking out for her because Rod's locked up at Rikers since Gatsby jerked his support. And Whitney was stalking us at Coney Island, for God's sake."

Devon looked dubious. "Whitney's stalking you? I thought they arrested her."

"She's out."

"Wow. You actually saw her?"

Steven sounded conciliatory when he said, "Somebody who looked like Whitney showed up in a picture the day we were at Coney Island."

Devon took a drink of his water. He squinted, like he was thinking it over. "But does that mean anything? A lot of people go to Coney Island. It's a popular place. Sounds like a coincidence."

It felt like gaslighting, and I wouldn't accept it. "You think? They arrested Edgar this week, and he's being held at Rikers—so far. But Larry is still out there. He's never been apprehended. And who knows—they might release Edgar on fifty dollars cash bail tomorrow. For all I know, Edgar will be waiting around the corner to push me in front of a bus this time."

I thought I saw Devon wince. But maybe not. "Wow. Damn. I was hoping that everything had kind of wrapped up. Diane left town. You hear that?"

I shook my head as I watched Devon toy with the bottle.

"And Larry's dropped out of sight. Whitney and Edgar got arrested for attacking you. I thought—you know, maybe that's it. End of story," he said.

I'd become so agitated that a pulse beat in my temple. "I'm afraid I don't share your level of confidence."

"But you understand my position. From where I stand, we're done. I want to leave it in the past. Actually, if I'd known that someone's still trailing you, I wouldn't have come out here today. I think we need to distance ourselves, or we'll be next."

Steven said, "Be next? So you agree with Kate, that there's still a threat? I've been trying to talk her down from this theory that someone's still out to get her."

"Distance," Devon said. "I think we have to forget we ever joined up with that group, pulled off the shit we used to do."

"We can't ignore what's happening," I said.

Devon gave me a wry smile. "I'm not ignoring it. I know what happened. It's why I want to back off. Like, really far off."

"That won't work," I said. "We have to confront it," I said.

"Really? Wasn't that your theory last time? You wanted to bring down Ian Templeton. Look at how that worked out." Devon lifted his water and chugged it.

Steven came to my defense. "None of this is Kate's fault, Devon. She was motivated by the same goal we all had committed to. Trying to correct some injustices."

"She waved a red flag in front of a bull when she pulled a heist on Templeton's yacht. That's my opinion, anyway."

Steven said, "Maybe we can do it better this time. Something subtle, not so 'in your face.'"

I blurted out, "Devon, you could hack into his business. See what Templeton's up to."

He snorted. "That's your idea of something subtle? Talk about a red flag."

I was losing him. He screwed the lid tightly on his water bottle. His face was closed, and he was about to bail.

"Seriously, Devon. Templeton's behind this. I'm not the only one who believes it. That's what Rod thinks, too. He told me that when I saw him at Rikers."

"I'm not really following your line of reasoning. I don't see where this endless pursuit works to my advantage," Devon said. He checked the time on his phone. "I've got to get back to Hudson Yards."

I exchanged a look with Steven. I said, "Hudson Yards? What are you doing there?"

He smirked at me. "Living there. Thirty-Five Hudson Yards. Tower E."

Steven and I yelped in unison. He recovered first. "Good God, Devon. How much are they paying you in tech? How the hell can you possibly afford to live in Hudson Yards?"

I couldn't fathom what the explanation might be. Thirty-Five Hudson Yards was a new skyscraper built near Chelsea and Hell's Kitchen. A rectangular prism rising a thousand feet into the sky, it was one of the most expensive places in the city to live. The top thirty-six floors housed multimillion-dollar condos. And Devon looked like his picture could be in a high school yearbook.

A little sheepish, he said, "It's my boss's place. He's at a tech conference in Amsterdam right now. It's not as glamorous as it sounds. I'm dog-sitting. I hate that fucking dog."

Devon pushed up his sleeve and displayed a large Band-Aid. "Teeth marks. Little fucker bit me yesterday."

"Ouch," I said.

He pulled the sleeve down and slid out of the booth. "Devon, please!" I said. "Don't go yet."

He cast a longing glance at the door. Seemed like he was eager to get away and wash his hands of us.

I couldn't let that happen because I needed him if we were going to take a shot at Templeton. "He's coming for us, Devon. I guarantee it. You just gonna wait for it to happen?"

After a moment's hesitation, he sat back down. "What am I supposed to do?"

I was thinking it over. "We have to take him down first. I have an idea."

Devon groaned and slumped over the table. "Not again."

"No, listen! Templeton's got a new cryptocurrency scheme. Something called Zagcoin. If we can buy in, we can expose him. You know it's got to be crooked, another Ponzi scheme."

"How can we afford to do that, Kate?" Steven's voice was soft and reasonable

"And why do you think there's anything wrong with his crypto? A lot of people are buying." Devon's tone was sharp.

I could feel my blood heating up. "Because everything he does is a scam! He's like Madoff, a wolf in sheep's clothing."

"Does she know anything about cryptocurrency?" Devon asked Steven.

Steven shook his head. I kicked him under the table and said, "How about this? I'll look into it, okay? And tell you what I find out. And we can see if we can figure out what the hitch is. That's not too outlandish, right?"

"Okay." Devon scooted out again. "I'll listen. That's all I'm committing to, for now. Let me know when you find the smoking gun. Steven's got my cell number."

As he hurried out, Steven nudged me. Trying to suppress a smile, he said, "Seriously, Kate. What do you know about cryptocurrency?"

"Nothing," I said. "But I'm about to have a crash course. Give me a few days."

"What kind of crash course? Where are you going for advice?"

I picked up my phone. "I think I'll get another coffee. You want one?"

"No, I've got to get back. But tell me, who's your investment guru?"

"I'm going to ask my mother's broker."

He looked impressed. "Your mother has a broker?"

"Oh hell yeah." I googled the name, and the business website popped up. "At Morgan and Goldberg. And they must be good. My mom has more money than any lawyer I know."

CHAPTER 22

AFTER STEVEN LEFT, I made a quick call to Morgan and Goldberg. At first, they shut me out and gave me a total cold shoulder. They refused to schedule an appointment until I dropped my mother's name. But after I used my mom as a calling card, I was told that her broker, Julie Wolfe, could make time for me that very afternoon.

I watched the clock in the deli as I used my phone to read up on Ian Templeton's new investment scheme. It was all over the media. Everyone in the financial sector was talking about it. I read everything I could find. Problem was, I could only grasp the basics. And I had no way of discerning whether or not his new investment was legitimate.

Only a short while back, there would have been an easy solution. I would have asked Whitney. She had a background in finance. A former Wall Street professional, Whitey had the ability to explain investments in a way that I could understand.

But I wouldn't be reaching out to Whitney, obviously. I had another resource, one that didn't pose a threat to my personal safety. I left the deli and headed for the train.

I got off the subway at the Wall Street station. The Morgan and Goldberg office was a couple of blocks away, near the New York Stock Exchange. The office was on the twentieth floor of a shining white art deco building built of limestone. Inside and out, the structure was beautifully maintained. By contrast, the Criminal Courts building on Centre Street looked like a grimy prison.

I stepped out of the elevator onto the twentieth floor, into a glittering office space. The receptionist who greeted me gave me a subtle once-over. She was much better dressed than I was. But that wasn't unusual, in my experience.

I said, "Kate Stone, here to see Julie Wolfe."

When the woman picked up the phone to notify the broker, I could tell there was a problem. After a brief conversation, the receptionist hung up and gave me a tight smile. "Ms. Wolfe wasn't expecting you. She was expecting Patricia Stone."

"What? No, Patricia Stone is my mother. Julie is her broker, that's why I called." After a pause, I added, "My mother referred me."

Maybe it sounded like a lie—which it was. The receptionist gave me a slow blink. "Ms. Wolfe is tied up. But you can talk to her assistant, Mr. Wagner. He's available. Or you can come back another time."

The snub made my temper flare. I could feel the heat crawling up the back of my neck. But there was no point in picking a fight with the receptionist. She was just the messenger.

I needed to control my ire and roll with it. Maybe the assistant would have the information I sought. "I'll see Mr. Wagner. Thanks."

It wasn't a bad trade-off, actually. Because when they ushered me in to see him, his windowless office made me feel more comfortable, more at home. It reminded me of the spot I'd shared with Bill Parker, not long ago. The assistant's office was a cleaner, better furnished version of the same tiny space we had shared in the DA's office. Wagner was an underling, and I know how to deal with underlings. I've always held that role.

As I settled into the chair facing his desk, he said, "So you're interested in cryptocurrency."

"Yeah! I'm just a beginner. Tell me about it."

"Okay." He sat up straight, folded his hands on the top of the desk. "Cryptocurrency is digital money. You know Bitcoin, right?"

"Yeah, generally. Explain it to me."

He seemed taken aback, like he'd encountered someone from a different planet. Maybe Wall Street types weren't accustomed to dealing with people like me, who had no understanding of the world of finance. "It's decentralized money, money that's digital and encrypted."

"Well, I know what money is."

"Right! It's decentralized, as opposed to, say, the dollar. The US dollar is managed by the federal government. Our country maintains the value of the dollar."

"I know that," I said. I didn't want him to think I was stupid.

He seemed encouraged. "With crypto, there's no central authority backing it."

I was already confused. "Then how is it worth anything?"

"It doesn't have intrinsic value. It's not backed by gold or silver, not issued by any country's government. It has value because people buying and selling it have invested trust in it. The value of currency is related to its utility and scarcity. Cryptocurrency has utility because electronic payment is easier with crypto than with currency. Digital transactions of crypto are fast. And it has scarcity. The currencies are limited, with a finite number available for purchase. That drives up the value."

Seriously, this was Greek to me, but I tried to follow along. "What about hackers?" I asked, thinking that Devon's particular skills might make a shortcut possible.

"There's always the danger, right? Since it's electronic, counterfeiters might want to mess around with it. Bitcoin has a security program to prevent that, called blockchain. You're familiar with blockchain?"

I shook my head, discouraged. Of course they would take steps to prevent people from hacking in. But Wagner was obviously warming to the topic. His eyes glowed as he described the many merits and detailed workings of blockchain. My mind wandered as I waited for him to pause for breath.

Finally, he did. He picked up a pen and tapped it on his desk, like he was beating out a rhythm on a percussion instrument. With an eager voice, he said, "So would you like to make a Bitcoin purchase?"

"No." I crossed my legs, leaned back in the chair, so I could gauge his reaction. "I hear Ian Templeton has a new investment opportunity. That's what I want to buy into."

His jaw dropped. Seriously, it looked like his glasses steamed up. He dropped the ink pen. It rolled toward me and would have fallen off the desk. I reached out and stopped it.

He cleared his throat. "Yes. Templeton is issuing new cryptocurrency. An ICO." And then he paused, hesitating.

"An initial coin offering." I'd read about it when I'd done my research that day. I was pretty sure it meant Templeton was sending new crypto into the world, for a price. "Tell me about it."

He said, "Well, it's a very exciting prospect, a lot of serious investors are pursuing it. And even celebrities are touting Zagcoin."

"Celebrities?" That didn't make sense to me. "Why would they care about promoting crypto? Seems like they're pretty focused on their own brand."

"It's all part of the excitement that's building around the ICO. Influencers, musicians, a film star—they're going on social media to talk about it."

"Huh. What do they say?"

"The primary draw for this cryptocurrency startup is Zagcoin's core product."

"What's that?"

"It's a card for spending cryptocurrency. It can be used like a debit card, to spend the currency in stores and businesses. This is a novel development. No one has done it before. Not successfully, anyway."

"Really." I crossed my legs, stared him down. "What does the SEC think about that?"

He let out a nervous cough. "You may not be aware, because

IPOs, initial public offerings in the stock market, are strictly regulated by the SEC. But ICOs, not so much. The crypto-currency area is so new so regulation hasn't caught up."

"I see." No wonder Templeton liked crypto. The government wasn't keeping a sharp eye out.

I decided I'd heard enough. So I nodded, trying to look confident. "That's it. That's what I want to invest in."

"You can't," he sputtered.

His response was intriguing. I wondered what reason he would give. Did his firm privately think it was a scam? Maybe Wagner knew that Ian Templeton was a crook. Templeton's criminal propensities might already be common knowledge at Morgan and Goldberg.

"Why not?" I asked.

He frowned. I caught him looking down at me from his seat behind the desk. Though he appeared to focus on my legs, I suspected he was looking at my worn-out shoes. He said, "Because you can't afford it. There's no way. Not for someone in your position. You have to invest in Tempcoin first, that's required. It's profoundly expensive."

That just pissed me off. It's the kind of attitude that makes the whole world hate Wall Street. How did he know I couldn't afford it? Maybe I was sitting on a fortune. Shoes don't always tell the whole tale.

Nonetheless, I tucked my feet under my chair. "Just give me the information I need, and I'll get out of here. Who do I contact to buy in?"

"Templeton formed a new LLC for the enterprise." The guy didn't have to look it up. He rattled the name off the top of his head. "Pyramid Investments, LLC."

Something pinged in my head when he gave the business name. It sounded familiar.

When I made the connection, it gave me a physical jolt. "Aw, shit," I whispered.

Pyramid Investments, LLC, had recently reported a stolen car.

The black Suburban.

The car that picked me up at LaGuardia belonged to Ian Templeton.

CHAPTER 23

Whitney

WHITNEY FLICKED A speck of lint from the sleeve of her jacket. She was dressed in professional attire. She had to stand in for Larry that day because Larry was passed out drunk in an alley. She privately suspected he'd imbibed to the point of unconsciousness to avoid the task he'd been instructed to perform.

What a chickenshit.

Larry had never been the right person for the job. He lacked intestinal fortitude. No one could accuse Whitney of cowardice. She had her flaws, but that wasn't one of them. That's why it fell to Whitney. They knew they could rely on her. She didn't shrink from unpleasant scenarios.

And she understood the situation, better than others. Her obligation to the group had not, in fact, ended.

When they freed her from Rosie's, they promised to look out for her. They had paid a commercial bondsman, taken over her legal representation, and were housing her in a new location. Her old landlord had initiated eviction proceedings. They were handling that action, too.

Now she was living in the East Village in an apartment over a psychic's in-home business, a medium named Lucy who advertised fortune-telling in her living room. She'd been tempted to knock on her door to see if she could tell what her future might hold.

But maybe, she'd thought, she was better off not knowing. Maybe she didn't want a glimmer of what fate had in store. Besides, the phony psychic didn't really know where Whitney would end up or whether she'd go back to jail.

She thought about her uncertain future as she rode in the front seat of a white Suburban, headed to a nursing home in Jersey. The guy behind the wheel of the SUV was chatty.

"How much are they paying you for this?" he asked.

Whitney ignored him. The question was inappropriate, she thought. Obviously, the young man was a novice.

When she didn't reply, the guy shot her a genial grin, a wide smile with one crooked tooth. "I'm just curious, is all. Because I already told them, I'm all in. I'll do whatever they need me to do. I get that I owe them for making my situation go away. But I can't keep doing this shit for free, not in the long term. I got bills to pay. Child support. You know."

Whitney didn't know. She'd successfully avoided parenthood. And she was amazed to hear that the guy was somebody's father. He didn't come off as the paternal type. Plus he had a dead look behind his eyes. It was discomfiting to see old eyes in such a youthful face.

"How'd you get tied up in this?" he asked.

She turned and looked out the window, hoping he'd take the hint. Whitney wanted him to shut up. She needed to get in the right head space, and his chatter was interfering with her concentration.

The Suburban pulled into the drive leading to Elfinwood Senior Living nursing home. There Whitney had to perform the task assigned to Larry. When they called her to pinch-hit, they said this one would be easy. Not like last time, they assured her. It would be a cinch. A piece of cake.

Because the old man was almost dead anyway. He was basically comatose, they'd heard. He just needed a little push.

When they'd said "push," Whitney had wondered whether the word choice was supposed to be ironic. A reference to other deaths they'd orchestrated.

The driver hit the brakes in front of the entrance. "They told me to drive around for a while, wait for a text from you. You're supposed to stand out here when you're done, waiting for me. No fucking around."

It was incongruous, taking orders from the guy. She faced him and narrowed her eyes. But he didn't quail.

The car roared away as soon as she stepped out. She buttoned her jacket before she pushed the buzzer on the intercom door. She was dressed in a lawyer's uniform, a dark suit with a white blouse. The costume had the added advantage of being commonplace, forgettable.

Out of habit, she patted her pocket. Since her release from Rosie's, she never ventured out unarmed anymore. The city was a shitshow, worse than it had been since the 1970s. Crazy people had overtaken the streets and the subways. Whitney carried a push dagger, a short, bladed dagger with a "T" handle. Whitney slid her hand into her pocket and grasped it. If she pulled it out, the blade would protrude from the front of her fist, between her index and her middle fingers.

She didn't think she'd need it inside the nursing home but it was reassuring to have it. Because you never know.

A woman's voice came through the speaker. "Yeah, how can I help you?"

When she bent over to answer, the wind blew her hair into her face. She didn't brush it away. "I'm here to see Victor Odom."

"Victor?" She sounded surprised. "Are you on his visitor's list?"

"I'm his lawyer. I work for Stone & Stone in New Jersey."

"Oh. Okay, then." The buzzer hummed, and Whitney pulled the door open. The woman at the reception desk waved her over.

"I'll need to see some identification."

She pulled out a New Jersey driver's license. It was a flawless imitation, meticulously executed. Gatsby was a stickler for details.

The receptionist held the license under a desktop lamp. "Patricia Stone, huh? Are you Stone? Or Stone?"

Whitney gave a tight smile. "Ha. Funny. It's a family firm."

She handed the ID back without further comment. Tense, Whitney waited to see whether she'd pick up the phone or seek information on her computer. If she researched the Stone firm, she would quickly discover that Whitney didn't look anything like the actual Patricia Stone. Her hand slid back into her pocket.

But the receptionist sounded unconcerned when she said, "Victor's in suite one twenty-two. If you're his attorney, I assume you know what to expect. Victor's not going to be talkative. You understand, right? He hasn't been too responsive since the stroke."

Whitney nodded, making what she hoped was an appropriately sympathetic noise in her throat. This visit was intended to silence Victor permanently. The old man had been in a coma for weeks. They'd waited impatiently for him to die of natural causes. And then: eureka! The old dude woke up. Those career cops were tough.

She kept her head down, ignoring the people she passed on the way to Victor's room. She dodged old folks slouched in wheelchairs and harried employees in nurse scrubs. They didn't look twice at Whitney.

When she reached suite 122, she pulled the door shut and locked it. The room boasted a single window, looking out onto a parking lot. She twisted the rod to shut the plastic blinds, making sure they were firmly closed.

Walking over to the hospital bed, Whitney looked closely at the shriveled figure under the sheet. At first, it was hard to tell whether Victor was breathing. She didn't detect any movement of the old man's chest that would be indicative of respiration. It would be really convenient if the guy would suddenly expire without assistance. It would make her day so much easier. And she could still claim credit.

But as she looked down on the wasted body, she could see signs of shallow breathing. Victor's mouth was agape, his eyes closed. He was just sleeping, it appeared.

Cautiously, Whitney slid the pillow out from under his head. She tried to do it smoothly and slowly, so the movement wouldn't disturb him. But when she freed the pillow, the old man's eyes cracked open.

When Victor saw the pillow in Whitney's hands, his eyes opened wide. He struggled to speak, but only a gargle came from his throat. With a bony arm, he tried to push the pillow away.

But the old man's fighting days were behind him. He was weak, one foot already in the grave.

Whitney wasn't a large woman, but she had little difficulty overcoming the struggles of the old man as she held the pillow over his face. As she watched his arms twitch and the movement still, she had to wonder. What did Victor Odom know that made this action necessary?

No one had bothered to share the information with Whitney. And she was savvy enough not to ask.

CHAPTER 24

Kate

AFTER I REALIZED that it was Templeton's car that had picked me up at the airport, I freaked. I immediately made a call to Detective Brennan at his Queens precinct house and left a message, reporting the new twist in my case. Apparently, Brennan didn't find the new facts as disturbing as I did. No response from him.

So I headed to Gravesend in Brooklyn. It was past time to bring Millie under my wing, as Rod had requested. With some urging, she agreed to pack up and leave the apartment they'd shared.

But my stay at the Essex House couldn't continue. Mom had communicated strong reactions to the text notifications she'd received from American Express. So I moved us into a new temporary living arrangement. In New Jersey.

On Thursday, we were comfortably settled in the great room of my mom's house. Steven was there, too. I'd asked him to spend some time with us because he had a calming influence on Millie and me. He was stretched out on the sofa, his head buried in the *Times*. Mom had the print copy delivered every morning, and he'd piled a stack of the most recent papers at the foot of the couch for easy access.

Millie sat cross-legged in Mom's favorite chair, eating rum raisin ice cream—also Mom's favorite—straight from the carton. I had dragged an ottoman up to the coffee table, upon which I'd spread print copies of current statistics on offenses committed by defendants released without bail. I'd intended to do my homework as I prepared a written memorandum in support of Rod's release. I'd filed motions in Rod's case and secured a setting on the court's docket for the beginning of the next week.

But my attention was drawn to the television screen. It was impossible to ignore. Millie had supplied the distraction. She'd turned the volume on max, and her voice was loud because she was arguing with the people onscreen, as if they could hear her.

"It's a toxic relationship," she said to the TV. "Your daughter isn't interested in affection! She just wants your money!"

When Dr. Phil tried to intercede in the battle on the screen, Millie hit the pause button. Frozen faces filled the screen, with Phil's mouth wide open.

Appealing to me, Millie said, "Where do they find these people?"

I studied the angry expressions captured onscreen. "I think the people who come on to the show apply online, asking him for help."

"They are beyond help. I should be in the studio, I could shut this down like that." She snapped her fingers, then picked up the spoon and pointed it at the frozen image of Dr. Phil's face. "He's not tough enough for the job."

I laughed at that. Steven folded the newspaper and said, "I found an article for you."

"Great," I said. I'd asked him to hang on to anything he saw about Templeton's cryptocurrency. "Is it Zagcoin?"

"Nope." He held it out where I could see. "Your friend Rubenstein is talking about the bail issues again."

That pulled my interest away from Dr. Phil. "What does he have to say? What's his position?"

Steven's expression was rueful. "That's hard to say. This reads like he's trying to take both sides, to make everybody happy. Which is impossible to do."

Though I'd spent three years complaining about Rubenstein when I served as his employee, I was more inclined to defend the DA these days. "He's probably trying to find a middle road."

Stephen shook his head, grimacing. "Sounds to me like standard political talk. Is he running for something? In the next election?"

I didn't have the answer to that. Had I heard office gossip, speculation that he wanted to be governor? Maybe.

"I still think you're crazy to get mixed up with him. You always used to tell me that Rubenstein is only concerned with his personal self-interest."

Steven folded the newspaper and set it down beside my statistics. "There's the article, if you want to read it. Hey, what do you want to have for supper tonight? I'm happy to cook."

I was relieved to have the opportunity to drop the Rubenstein topic. We walked into the kitchen together to open the pantry and the freezer, check out our options. Then we returned to the great room and sat side by side to make a grocery list. It was a pleasant domestic exercise, talking about the dishes Steven could prepare.

We'd enjoyed some relaxing days in New Jersey. It was nice playing house, surrounded by the comfort my mother's big home offered. I'd always mocked her choice to live in a gated community, but under the circumstances, it was nice to know that someone was minding the gate. The stress and angst of the past week had fallen out, like wrinkles under steam. Everything was deliciously chill in our little world.

And then I heard the whirring noise that the garage door made when it opened.

"Oh, shit," I said.

Millie's head jerked around, facing me. "What? Is someone breaking in?" Her voice went up an octave. "It could be Whitney. Dial 911!"

My mother burst into the kitchen through the garage entrance. She paused for one second before shouting out my name.

"Kate! What the hell is going on?"

And just like that, our peaceful interlude came to an abrupt end.

I scrambled off the sofa, hoping to intercede before she discovered my houseguests. I suspected she would make a scene, pitch a fit.

I wasn't fast enough. My mom appeared in the entrance to the great room. When she saw us, her eyes widened, and her mouth narrowed into a thin line that boded ill.

"What are these people doing here? This is my home, it isn't an Airbnb."

"Jesus, Mom," I said, feeling as chagrined as a teenager who'd been bawled out in public. "Don't be rude to my friends."

Leo came in behind her, pulling two wheeled suitcases, one in each hand. His face lit up. "Hey, Kate! Good to see you."

I gave him a quick hug. My mother did not look like she wanted an embrace, and I wasn't in the mood to offer one. "Leo, have you met Steven and Millie? I know you've heard me talk about them."

Millie waved from her spot in Mom's chair but didn't get up. "Hi, Leo. And Mrs. Stone."

Steven had risen from the couch. He smiled as he greeted Leo with a handshake. To my mom, Steven said, "I've heard so much about you from Kate, Mrs. Stone. It's a pleasure to meet you."

Mom snorted. She's no fool. She could guess that the conversations Steven and I had concerning my mother weren't always flattering.

She looked like she wanted to pounce, to go on the attack. I followed her eye as she looked down at the carton in Millie's lap. "Is that my ice cream?" she demanded.

Millie dropped the spoon inside the empty carton. "It was delicious. Hey, Mrs. Stone, I want to thank you for letting us stay here. I really appreciate it. You're a lifesaver." She paused, infusing drama into her voice, and added, "And I mean that literally."

Mom pinned me with a furious glare as she repeated Millie's words. "You're all staying here?"

Leo chimed in, sounding like a kid on Christmas morning. "Really, you're staying here? Cool."

I had to defuse the situation. "Mom, could I talk to you for a minute? In private?"

My mother wasn't totally crazy. She knew the danger that had been hanging over me. If I had the chance to explain, I thought she would surely be reasonable.

She turned on her heel and marched up the stairway to the second floor. As we walked into her bedroom, I was thankful that Steven and I had used the guest room, and that Millie had taken over Leo's bed. If my mother had walked into her boudoir to find an unmade bed with rumpled sheets, she would have lost it.

After I shut the door, I started to say, "I should have told you." At the same moment, she spoke, saying, "You should have told me."

Well, at least I knew how her mind worked.

She didn't bother to lower her voice. "You know how I feel about those people. They're trouble, bad news. I've advised you to stay away from them, and you let them take over my house? Did I not make myself clear?"

I sat on the comforter, patting the spot beside me on the bed. She didn't accept my invitation to sit. Instead, she towered over me, waiting for my explanation.

So I launched into it. "There's been some weird shit going on, since I came back."

"With Bill Parker, you mean? Your friend in the DA's office? He's the reason you went tearing off from the resort and left us behind in Florida. Am I right?"

"It's not Bill. He's fine. But there's other stuff. Millie's

161

boyfriend got picked up on a crazy charge, and she's alone. She doesn't feel safe."

"So why doesn't she stay with you in your apartment? The cozy studio you love so much in Manhattan. You've assured me repeatedly that it's superior to living in New Jersey."

"My place was vandalized, Mom. While we were in Florida."

She flinched. I saw the anger recede, replaced by worry. "What? Vandalized how? What did they do?"

"I found a dead rat in my place."

Breathing out sigh of relief, she sat beside me on the bed and took my hand. "Kate, honey, that's New York. The damned rats are everywhere, you can't avoid them. It's one of the reasons I left the city behind."

I shook my head. "It was intentional, Mom."

"Really?" She looked skeptical. "How can you distinguish a dead vandalism rat from one that died of natural causes? I'm not sure I could spot the difference. Did it scrawl a message on the wall before it died?"

She thought she was so damned smart. It always rubbed me the wrong way. "Because my bed was pulled down and the rat was tucked inside, under the covers. A rat would have to be over five feet tall to pull that off, and this one wasn't that big."

"You're sure you hadn't left the bed down."

"I'm sure." I'd given it some thought, and I was pretty certain. "And that's not all. Whitney Novak is out."

Her face blanched. "You're joking."

"Nope. No joke."

"That's not possible. She was supposed to be held without bond."

"Callahan let her out. It's the new bail reform policy."

My mother's hand was still wrapped around mine. She squeezed my fingers so tightly I was afraid they'd break. "Son of a bitch. I'm gonna kick his ass."

Her face was scary, but I appreciated it. When she directed her Patricia Stone brand of fury at someone on my behalf, it felt exceptionally comforting.

"And remember the car at LaGuardia that took me for a ride—the one you didn't send? The vehicle belonged to Ian Templeton's business."

I didn't add that he'd reported it as stolen. I was trying to make my case to her.

"Hmm. That's unsettling," she said.

I hoped she was coming around. "So you see? We didn't feel safe, so we thought we'd crash here. Since you were on vacation, I didn't think we'd bother you."

She released my hand and patted my knee. She said, "It's just temporary, then. Until we can work out a solution."

"Oh, totally. Temporary, God, yes."

She sighed as she stood, tugging off her jacket. "I need to shower, to wash the filth of the airplane off before I catch something. Kate, *you* can move back in, obviously. For a while. But these strangers? I can put up with this for one day. They have twenty-four hours to come up with a solution before my hospitality runs out. Now run back downstairs."

"Sure, I'll give you some privacy. Hey, Mom," I said, pausing on my way out of the room. "I didn't expect you home yet. Weren't you supposed to stay through the week, and come home on Saturday?"

"Our plans changed." She dropped her jacket into a hamper

for dirty clothes. "I had to come back early. You remember your father's partner, at NYPD? Victor Odom? He died."

"No kidding? Sure, I know Victor. Why'd you have to cut your vacation short for that? What's it got to do with you?"

"I'm the executor of his estate." Before she stepped into the bathroom, she sighed. "No rest for the weary."

CHAPTER 25

THE DAY OF reckoning had come. Millie and I were moving out of my mother's house and into my place. So I had to sanitize my apartment, to clean it so thoroughly that I could make the rotting rat a distant memory. I'd purchased the necessary tools. I had a bag of brand-new cleaning supplies. I'd even purchased a bottle of chlorine bleach, to add to the washing machine while I did laundry. Steven had recommended it, based on the laundry challenges they experienced at the BoHo. He assured me it would eliminate lingering odors.

I was killing time because I wasn't quite ready to face the task. I stood in front of my apartment building, smoking a cigarette. But I wasn't a smoker—not really.

I didn't qualify as a smoker, I honestly believed that. Because I never actually purchased cigarettes. The last time I'd paid money for a pack of cigarettes was when I was studying for the New York State bar exam. That was over three years ago.

But I liked to bum a cigarette once in a while. Sometimes, I'd catch a whiff of tobacco from a smoker on the street, and it would give me the urge. I know—they are unhealthy, noxious, a terrible habit. But I didn't have the habit. I'm not defending the use of tobacco products. Everyone knows they can kill you.

My father smoked. Marlboro Reds, a pack a day. He was dead, but smoking hadn't killed him. Maybe it would have, if he'd lived long enough.

I'd just blown out my third puff of smoke when Edie ambled up, pulling her utility cart behind her. She squinted up at me through her cat-eye eyeglasses. "Oh Kate, no. You smoking again?"

Her reproach made me want to hide it behind my back, like a kid confronted by a teacher in the school restroom. I stifled the desire to drop the cigarette.

Edie shook her head at me, clicking her tongue with a tsking noise. "Well, it's probably all the pressure. From that high-stress job of yours."

I had to set her straight. "Edie, I don't have that job anymore. I left the DA's office a couple of months ago."

It wasn't quite a lie. I did leave the DA's office. Not voluntarily, I was fired. But I left.

"I didn't know! You should've told me, I'm still telling everyone we've got an ADA in the building, right down the hall from me. So what're you doing now?"

I sucked on the cigarette. Inhaled the smoke, blew it out. "For now, I guess I'm working for my mother's law firm. In New Jersey."

She made a face. "No, that's no good. The commute will kill you."

She was right about that. It took almost ninety minutes

to get to my mother's office, tacking on an additional three hours to the average workday. By comparison, the train ride from Morningside Heights to the Criminal Courts building in lower Manhattan had been a breeze.

I'd never intended to practice the area of law that my mother had carved out for herself. I'd always sworn that I'd never do a criminal trial practice, even though it was a common jump for lawyers after spending time on the prosecution side. But I never envisioned myself taking that role. I had only taken the job with Mom's defense firm as a last resort when Frank Rubenstein fired me for flaking on the anger management therapy he'd imposed as a condition of my employment. I had to crawl to Mom so I could pay my bills. Mom had always pushed for me to go to work for her, but I had done it out of necessity rather than a desire to assist criminal defendants.

I'd always been a passionate advocate for victims of crime. I wanted to take up the cause of the abused, rather than the abuser. Just like my father had. That's why I'd agreed to join up with Steven's group. In hindsight, it was a huge mistake.

And as I stood there on the sidewalk, I had a eureka moment. Maybe it was the nicotine, because I realized with crystalline clarity there were people on both sides of the criminal justice system who deserved a passionate advocate. The obstacles Rod faced and the conditions I'd witnessed at Rikers had caused a turnaround in my perspective.

And now, another opportunity presented itself. Rubenstein had opened a door for me with the appointment to the advisory group. With the wide array of legal professionals in that circle, someone would surely offer the kind of practice I could get excited about. I liked fighting for underdogs. There were a lot of them in my city, on both sides of the courtroom. People like Rod.

My spirits rose as I clutched at the vision. I felt like I was going to get my career back.

"You have a fair point, Edie. I need to look around. Maybe I can find something closer to home," I said.

The first meeting was coming up and there was a big advisory board event scheduled at the World Trade Center. Soon, I'd be rubbing shoulders with attorneys who had influence in the New York Bar. I vowed to keep my eye peeled for an opening.

Edie reached out her hand, her arthritic fingers making a crooked peace sign. "Here. Give me a hit."

Surprised, I handed off the cigarette. She took a quick puff and then dropped it onto the sidewalk, crushing it under the sole of the Skechers she wore on her feet.

"Enough of that stuff. You don't want that monkey on your back, believe me. My brother was a smoker. Emphysema took him when he was young, barely seventy-five."

Seventy-five sounded ancient to me, but I didn't volunteer an opinion. Edie pulled the front door open and dragged her cart over the threshold. "Come on up, honey. I'll introduce you to Pierre, my new roommate. He's a real beauty."

I followed her. I was in no hurry to reach my apartment. Once I arrived, I'd have to start scouring the place like a scrubwoman.

When we stepped out of the elevator and onto the sixth floor, I gave the air in the hallway a tentative sniff. There was a definite improvement in the air quality. I only detected a lingering funk.

Edie caught me catching a whiff. "They must have taken their trash to the chute, whoever it was. Probably that man in six-oh-two, he always looks sneaky. Like he's hiding something. God only knows what he has stored in his place."

She unlocked her door. When she opened it, she waved me in. "Hurry! Don't let him out."

I scurried through the door. She followed, dragging the cart, and locked the door behind us. She kicked off her shoes and padded around the small living room in her stocking feet. "Pierre! Mom's home!"

I looked around, but Pierre didn't appear. Edie looked up at me, with an apology behind the eyeglasses. "Don't feel bad, honey. He's still shy around strangers. It takes a while for a feral boy to warm up. Have a seat on the divan, I'll get you a soda."

A short sofa, without a back or arms, sat against the wall. A flat pillow lay at one end. It was sprinkled with gray hair.

I suspected that Edie was going bald until she walked back into the room, clutching a gray-striped tabby cat.

"Voilà!" she said. "Kate, this is Pierre. He's my new baby."

The cat made an inarticulate noise that sounded like he didn't appreciate the description.

When she lowered herself onto the divan, the cat struggled to escape. Edie held on tighter.

"Just look at that face. Did you ever see such eyes? Like emeralds. And he has a distinct 'M' on his forehead. He could be a model, he's so handsome." She kissed the top of his head. Pierre made a rumbling sound. Might have been a purr. Could've been a growl. I kept my distance.

"You want to pet him?"

I looked into those green eyes. There was a definite warning in them. My mother never liked cats, wouldn't let me have one. She always said the only reason cats don't eat their owners is that they're not quite big enough.

The cat had some indefinable quality, though. He made me want to hold him, even though I was likely to be sliced to ribbons if I tried. Fascinated, I watched his claws as he kneaded Edie's arm. Fortunately, she wore a fleece jacket.

"I think I'll let him get used to me first," I said.

She released him, and he sailed out of her arms, landing on all fours on the hardwood floor. The cat scampered under a skirted armchair. "That's his hidey-hole," she said. She used a singsong voice, like she was talking to a baby.

Edie returned to the kitchen and emerged carrying two glasses of soda in battered plastic tumblers. After I took a sip from the glass she handed to me, I asked, "What happened to your other cat? The black one?"

Her face fell and her thin shoulders sagged. "Camille died. Kidney disease."

She sounded brokenhearted, like she'd lost a family member. I guess she had.

Edie took a deep breath and gave me a wobbly smile. "She had a good life. Nineteen years. And she sent me a new cat after she passed. I put Camille down last month, and just a week later, Pierre was out by the trash can on the corner, begging for something to eat."

Pierre's tail peeked out from under the skirt of the chair, did a quick flip, and disappeared.

Regaining her good cheer, she said, "I'm glad to say I've

got a mouser again. You know, the rodents won't go into an apartment where a cat lives. They know there's a predator in the place."

She sipped her soda and put the glass down on the coffee table, then turned to me. "I didn't let him in. Did you?"

I tried to follow the conversational thread. Were we talking about cats? "Who? Pierre?"

"No! The exterminator. He was going from door to door on the sixth floor, knocking. He wore a uniform, said the landlord sent him to check for infestations. And to spray, set out traps."

"You're kidding." I was astounded.

"I'm not. He came to my door twice."

It was unbelievable. Our landlord never bothered with pest control. We learned to live with cockroaches. To visitors, I joked about adopting them as pets.

I wondered what motivated such a monumental change of policy. Was it the rat? *My* rat?

And then it occurred to me that Mom could've been right. Maybe I'd been overly paranoid about the presence of the dead rat. It was possible that discovering vermin in an old apartment that's been vacant for a week or two isn't outside the norm. I wasn't 100 percent sure that I'd put my bed away.

"Edie, have you seen any new pests on our floor? Rats, maybe?"

"You'd be more likely to see a rat in a first-floor apartment. Rats start from the ground and go up. They don't wanna make friends, they want to eat. Take away your trash to keep them out, you hear me? Don't let it sit around."

A small bag of cat treats sat on the coffee table. She picked them up and shook the bag. When it rattled, the cat's head popped out from the corner of the skirt.

Edie gave me a curious glance. "So did you let him in? To inspect your apartment?"

"No. I wasn't here when he knocked. Maybe he came while I was in Florida."

"Well, I don't let strangers in, I don't care what reason they give. We're women, living alone in the city."

She shook the bag again. The cat crept out, keeping his eyes fixed on the bag of treats.

I said, "That's an excellent policy. My father would've approved. Dad always said that I shouldn't let a stranger into my apartment, no matter what."

The cat hopped onto Edie's lap, purring loudly. After he bumped her hand with his nose, she shook some dried nuggets from the bag and the cat ate them from the palm of her hand.

"He asked about you. Wanted to know when you'd be home, whether I knew when you come and go."

That gave me a sinking feeling in my gut. My throat was suddenly dry, and my voice cracked when I said, "What did you tell him?"

"Nothing! Do you think I'd tell some strange man your business?"

I digested the statement. "Did he leave a business card? Give you a name?"

I hoped so. I prayed that he was legit, a real card-carrying pest control professional.

"No. I didn't give him the opportunity. Like I told you, I didn't give him the time of day."

I needed more information. Because I couldn't help but

worry. It could have been Edgar, who shoved me into the subway. Or Larry, who lured me there.

I swallowed. "Can you remember what he looked like?"

"Oh, he was a nice-looking fellow. Young man, probably in his twenties. Didn't look old enough to know what to do with the canister of chemicals. But when you get to be my age, everyone looks young."

That was a relief. Larry was middle-aged, a nondescript, graying man who carried extra weight around his middle. And Edgar, in his late thirties, would have made a distinct impression on Edie. Besides, he was currently locked up.

"Yeah, he was a looker, if you like the type. He could be in the movies. Dark hair, beautiful smile."

She bared her teeth, tapping her eye tooth with her fingernail. "Just one tooth out of place."

Shit.

Millie and I would have to keep our guard up. The man she described could absolutely be the driver from LaGuardia.

Sitting on Edie's couch, I envisioned it. In my mind, I saw the guy dressed in a pest control uniform, knocking at my door. Unlocking it and walking into my place, carrying a bag with him. Dumping a dead rat out of the bag and onto my bed. Pulling the blanket to cover it.

Surprise!

The old fury surfaced, energizing me. The guy was sneaking around my apartment. The driver of the black Suburban registered to Ian Templeton's crypto business.

Stolen vehicle, my ass.

It was time to contact Steven and Devon. No more playing the game of "wait and see."

CHAPTER 26

I PERCHED ON the seat of a long white couch, looking out at lower Manhattan. The floor-to-ceiling windows offered an astounding vista, like a postcard in a souvenir shop. I had a clear view of One World Trade Center, with its spire jutting into the blue sky.

"Incredible," I whispered. "How do people who live here get anything done? It would be tough to tear yourself away from the windows."

We'd come to visit Devon in his temporary residence on the sixty-seventh floor of the tower at Hudson Yards, intending to pitch a coup. So far, all we'd done was gawk at the view.

Millie walked in from the hallway and said, "The bathroom is real marble. And you can look out at the Hudson River from the bathtub."

"I've got to see that," I said, rising from the couch.

"I went into a bedroom, and there's a fur throw on the bed. It's got to be imitation, right? And you can see the Chrysler Building from the bedroom window."

"Show me," I said.

She struck a pose and affected a broad New York accent as she belted out, "You're all gonna clean this dump till it shines like the top of the Chrysler Building!"

When I gave her a blank look, she said, "Miss Hannigan? Act one of *Annie*, right before the orphans sing 'It's a Hard-Knock Life.'"

"Jesus," Devon said. "Could you lower your voice? And quit snooping around. This is a private residence—and it's not mine."

Devon was on edge. He had been since we arrived. He hovered over us, fretting that we'd leave a water ring on the glass coffee table or a mark on the rug. He'd instructed all of us to remove our shoes at the door. It was easy to understand why. The living area was white: furnishings, rug, even the art on the walls.

A bulldog waddled into the room, walking with a side-to-side gait. He went straight to Steven, who patted his wrinkled brown and white head.

"What did you say his name was?" he asked.

"Bruno," Devon said.

"Bruno," Steven crooned. "You're a lucky dog, aren't you?"

"He's so ugly," Millie said.

"He cost a fortune." Devon cast a resentful gaze upon the canine. "Bloodlines, apparently. His father was best in show."

He didn't look like a show dog. His tongue lolled out of his mouth. As I watched, a long string of saliva dribbled out.

I said, "He just spit on the rug."

"Shit!" Devon grabbed a box of wipes and knelt on the rug, scrubbing at the wet mark. When he finished the cleanup, he sighed and sat down on the floor. "This is kind of stressing me out. Bruno's not used to strangers. And it's my boss's home you're wandering around. So let's get down to it."

"Absolutely, you're right." I returned to the white sofa, sitting where I could face him. "So here's the deal."

Devon met my eye. "Ian Templeton?"

"Yeah. I've looked into the new crypto offering. I think it's a pump-and-dump scheme."

"What's that?" Millie sat on a piano bench and plucked the keys of the baby grand, also white like the rest of the furnishings.

"It's a crypto scam. The coin's founder—Templeton, in this case—introduced new cryptocurrency. Then he spread false information about it to pump up the price by making a buying frenzy. And Templeton will make a ton of money when he dumps his shares of the crypto at the inflated price."

Devon said, "Yeah, well. That hasn't happened yet."

Engaging Devon's interest would pose a challenge. I soldiered on. "What I don't get is the tie-in to his other currency, Tempcoin. You have to invest in Tempcoin first and then use it to purchase the new crypto, Zagcoin. But one thing is certain. It's going to be a worthless investment, and people will be ripped off."

Steven said, "And Templeton will walk away with a fortune. Like he always does." He patted the dog again. Bruno licked his arm, leaving a shiny wet spot. Devon handed him a wipe.

Devon's voice had a note of doubt when he said, "So a bunch of people with money to spare get swindled by Templeton's worthless investment. That's too bad, hard luck for the victims. But what's it got to do with us? He's not risking our money. What have we got to lose?"

"Everything." I felt my face heat up. "Ian Templeton poses a threat to our personal well-being."

Millie said, "Templeton put Rod in jail. And he sent some hood out to snatch Kate at LaGuardia."

Devon's brow wrinkled. "You haven't told me that before. It was Templeton?"

"Yeah," I said. "I just learned about the connection. Pyramid Investments is Templeton's new LLC. And Pyramid Investments owned the car that picked me up."

Devon looked thoughtful. He bent over the rug, checking the spot Bruni had soiled. Then he directed a question to Steven. "What do you think?"

He said, "I think you should hear Kate out. So far, retribution has been aimed at Rod and Kate. But I don't think that means we're in the clear, Devon. It makes sense that we're all vulnerable."

I jumped in, hoping to bring Devon around. We couldn't launch an attack without his tech skills. "We need to go to Templeton's office. Check it out. Maybe you can hack into his business computer, like we did on the yacht. Plant malware, something like that."

"That's a stretch," Devon said. "I can't hack it remotely without access. He's got high-level cyber protection in place. And it's not like we're going to meet with him personally."

"Why not?" I said.

He pulled a disbelieving face. "Why would he let us in? You just told me he's chasing after us."

"I'm not saying we'll march in under our own identities.

We could pose as people he'd want to talk to. He'd surely let an investor in. Someone big, with lots of money. Maybe a rich doctor." I glanced at Steven.

He laughed. "I'm the poorest doctor in the city."

Devon said, "Better come up with another idea for a prospect. Someone who could get through the door."

Mille pounded the piano keys, making discordant sounds. "We could get a social media star," she offered. "Kate told me he's using influencers to sell the crypto. We get an Internet celebrity."

"Who?" Devon asked.

"Me."

Steven laughed. "Millie, we love you. But you're not a celebrity."

"I will be." She looked smug. "After Devon boosts my following on Insta. You could do that, right?"

Devon looked thoughtful. "Yeah, I probably could. It would be phony—bots, international accounts. But as far as numbers, I can do that."

"Your real account?" I asked. Rod wouldn't like this, I was thinking. I was supposed to keep Millie out of harm's way.

"It's my professional persona. A stage name: *Divalicious*. Lots of stage pics. In costume." She started playing "Chopsticks." Apparently, her musical gifts did not include the piano.

"I could dress up, something outrageous. You all could be my entourage. We go to the office under false identities. Meet him, break into his computer, figure out how to undermine his crypto." She hit the piano keys again. "It would be a performance."

Actually, it wasn't a bad idea. Except for the fact that it put

Millie in the eye of the storm. "Do you think we should check with Rod first?" I asked.

"I'm doing it for Rod," she said. "Devon, you start building me up today. And I'm going to call that Pyramid Investment office."

"Really?" Steven said.

"Yep. For an appointment for two days from now." She pointed at me. "Because tomorrow's out. Right, Kate?"

"Right." I said.

The next day, I was going to court.

CHAPTER 27

THE DAY AFTER our meeting at Hudson Yards, I walked into the Criminal Courts building with Millie in tow.

Despite the pro-defense eureka moment I'd recently experienced, my new path in criminal defense was rocky, far trickier than I'd ever realized. Determined to follow correct procedure, I'd entered my appearance as Rod's attorney of record. I'd gotten the case out of Callahan's court; that was crucial. Then I filed a motion for release on recognizance in his case, along with a motion to shorten time, and had it set on the judge's docket.

But I wanted to secure the support of the prosecution before the motion was heard, and chasing down the right assistant DA with the power to assist posed a challenge. Donald Rudd, who'd been referred to me by Rubenstein, was back from his conference but he wasn't responsive to my calls or emails. I finally played my card and dropped Rubenstein's name. That got me a return email and a brief conversation over the phone. He'd agreed to meet with me in court before the motion was taken up.

Millie had insisted on coming with me to court.

It was a bad idea to permit her to accompany me to the hearing so I had tried to talk her out of it. She insisted and would not be dissuaded from her mission. She absolutely had to see Rod. She said she wanted to help.

Millie wouldn't be able to assist. But though I tried, I couldn't convince her to stay away. For a nice girl from the rural Midwest, she could be incredibly stubborn.

Inside the lobby of the courthouse, I made my way to the employee security line, moving on autopilot. When I reached for my DA's office ID, I stopped short. It was a tough habit to break. I turned on my heel and led Millie to the public entrance.

The security guard was friendly and didn't give us a hard time. Millie gave him a tragic look before she walked through the metal detector. "I'm here to get my boyfriend out of jail," she announced.

Her voice boomed in the vaulted space, bouncing off the marble walls of the two-story lobby. The guard shook his head ruefully. "Might want to think about getting a new boyfriend," he said as she passed by.

She swung around with fire in her eye. "What did you say to me?" she demanded. "What's that supposed to mean? You don't even know him."

I grabbed her elbow and pulled her to the bank of elevators. *Bad idea*, I thought yet again. Millie was geared up to put on a show. And when she made a bid for attention, no one on earth could shut her down.

We walked up to the courtroom right on schedule. It was just past two fifteen, and the judges would be returning from the lunch break. I'd explained that to Millie earlier in the day.

She yanked on the handle of the courtroom door. It was locked. "There's some problem. We can't get in," she said.

"They'll open up in a minute."

But Millie was nervous. She peeked through the window into the courtroom and said, "I hope we're not too late."

"We're fine."

"This timing doesn't make any sense. My sister worked at the county courthouse back home. The court shut down from noon to one for lunch. Anyone who missed the one o'clock docket could be held in contempt. No one in the county stayed out for lunch until two fifteen."

"Millie, this is the city. It's different here."

Just then the bailiff unlocked the courtroom door. He looked surprised to see me. "Kate Stone, where have you been? Haven't seen you around."

"Hey, Lester. I'm back. Working on the defense side today."

He held the door open, and we walked in. I asked, "Have you seen Donald Rudd? We're taking an appearance up before the judge."

"He was hanging around here before we broke for lunch. That's all I know."

One of the other uniformed bailiffs called out to Lester, and he hurried away. An assistant DA walked in with a couple of defense attorneys chasing after him. I thought I would join them and ask the ADA about Donald Rudd's whereabouts.

"Millie, just take a seat back here by the door. I'm going to talk to some people."

Millie took a hesitant step toward the old wooden bench on the left side of the aisle. "You really want me all the way back here?"

"Yeah. Make yourself comfortable. It may be a while."

She sat, looking glum. "But you're going to be up there at the front? I don't understand."

Millie showed signs of a bad case of FOMO, but I knew it would be best for all concerned if she could stay out of the way. I gave her shoulder a reassuring pat. "You'll be able to hear everything that goes on. They have a sound system."

I didn't inform her that the sound systems in the courtrooms were glitchy. No point in borrowing trouble.

She pointed at the graffiti etched into the wood on the back of the bench directly in front of her. Sounding scandalized, she said, "Do you see that? Who would dare to vandalize a court of law? My sister would never believe it."

Over the years, most of the benches had been defaced by unhappy people using sharp implements to leave angry messages behind. I'd never paid much attention to it. Millie leaned forward, running her fingers over letters dug deep into the wood that read: "DIE BITCH."

I got that prickly feeling that comes when my superstitions flare up. I started to rub the skin by my thumb. But at that moment, the courtroom door opened, and Donald Rudd marched down the center aisle.

"Gotta go," I whispered to Millie, and then I followed him to the front of the courtroom.

I called out, "Donald! I'm Kate. We talked over the phone. I'm here on the People versus Rodney Lamar Bryant."

"Bryant?" He paused, his brow furrowed, as if trying to recall. "Is it set for a plea?"

I wanted to punch him. How had he already forgotten our conversation?

I said, "No, we need to work out the issue of bail. Rodney is being held in detention at Rikers. It's an error, some kind of fluke. He's just charged with a misdemeanor, so he shouldn't be in there at all. I'd like to get him released without bail."

Rudd carried an armful of hard files. He sat down on the first bench of the spectator seating and started to rummage through them. I was wondering whether he'd forgotten to bring the file to court when he finally pulled it out. He opened to the first page and studied a roster of handwritten scribbles.

"He was arrested on an assault charge a couple of months ago," he said.

"That's right."

"And the judge set bail, and he made bond with a commercial bonding company. That's what I'm seeing here."

I was aware of that. It happened immediately after we crashed the party on Ian Templeton's yacht. Millie and I got away, but Rod was busted. And he put up a good fight with the security guards before they handed him over to the police.

"And that's the only charge he's being held on now," I said. "Misdemeanor assault, not a felony."

"Yeah, looks like it."

"So he shouldn't be held at Rikers, right? He should be out."

He flipped through the pages in the thin file. "Oh, here's the problem. Looks like the bonding company pulled out. They revoked the bond. Told the court he wasn't complying with conditions. Thought he was a flight risk."

I knew that the bondsman had taken steps to revoke his bond. Clearly, our benefactor's protection had disappeared, and this was the outcome for members of the group who fell from favor. The indemnitor had decided to kick Rod to the curb and put him behind bars. And it put us in a vulnerable position.

There was no way to explain the situation to Rudd. I tried to play it cool. "So? It's a misdemeanor charge. He's presumed innocent. There's no need to lock this guy up pretrial."

"Hmmm." He continued to scan the notations on the pages in the file. Watching him, I started to worry. Were new charges against Rod in the works? We didn't really know what we were up against, didn't know who was pulling the strings. As I waited for him to weigh in, I grew increasingly nervous. My voice cracked when I said, "Come on, Donald. This is New York, not Alabama. We have bail reform in this state. Requiring cash bail is a way to penalize people for being poor. You know that."

"Where's that coming from?" Rudd looked at me with a wary expression. "You were with this office for three years, right? We've all seen the damage done by bail reform in this city."

"But not this guy. He's a vet. Served his country."

"Yeah, well, we get a lot of crazy vets coming through the criminal courts. Hell, Kate, you know that."

I attempted a cajoling tone. "Donald, he's a friend of mine."

He shut the file and slapped it down on the wooden bench next to him. "Take it up with the judge. I'll stand silent. That's the best I can offer."

At that point, the judge emerged from chambers with his robe hanging over his arm. We weren't appearing before Callahan. Because I'd filed for a change of judge, we were taking the case up with Judge Robertson instead. He had a reputation for being reasonable and even-handed. I hoped he wouldn't rubber-stamp Callahan.

Judge Robertson donned the black robe as he chatted with the court reporter. After he zipped it up, he ambled over to the bench and took his seat.

The bailiffs were still chatting with one of the clerks, laughing about some private joke. The judge said, "Okay, let's get started. Court is in session."

When he spoke, his voice rang out, making me want to cover my ears. The sound system utilized in the courtroom was set at a punishing volume.

The clerk handed a file to the judge. He opened it and said, "In the case of Rodney Lamar Bryant, are the parties present?"

Rudd and I walked up to the dual podiums facing the judge.

The judge frowned down at me. "Is your client late?"

"No, your honor. I'm Kate Stone, counsel for Rodney Lamar Bryant. He's not late. He can't be here. Mr. Bryant is detained at Rikers."

Rudd said, "I'm here on behalf of the People, your honor."

The judge sighed. "Okay then, we're doing this remotely. Bailiff, can you get him on the screen?"

A large video monitor sat in court, angled toward the bench. I went up on my toes and leaned over my podium, but I couldn't get a view of the screen.

The judge squinted his eyes. "Bailiff, turn on the microphone and camera. Is that him? In the corner? Bailiff, did you get the spelling of his name right? Is that him?"

Apparently, the tech side of the courtroom proceedings was experiencing difficulty. The judge spoke directly into his microphone, the sound loud enough to burst an eardrum, making me wince again.

"Mr. Bryant, can you see me? Hear me?"

I still couldn't see Rodney, but a garbled voice came through the sound system. "Can't see you very well, but now I can hear you, Judge."

The judge turned to his clerk and gave her a nod before looking back into the monitor. "Mr. Bryant, we're going to do your court appearance remotely. Is that all right with you?"

"Yes, your honor." At last, the system picked it up clearly. It was Rod's voice, I was certain.

Millie heard it, too. "Rod!" she cried, her voice sailing through the room. "Baby, I'm here!"

I turned around to see her running down the aisle toward me. Giving her a stern glare, I whispered, "Millie, sit down!"

Though I didn't mean to share the remark with the courtroom, the microphone at my podium picked it up. Mortified, I jerked back to face the judge. "Your honor, Mr. Bryant is being held at Rikers pending trial on a misdemeanor charge. The pretrial detention is an illegal violation of state bail policy. I urge the court to grant my motion for an ROR. We request that he be released today."

Millie reached the front of the courtroom and stood at my shoulder. I covered the mic with my hand this time. "Sit. Down."

The assistant DA spoke up. "The people have no objection, Judge."

I was relieved to see the judge nod, looking amenable to the defense request. And he didn't seem rattled by Millie's outburst. He ran a fairly informal forum in his court. But as he glanced over the file that lay on the bench, he paused. His eyes darted across the page. He cleared his throat and coughed into his hand.

After a long moment, he said, "Mr. Rudd, are you sure the people don't want to speak to this issue?"

Rudd and I exchanged a look. He was baffled, I could tell. There shouldn't be any cause for debate. Under state law, Rod was entitled to the release. Judges didn't have much discretion under the new bail reform statute.

As the moments ticked by, I was growing distinctly uneasy. Millie picked up on it. She tugged on the sleeve of my jacket. "What's happening?" she said in a loud stage whisper.

The judge continued. "Because, from my file, it appears that there have been incidents in detention. Violent assaults allegedly committed by the defendant against fellow inmates since he's been in custody."

Rod's voice crackled through the speaker. "Your honor, I had to defend myself—"

Millie was quicker to the draw than I was. "Rod! Don't say anything!"

Donald Rudd was tearing through the pages of the DA's file, trying to find what he'd missed. "I want to amend my position, Judge. The people oppose the release."

I jumped right in. "The DA's position has no bearing on the matter. State law requires the court to release him." In my agitation, I'd forgotten to modulate my voice. My loud volume made the microphone screech in protest at the end of my argument.

Robertson removed his eyeglasses and rubbed his forehead with a pained expression. Maybe I'd given him a headache.

He said, "I think this is an appropriate case for release conditions."

I kept my mouth a safe distance from the microphone. "Your honor, the law supports the defense—"

He cut me off. "I'm talking about nonmonetary release conditions. Under the circumstances of this case, I believe I should consider certain restrictions that will ensure Mr. Bryant's appearance in court."

"Yes, your honor," Rudd said.

But I was wary of the judge's proposal. "What restrictions? Mr. Bryant will comply with any reasonable request. We request that the court state the restrictions on the record, and we'll go forward with the release."

The judge grimaced. "I think it merits some thought. I want both parties to weigh in with written suggestions. We'll take the matter up again in two weeks." The judge closed the file. "Next case."

"No!" Millie shrieked. "Rod! I have to see you. I need to talk to you!"

I wanted to see him, too. I needed to eyeball him to make certain he hadn't been physically harmed. I left the podium and ran up to the bench, hoping to get a look at the monitor and communicate with my client. But the screen was dark.

Rod was gone.

Looking back, that was definitely an omen.

CHAPTER 28

CONDITIONS IN MY studio apartment had grown crowded. After Mom booted us out of her house in New Jersey, Steven had returned to his bachelor accommodations at the shelter. But Millie was still at loose ends due to my inability to get Rod out of Rikers. She went into a deep funk after the court hearing. Mad at the judge, mad at the world—kinda mad at me, too. Part of the burden the defense attorney bears, I was learning.

But she couldn't live alone, not right now. So I still had a roommate. And because I had a roommate, I had a frequent visitor.

Millie sat on the sofa with my brother Leo close beside her. They were huddled together over my laptop, watching old episodes of a TV comedy—*Friends*, from the sound of it. Leo was laughing uproariously at the dialogue, but Millie looked subdued. Worrying about Rod, I suspected.

A pizza box lay on the coffee table because Leo had surprised us by delivering dinner. Two big slices still remained in the box. I hoped they'd go uneaten because I had designs on them. Cold pizza was a breakfast delicacy at my place.

As I eyed the box, wondering whether it was too soon to snatch it up and take it into the kitchen, Leo glanced up at me. "You want to watch with us, Kate? There's plenty of room for you."

He scooted on the couch, edging closer to Millie, as he patted the spot beside him on my battered sofa. She didn't appear to notice, just remained focused on the screen.

I was fairly certain that I knew what the draw was for Leo, what had brought him to my apartment in Morningside Heights. He'd visited daily since he and Mom had walked in on us in my mother's living room. Whether Millie had caught on, I didn't know. I hoped not. She hadn't said anything.

Leo and I needed to have a talk, but we couldn't do it in my one-room space. I resolved to call him the very next day, to nip his crush in the bud. Millie had a boyfriend, one who could flatten Leo without exerting himself. And Rod wouldn't remain in Rikers much longer, not if I could help it.

I wanted to take Rod's case up with Rubenstein. After I'd filed my written suggestions with Judge Robertson, I'd cc'ed them to Rubenstein with a long email describing the outcome of the hearing, but I was waiting to hear back from him. If he didn't respond, I planned to hit him up when the advisory committee met. I'd received notice that there would be a formal gathering on Friday outside the Oculus. It would be a showy press affair with a cocktail reception following. Rubenstein was a hard man to run down, but the reception should provide the opportunity I needed.

I looked at Leo, sitting shoulder to shoulder on the couch with Millie. He was gone on that girl, totally smitten. "I'm not interested in the show, thanks, Leo. You two can spread out. I'll sit right here."

I dropped into the other seat in the room. It was my dad's recliner, the chair I'd inherited from his place after he died. I figured that, if I put my earphones in, it would drown out the laugh track from their program.

But someone pounded on the apartment door before I had the chance. A man's voice called out, "Kate? You in there?"

Millie looked up at me, startled. Rising from the chair, I reassured her. "It sounds like Bill. He's a friend of mine. Nothing to worry about."

I went to the door and checked the peephole, to be certain. He stood in the hallway, adjusting his glasses.

I was surprised to see him. Bill lived in Brooklyn, and rarely came to my neighborhood. It took a minute to unfasten the locks I'd installed. When I opened the door, Bill looked over my shoulder, into the room. Sounding sheepish, he said, "Guess I'm interrupting. Sorry, Kate. I didn't think you'd have people over. Is this a bad time?"

"No, come on in. What are you doing?"

He walked in. Standing uncertainly just inside the doorway, he shoved his hands into his pockets. "I've got a meeting, just about a block away from here, and I'm early. I thought I'd see if you were home. I figured we could talk, catch up."

"Great, glad to see you. You know my brother, right? And this is my friend Millie. Millie, Bill and I worked together, back when I was in the Manhattan DA's office."

She fixed him with a resentful glare. Representatives of the

DA's office were low on her list since she had accompanied me to court. But Leo was friendly.

He said, "Hey, Bill, I brought some pizza. You want a slice?"

I wanted to shut the cardboard box, wished I'd stowed it in the fridge before we had a new arrival. I was relieved to see Bill shake his head.

"I'm good. Just dropped by to say hello, that's all."

He walked over and sat in my dad's chair. That exhausted the seating options, so I sat cross-legged on the floor. "Did you say you've got an appointment up here? Where are you going, Bill?"

"It's a meeting."

"Really?" I was curious. "Is it work?"

"No, not business. It's that thing I told you about." Sneaking a glance over at the couch, he sounded self-conscious when he added, "My therapy."

"All the way up here? I thought you met in Midtown."

"We do. This is more like a social gathering. One of the guys in the support group is a musician, plays the saxophone. It's a jazz night at a bar on Broadway, so we're meeting up there to hear him play."

Millie's left hand clutched the arm of the sofa. "What kind of support group?"

Bill cleared his throat. "It's some people who are working to overcome their anxiety."

His face flushed when he spoke, like he was embarrassed to announce it. But both Millie and Leo perked up.

"What kind of anxiety?" Millie asked.

"All kinds. Social, performance anxiety, generalized anxiety. We talk about it in group. Learn about tools to control it.

If you have the issue, it's helpful to know you're not the only one who struggles with it."

Millie tapped the computer keyboard with a finger, muting the sound. "I suffer from anxiety. For *years*. Seems like I've been battling it forever."

My brother turned to her. "Really? That's unbelievable."

She gave him a chilly look. "Why do you say that?"

"Because you're so ...." He didn't finish the sentence. Instead, he lifted his shoulders in a shrug and confessed, "I have test anxiety. Always have, ever since I was a kid."

Maybe it was wrong of me—in fact, I'm sure it was. But I didn't want to hear Leo reveal the trouble he'd had with the New Jersey bar exam. He had taken and failed it, more than once. It was a sore spot with our mother, and the topic always set me on edge. Out of long habit, I changed the subject.

"Hey, Bill, what's the word on Ian Templeton? Has anything surfaced at the DA's office?"

He gave me a baffled look. "Like what?"

"Like a criminal charge. What do you think? He's a crook, I've told you that so many times, I'd think you'd recall it. I hope to see an announcement of his downfall any day, but I'm always disappointed."

He edged forward on the chair seat of the chair, like maybe he was preparing to make a hasty departure. In a quiet voice, he said, "Kate, you know I can't talk about particular cases or ongoing investigations. It's a conversation we can't have. Cam is adamant about that."

His shoulders sagged, like he was carrying a heavy load. He looked like he was down about something. It was a marked contrast from the last time I'd seen him. "How's it going in the new division? Are they treating you right?"

He grimaced and started to say something but then appeared to change his mind. I nudged him. "Come on, Bill. You can tell me anything."

With a mirthless laugh, he said, "I guess it's like any new position. There's always a honeymoon period at first. But it can't last forever."

For Bill's sake, I was sorry the honeymoon was over. "Are they dumping the crap cases on you? Because that's pretty typical for the new guy."

"Not that exactly. It's not just weak cases. I'm used to that."

"Is it Maya? Or the division head, Cam? Honestly, he seemed like a dick."

A shadow crossed his face. "Maybe I'm not cut out for white collar, after all. I was thinking about moving on. Do you like what you're doing—the defense work?"

I was astounded. Last I'd heard, Bill was thrilled with his new assignment. "Criminal defense isn't a picnic. And defense work was never your aim. So what's up? Tell me."

He started to speak but then hesitated. I thought he was going to confide in me. But he shook his head and rose from his seat.

"I'd better head out, don't want to be late." As he walked by the couch, he said to Millie and Leo, "Hey, if you're interested, you all should check it out. Our support group is always open to new members."

Millie unmuted the laptop. "No thanks. I'm not into support groups. Bad experience. You don't wanna know, I guarantee. Long story."

That was an understatement. Leo shook his head at Bill, smiling. "Yeah, we're tied up here tonight. Streaming old *Friends* reruns."

Millie turned to my brother. "You should go."

Taken aback, he said, "Really? You think?"

"I do. It would be good for you."

As she pulled the computer onto her lap, I realized that, apparently, Millie was cognizant of Leo's affection.

My brother looked over at me like he was undecided. I thought it would provide a distraction from his unrequited crush. "Yeah, check it out. If nothing else, you can drink a beer and listen to live music. Sounds like a good time."

He rose from the couch. In a reluctant voice, he said, "If you really think so."

I followed Bill and Leo to the door. When I opened it, a streak of gray flew past my feet.

Millie's face lit up. "It's the cat, the old lady's cat from next door."

Edie's cat hopped onto the couch and settled beside her. Millie stroked his striped fur, murmuring baby talk to the feline.

Bill gave me a rueful look and said, "Good to see you, Kate. I've been missing the time when you and I shared our office. Feels like those were the good old days. You know what I mean?"

"I do." His forlorn expression troubled me. "Bill, we can get together anytime. I'm really flexible these days."

He smiled before he walked away with my brother at his side.

When I shut the door, Millie had the cat on her lap and her phone in her hand. As she swiped the screen, her face lit up.

"What's up?" I said.

She grinned and held the screen up. "Voice mail message. We've got an appointment with Ian Templeton in his Wall Street office. They even gave me directions. It's down the street from *Fearless Girl.*"

CHAPTER 29

Whitney

WHITNEY NOVAK WAS taking her afternoon cigarette break.

It was a luxury she afforded herself, a peaceful moment in a life that had gone haywire. Near the office, she had a regular spot she always ducked into, right at the corner of the steps leading up to Federal Hall. Since they closed the building, the sidewalk didn't get so much foot traffic. She had an unobstructed view of the New York Stock Exchange. Whitney could gaze out, reflecting on happier times.

She pulled a crumpled pack of Marlboro Reds from the pocket of her trench coat. Only two cigarettes remained, but that would have to satisfy her, at present. They'd expect her to report back to her cubicle in fifteen minutes. She didn't have time to hunt down another pack.

She lit the smoke with a Bic lighter. On that afternoon, she didn't have to worry that her habit would offend passersby. Not many people were strolling by her on the cobblestones of Broad Street. But predictably, pedestrians flocked to the bronze statue half a block away from her.

Whitney was no fan of the bronze sculpture, the little pony-tailed figure standing with her hands on her hips, staring down the New York Stock Exchange. When the city had placed the *Fearless Girl* statue in that spot, Whitney had been vocal in her opposition. She'd sounded off to anyone who would listen. It was phony, she claimed, and gave a false portrait of reality. Why pretend that a kid could intimidate the big board?

And the implication, urged by others, that the child represented women's power in the boardroom? That was a farce. Women were still playing catch-up in the financial sector. And those, like Whitney, who had the grit and fortitude to rise in the world of finance, bore no resemblance to the kid in the little bronze dress. Women like Whitney had to be like the bull. The *Charging Bull*, the bronze sculpture on Broadway—now, that was a statue Whitney could relate to.

Because Whitney disliked *Fearless Girl*, she usually paid no attention to it. That's why it was such a shock to spot Kate Stone that day. It was more than mere coincidence. Whitney didn't believe in coincidence, anyway. She never left anything to chance. Life had taught her that, long ago.

Looking down the street, Whitney shook her head in amazement. Because there she stood, the unbeatable Kate Stone, just feet away from the statue. She was wearing a black suit that Whitney recalled was part of Kate's limited professional wardrobe. Kate held her phone, standing by the statute like she was some tourist from Small Town, USA, one who had never before traveled to New York City and wasn't likely to return.

Whitney pulled out the second cigarette and shoved the empty pack into her pocket. As she lit it, she thought about her options. She hadn't expected to encounter Kate here. What Kate was doing in the Financial District, Whitney couldn't fathom. The woman had always been unapologetically dense when it came to money, and she purported to disapprove of people who had too much of it. That had motivated her attacks on Templeton, and on his associates. Kate had claimed to despise Ian Templeton because he made his money by trickery and illegal schemes. Whitney always had her doubts about that. She thought it might have been a simple case of jealousy, resentment against a man who had amassed a financial fortune.

Standing alone on the corner, Whitney tried to deduce the reason for Kate's presence on Wall Street. She eliminated the improbable explanations, one by one. Kate wasn't an out-of-towner, checking out famous sights for a Facebook post to impress friends back home. She had no interest in finance and no money to invest. That only left one explanation. Kate was still trying to bring down Ian Templeton.

A plan was afoot. Whitney could sense it, feeling the vibrations. She tossed her cigarette onto the curb. As she stood, still watching Kate from a distance, a woman holding a child by the hand approached her. With a tentative smile, the woman said to Whitney, "We're looking for the statue of the little girl. My daughter wants to see it. Is it near here? We're from out of town."

Of course you are, Whitney thought. She was unhappy with the interruption. She wanted to be alone with her thoughts. She refused to make eye contact with the tourist as she said, "They moved it."

Hearing the child protest as the mother led her away,

Whitney didn't feel a shred of remorse. *What do they think I am?* she thought. *A tour guide for the hop-on, hop-off bus?*

Kate Stone had changed position while the mother distracted Whitney. She stood beside the statue at that point, holding her phone up high.

Whitney cackled at the sight. *Really?* Kate was taking selfies with *Fearless Girl*? This was comical, much better than watching standup at the Comedy Cellar. Far, far funnier.

Whitney experienced an epiphany, a flash of inspiration. She could put an end to the Kate Stone saga that very afternoon. She was carrying the push dagger in the pocket of her trench coat, next to her cigarettes. Whitney slid her hand into her pocket and grasped the handle with a firm grip. In her mind's eye, she could see the blade protruding from the front of her fist.

The dagger was razor sharp, Whitney saw to that. She provided faithful maintenance to the blade. She cast an assessing eye at Kate, looking at the way her neck rose from the jacket of her black suit. It was a long neck, totally exposed and vulnerable. Whitney could make a run for her, right then, at that very moment. While Kate posed for her selfie, or maybe checked the picture on her phone, Whitney could step up to face her, slit her throat with one slice of the dagger, and walk away.

While she considered it, another person joined Kate as she posed by the statue, blocking Whitney's view of the target. Whitney couldn't see the interloper's face. It looked like a young female, taller than Kate, with garish, multicolored hair pulled into high pigtails. They stood shoulder to shoulder as Kate held the phone overhead and took pictures.

That change of circumstance made Whitney reconsider. The presence of a close witness altered things. Fatal incidents and executions needed to be tidy, performed with efficiency and forethought. Also, cameras were everywhere. The spot was far too public. She shouldn't be impulsive. It wasn't smart.

Besides, it would be more interesting to see it play out. Kate had a new game plan, that was certain. It would come to some bizarre, climactic finale. That's how Kate rolled.

And when the drama reached its pinnacle, *Charging Bull* would mow down *Fearless Girl*.

Because that's how it worked in the real world.

Whitney released the dagger and let it rest at the bottom of her pocket. She pulled the empty Marlboro pack from her pocket and tossed it into a trash can on the corner.

Time to go back to work. She whistled as she walked away, feeling better than she had in a while. She felt positively sociable. Maybe she'd even hit another support group meeting and chat up the new kid.

Kate Stone's brother looked like a guy who needed a friend.

CHAPTER 30

MILLIE AND I were early. We'd agreed to meet up with Steven and Devon on Broad Street in Lower Manhattan, by the *Fearless Girl* statue.

"Let's take pictures while we wait," Millie said, "and I'll post them on Insta."

I pulled out my phone, but it hummed before I could take a picture.

It was Mom. I almost didn't answer. After four rings, I relented. "Hey, Mom! What's up? Are you getting caught up on your cases, now that you're back?"

Her response was tart. "I'm trying. It would be easier if I had some help. Are you coming into work today?"

I wasn't. Not today, not tomorrow. I wasn't eager to return to her New Jersey office. But I didn't have the nerve to tell her I'd been planning to seek out alternative employment. "No, can't come in today."

"Why not? Where are you?"

"I'm in the Financial District." It wouldn't help to lie about my whereabouts. She knew Leo and I had a location sharing app.

"Why? You don't have any money, other than what I give you. Do I need to remind you that I'm paying your salary? Which requires you to actually come in and do some work?"

"I'm just looking into something. Getting advice on crypto."

She scoffed into the phone. "Here's some good advice. Don't buy it. So why haven't you been in the office all week?"

"I couldn't come in. I was busy. I had a hearing in court, and I was cleaning the apartment before that. Because you wanted me out of your house."

"So you'll be in tomorrow?"

"No." I glanced around but didn't see Steven or Devon. "Tomorrow's the big press conference to introduce Rubenstein's advisory committee. You'll probably see it on the local news."

"Will you be in next week? Think you can work it into your busy schedule?"

"Yeah, sure." I ended the call before we got into a fight.

I took the selfies and then handed the phone off to Millie. As she scanned through them, she frowned. "Maybe we need to cut you from the shot. You don't really fit the image I'm trying to portray."

Chagrined, I enlarged the picture to remove myself. I'd tried to dress the part for our Templeton appointment when I chose the black business suit. Checking my appearance in the spotty mirror of my apartment, I realized I was sorely in need of an update. I also planned to wear it to the swanky advisory committee event at the Oculus on the World Trade Center campus. But I was thinking that I'd look like someone who wandered in by mistake.

I handed the phone back to her. "Better?"

She smiled as she texted the image to her phone. While she tapped the screen, I said, "Tell me again, so I understand. Exactly what persona are you going for?"

"I'm fluid," she said. "But right now, it's a Harley Quinn vibe."

She tossed her head, making the pigtails twirl around. One side of her hair was dyed pink, the other aqua—a temporary rinse, she'd informed me. Her eyes were smudged with black, and she'd painted a wide coat of scarlet lipstick on her mouth. Millie was dressed in a costume she'd once worn to portray a prostitute in *The Threepenny Opera*. Her scandalously short skirt displayed the tops of the fishnet stockings she wore with white ankle boots.

"You want to look cartoonish?"

"Right!" She shot a dubious glance at me. "You're too dowdy to be my manager or publicist. I'm going to recast you."

The comment stung. I was tempted to make a tart reply, but just then Steven and Devon joined us. When Devon saw Millie's costume, he laughed. "Wow. If I didn't know better, I'd think you were Margot Robbie."

"Thank you. I'm always glad to be mistaken for Margot."

She grabbed Devon in a hug and kissed him on the cheek. As she wiped the red lip print from his face with her thumb, she said, "Devon, you're a genius. You got my followers almost to five hundred K. You're going to make me a star. I think we should do TikTok next."

Steven's eyes widened. "Half a million? Jesus, Devon."

He shrugged. "I didn't grow it organically, you understand.

So the numbers don't signify real followers. But Templeton won't know that."

I checked the time. We'd agreed that we shouldn't be too prompt because it might be a mistake to seem eager. But we couldn't make a man of Templeton's stature wait for long.

I said, "We've got a few minutes to do recon. Millie, give us a run-through."

"I'm the Divine Miss M, aka Divalicious, a new musician on the rise with a strong social media base. Steven's my manager because he looks kinda hip. Devon is perfectly technosexual, so he'll play my publicist. Kate looks like…" Her voice drifted. "A really poor secret service agent. So she's my bodyguard."

"Fine." I wasn't going to snipe about my changing role in the proceedings. It didn't matter. "You're going to ask him about the crypto investment and have him pitch it to you in detail. I'll be recording it on my phone."

Millie said, "I'll get him to talk. And I'll act like I'm seriously impressed."

Steven said, "Millie, if he asks you to boost his crypto on social media, pin him down. Make him specify what you should do."

"If he doesn't ask, then volunteer. And keep him talking," I said. "We want to hear him lie, making misrepresentations about the crypto scheme. So we'll have evidence of fraud."

Steven said, "Devon, what will you be looking for?"

He frowned, looking thoughtful. "While we're in the office, I'll get information on his IT systems, see what operating systems they use at Pyramid Investments. When I gain more insight, it should be possible to hack in."

"And you'll try to upload spyware?" Steven said.

"Well, yeah. Ideally, if I could plant spyware, I could have access to everything. But the preliminary step is to get inside and observe."

I wished he could envision a way to hack the system in the initial meeting. But I understood that it might be impossible to pull it off in his business office, under Templeton's nose with his employees all around.

"Or we can proceed with our plan B. I can just take his cell phone," Millie said, as she touched up the red lipstick, using her phone screen as a mirror.

Devon barked a laugh. "Sure, why not? With his phone, I could crack him wide open."

"Let's do it, regardless of what you find. Move the cell phone to plan A. It's not that hard. I used to pick pockets, you know. Kate and I were pretty good at it."

The day before, Millie had proposed that I lift the phone, but I refused. The suggestion made me jittery. "I'm glad you're in charge of that. There's no way I could pull it off. I'm out of practice."

"I've still got the magic." She gave me a nudge as she walked around me on the pavement and then held something up with a flourish.

It was a cell phone. My cell phone.

I took it from her hand and said, "You're good, Millie. I give you props. Want to rehearse it again? You can practice what you'll say."

"I don't need to rehearse any lines. It's improv," Millie said. Her confidence was contagious. Well, almost contagious. I still battled uncertainty.

I stared down the street, gazing up at the tall building

where Ian Templeton's offices were located. Light reflected off the windows, making them glisten in the sun so that I couldn't see inside. It gave me an edgy feeling, like I was running in to fight an invisible foe.

Steven said, "What do you think, Kate? We've been talking this through for the past two days. But if you're having second thoughts, we'll walk away."

"No!" Millie clutched my arm. "Rod thinks Templeton's behind all of this, right? He put Rod in jail, and now he's going to chase all of us down."

I nodded. Millie's expression hardened. She said, "Then we can't blow off this opportunity. Let's go get the evidence. This is our way out."

Millie was right. I just needed to screw up my courage and get my head straight.

"Let's get him on the record," I said.

We followed Millie, playing entourage to her celebrity role. Heads turned as we walked through the lobby. The elevator took us to the top floor of the building where Templeton's offices were housed.

The elevator opened into a minimalist lobby, furnished with white tile and aqua leather sofas and chairs. The receptionist sat behind a long white counter. She didn't blink as Millie sauntered up with the three of us in tow.

"I have a meeting with Ian. I'm a little late, I think."

The receptionist rose, ushering us through glass corridors into a large conference room where a polished table was surrounded by twelve leather chairs.

"Have a seat," she said. "Mr. Templeton will be here shortly. Can I get anyone a beverage?"

We all refused—except Millie. She tilted her head, thinking. "A vanilla Coke Zero for me."

I hid a smile. The diva was in character. She'd never consumed a Coke Zero in the whole time I'd known her.

When the receptionist shut the door, Steven pulled out a chair and collapsed. "Kind of surreal," he said.

A computer docking station was installed on a credenza against the wall. Devon strolled over to it, inspecting it. I joined him. "What do you think?"

He shrugged. "Thinking about network connectivity. Also—"

Devon froze and didn't complete the sentence. He raised his eyes to the ceiling where it met the corner of the room. In a bare whisper, he said, "Cameras."

I whirled around. There were cameras in all four corners.

Devon was whispering again. I stood close to him, so that I could make out what he was saying.

"Yeah, I recognize the kind of system he uses. But I'm not hacking in while I'm under surveillance. If I do, they'll put me in a cell at Rikers, too."

I turned, catching Steven's eye. He glanced up at the camera; he'd also observed that security was watching us. Mille was sitting on the table near him. He waved her over and whispered. I saw her frown.

She hopped off the table and walked up to Devon and me. "I can still get his phone, and Devon can get info from it. When he comes in, I'll give him a big hug, do my thing. No problem."

We didn't have a chance to talk it over. The door opened, and a new employee entered, a woman wearing wire-rimmed eyeglasses under a fringe of dark bangs.

She held a can of vanilla Coke Zero in one hand and a short tumbler of ice in the other. She presented the beverage to Millie, who promptly popped the top and drank straight from the can.

The woman's regretful expression was carefully manufactured. "So sorry. Mr. Templeton is tied up. He asked me to convey his apologies."

The fuck? I stepped up, ready to demand an explanation.

Mille beat me to it. "How long does Ian expect me to wait?" She set the can on the conference table.

"He's not available today, unfortunately. But he appreciates your interest and thanks you for coming by."

Steven rose from his seat. He and Devon stepped toward the door. But Millie didn't budge. "When are we going to reschedule? Because I'm booked up. I'm flying to LA next week. Got a meeting with CAA."

Again, the woman offered her sad smile. "I'll pass along the information. Maybe Mr. Templeton will have more availability when you return."

Millie grinned, looking like a cartoon villain with her clownish smile. "Maybe I'll have a better offer by then. Or change my mind." She lifted the can, swigging down another swallow, and handed the Coke Zero to the assistant. "Give Ian a message."

"Certainly." The woman smiled again.

"Tell him I'm free for cocktails Saturday night. He can drop by my place."

I almost gagged. The studio? In Morningside Heights? Millie must have lost her mind to let him invade my apartment.

210

The woman was speaking in a condescending tone. "He's very busy."

"Who isn't? I live at Thirty-Five Hudson Yards. Tower E."

The woman's eyes had widened, the lenses of her glasses magnifying the reaction. "What was the address?"

Millie repeated it and added, "Tell him I make a great Negroni." She flounced out of the office without a backward look, and we followed, single file. We remained perfectly silent as we left the office, rode the elevator down, and exited the building.

On the steps, Devon erupted. "You're throwing a party at my boss's condo? Have you lost your mind?"

Steven said, "Let's move away from the building, okay?"

As we walked down the street, Devon continued his tirade. "You're gonna get me fired. I can't believe you'd pop off with that suggestion without even asking me."

Steven said, "Devon, calm down. What are the odds that Templeton would actually come over? We got the brush-off today. He ghosted us."

Millie was lagging behind us on the pavement. I heard her laugh. When I turned my head, she was dancing on the sidewalk. Pedestrians were giving her a wide berth.

She held her phone out and read aloud, "'Miss M, my sincere apologies for today's inconvenience. See you Saturday at five.'"

I gasped at her. "You're kidding."

She waved the phone. "'P.S. Love a Negroni.'"

I grabbed her and gave her a hug. "Millie, you're brilliant. Jesus! I owe you."

She squeezed me and said, "Just get Rod out of Rikers,

that's all I ask. Maybe you'll talk to Rubenstein tomorrow, at that committee thing."

Devon clearly didn't share our glee. He looked like a thundercloud.

As I stepped away from Millie, she skipped ahead. Steven and I walked beside Devon, offering reassurances.

Steven said, "It'll be quick. He won't stay long. If he comes at all. He stood her up today."

Millie whirled around and said, "Oh, he'll come. The Hudson Yards address was magic. He thinks he's got a live one on the hook—young, rich, and dumb. The perfect sucker."

Devon groaned. I put an arm around him and gave him a pat. "Don't be so dramatic! Millie will make him a drink, give him a hug. Take his phone and send him on his way. What's so hard about that? What could go wrong?"

"Everything. It sounds like a disaster. You think he's not gonna miss his cell phone? And he'll know exactly where he lost it—my employer's condo. How will I explain that to the boss?" Devon was quiet for a moment. "But if Templeton actually shows up, and we manage to keep him inside the condo for a while, we may not need the physical phone."

"Really?" I said. "Why not?"

He was thinking. I could see the wheels turning. "Bluetooth."

CHAPTER 31

IN THE SHADOW of the Oculus on the World Trade Center campus, a temporary platform had been constructed for Rubenstein's press conference. I sat on the middle row of a section of folding chairs they had set up behind the platform. Surrounded by a glittering collection of high-profile attorneys and community leaders, I tugged at the belt of the dress I had borrowed from Millie that morning, after she declared my wardrobe unsuitable for the occasion. Millie and I weren't built the same, and the dress was an imperfect fit because I didn't fill out the bodice. But the garment was spotless, fresh from a dry-cleaning bag.

She'd also lent me a pair of matching navy-blue shoes. I decided to wear them because they were shiny, practically new, as opposed to any of the footwear choices available in my closet. Millie's shoes were about half a size too big, however. She advised me to stuff the toes with a wad of newspaper. I read things online. I didn't have a newspaper.

So I used a crumpled paper towel instead. The substitution was unsatisfactory because, not only was the wadded towel uncomfortable, it didn't keep my heel from slipping out of the shoes when I walked.

I looked around at my fellow committee members, and a sense of wonder overwhelmed me. The committee was made up of older, prominent, experienced professionals. Without exception, they possessed established profiles in criminal justice, law enforcement, and social justice.

And then there was me. In that group, I was the odd duck, the person who didn't fit.

Rubenstein was working the crowd. He'd seated the crown jewels of his committee in the front row, and he walked from one end to another, greeting them and shaking hands. He was upbeat and jovial and didn't exhibit any performance jitters as he chatted up a retired New York State appellate judge who had briefly served as a White House staffer for one of the Bushes. I couldn't remember which.

I wondered whether he'd make it down to my row. My efforts to schedule an appointment with him were still unsuccessful, and though I'd spent hours devising a memo of arguments and suggestions on Rod's behalf and sent it to him, I hadn't had the chance to make a face-to-face pitch. But maybe that would change. If the opportunity presented itself that day, I intended to grab hold of it.

With my eye on the DA, I watched as Rubenstein's publicity director came up behind him and interrupted, whispering something in his ear.

Rubenstein nodded and walked over to the videographer. After I had sidled over in my chair to keep him in my sights, the woman seated next to me turned and gave me a curious look. "Do I know you?"

The question made me defensive. "I don't know. Do you?"

She raised a brow at my effrontery. "Do you have an advisory position, or will you be serving on the committee in a clerical capacity?"

The fuck? I gave her a level look. "I was handpicked by Frank because of my specific background in criminal justice."

"Really." She looked at the shiny shoe that was hanging off my foot and cracked a hint of a smile. "I had you pegged for a representative of the ACLU."

Believe me, she didn't intend it as a compliment. An angry knot formed in my throat, and I sat up straight, preparing to fling a barbed comment back at her.

But she startled me with her next question. "Do you think he'll announce his candidacy?"

I said, "For what?"

She whispered it. "Governor."

I wanted to hear more, but Rubenstein was walking up the stairs of the platform. The show was about to begin. A polite round of applause heralded his remarks.

Camera lenses aimed at him. I couldn't see his expression, just the back of his head. I wondered whether Rubenstein was smiling, or whether he thought the occasion called for a somber face.

He spoke into the microphone. "Ladies and gentlemen, thank you for coming out today. As one of the primary law enforcement officials of our magnificent city, I'm obliged to convey unhappy news. Since our state bail reform laws took effect in 2020, the crime rate is rising in New York."

Solemn face, I thought. He'll smile for the cameras later.

"The data is clear, we can't ignore the numbers. Our city saw a thirty-eight percent increase in crime since the same period a year ago. Violent crime is up. Robbery, rape, assault, all on the rise. Shooting incidents increased by thirty-two percent."

His voice, amplified by the sound system, soared over the World Trade Center campus. The event had drawn a number of onlookers—curiosity-seekers, in addition to the press. Two young men were shouting back at Rubenstein, but their voices were drowned out by street noise and the loudspeakers cranking up the audio.

Rubenstein continued. "As a public servant, I appreciate the work that the state legislature did on bail reform. And I sympathize with the purpose of the legislative changes. People who have been arrested and charged with a crime are presumed innocent until proven guilty. That is one of the hallmarks of our justice system. Too often, the person's ability to leave jail after they are arrested depends on their individual economic status. People with money to pay cash bail can secure their freedom. But the poor, the indigent, are forced to remain incarcerated while they wait for trial."

His voice rose with emotion. "It's a class distinction, discriminatory because people are penalized for being poor."

At that point, some catcalls and boos rang out from onlookers. I wore a poker face, kept my eyes on the back of Rubenstein's head. As I sat like a polite statue, it struck me that I'd never before behaved in such a decorous fashion. I knew that the role I'd been assigned that day was comparable to one a politician's spouse performed during a campaign. It didn't suit me, I was getting fidgety. I was glad my duty would end in an hour or so.

As Rubenstein's remarks went on, he transitioned from compassion for the accused to standard law-and-order cheer-leading. He talked about the duty of his office to protect citizens' personal safety and their property. While he spoke, my mind wandered. I pondered the possibilities of our up-coming meeting with Templeton at Hudson Yards. Devon was devising a plan based on the security already in place in the tower. If Templeton actually came and we were able to keep him on the premises for a sufficient length of time, Devon had a shot at accessing his phone remotely. It was mind-boggling to think that such a thing was possible. But if he managed to hack in, we felt certain that we'd find incriminating statements and material on the device.

Unfortunately, the plot wasn't strictly legal, and that element made me cringe. Maybe my ambitions were too con-flicted. I wanted to bring Templeton down, for our personal welfare and the general good, but also to uphold my ethics in the legal profession and take action that would've made my dad proud. Was that an impossible goal? And it was impera-tive that I attain justice for Rod. Rubenstein was holding a reception for us later that day. That would create a chance to bend his ear.

Rubenstein was moving on to introductions. He started with the committee chairs seated on the front row. I checked my dress, uncrossed my legs and slid my feet into the over-sized shoes. People rose as they were introduced. I wanted to look good for the camera.

When he came to me, I was shocked to receive a special

shout-out from Frank. "And the youngest member of the advisory board, a former member of my staff, now practicing criminal defense: Kate Stone."

With a smile frozen on my face, I stood. Once I was on my feet, I had a better vantage point from which to view the onlookers. A fair-sized crowd had assembled. After a moment, the smattering of applause I received died out. I was ready to sit back down.

But someone caught my eye. A disheveled man bundled into ragged, mismatched clothes stood on the edge of the crowd. He was an unlikely onlooker for a DA's press event. He looked just like the people Steven served. I didn't want to make him self-conscious, and so I glanced away. But something made me take a second look.

The smile I wore dropped off my face. The man resembled Larry, the engineer who'd belonged to my vigilante group and who'd lured me to the subway on the day Edgar had pushed me onto the tracks. Taking a longer look, I realized that it absolutely was Larry standing at the edge of the crowd, dressed like a member of the unhoused community. And when I zeroed in on him, I noted he had a companion. The guy from LaGuardia who'd driven the Suburban.

I didn't stop to think or attempt to make a plan. I hiked up the skirt of my borrowed dress and plowed down the row, stomping on my fellow committee members' feet. As I charged through the chairs that blocked me from my prey, I shrieked like a madwoman. "Get out of my way!"

CHAPTER 32

WHEN LARRY SAW me coming for him, he froze. His eyes widened as I stumbled over the feet of my fellow committee members.

"What the hell are you doing?" The man seated at the end of my row raised his arm, as if he intended to stop me.

The spiked heel of my borrowed navy-blue shoe jabbed into his foot. It must have hurt. He yowled like an angry cat.

Larry didn't move until he saw me emerge from the tangle of seats. His companion, the dark-haired driver, tugged at his arm, shouting something I couldn't make out. I'd almost reached the spot where they stood on the fringe of the crowd when they turned and ran, skirting the loose circle of onlookers.

People scuttled out of our path as I pursued them. Larry lagged behind the ponytailed guy, couldn't keep pace with the younger man. I almost had him, was only a couple of arm's lengths away when I got tripped up. My foot slipped out of Millie's shoe, giving my ankle a nasty twist. Snatching the shoe off the ground, I hopped on one foot to slip it back on while the men made their way to the entrance of the Oculus.

My ankle slowed me down, but I trailed them as fast as possible while wearing a loose pair of stiletto heels. When I ran through the sliding doors of the Oculus, I paused, looking around.

Every time I stepped inside the station, it took my breath away.

I had entered the terminal for the World Trade Center complex, a transportation hub for New Jersey train travel and the New York City subway lines. The Oculus was built to replace the station house destroyed on 9/11. Designed by architect Santiago Calatrava to look like a dove taking flight, its white steel arches soared upward 164 feet from the ground. The all-white interior of the building was illuminated by a long rib of skylights providing natural overhead light. It kind of felt like walking into some artist's dream rendering of heaven.

The white surroundings made it easy to spot Larry as he stumbled down the escalator. I made an awkward dash to follow him, but I didn't move swiftly enough. Two teenage girls slipped onto the escalator first. Carrying bags from H&M and Banana Republic, they effectively blocked the steps that they occupied. As I shouldered my way past them, one of the girls shouted in protest.

"You trying to get someone killed? You're busting the line, bitch!"

I didn't stop to exchange fighting words, because Larry was getting away. I kept up the pursuit, dodging shoppers and transit passengers as I trailed Larry. When I saw Larry pause to look over his shoulder at me, I shrieked his name.

"Larry! I want to talk to you!"

He stopped in his tracks, which surprised me. Panting for breath, he bent at the waist with his hands on his knees. As I trotted up to him on my wobbly shoes, his face crumpled, like he was about to cry.

I was winded when I reached him. But questions tumbled out before I could catch my breath. "Larry, what the fuck is going on? Who's that guy you were with? Did you know he tried to run off with me at the airport?"

Larry looked like the image of misery. His clothes were tattered and dirty, his thinning hair standing on end. As he gasped for breath, I could smell the stale booze from last night's bender.

"It's not my fault," he said. "I never wanted any of this to happen."

"Wanted what to happen? Who's behind this? I'm entitled to know."

He turned and began to lope away. I heard him speak in a mournful voice. "Sorry, Kate."

I wanted to demand Larry specify just what he was apologizing for. Was it something that had already befallen me or something that I still had occasion to dread?

I got my answer when someone tackled me from behind, taking me down onto the floor.

CHAPTER 33

THE HIT TOOK me by surprise. I barely got my hands out in time to break the fall.

Stunned, I lay on the white tile floor of the Oculus, gasping for air. My attacker hopped back up and took off running.

A middle-aged woman stepped over and asked, "Are you okay?"

Before I could answer, I heard someone else weigh in. "Serves her right! She was messing with that poor old dude. Did you hear her trashing him?"

One of the teenage shoppers had followed me and was apparently glad to see me get my comeuppance. As I scrambled to my feet, she taunted me. "Karma's a bitch, bitch!"

Larry had managed to disappear while I had been laid out on the floor. The ponytailed LaGuardia driver was in my sights, but he had a fair lead on me. Undeterred, I pushed my hair out of my face and chased after him. What I intended to do with him if I caught him, I hadn't decided. But I was in the mood to kick somebody's ass.

Bypassing the escalator, the LaGuardia driver ran for the stairs. I followed, scrambling up the steps in those goddamn wobbly shoes. I saw him escape through the doors of the Oculus that exit onto the street.

I shoved past the people who were blocking the doorway, ran onto the pavement outside and came to a dead stop. I thought I had lost him.

Pacing under the white beams, I scanned the sidewalks. Although I couldn't see anyone running away, I thought maybe he was trying to blend in with the rest of the pedestrians. The Millennium Hilton was directly across the way, and he might have taken refuge there. Squinting, I peered at the entrance of the hotel, but he wasn't hanging around outside or on the steps leading to the hotel doors.

Feeling dejected, I turned to make my way back inside the Oculus when I heard horns blaring. I spun back around just in time to see the dark-haired guy narrowly miss being struck by a city bus as he ran against traffic at the intersection of Fulton and Church Street.

I kicked off Millie's shoes and ran, following him onto the street. Traffic had slowed when the bus came to an abrupt halt to avoid hitting the guy, and a symphony of angry horns rang in my ears as I narrowly dodged a yellow cab before I made it to the opposite sidewalk. I could see him ahead of me, running by the graveyard of the old St. Paul's church. He must have sensed I was in pursuit because he paused to check over his shoulder. When he saw me following in his tracks in my bare feet, an odd expression crossed his face.

He hopped on the stone foundation of the high black wrought iron fence that surrounds St. Paul's on all four sides.

Reaching overhead, he grasped the spiked cast iron spear points protruding from the top of the high fence. With an audible grunt, he hoisted himself over the fence and dropped onto the ground.

The black iron fence was tall, stretching over my head. But I thought, if he can do it, so could I. I grasped the vertical metal spires and slid my feet over the finials adorning the horizontal support. I quickly learned that climbing a spiked fence without footwear was a tricky proposition. The old fence had pointed barbs at the top and the bottom, so my foot- and handholds were painful. If I hadn't been pumping some serious painkilling adrenaline, I would have given up. But I could see him, turning back to laugh at me as I made my third attempt to scale that fence.

The third time was the charm, although one of the pointed spikes scraped a gash in the back of my thigh. And when I jumped away from the fence, Millie's dress snagged on one of the spears welded to the top. So when I landed on the ground, a fair portion of my skirt remained on the fence above me, waving like a navy-blue flag.

I stood up in the churchyard. Though I'd grown up in the city, I'd never been inside the fence before. It was an eerie experience, like being transported back in time. The chapel is the oldest public building in Manhattan, built in the 1700s. Most of the churchyard that surrounds the building on all sides is a graveyard, with hundreds of ancient stone markers jutting out of the grass.

The guy I'd chased was hiding behind a burial vault, his dark hair visible behind the marble. Once I had him in my sights, I tore across the churchyard, shouting curses at him, using words that aren't generally uttered in a religious setting. As I approached his hiding place, he jumped up and peeled off, vaulting over the stones to distance himself. I could hear him shouting as we ran, something about being chased by a crazy, half-naked woman. But he should have been watching the ground instead of taunting me. He tripped over a crumbling grave marker buried down deep in the grass. And that time, he went down, instead of me.

CHAPTER 34

THE FALL MUST have stunned the dark-haired man, maybe he struck his head on something. Because he was slow to recover, and by the time he started trying to get to his feet, I managed to pin him. His breath expelled with an audible "oof" as I tackled him to the ground and jerked his hands behind his back. When he struggled, I jerked one hand higher, to subdue him. I was determined he wasn't going anywhere until I had some answers.

"Why do you keep coming after me?" I asked him. "Who's putting you up to it?"

He turned his head to the side. When he scowled, he flashed the crooked eyetooth. "I never laid a hand on you. I was on the street today, and you started chasing me. You're a fucking psycho."

He renewed the struggle and I tightened my hold. Tugging his wrist farther up his back, I ground out, "Tell me who sent you to LaGuardia."

"Your mother."

I wanted to scream with frustration. Even with the guy at my mercy, I still couldn't uncover what I needed to know.

I persisted. "Is it Templeton? Is he paying you? Or did they pull you into their circle, like they did me? I promise you, it's not going to work out like you think it will."

He quit fighting me. His muscles relaxed, his body went limp. "I swear to God, your mother said to pick you up at the airport. When we were in the car, you got paranoid for some reason, and started choking me. You made me crash the car."

When he gave his version of the airport pickup, stars floated in front of my eyes. Maybe I was hyperventilating, from the chase and the stress. I felt breathless, and my voice came out in a whisper. "That's a lie."

He lay passive and unmoving beneath me. After a moment of silence, he said, "So what now, what are you going to do with me? We gotta hang out like this all day?"

I didn't know what to do next. I couldn't dial 911. My phone was by a folding chair outside the Oculus, resting inside the prim clutch handbag that matched Millie's shoes. I gazed out, looking through the wrought iron fence, hoping to spot an NYPD patrol car. Predictably, there were none in sight. It was like that old saying, never a cop around when you need one.

My dad used to mimic that line, as a joke. It wasn't particularly funny then, and certainly wasn't funny now. But it was ironic, as it turned out. Because just as I was mentally bemoaning the scarcity and absence of law enforcement in my situation, a hand grasped my arm and jerked me off my prisoner with such force I thought my shoulder had left the socket.

I scrambled to keep from falling down. A uniformed officer kept the firm grip clamped around my upper arm. Getting my bearings, I observed someone standing behind the cop. It was an ancient man wearing a clerical collar. The priest pointed at me with a liver-spotted hand.

"Those young people are desecrating a sacred spot. This is holy ground. Officer, I want both of them arrested for trespass."

My captive rolled over onto his back and started to crab-walk away from us. I couldn't believe it. The dude was going to escape, yet again.

I tried to jerk my arm away, but the cop tightened his grip. I turned to him and said, "Don't let that guy run. You need to arrest him. He tried to abduct me!"

The cop gave me a dubious look. "That's not what this witness saw, ma'am. He said you tackled the guy on church property. And I witnessed the two of you rolling around in the grass. You had him pinned."

"That's right," the ponytailed guy said, as he scooted farther away. "I don't even know that woman. She attacked me out of nowhere."

The pitch of the priest's voice rose to a shriek. "St. Paul's is a historic landmark, it's only open to the public on specific occasions at designated hours. We can't have people rioting amongst the graves. It's indecent."

I looked up, trying to gauge the cop's reaction. He wasn't much older than I was, so maybe he'd be willing to hear me out. When I studied his face, I thought he might be struggling to keep from laughing out loud.

And that made me angry. Because while the cop was enjoying

the situation, the guy I had painfully chased down jumped to his feet. I screeched, pointing at his retreating figure.

"Goddamn it, Officer! Are you going to just let him get away?"

The priest intoned, "Don't take the Lord's name in vain on consecrated ground!"

And that did it, it broke the cop. He doubled over, braying with laughter and loosening his hold on me. I broke away, chasing my target over the uneven ground.

I didn't have a fair chance to catch the guy. He was wearing shoes, and I was barefoot. My feet stumbled over the rough terrain. In addition, my escape spurred the officer to pursue me. I heard him shout as his feet thundered behind me. "Halt! You're resisting a lawful arrest! I have a stun gun!"

If my brain had been working right, that threat would've stopped me. But I was focused on the chase. My prey made it to the fence, scaled it, swung one foot over the top. I doubled my speed, keeping my eyes on his getaway. My bare foot slammed into a broken sarcophagus sunk low into the ground, and I fell, landing on my face.

CHAPTER 35

THE COP DIDN'T believe me, not at first.

Admittedly, I didn't make a convincing case as I lay sprawled across the stone sarcophagus. It was a good thing that it lay low to the ground. If it was higher, I might have broken a bone. Or maybe my neck.

The officer had me at a disadvantage as he pulled my hands together behind my back and cuffed me. While I tried to catch my breath—because the tumble over the ancient stone knocked the wind out of me—the cop launched into a recitation of my *Miranda* rights.

"You have the right to remain silent," he said as he tugged the cuffs to ensure they were securely fastened. "Anything you say can and will be used against you in a court of law."

I was intimately acquainted with the language of the warning. Three years in prosecution will do that for you. I tried to sound professional as I said, "I understand my rights and I waive them. Let me tell you what happened out here, Officer."

The old priest toddled up to us and stood nearby; his lace-up oxfords weren't far from my head. "I was a witness, Officer, I saw it all. Don't let that young woman deceive you."

The cop ignored both of us. "You have the right to an attorney. If you can't afford a lawyer, one will be appointed to represent you."

I tried to roll over, so that I could make eye contact with him. Maybe, I thought, if we were able to communicate face-to-face, he could see I wasn't nuts, and he'd believe me.

"I'm a lawyer, Officer. I spent three years in the Manhattan DA's office."

I heard the priest make a snort of disbelief. "You can't credit anything the woman says. She must be unbalanced. Just look at her."

I managed to roll partway onto my hip. The cop wasn't having it. He shoved me back onto my stomach and pressed his knee in my back.

I tried again. "This isn't what it looks like," I said. "The real criminal is getting away."

I heard the cop sigh before he continued. "If you decide to answer questions without an attorney present, you may stop the questioning at any time."

In an encouraging voice, I said, "That's great! You nailed it, Officer, that's really gratifying. I'm serious. A lot of defendants claim that the arresting officer never advised them of their rights, or they allege that the officer left pertinent portions out of the warning. I'm so glad to know that you are proving them wrong."

He went on, as if I hadn't spoken. "Do you understand your rights?"

"Oh, yeah. Hell yeah. I wrote a paper on *Miranda* in my third year of law school."

His voice sounded curious. "Are you really a lawyer?"

"Yes. Swear to God." I strained to turn my head, trying to catch a glimpse of the guy who held me down. He was easy on the eyes. Handsome, in that clean-cut, square-jawed way. Under other circumstances, I might have asked him to join me for a drink.

Earnestly, I said, "I'm serious. I understand my right to silence and to counsel, and I'm ready to waive them, so I can explain what happened. I can clear everything up, if you will just listen to me for a minute."

The old priest started to object, but my Central Casting cop shut him up this time. That was a good sign, I thought.

Keeping my voice meticulously pleasant and respectful, I said, "May I sit up, Officer? I'm not going anywhere, I promise. I've done all the running I intend to do today."

I felt the pressure of his knee leave my back. With a sigh of relief, I rolled all the way over and sat on the flat stone. That's when I saw that I wasn't adequately covered. I'd clearly left a significant portion of my skirt behind on the fence. I was wearing thong underwear, and it was on display. And that meant that my butt had been on display a moment earlier, when I was lying on my stomach. I'm not particularly bashful, but if my hands had been free, I certainly would have pulled down the remaining tatters of my skirt. As it was, I looked like a crime victim on the cover of an old pulp fiction paperback.

The priest turned his head away from the sight of my indecent attire. The cop kept his eyes on my face, which was decent of him, considering.

I said, "I'm a member of Frank Rubenstein's jail reform advisory committee. That's what I was doing downtown this morning. I was at the press conference."

The cop looked skeptical. "You mean that outdoor press thing they had over at the World Trade Center campus? You were over there?"

"Yeah, right in front of the Oculus. I'd just been introduced when I saw the guy who ran off. He was in the crowd, and I wanted to apprehend him. I'm a crime victim, he tried to abduct me."

The priest looked like he'd been sucking on a lemon. "Officer, I'm a witness. The young man was fleeing from her, I saw it. If there was an abduction attempt, she's the perpetrator, not that young man."

"No, you gotta let me explain," I said.

The priest went on, as if I hadn't spoken. "And the young man was fully clothed. This woman came onto the church property in a state of partial undress and has continued to engage in indecent exposure."

"Completely unintentional," I said, trying to give the cop a rueful grin. "My dress got torn when I climbed over the fence. I don't recommend jumping the fence, by the way. If I ever come back, I will absolutely walk in through the designated entrance. Cross my heart."

The cop tried to hide a smile. He had a dimple in his left cheek. *Shit*, I thought. *Not fair.* A man shouldn't get to look that good, especially when I was in my current condition.

I said, "If we go back across the street, you can ask Rubenstein yourself. He'll vouch for me."

As soon as I made the statement, I wondered. *Will he?* I

thought so, but I couldn't be 100 percent certain. Given our history, relying on Frank Rubenstein for support involved a risk. It was never guaranteed.

The officer squatted down on his haunches, looking at me face-to-face. I read the name tag under his badge: Jankovich.

"Do you have any identification?" he asked me.

"I do!" I announced, thinking with triumph that we were making solid progress. "But it's in a purse, over by my seat at the press conference."

At least, I hoped it was still there. In my mind's eye, I could see my father's face, looking at me with disapproval. He would have chewed me out for running off without an ID on my person.

I looked down at the tattered dress. "I don't have it on me at the moment, Officer Jankovich. As you can see."

He shook his head. "And your shoes?"

"On the sidewalk, other side of the street. I kicked them off before I made the climb." Also a maybe. It was possible that someone had viewed the navy heels as a gift from Providence. Possession being nine-tenths, and all that. Which has always been a misstatement of the law, but people continue to repeat the saying like it was true.

"I really appreciate the opportunity to show you that I'm legit. Did I mention that my dad was a cop with the NYPD for thirty years? Morris Stone, at the Twentieth Precinct."

And that's when everything turned around. Those were the magic words. Why hadn't I spoken them earlier?

Officer Jankovich grasped my elbow and helped me stand up. "I guess there's no harm in going across the street to check it out."

CHAPTER 36

OFFICER JANKOVICH ESCORTED me through the tombstones. He kept a firm hand on my arm without squeezing it too tightly. When I tripped over a chunk of gravestone with a heart chiseled into the granite, he caught me before I fell.

We passed through the gates of St. Paul's. He marched my shoeless feet down the sidewalk on Fulton Street, along the wrought iron fence marking the perimeter of the churchyard cemetery. When we approached the curb, I cast a wary eye down at the street. A variety of perils awaited me: green shards of broken glass were scattered around a murky puddle that had pooled in the gutter. A step away, someone had ignored the waste can that stood nearby and tossed a half-eaten sandwich onto the street.

The cop shook his head in disgust. "I just don't get people who can't be bothered to pick up their own trash."

And then he glanced down at my feet. "Yeah, this isn't gonna work."

He pulled the keys from his duty belt and uncuffed me.

"Don't you dare run off on me," he said. After reattaching the handcuffs onto his belt, he scooped me up in his arms and carried me across the street.

I'm not kidding when I say that it was a novel experience for me. I've had my share of intimate encounters, but I'm not the type of woman who gets literally swept off her feet. Under those circumstances, however, I welcomed the heroic gesture. I wasn't about to complain or accuse the officer of resorting to a show of toxic masculinity.

Despite my gratitude for his exertions, it was kinda unnerving to be carried through the streets like a swooning heroine from a historical romance novel. As we made our way back to the Oculus, I felt compelled to break the silence.

I tried to make a little joke. "Is this standard procedure?"

He didn't break his stride. "Nope."

"Well, I genuinely appreciate it. You are going above and beyond the call of duty today."

"You're right. I am." He stopped to readjust his hold on me. "You're heavier than you look."

I wasn't sure how to take that. "It's probably muscle weight. I work out pretty regularly." When he didn't comment, I added, "Kickboxing."

But I hadn't been to the gym in a while. Maybe I was getting out of shape. I made a mental vow that I'd get back into my routine, just as soon as I unknotted all of the various dilemmas I'd taken on.

As we approached the grounds of the World Trade Center, I said, "Hey, Officer, you can put me down now. Really, I can walk from here. No more streets to cross. And I promise I won't run."

He didn't respond, just kept walking. I could have tried to break his hold, but there was nothing to be gained by fighting him. He might tase me for resisting.

When we turned the corner at the far end of the Oculus, I saw that the press conference at the Memorial Plaza had concluded. The crowd had thinned out. Only Rubenstein and his team remained, chatting with a handful of committee members.

When Frank caught sight of me, his eyes widened. He pushed through the circle of supporters and strode up to meet us. I saw that he held a navy-blue clutch bag in his left hand.

"Kate! Are you all right?"

"I'm fine." I pointed at the bag he held. "I believe you're carrying my purse. Thanks for taking care of it."

Jankovich set me down as Rubenstein handed over the bag. He sounded like the old irate boss I remembered as he demanded, "Why did you run off like that? Where did you go?"

Before I could reply, he said to Jankovich, "Officer, has there been some kind of incident?"

"This woman was creating a disturbance in the churchyard at St. Paul's."

I didn't appreciate his description of the circumstances. Apparently, we hadn't bonded as much as I'd hoped during our walk from the church.

"Disturbance?" Rubenstein looked down at my torn dress, muddy knees, bare feet. "What kind of disturbance?"

"A physical altercation. More specifically, I'd have to say it looked like a wrestling match to me."

Wearing a pained expression, Rubenstein closed his eyes and muttered, "Oh, shit."

"When I broke it up, she didn't have any identification on her. Or shoes on, for that matter. This woman claimed to be the victim, but from all appearances, she was winning the fight." He paused before adding, in an inquiring tone, "She says you'll vouch for her?"

I unzipped the bag and offered my driver's license to Jankovich. "I was telling you the truth. See? I'm Kate Stone, I was at the DA's press conference. Everything checks out. I used to work for Rubenstein—isn't that right? You tell him, Frank. He doesn't believe me."

Instead of providing the necessary information, Rubenstein focused on me with a rueful glare. "You were in a fistfight over in that church graveyard?"

"I didn't hurt him! I was just trying to apprehend him, to hold him until a policeman could arrest him. The guy was the Suburban driver, the one who tried to take off with me from LaGuardia. We talked about that, remember? You said you'd read the reports. The police are looking for him, I think they're checking out street cameras for facial identification at the precinct in Queens."

Jankovich pulled out a smartphone. "Is there a warrant out for the guy?"

"There would be, if they could figure out who he is. Today was a missed opportunity. I had him, was holding him on the ground."

"Why didn't you tell me that before he took off?"

"No one was listening to me!" The frustration triggered an emotional response. My eyes burned, and I felt like I was about to cry. Horrified, I blinked back the tears, turned my back and swiped at my eyes. I pinched the web of skin by my thumb. *Get a grip, Kate.*

The cop held on to my ID, entering the information into his device. To Frank Rubenstein, he said, "The caretaker at St. Paul's Chapel wants her charged with trespassing. He was pretty upset, but he'll get over it. I'm not inclined to issue a citation for the incident."

I rubbed my nose, afraid that it would drip. Partly mollified, I said, "Okay, good. I appreciate that."

The cop tucked the phone in his belt. His voice was warmer when he asked me, "You need me to take you somewhere? Drop you at home? I can get the patrol car."

Honestly, I was tempted to take him up on the offer. And not only because I didn't relish the prospect of descending barefoot into the subway, wearing a ragged dress. I suspected that if I accepted the ride from NYPD, I'd enjoy the view of the driver. We could get better acquainted.

My conscience pricked me. I had a romantic partner. We'd never discussed it, but I assumed we were exclusive. If Steven started catting around on me, I wouldn't appreciate it.

The dilemma was resolved by Rubenstein. He had other plans for me. "I'll take over, Officer. I can transport Ms. Stone safely home." He pointed, indicating the corner of Greenwich Street and Fulton, where his driver stood waiting beside a shiny black Bentley.

I couldn't believe it. I was about to hitch a ride with Rubenstein in his private car.

CHAPTER 37

I SLID ACROSS the leather seat, grateful for the opportunity to get off my feet. Frank's car was a luxury vehicle, so opulent that it made my mother's Lexus look like a soccer mom's knockaround minivan by comparison. I breathed in the scent of the interior, an intoxicating combination of leather, polish, and subtle notes of lavender and sage. Frank utilized a car air freshener, a device that bore no resemblance to the cardboard pine tree dangling from the rearview mirror of the car I used to drive. Back when I had a car.

As he settled beside me into the seat, I thought I would offer a compliment. "Frank! You're pimping your ride with one of those prestige car fragrances. It smells great in here. Wish my apartment could have the same ambience."

He had barely buckled himself in before he laid into me.

"Kate, how could you?"

So the ride wasn't going to be as jolly, friendly, and upbeat as I had hoped. Nonetheless, I kept my voice pleasant. "How could I what? Specifically, what are you objecting to?"

"Specifically? You made a scene, Kate. Disrupted my press conference by jumping out of your seat and tearing across the venue in a wild chase. You looked unhinged, frankly. I've never been so embarrassed."

Ah. Here we were again. Frank was minimally concerned by the impetus to my actions, far more focused on how they affected him in the public eye. Our relationship hadn't changed, after all.

He raked his fingers through his hair, disturbing the carefully coiffured press conference hairdo. He must have used a fair amount of product to ensure his hair would be weatherproof because a stiff lock of hair was standing straight up.

He continued, "I had to pull strings to get you that appointment. Are you aware of that? It wasn't easy."

That hurt my feelings. But I covered up, put on my tough face. "Really? You informed me that I was an ideal candidate for the advisory board. You asked me to serve, it was all your idea. I didn't beg you for the opportunity, you talked me into it."

He didn't address my extremely salient point. "And you're fighting again. Right? The young officer from NYPD got his story straight, didn't he? You knocked a man to the ground and pinned him."

That much was true, but I adamantly refused to hang my head over it. "I sure as hell did. Since no one else has apprehended him. Jesus! Do I have to do everything myself?"

That was intended to generate a laugh. A smile, at least. But Frank wasn't amused. He said, "If you believed that he was the perpetrator of a crime against you, you should have handled it through the proper channels. You're not a law enforcement officer, Kate. You can't just take the law into your own hands. This isn't the Wild West."

"I wanted to hold him until a cop arrived. That was the plan."

He looked me up and down, shaking his head with an expression of disapproval. "And look at you. Look how your plan worked out. It's a wonder you're not in the ER."

As I looked down at my dirty feet and the shredded dress, I became uncomfortably aware that Millie wouldn't be happy with the way I had treated the clothes I borrowed from her. With a rueful grin, I said, "I guess this means you're not taking me to the after-party."

Frowning, he turned away and looked out the tinted window. When he didn't respond, I let out a dramatic sigh. "I'm missing the cocktail reception. That's killing me. The only reason I agreed to do this was the free drinks."

Frank continued to stare out the window. As the silence dragged on, I grew miffed, unhappy with the lecture I'd received. It was clear that Frank had no appreciation for the situation I found myself in.

The driver stopped at a light. I checked our location and estimated we were roughly fifteen minutes away from my apartment. The time line would be longer if we got snarled up in traffic. And I didn't intend to waste it because I finally had Frank in my clutches. He would be a captive audience until we reached my neighborhood.

"So, Frank. While we're here, just the two of us. I'd like to raise an issue. My client, Rodney Bryant—we talked about him in your office—is being held in pretrial detention at Rikers. On a misdemeanor charge. I'm hoping you can help me with that. Did you read the memo I emailed about it? Because you didn't acknowledge receipt."

Looking weary, he closed his eyes. "I don't negotiate these minor matters, Kate. It's not my role. Didn't I refer you to a member of my staff?"

"You did! Didn't really work out for me, that's why I'm hoping you can intervene. I think that, if you personally communicate your position to the judge, telling him Rod's a candidate for a no-cash-bail release, he'll be persuaded."

He sighed and didn't respond.

I tapped my phone, pulling up the email I'd sent. "I'm going to resend this memo, so it will be at the top of your inbox. When you look at it, Frank, you're going to see that I'm taking all of my arguments for Rod's release from the statements you've made to the press regarding this issue. It's like I'm quoting you verbatim."

"So you and Rudd didn't take this up in court before the judge?"

"Yeah, we did. It didn't quite go as planned."

"What did the judge do?"

I was about to lose him. I could feel it. "The judge reset it. Says he wants to consider nonmonetary conditions of release. But Frank, he's still locked up in there. It's not right."

"Then there's nothing I can do. This is the judge's call. Once the judge decides on the conditions, get your client to agree to them. And to comply with them, after he's out. But I think you're ignoring the real issue. Ultimately, the man will face the underlying criminal charge. He'll go to trial. Maybe you should concentrate on getting a good plea bargain instead of chasing the pretrial release. Or, for that matter, chasing random people down on private property."

So that was it. He was still upset about the St. Paul's rumble. "Frank, I know it bugs you when I go off. You are disturbed by my angry reactions."

He glanced over at me, made eye contact. "That's right, I am."

"But what if my anger is justified?" If he wouldn't help with Rod, maybe I could make headway on another topic. "The guy I was running after, I don't think he's some random criminal. I think he's connected to a huge figure who needs to be toppled."

"Excuse me?" Frank didn't look convinced.

"I'm serious. A person needs to be toppled by you, Frank."

I stopped. Dramatic pause.

Deadpan, he asked, "Are you going to tell me what you're talking about? Or am I supposed to guess?"

"Sure, I'll tell you. I think that guy I was chasing is a henchman for Ian Templeton."

Frank's face didn't betray any reaction but his voice was dry as he asked, "And why would Ian Templeton need a henchman?"

"Because he's a criminal."

"And he's interested in you? To the point that he's hiring criminals to go after you in public? Kate, please. That betrays a disturbing grandiosity on your part."

"I know, it sounds bonkers. But when you think of the things that have happened to me, Frank, it all ties in to Templeton. I went after his employee last year, as you may recall. Remember the assault trial?"

"The one you lost?"

I ignored that. "You know the car that picked me up at LaGuardia? It was owned by Templeton's company. Pyramid Investments."

"I read the report. It was a stolen car."

"He ran a major Ponzi scheme last year, got rich while people went broke. There are glaring irregularities, major white-collar stuff. Why isn't your white-collar department going after Templeton? Why is he getting a free ride?"

Talking about Templeton made me shiver. My arms erupted into goose bumps. Whether it was the topic of conversation or the air conditioning, I wasn't certain. Frank tapped the driver on the shoulder. "Turn the temperature up in the back seat, it's too cold back here."

To me, he said, "I wish I could tell you what every division in my office is investigating, but I can't. You know how many lawyers work in the Manhattan DA's office."

I wasn't about to let him off the hook. "Templeton has a new crypto scheme, it's all over the papers. Have you seen it?"

"I haven't paid much attention. But he's a financier, that's his profession. Unless someone shows a pattern of criminal activity, or at least until we receive complaints, our office wouldn't be involved in his business practices."

I knew the white-collar division wouldn't go after him. The members of my anonymous band of vigilantes had sent the white-collar unit direct evidence of Templeton's Ponzi scheme months ago, and they hadn't touched it. We had a shot at nailing him on the crypto scam in our upcoming meeting at Hudson Yards though. If I had a chance to bypass the lawyers in that division and go straight to the top, I needed to grab it.

"Frank, what if I was able to obtain convincing evidence of criminal activity on the part of Templeton's new ICO?"

"How? Do you have any evidence?"

At that moment, I didn't. But I was so close. "What if I did? What would you tell me to do?"

His eyes narrowed as he looked at me. After a moment, he lifted his shoulder in a negligent shrug. "Okay, I'll bite. If you can find evidence of criminal wrongdoing in Ian Templeton's new crypto investment scheme, bring it to me."

"Seriously? To you, not to somebody under you, someone else on your staff?"

"Directly to me. I'll give it my personal attention. That's a promise."

He looked like he meant it. I intended to get evidence soon, at Hudson Yards, so I wanted an ironclad guarantee. I couldn't demand one, but I came as close as I dared.

My voice held a challenge. "Don't make promises you can't keep."

Finally, he broke into a smile. "I never do," he said.

CHAPTER 38

WHEN RUBENSTEIN DROPPED me in front of the apartment, I was pumped up about the possibility of finally nailing Templeton. I wanted to tell Millie about it, so we could plot out the interaction at Hudson Yards.

The elevator had a piece of paper taped to the door. "Out of order." I limped up the six flights of steps. When I reached my apartment, I was breathing hard.

I unlocked the door and stepped inside. Millie was stretched out on the couch with the laptop. When she saw me, her face registered shock.

"What have you done to my dress?" she demanded.

I couldn't fault her reaction. The dress was ruined. "Sorry about that, Millie. I got into a scuffle that was pretty intense. But oh my God, I almost managed to catch the guy from LaGuardia. I was this close."

I held up my thumb and finger, pressed together for her benefit. She didn't catch the gesture because she was looking down at my feet.

"Where are my shoes?"

"Oh, yeah. Yikes. Really sorry." I'd almost forgotten. "I lost them along the way."

Her face puckered in distress. "That was my audition outfit, Kate."

"I'm sorry, Millie. I feel terrible about that, just awful." I still had the navy-blue clutch bag. It had come through the day unscathed. "Here's your purse."

She didn't reach out to take it. "You said you were going to some kind of press event for that group you've been invited to join. You told me it could help Rod, that you were going to take up his case with Rubenstein. But you ended up chasing some guy around and getting in a fight?"

It did sound crazy when she put it like that. "I was telling the truth. I did think being on the committee might help Rod. It still could help, maybe." I wasn't sure how, but I intended to give it some serious thought. "But I just talked to Rubenstein, and he gave me some exciting news."

"About Rod's case?"

"No, not about Rod. About Ian Templeton."

"Oh." She shut the laptop and rose from the couch. Walking to the kitchenette, she pulled a cold can of Diet Coke from the fridge. I checked the bottom of my feet. The sight was scary. "I'm gonna hop in the shower," I said, heading for the bathroom.

She popped the top of the can and took a sip. "Your mom was here."

I froze. Turning back to Millie, I said, "Who?"

"Your mom."

I walked back to my chair and sat down. "What do you mean, here?"

"Here. In your apartment."

I couldn't believe it. In the three years since I'd moved into my place, I couldn't recall my mother ever entering the apartment. "But the elevator's broken. My mother climbed six flights of stairs?"

"I guess. She didn't mention anything about the elevator."

"You're kidding, right? It's a joke." I got up from the chair, went back to the bathroom, and turned on the hot water.

Millie's voice followed me. "I don't know why you complain about her so much. She's great."

I stepped out of the bathroom, to see whether Millie was messing with me. But she sat on the couch sipping from the can. She held it up. "She brought a twelve-pack. As a housewarming gift for you. Said you used to love it."

I did love Diet Coke, when I lived at home in New Jersey. I drank it every day, sucking it down like nectar. After I moved into the city, I broke the habit. Carrying groceries to the sixth floor will whittle down a shopping list.

"So she actually came inside? And sat somewhere?"

"Sure." Millie pointed at the recliner I'd inherited from Dad. "She sat right there."

The shower was still running. I needed to hop in before the hot water supply petered out.

I stepped back into the bathroom, saying, "If this day gets any weirder, I'm going to go to bed and start over."

Before I shut the door, Millie said, "Don't you want to know what she said?"

I stood in the doorway, anxious to scrub off the dirt of the St. Paul's graveyard. "What did she want?"

"She didn't want anything. She's taking Rod's case."

That got my attention. I cranked the faucet off, stepping back in the room. "But I'm representing Rod."

"I appreciate that, Kate. I kinda hesitated to bring it up, because I don't want to hurt your feelings. But your mom thinks she can get him released. I'm really relieved she'll be stepping in to take over."

I should've been relieved, too. But I had that knee-jerk reaction that surfaces when my mother tries to control my life. "Don't get your hopes up, Millie. If my mom could turn it around, that would be great. But Rubenstein personally told me that it's impossible. Nobody can force the judge to change his ruling."

"Your mom can."

Millie actually beamed at me. She appeared to be in better spirits than I'd seen since my return from Florida.

"She's really cool, Kate. She has a way of inspiring confidence. Patricia gave me a good feeling."

My voice held a note of doubt as I said, "I'm glad to hear that."

She squeezed the aluminum can in her hand. It made a funny metallic noise. "She said to tell you to be sure you get to work on time Monday. Okay? So you and your mom can strategize about Rod. Nine o'clock, don't be late. Mom's orders! I promised to get you out of bed on time."

Great. I could feel the resentment wash over me. My mother was manipulating me again, using Rod's incarceration and my friendship with Millie as a tool to make me do her bidding.

All of my former excitement from the day's events was dissipating. This new development might give Millie hope, but it would be temporary. I didn't believe Mom could work a miracle for Rod. She was setting Millie up for disappointment. And I couldn't pretend that Mom would magically spring him out of Rikers.

So I tried to change the subject. "Rubenstein gave me a ride; can you believe that? In his private car."

"Cool. Was it a limo? A stretch, like we rode to the party on Templeton's yacht?"

"No. Just a regular car. But I told him we were going to get the goods on Templeton. So after we meet at Hudson Yards and put our information together, he's gonna look at it, personally."

She didn't respond. The laptop was on, and she was streaming another TV show. I raised my voice to get her attention. "We need to plan out the Templeton meeting. Devon will handle his end, but you still need to encourage him to make his pitch. So we'll want to anticipate that. Have a firm vision of how you'll handle it."

"Sure. After you get cleaned up, I'm ready." She upped the volume on the laptop.

I shut myself in the bathroom and glanced in the mirror. "Good God," I said. My reflection was so frightening that I barely recognized myself.

All of the energy that had sustained me through the day's confrontation disappeared. When I shed my clothes and stepped under the shower, I felt limp and battered and weary.

But I needed to get back in fighting shape. I'd be face-to-face with Ian Templeton the very next day.

CHAPTER 39

Whitney

AFTER THE DEBACLE at the Oculus, Whitney was instructed to find Larry. It didn't take long because she knew where to look. She stood half a block away as he exited a liquor store on Amsterdam, carrying a brown paper bag.

Maintaining a comfortable distance, she followed behind until he ducked into an alley. At the narrow entrance, she peered down the alleyway where Larry sat under a fire escape, leaning against a brick wall. As she headed toward him, he tucked something inside his jacket, pulled his knees up, and bent his head down.

She assumed he hadn't yet recognized her. Whitney was dressed as a woman of the streets, in baggy clothes with the hood of a sweatshirt pulled over her head.

She gave him fair warning as she approached, calling out, "Hey, Larry! Drinking alone?"

His head jerked up. He wore a surprised expression. She grinned at him, hoping to set him at ease. When she reached the spot where he sat under the fire escape, she squatted on her haunches, facing him.

"So this is where we're hiding out these days? Larry, I gotta be frank. Slumming isn't cool." Whitney grunted and groaned as she joined him on the pavement by scooting back against the wall so that they sat side by side.

He glanced over at her and asked, "How did you find me? I deleted the app. I turned off my phone. Kind of hoping for some alone time today."

"You're not hard to track, Larry. You are a creature of habit, you see."

She could see that one of his hands was tucked inside his jacket, out of sight. She reached over and jerked up the hem of his coat, revealing a half-pint bottle of cheap Scotch. It looked like he'd already consumed about a quarter of the contents.

"Shit, Larry! Ambassador? You've hit a new low."

Larry lifted his shoulders in a shrug. He unscrewed the bottle and took a swig. "I won't pass it to you, then. More for me."

"So are you having this private cocktail party to drown your sorrows over the botched performance you gave today?"

The question must have rattled him because his rheumy eyes widened. "Who told you?"

"Eh, I'm a snoop. You know that."

Before he spoke again, he tipped back the bottle and swigged, as if he needed to fortify himself. "It didn't work out."

"Why did you blow it?"

He grimaced and looked away. "I wasn't comfortable with the whole thing. I don't know why they're picking me for this strong-arm stuff. That new guy would have been a better choice. I'm no assassin."

"He was a backup. He wasn't armed. You were."

"We were supposed to do it after the speeches were done. But Kate bolted out of her chair, came running for us, right in front of the cameras. We had to abort the plan."

Whitney digested his statement. "Kate is an unpredictable target. No question about that. That's why you needed a plan B."

She watched Larry lift the bottle to his lips. He was sucking the whiskey down so fast the half-pint wouldn't last long.

He wiped his mouth with the back of his hand and said, "Plan B? Really? Hell, Whitney, I'm too old for this shit. It's not my nature."

"You didn't have a problem taking her to the subway that day."

He tipped the bottle and chugged from it. "That was different. I didn't hurt her."

Whitney kept her tone brisk. "I see. So you only follow the orders when they fit your personal boundaries."

"Yeah, I guess so."

"But Larry, you understand that Kate poses a problem for us, right? It has to be addressed."

He lifted the bottle again, but it was empty. When he couldn't get a swallow, his body started shaking.

Whitney patted his arm. "Settle down, pal. I come bearing gifts." She pulled a pint from the front pocket of her sweatshirt. "I got your back, see? Johnnie Walker, a far superior beverage. This will cheer you up."

Larry looked grateful as he took the bottle. When she said, "Drink up!" he obeyed.

Whitney kept a close watch as he relaxed and set the bottle carefully between his legs. A fleeting smile crossed his face.

"Feel better?" she asked.

When his eyes glazed over, she braced against the brick wall and pushed up to stand. Brushing off the seat of her pants, she said, "We deal with assets and liabilities. You were an asset when the group was able to utilize your engineering expertise."

He slumped and dropped onto his side on the dirty pavement.

She waited. "You awake, Larry? Can you hear me?"

She nudged him with the toe of her shoe. He didn't respond. She addressed him anyway. "You fell down the rabbit hole, friend. Now you are a liability."

When the convulsions started, her mouth turned down. "So long, pal."

Whitney leaned against the wall, watching until Larry stopped moving. She bent over to pick up the Johnnie Walker bottle, just in case some ambitious investigator might take a look. Unlikely, but it was a possibility. She tucked it back inside her sweatshirt. She would drop it in a trash can a couple of blocks away.

The wind whistled down the alley as she pulled the string of the hoodie tight to hide her face while she walked back to the street.

CHAPTER 40

Kate

I STOOD AT the wet bar in the Hudson Yards condo with my back to the windows offering the view of Manhattan. My cell phone provided instructions for crafting a Negroni cocktail.

On the bar, I'd assembled bottles of gin, Campari, and sweet vermouth. A sliced orange sat next to the ice bucket.

I pulled four tumblers from a shelf of barware. "Devon, are these the right size?"

He appeared at my side, looking perturbed and anxious. "These glasses are Baccarat crystal." He set two back on the shelf. "Only Millie and Templeton need to drink. You're a bodyguard, remember? And you better not chip these glasses or you'll have to replace them."

Millie joined us. "Devon, don't sweat this minor stuff. Your role is breaking into his device." She bent over a charcuterie tray we'd purchased for the occasion and plucked the center from a rose made of sliced salami.

Devon looked at her in disbelief. "Really? You're eating the appetizer before he gets here?"

She swallowed it down. "I'm playing a part. My character would totally feel empowered to mess up the food before he arrives."

If he arrived. I checked the time. It was getting close to five o'clock. He'd confirmed the appointment when Steven contacted him about the security procedures in the building. But we wouldn't know for certain until he actually walked into the lobby.

Steven must have noticed that I was watching the clock. He said, "It's early, Kate. He won't be on time. It's a power thing."

I was about to reply when a forlorn howl echoed through the space. Bruno was locked up in another room. And he wasn't happy about it.

"What are you going to do about the dog, Devon?"

"Give him some salami," Millie said, deconstructing the rose and placing slices on a napkin. She held it out to Devon. "Dogs love it."

"Are you crazy? He eats a special diet." He took the napkin and tossed it in a waste basket under the bar. "I've got him in the office. I'll be back there, so he'll quiet down. Maybe."

Millie shrugged. She turned to Steven and asked, "Do you think Templeton will call you for the building access? Or me?"

"I told him to call me, but you should be prepared. Supposedly, you live here."

The entrance to the residential part of the building was controlled by state-of-the-art audio and video surveillance. It had Bluetooth-based security, which required anyone accessing the property to accept a Bluetooth link and download an app. If Templeton wanted to come into the building and ride the elevator to the sixty-seventh floor, he had to use his cell phone.

Devon would have the opportunity to hack into the phone with a custom Bluetooth link he created for this purpose. When Templeton entered the property, he would open his Bluetooth, scan the device options, and select "Hudson#6702." And then we'd instruct him to reenter his phone password so Devon could capture that magic key.

With that key, Devon would connect the phone to Devon's computer and x-copy the contents using a backup routine. He would then have copies of everything contained on Templeton's phone—contacts, emails, messages, pictures, OneDrive files, and saved passwords. The passwords would also grant Devon access to Templeton's various login credentials so he could access personal apps, websites, and financial account portals.

Devon had explained that it was just a fishing expedition. There was no telling what could be accessed, and Templeton would eventually figure out that something was wrong, especially when two-party authentication notices began to flood his phone.

But Devon said he would probably focus on the existing contents, hoping that the downloaded OneDrive files showed the financial data and reports we were looking for. After he studied the contents, he would know whether he'd need to venture through other website portals. If so, he could just hijack the phone entirely and report Templeton's phone as stolen, rendering it useless.

Then he would change all the existing passwords. That

would give him several hours of hacking into the various accounts, especially if he did it when the rest of the world was asleep.

It would take hours for Templeton to regain control over his phone after the breach. It would take days for Templeton to recover from Devon's dabbling. And that depended entirely on how much Devon wanted to fuck with Templeton.

But the first thing to be erased on Templeton's phone would be tonight's Bluetooth link to Hudson#6702. *Leave no trace.*

Millie checked her reflection in a mirror hanging over the wet bar. "That makes zero sense to me. Glad to hand that role to you, Devon. I'll just play my part."

Devon said, "You'll need to get him to hang around for a while, Millie. It's going to take time to back up his cell phone on my laptop."

She fluffed the blue side of her hair, tightening the pigtail. "How long?"

"I'll probably pass on the pictures and videos, so maybe fifteen minutes. Can you do that?"

I glanced at her reflection in the mirror. Her face betrayed no ambivalence.

"Guaranteed," she said.

"Who's making the drinks?" Devon asked, as he pushed the Baccarat tumblers out of harm's way. "Kate?"

Millie said "Bodyguards don't make drinks. I'll do it."

"No," I countered. "You need to get him to talk. We want to hear the pitch, that's a crucial element of fraud."

Steven said, "I'll do it."

"Really?" I said. "Cocktails aren't your specialty, Steven.

You don't get enough practice." I picked up the Campari bottle. My mother had unknowingly paid for the high-end liquor with her American Express. She would flip when she saw the bill for the charcuterie tray, too. Crazy that salami and cheese and some grapes could cost a fortune.

We were headed into an argument over the bartending process when the speaker by the condo door rang. All four of us fell silent as our heads turned toward the sound.

"Templeton to see Miss M."

Steven ran over to the door. "Mr. Templeton, this is Steven, Miss M's manager. Hudson Yards security uses Bluetooth to access all areas, including the elevators. You need to go to Bluetooth on your phone and connect with our unit link, Hudson#6702."

He looked to Devon, who nodded.

We heard the voice again through the speaker. "Yeah. Got it," he said.

My heart had starting pounding in my chest. I squeezed the skin by my thumb, thinking, *It's really happening.*

The speaker said, "Isn't working."

Oh God. I felt Millie's hand seize my arm, her fingers squeezing in a bruising grip.

Devon whispered instructions in Steven's ear. Steven repeated the message into the speaker. "Try reentering your phone log-in credentials. And then try again."

"Got it," the voice said. We could hear the clicking sounds from the lock assembly.

We stepped away from the speaker. Millie's hand still clutched my arm. We exchanged a panicky glance.

"He's really here," she whispered.

The show was about to begin. I almost wished her luck but caught myself in time. Millie had once informed me that in the theater world, saying "good luck" was bad luck. Actors were a superstitious group.

I respected that. "Break a leg," I said.

CHAPTER 41

IT WAS TOO late to have second thoughts. So I followed Millie back to the bar, watching as she freshened the scarlet lipstick.

I whispered, "Will he recognize us? From the yacht?"

She shook her head, making the pigtails bounce. "We were high-society party girls on that boat, dressed to the nines. He won't place us. I mean, look at you."

She turned to study me. I'd worn another suit, tan jacket and pants over a black blouse. "You're drab, invisible. He won't recognize you."

I knew she meant to be reassuring, but Millie's assessment stung a little. When my financial situation improved, I intended to revamp my clothing style.

The doorbell rang. Devon disappeared, heading back to the office where Bruno waited.

I hung back, watching as Steven opened the door.

Templeton looked older than I remembered. His hair was liberally sprinkled with silver, and his suntanned face was lined. But he dressed like a glossy *GQ* ad and carried himself with the ease of a younger man as he stepped into the foyer.

Steven was greeting him when Millie tore up to the door.

"Ian!" She embraced him and then grabbed his neck in both hands and kissed him hard on the lips.

Watching in fascination, it struck me that I'd seen that move before, in a mafia movie. Millie had given Templeton the Michael Corleone kiss of death.

She had him by the hand and was pulling him to the white couch. "Hey, Steven! Make us a drink. Maureen, you wanna bring a snack over here?"

Millie had coined the name "Maureen" for me, announcing that it was perfect for a bodyguard. I joined Steven at the bar. He was studying the bottles, as if he needed direction. "I can make it," I said.

Millie must have heard. She called out, "No! That's not your job, Maureen! Last time you made a drink, it tasted like piss. You can bring us a snack."

Maintaining an impassive demeanor, I delivered the charcuterie tray. After I set it on the glass table in front of them, Millie frowned. "Where's the napkins? Ian's got a little lipstick smear."

She wiped his upper lip with an index finger. I returned to the bar for the napkins, wondering whether Millie was overdoing it.

Steven had his phone out, searching for the recipe. I murmured, "One part gin, one part Vermouth, one part Campari. With an orange."

When I returned with the napkins, Millie was sitting sideways on the sofa, facing Templeton. Setting her elbow on the top of the backrest, she leaned close to him. "Ian, I want to hear about crypto. I love that word. It sounds so sexy."

When he smiled, his eyes crinkled. It looked genuine. Maybe Millie was playing him just right. He had carried a brown leather portfolio into the room with him. He opened it and pulled out a sheaf of paper.

"I hoped you'd want to discuss it, Miss M."

"Ian, just call me M. We're already friends."

"M, then. I brought you a copy of my white paper." He handed them to her.

Millie gave the papers a brief glance before she tossed them on the sofa cushion. "Yeah, they're white." She smiled at him, displaying all her teeth. "Tell me about it. Give me the pitch. I'm an auditory person. Performers usually are."

He didn't seem to be put off by the demand. "M, my business is launching new crypto. We're calling it Zagcoin. You've heard about it, right?"

She nodded, scooting closer to him.

He said, "People are excited about it. It's going to be a static supply and dynamic price offering. Our goal—as you can see on the white paper—is to raise four billion dollars the first year."

Steven approached with the cocktails. After he set them on the table, Millie raised hers high in the air. "Cheers!" she said. When Millie tasted it, her face puckered with disgust. Picking up both glasses, she handed them back to Steven.

"You didn't do it right. How many times do I have to tell you? You have to stir it, Steven. Throw these out and try again."

Without comment, Steven walked away with a glass in each

hand. Millie turned back to Templeton. "What else does it say in the white papers? Tell me about the four billion."

"The funds will be reserved in an escrow wallet."

"What's that?"

"It means it's held by a fiduciary. M, a fiduciary is someone you know you can trust."

When I heard that line, I had to struggle to keep a straight face. I kept a side-eye on the white sofa.

Templeton gave Millie a warm smile. She tilted her head, like she was thinking. "I heard you have to buy another coin to invest. How come?"

"That's true," he said. He crossed his legs. I wondered if that was a "tell." "It's necessary to purchase Tempcoin to invest in Zagcoin."

"Yeah, but why?"

"It's involved in the technology side of the new offering. Kind of complicated, don't want to bore you. It's all in the white paper. But it's the required currency for the initial funding."

Steven delivered the new cocktails and waited while Millie sampled hers.

"Better," she said.

Steven walked away and took a seat across the room. I remained by the bar, where I could keep an eye on my phone to ensure it was recording the conversation.

Millie said, "You've got some cheerleaders out there on social, I saw that. So if I get involved, can I help with promotion? You know, a lot of my followers won't understand the financial talk, the terms you're using."

"You should tell them about the core product—a card, like

a debit card, they can use to spend crypto like cash. You can pitch how easy it would be. Can you sell that?"

She laughed out loud. "Love it! Everyone relies on a card, am I right? Have you named it? Maybe I'll drop the name as a teaser."

"Not yet. Maybe we can work on that together. You strike me as a creative, an innovative thinker."

She scooted even closer to him, and picked up his left hand. There was no ring on it.

"You married?" she asked.

"Not currently."

"Who's your girlfriend? Maybe I know her."

His hand closed over her fingers. "M, are you flirting with me?"

The tinkling laughter she produced was reminiscent of Marilyn Monroe. "I like older guys. I can't help it, I've got daddy issues."

He laughed, putting an arm behind her on the couch. I stood at my station with my eyes averted, like an unwelcome chaperone. I wondered how many minutes had gone by. Millie was putting on a great show, but she couldn't keep it up indefinitely.

My phone vibrated. I took a peek. A text from Devon appeared on the screen.

I've got it.

When I sneaked a glance at Steven, he was already focused on me with his phone in his hand. He'd received it, too.

I cleared my throat and stepped away from the bar.

"Miss M, you have another appointment."

"Oh! Shit." She grabbed Templeton's hand and clutched it to her chest. "I don't want to go. This was so fun."

Templeton looked startled. He uncrossed his legs and shifted on the sofa. "I have a lot more information for you. We need to discuss the terms of your involvement, expectations on both sides. If you're serious about helping Zagcoin on your social media platform."

Steven crossed the room and picked up both cocktail glasses. "Miss M has a meeting with a network. You understand."

I took a step toward the white sofa, holding up my phone. "The car is waiting for you, Miss M."

I was tempted to add, "It's a black Suburban." But it was an inopportune time to be a smart-ass.

Millie hopped off the couch and pulled Templeton to his feet. Linking an arm in his, she walked him through the foyer. "When I get back from LA, we've got to do this again. It was definitely fun. I want to get to know you better. There's a hot club in the East Village, I'm going to take you there."

At the door, she wrapped her arms around his neck and laid a long, hungry kiss on him. When she let him go, his mouth was smeared with red lipstick.

It looked like he was dripping blood.

After she shut the door behind him, Millie leaned against it for a minute. Then she ran to the wet bar and spit into the sink. I watched with growing concern as she grabbed the gin bottle, took a swill, and gargled with it.

After she spit out the gin, she coughed violently on her way back to the white living room couch. She rubbed her mouth with paper napkins as she collapsed on the cushions.

I came to her side and stood over her. "You were brilliant," I said.

"Brava," Steven called.

She let out a shuddering breath. I heard a door open, and Bruno came waddling in, followed by Devon.

"What did you get?" I said.

"I've got to go through it. It'll take a while."

It wasn't the response I'd expected. I wanted an answer, impatient for a revelation. "But when will we know what's on the phone? Did you see anything incriminating?"

"Jesus, Kate. I'll let you know." He snatched the lipstick-stained napkins off the table. "You all really have to get out of here before I get busted."

I kept my mouth shut. Didn't argue with Devon. But it was tough.

Jesus, I hate to wait.

CHAPTER 42

WE DIDN'T HEAR anything from Devon the next day. I was wild with impatience, but Steven counseled me to respect the process. He assured me Devon would be in touch after he had time to sift through the information on Templeton's phone.

On Monday morning, I tried to think of other matters while I took the train to New Jersey. Like, for example, what my mother was plotting when she had crashed my apartment the week before.

Mom hadn't followed up the surprise visit to my apartment with a call or text. And I'd been too preoccupied to contact her. So I didn't know whether we were playing some mother-daughter power game.

The sun was bright as I strolled up to her one-story office building in the city's business district. On the sparkling glass storefront window, bold black painted letters read: "Stone & Stone, Attorneys-at-Law."

The sight should've prompted a twinge of chagrin. One of the Stones wasn't carrying her weight. I hadn't darkened the door of the law office in weeks.

A jaunty bell tinkled to announce my arrival when I walked through the door. Ethan, my mom's assistant, sat behind his tidy desk in reception, looking impeccably groomed. By contrast, the front of my skirt was splattered with a large coffee stain caused by a sudden train stop.

Ethan glanced up. "Look who's here."

I breezed in, passing his desk en route to Mom's office. "Surprised to see me?"

"No. Your mother is expecting you. She said to go on in."

So. I was right, there was a contest going. I felt a surge of adolescent rebellion as I walked into her office and dropped into a chair in front of the desk.

Mom was poring over something on her computer monitor. It was angled away from me, so I couldn't see what held her attention.

After a couple of minutes, she pulled off her reading glasses and let them dangle from a beaded chain she wore around her neck. Her eyes went straight to the coffee stain.

"Good God, Kate. You're a professional. Do I have to remind you to wear clean clothes to work?"

"It's clean." That was a relative truth. My mother and I defined the term differently. "The train was jerky today, made me spill my coffee."

She sighed. To needle her, I crossed my legs, so that she could get a good look at the dark brown stain. "Millie told me you dropped by on Friday."

"That's right. I came to visit you. You were out."

"I was at the advisory committee press conference. I'm sure I told you about it. It was a major deal. Got a lot of media attention."

"Apparently." She pushed the screen where I could see it. The monitor displayed an image, a picture of me from the back, chasing Larry and the dark-haired man into the Oculus.

I wanted to slide down in the seat, but I gripped the arms of the chair to remain erect. In a lofty tone, I said, "Social media is so juvenile."

"This is on Twitter. There's a video on TikTok. They set it to music."

"Really? That's a first. For me," I added. "I'll have to check it out. See how many views it got."

She gave me a tight smile. "You have a habit of forcing your way into the public eye, Kate. I hope you'll overcome it. It doesn't serve your client's interest when you play the fool."

That stung. I was working on a comeback when she tossed a file at me. "I've entered my appearance as your cocounsel in Mr. Bryant's case. Your friend Millie asked me to help him out."

"Did she?" Millie had made it sound like it was my mother's suggestion.

"She has reservations about whether you can effectively represent him. She's growing impatient, with her young man in lockup. She's quite attached to him. Very concerned for his welfare. I'm sure you understand."

I was injured. I thought I was doing my best to help him. "I'm taking care of it. Rodney's in an impossible situation, Mom."

"Impossible? Really? Is that your legal conclusion?" She popped the eyeglasses on the bridge of her nose and stared over them. The scrutiny made me squirm.

"I saw him in Rikers and appeared in court to demand his release. The judge put me off. It's reset, week after next."

Her eyes were unblinking. "So you gave up."

"It's not like that! Frank Rubenstein told me—"

She cut me off with a harsh laugh. "You're taking advice from the district attorney? What kind of defense lawyer are you?"

I could feel the heat in my face. She had me pinned in the corner. No one could intimidate me like my mother; she had twenty-eight years of experience. "Will you just listen to me, Mom? Frank talked to me about it. He says there's nothing I can do."

"Frank? You and the old boss are first-name pals? Are you lunch buddies yet?"

There was a spark of malice in her mocking tone. She was having way too much fun at my expense. I gave her the stink eye.

Maybe she realized she was pushing too far. She eased back in her chair. "I'm stepping in to show you how it's done, Kate. Don't want you committing malpractice when you're covered by my insurance policy. And your friend appealed to my maternal sensibilities. She has a certain charm. I liked her, after I convinced her to lower her voice."

She made a comical grimace as she said, "Do you think Millie's aware of how loud she is? Her voice bounces off the walls."

I lifted my shoulders in a shrug. "Pretty sure she's proud of that."

Millie's powerful voice was the instrument that carried her to Manhattan. I recalled telling my mother the story, but she'd probably tuned me out.

"I see you had the sense to get the case away from

Callahan. I don't trust that old scoundrel. We'll go see Judge Robertson in his chambers tomorrow at eleven o'clock. Saul Robertson and I go way back." She stared pointedly at the coffee stain. "Wear something appropriate. Do you need a new suit?"

I did, in fact. But I was too stubborn to admit it. "I'm fine."

"Good. Because you need to run an errand for me tomorrow at First Central Bank, and I don't want you walking into the building like the Little Match Girl. They'll call the cops on you."

I didn't tell her I'd had a near-arrest just days before in the graveyard at St. Paul's church. The timing felt poor.

"Why do you need me to go to the bank? Nobody does bank business that way anymore. Can't Ethan just scan something for you?"

Frowning, she said, "Not this. It's related to the Victor Odom estate. He has a safe-deposit box at the bank's Midtown location."

I hadn't really been surprised by the news of Victor's passing. When I visited my dad's old NYPD partner at the nursing home in the past year, he looked like he was at death's door.

"Okay. Give me the key to the safe-deposit box, I'll stop at the bank on my way to the courthouse tomorrow."

"I don't have the key. It's not in his personal effects."

"Then how am I going to get into it?"

"They'll have to drill it open. I've made the arrangements. You just need to be there at nine o'clock."

The errand was starting to sound like a pain. "How long will it take?"

"A while. I want you to get there early, when they open, so

you'll have time to meet me at the courthouse afterwards. You don't want to be late to court."

I wanted to weasel out of the task. "Shouldn't you do it? Since you're the personal representative, the attorney for the estate. Seems like it should fall to you."

She gave me a level look. "I'm sending my law partner. Because I need to protect my valuable time."

That took me back. I didn't realize we were partners. I assumed I was a poorly paid legal associate. "This is news. What's my cut of the partnership?"

"Nothing, so far. It's zero, until you start putting in some effort."

For the first time, I felt more enthusiasm for the position I'd taken out of desperation. Maybe I didn't want to join up with a Manhattan defense firm, after all. My mother's firm was undeniably profitable, and she could provide a hands-on instruction in effective legal defense.

"What's inside the safe-deposit box? Just so I'll be prepared."

She turned back to her keyboard, pulled up a legal document and hit print. The pages churned out of her printer as she said, "No idea. I guess we'll find out tomorrow."

CHAPTER 43

I KNEW MY mother was serious when she'd counseled me on my professional attire at her office the day before. So I wasn't wearing rags when I walked through the door of First Central Bank on Thirty-Ninth and Broadway. But I didn't look like a figure from the *Style* section either.

When I'd sorted through the scant offerings in my closet that morning, I had asked Millie if she had anything I could borrow. She answered with an eloquent look. Apparently, she was holding a grudge over the destruction of the last outfit I'd borrowed from her.

So I pulled a dress from the back of the closet, a relic from law school I'd worn to a classmate's wedding. I'd purchased it at T.J.Maxx, not because I liked it, but because it was hanging on a clearance rack, priced at 75 percent off retail value. I concluded that no one in the whole city wanted to wear the garment. It was a wrap dress, a good fit on me. But the fabric was pink, with a multicolored paisley pattern.

I held the dress up to my shoulders and assessed the reflection in the mirror. It was definitely not courtroom attire.

The only advantage the dress could claim was that it was perfectly clean. Wrinkled, but clean.

Millie was standing behind me. Our eyes met in the mirror. Sounding doubtful, I said, "What do you think?"

Her face lit up. "I like it! My married sister in Oklahoma has a dress just like that."

That comment almost talked me out of it. I was ready to shove the pink paisley dress back into the closet and wear the black suit that was stuffed into a dirty clothes hamper. But I checked the time. The bank was opening soon, and I didn't want to run late. My mom had given strict instructions. We had a golden opportunity, a chance to pitch Rod's case before the judge, in chambers.

So I tried to carry myself with dignity as I strolled into the bank in my multicolored frock. The security guard winked at me; that was alarming. The dress I wore was like a flashing sign: "Don't take me seriously."

I had to go through multiple levels of evaluation with the bank security staff before they gave me access to Victor Odom's safe-deposit box.

After I'd provided documentary proof to the bank's satisfaction, a middle-aged woman dressed in black told me to follow her. When the bank employee let me into the vault, I said, "This is probably a novel situation, am I right? Seems like people don't lose track of keys to safe-deposit boxes."

She gave me a conspiratorial look. "You'd be surprised."

When we stepped in front of the wall of boxes, I said, "Which one is it?"

She pointed to one of the boxes. "This one belongs to Mr. Odom. Number 11013."

I was startled to see it. I assumed Victor would have a little box, maybe to hold some important papers, or old wedding rings, something like that. He'd been married three or four times. A guy with that many ex-wives might want to hide his valuables.

But the box she indicated was huge, the biggest size available in the vault.

"Are you sure?" Because I thought there must be a mistake.

She handed me the paperwork, from my mother's law office. "There's the number. It's consistent with our records. The locksmith is here. Have a seat, it will only take a few minutes."

I sat in a chair by a small metal table and watched the locksmith drill the lock. When he was done, he swung the door open and stepped away from the box. The bank employee said, "You'll need to take the contents with you."

I brought my briefcase along, as my mother had ordered. Like Mom, I figured it would serve the purpose. But from the size of the box, I should've brought a steamer trunk. What the hell did Victor have in there?

When I dragged the heavy box from its place in the wall and opened it, my first reaction was shock. The box was stuffed with cash, packets and packets of hundred dollar bills.

I glanced over at the woman in charge and quipped, "Wow! Looks like Victor robbed a bank."

She didn't laugh, which was understandable, considering the setting.

Assessing the contents of the box, my next response was a jolt of exasperation. How the hell would I manage to stuff all of that money into my briefcase?

CHAPTER **44**

I PULLED UP to the Criminal Courthouse in an Uber. Because there was no way I could walk down into the subway with all that cash in my possession.

It wasn't limited to the briefcase. There was too much of it. The bank had to give me additional bags—a handful of those zippered bags with the bank logo, designed to hold cash. Once I'd filled them, they created such a bulky armload that the bank offered me a black plastic trash bag. I was toting a Hefty bag full of currency, in addition to the bills stuffed into my briefcase. I was a walking target for a mugger. Climbing the front steps of the courthouse, I felt like a flashing sign over my head spelled out "ROB ME."

Fortunately, the criminal courts security personnel knew me. When my buddy Ahmed checked out the briefcase and the trash bag full of cash, his eyes popped out of his head.

He took me by the elbow after I walked through the metal detector and pulled me aside.

"What the hell, Stone?" he said in a shocked whisper.

"It's not mine!" I said.

Bemused, he looked over at the bags of money. "Then who does it belong to?"

I spoke in a low voice. "Ahmed, my mom has a new probate case. The guy just died, and she told me to empty out his safe-deposit box before I met her at court. We've got a chambers conference with one of the judges."

It was the plain truth. Ahmed said, "That sounds conceivable. I guess." But he looked doubtful.

I said, "Can you honestly think of any other explanation for me to have that kind of cash? You've known me for years."

I was afraid we might be attracting attention. I scooted closer to the loot. If someone grabbed it, my mother would lay the blame at my feet.

Ahmed said, "You're probably doing defense work, now that you're not an ADA. You sure that money's not dirty? Connected to a criminal enterprise?"

In fact, I wasn't sure. But I lied. "Cross my heart."

He handed me the trash bag and the briefcase. "Whoever died must have been made of money. He had the golden touch, right? I'd like to be in the business he was in."

I just nodded. Didn't tell Ahmed that he was in a similar line of work as the late Victor Odom.

Which raised the question I'd been chewing ever since they drilled Victor's box open. What kind of side hustle was my dad's old partner into, to come by all that cash?

I went to the elevator bank and rode up to the courtroom. My mom was sitting on a bench in the hallway outside Judge Robertson's court, having an animated conversation on her cell phone. When I trundled up with my hands full, she gave me a stare of horror and cut off her call.

"What are you wearing? You look like a character out of a Tennessee Williams play. Why can't you dress like a lawyer?"

I'd been so intent on protecting the money that I'd forgotten to brace myself for the ridicule. Deadpan, I said, "I love this dress. It's my favorite."

When she smirked at me, I hoisted the trash bag and dumped it on her lap.

Her face wrinkled with pique. "Don't dump your trash on me, Kate."

"It's Victor's. The contents of his safe-deposit box."

She gazed up at me like she was checking to see whether I was kidding. When I nodded, she untied the top of the trash bag and peeked inside, reached in, and unzipped one of the bank bags.

And then she gasped. "Oh my God."

I dropped the briefcase beside her on the bench. "This is the rest of it."

She shoved the trash bag aside and lifted the briefcase, groaning at the weight. Before she opened it, she said, "This is crazy."

"Yeah."

She flipped the latches and lifted the lid, just high enough to spy the contents. After she glimpsed the stacks of hundred-dollar bills bound together with brown paper bill straps, she slammed the briefcase shut. As she locked it, I heard her murmur, "Victor, what were you up to?"

I was wondering the same thing.

She stood up, grasped my briefcase by the handle, and instructed me to tote the remainder of the money. "We'll have to carry it into chambers. I'll think of some explanation."

"Right."

As she marched into court, I followed her, carrying the trash bag over my shoulder like Santa's bag of toys.

Judge Robertson's clerk led us straight back to the judge's private office. Nobody messed with my mom; there were no complications, no delays.

The judge was in his shirtsleeves. He rose as we entered. "Hey, Patricia! Good to see you. It's been a while."

She shot him a toothy smile. "Too long."

"Have a seat." He waved a hand, indicating a couple of worn office chairs facing his desk.

Mom eased into a chair and crossed her legs, like she was a femme fatale in an old film noir movie. "Judge, have you met my daughter? Kate has joined my firm."

He cast a doubtful glance my way, like he'd never seen me before. "Nice to meet you, Kate."

I was starting to tell him I'd appeared before him the week before, when Mom interrupted. "I have to apologize, your honor. Kate's moving her personnel files from her old DA's office. I'm so sorry to have her drag things into chambers. Hope you'll forgive her."

He gave the trash bag a bare glance. "No problem."

Mom pulled a file folder from her bag. As she perched the reading glasses on her nose, she said, "Thanks so much for agreeing to see me, Saul. I've entered my appearance on behalf of a young man who's being held at Rikers—a family friend."

I slid down in my chair, chagrined. Was my mother actually trying to woodshed the judge? It wasn't ethical to take up a case with a judge unless the other side was present. And no representative from the DA's office was with us; it was just the three of us, Mom and Judge Robertson and me. Any minute, he was going to shut her down, and I'd be forced to witness it.

Blithely, she went on, as if her professional ethics wouldn't be called out. "There's no reason to hold him. He's clearly entitled to release under the state statute, and no extraordinary circumstances justify pretrial detention in Rodney's case. He doesn't have a criminal history. Good God, Saul, the young man is charged with a misdemeanor. And I'm almost certain the state's witness won't appear. I anticipate they'll dismiss the charge."

Wait—what? Was she blowing smoke? I didn't know anything about a recalcitrant witness. If the state's case had a hole, no one told me.

"If you'd go ahead and release him, you'll be my personal hero." She beamed at him and held out a document.

I was incredulous. What was going on? What planet was I on?

I waited for the judge to berate her and escort us out of the office. Instead, he took the sheet of paper from her hand, turned to his monitor, and started tapping on the keyboard.

"You make a convincing case, Patricia. But you always have. It's part of your charm."

"Saul. Stop that, I'm blushing."

Oh God. She was flirting. I thought I might throw up.

The judge said, "Rodney Lamar Bryant. That sounds familiar. Seems like someone appeared on his behalf the other day."

Someone? I opened my mouth to inform him that I was the counsel for defendant who'd appeared on his behalf. My mother silenced me with a sharp kick to my ankle.

I almost howled. Grabbing my injured ankle, I rubbed the sore spot, waiting to see what would happen next. I expected to hear the judge inform my mother of the updated information I'd received when I appeared, that Rodney was being held while the judge pondered release conditions because he'd committed violent assaults on other inmates.

But he didn't say anything about recent assaults. He stared at the screen, clicking the mouse. My hopes started to rise.

Maybe my mother was a magician.

Since we'd walked into his chambers, the judge acted like he was taking orders from Mom. It was a strange reversal of power, as if he was a genie devoted to granting her wishes. But if it worked, that was good for our side. I started rooting for victory. *Come on, Saul*, I thought. *Listen to your old pal Patricia. Let Rodney go.*

When he turned away from the computer, he wore a strange expression on his face. My hopes sank with a thud. I figured I could predict what he was about to say. Rod wasn't leaving Rikers.

I was wrong.

"Patricia, you're not gonna believe this."

"What?"

"Rodney Bryant isn't at Rikers. He escaped."

CHAPTER 45

MY MOTHER CHARGED toward the bank of elevators, clutching my briefcase. As I tagged along behind her, I heard her mutter.

"Jesus Christ. That's a first."

She reached the elevators and punched the down button. When the doors didn't open immediately, she pushed the button so hard I thought the plastic cover might break.

"That's what I get for being the nice guy. When will I learn? Never represent someone who hasn't paid in full."

She swung around so fast that her glasses fell off her face. Maybe that's why she kept them attached to a chain.

"People who don't pay for services have no appreciation for the representation you provide. Remember that!"

I felt obligated to speak up in defense of Rod. "Mom, it wasn't personal. He didn't even know you were involved."

The elevator doors opened to a full carload of bodies. When my mother tried to shoulder her way inside, I tugged her arm.

"Uh, Mom. It's going up."

"Shit," she hissed. She stepped back and jammed the down arrow again.

While we waited, I spoke, more to myself than to her. "Sure hope Rod's going to be all right."

"All right?" She gave me a look of disbelief. "Escape from confinement. He committed a felony, and every officer in New York is looking for him. Do you think that's going to end well?"

Her words sent a chill through me. I wondered how I could break the news to Millie. She was going to be devastated. As my anxiety level ratcheted higher, I wanted to rub the skin by my thumb. It was tough, with a trash bag of money in my fist, but I tried.

My mother caught sight of the movement. As she glanced away, she said, "Are you still doing that? After all these years?"

I jerked my hand away and hid it in a fold of fabric of the pink dress. "What do you care?"

"I told your father when you were a baby. He was just trading one bad habit for another."

I didn't understand. "What are you talking about?"

She sighed. "You were a thumb-sucker. Your father taught you to rub that piece of skin instead, to save your teeth from being displaced."

I was dumbfounded. I had no recollection of that. I didn't know when I'd adopted the habit. I'd done it as long as I could recall.

The door opened and Mom sighed with relief as she stepped into the elevator. I was about to follow when a voice called out, "Kate! I need to talk to you!"

It was Bill. I turned, saw him running down the hall toward me.

My mother screeched "Kate!" as the elevator doors shut, separating us.

When Bill stopped beside me, he was breathing hard. "God, I'm glad to see you."

As I checked him out, his appearance troubled me. He'd lost weight; his suit pants hung loose around the waist. His complexion was white as paste, and he had a rash around his eyes. Bill always broke out in hives when he was under stress.

"What's up? You okay, Bill?"

He took my free hand and commenced to pull on it. "Come on, let's find a place to sit. I need to talk to you."

I was always up for a conversation with my old coworker, but I was in a tight spot that day. "Bill, my mom's waiting on me. I've got to go downstairs to meet her."

As if I'd conjured her, my phone pinged. I pulled it out. It read: Get down here NOW!

An elevator opened, and I walked over to enter it. Bill followed me. As the doors shut us inside, he said, "You were right. Everything you said, you were absolutely right."

Those are words I love to hear. But I didn't know what he was talking about.

He must have read my confusion. He went on, his voice shaking. "That support group. It's dodgy, there's something wrong with these people. They're fundamentally flawed, unethical. You wouldn't believe what they're trying to make me do."

The car stopped on the fourth floor. As it started to open, Bill hit the close door button. Someone waiting on four started protesting as the doors shut before they could enter.

"They have no respect for the law. They're planning criminal escapades—and they wanted me to participate, think I should advise them. Can you believe that?"

Hell yeah. I absolutely could. "What did you tell them?" I asked.

He dropped his voice. "I told them no, absolutely not. And I said I wasn't coming back. I won't be, either. Some of these people are batshit crazy, I don't want to have anything to do with them. And now they seem to pop up everywhere I go."

It wasn't lost on me that Bill's judgment was superior to mine. I hadn't cut my dodgy support group off until they tried to off me.

We landed on the main floor. As the door opened, Bill grabbed my arm. "I'm worried about your brother."

My mother stood in the lobby, staring daggers at me. I pushed the button, hit the top floor.

As we started to rise, I said, "Is Leo tangled up with them?"

"He thinks they're great. He won't listen to me. You've got to get him to disassociate, cut them off."

My stomach lurched; I thought I might throw up. Leo was naïve, impressionable. He'd be so easy to manipulate.

My phone rang. It was Mom. I swiped the screen. "Get your ass down here immediately."

"On my way," I said. And I ended the call.

To Bill, I said, "I'll talk to Leo. He'll listen to me."

He sighed, looking partially relieved. "Good. That's good."

As we rode down, I got an uneasy twinge when I observed him. He was on the edge.

"You sure you're okay, Bill? Is there anything I can do?"

"Yeah." He met my eye. There were dark circles, magnified

by the lenses of his glasses. He looked like he hadn't had a good night's sleep in a long while.

"We need to have a long talk."

"About Leo?"

"Nope. About Ian Templeton."

When Bill spoke that name, my breath hitched, and I had to stifle a gasp. *Finally, he caught on.* "Yes—please."

"That Ponzi scheme you kept talking about? I think you're right. I'm trying to convince Maya."

I clutched his arm. "His crypto ICO is a scam, too. I'm gonna have evidence that will bust it wide open."

We were back on the main floor. This time, when the doors opened, my mother was ready to pounce. She stepped into the elevator, grabbed my arm and pulled me out with her.

In a low growl, she said, "I'm parked in the garage on Centre Street, three blocks away. We need to carry Victor's property together. Are you aware that we have over a million dollars in our possession?"

I had no idea. Didn't stop to think how my mother could calculate that figure without counting it. How would she know what a million dollars in cash looked like? Maybe she'd seen it on TV.

I was dying to pick Bill's brain about Templeton, but it would have to wait.

I said, "Bill, can we get together? Tonight?"

He sighed again, looking relieved. "Yeah. Want me to come by your place?"

"No!" Millie would flip out when she heard about Rod. We needed to respect that. I seized onto another meeting place. "Let's meet at Craftsman."

The Craftsman was my neighborhood watering hole and one of my favorite dives. I added, "You can take the One Train to 125th Street."

"I know how to get there. What time?"

My mother was literally dragging me away. I said, "Eight o'clock, okay? That's when the music starts. We can talk about anything, no one will hear."

He gave me a thumbs-up. I waved as Mom pulled me toward the Centre Street exit with an iron grip on my arm.

CHAPTER 46

AS I CLIMBED out of the subway at Broadway and 125th and headed home, my physical load was much lighter than it had been at the courthouse. My mother had taken custody of the cash. I had helped her dump it in the trunk of her Lexus, and Victor's haul was headed to New Jersey. I was glad to wash my hands of it.

My mental burden, however, was weighing me down. As I rode the subway uptown, I had called Leo once and texted twice, but he didn't answer. When I had looked for him on the location app, it didn't locate him. Was it possible that he'd turned it off? That would be completely out of character.

I pulled up the local news and pored over the reports of the Rikers escape in the *New York Post*. The headline splashed across the web page read: "Daring Duo Escapes from Rikers." Rod had a partner in the escape, a Russian mobster was also missing. That gave me something new to worry about as I recalled that Rod had been forced to share a cell with some Russian criminals. The *Post* ran their mug shots. According to the article, the photos had been sent to the cell phone of every officer in the NYPD. Rod's mug shot was a good likeness. He wouldn't be difficult to recognize.

When I turned onto Claremont and my apartment building came into view, I had a sinking feeling. I had to face Millie, who was sitting inside my studio awaiting good news. She'd been cheery before I left that morning, certain that my mother was going to work some magic on Rod's behalf.

As I reached the front stoop to the building, I met Edie. She was struggling to get her shopping cart up the steps.

"Let me give you a hand with that," I said.

She gave me a bright grin. "Thanks, Kate! Hey, you're looking good today. You should wear more colors like that, it brightens you up. I don't know why young people go around in black all the time, looks like they've just come from their grandpa's funeral."

As I followed her through the front door, I noticed a big smudge of dirt on the seat of her lavender capri pants. I could've alerted her to it, to illustrate the rationale behind my sartorial choices, but I kept my mouth shut.

Inside the lobby, I handed off the shopping cart. She pulled it behind her as we walked together to the elevator.

"Since the old lift is working today, I decided to make my grocery run. Besides, I was running low on cat food. Wet food and dry. You remember that nursery rhyme? About Old Mother Hubbard?"

I didn't. My mom wasn't the Mother Goose type of parent.

When the elevator door opened, we stepped inside, and I hit the button for the top floor. The car began its slow ascent. Edie kept up a running thread of chatter.

"I guess my sweetie has been coming by your place to visit.

Pierre will make a cat lover of you, you'll be adopting your own baby before long, I bet."

I grimaced. "Probably not, Edie. I think it's my roommate he likes. A friend is staying with me, she's taken a shine to your cat."

"Yeah, we met in the hall. Such a pretty girl. Not from around here, right?"

"No. God, no."

The elevator ground to a stop on the third floor, and the door opened, rattling in its track. An old man stepped up, preparing to join us.

Edie pushed the close door button. "We're going to six. You'll have to wait."

He protested as the door shut in his face, but the sound of his voice was drowned out by the elevator as we resumed our ascent.

Edie said, "We got a lot of action on our floor these days, don't we?"

I looked down at her, not entirely certain what she meant. "Do we?"

"Yeah, all the coming and going at your place. You got that nice Mexican boyfriend. And your roommate, the big blond girl. Your brother always comes and goes. What's his name?"

"Leo."

"Yeah, that's right: Leo. Such a nice boy. He's a lawyer, too, right?"

"Not quite." I didn't volunteer additional information. Leo would pass the bar exam someday.

"He looks a lot like you. Always helps me with whatever I'm carrying. He took my laundry basket for me one week. A lot of boys his age aren't so well behaved, not like it used to be. I remember when they'd jump up to offer their seat on the subway to a woman my age. Nobody does that anymore."

Finally, we arrived on six. I held the door open as she struggled to pull her cart in the hallway.

When she stepped to put her key in her apartment door, she said, "I guess you got more company. I don't see how you fit everybody in there. Must be like sardines in a can at your place."

She pushed the door open. I saw the cat. He was perched on the back of her divan, with his eyes fixed on the door. At the sight of Edie, he made a loud yowling sound, like he was bitching about something.

I said, "No more company. I'm full up."

Edie winked at me. "I bet you are. Your boyfriend's gonna be jealous."

She wasn't making any sense. I moved on down the hall, figured the conversation was over. But her cat darted into the hallway. Edie stepped back into the hall and snatched him up. I couldn't believe the old woman could move that fast.

She clutched the cat to her chest and dropped a kiss on the top of his head before she gazed at me over the frames of her eyeglasses. "Don't know how you do it. You're putting out catnip to get all those good-looking men hanging around your door."

Before she returned to her apartment, she said in a loud whisper, "I saw that big Black man who showed up at your door this morning. Wearing nothing but his pants. Whew—I almost ran a fever, just looking at his build. He oughta be in the movies!"

CHAPTER 47

I SHOULDN'T HAVE been surprised. I'd had fair warning.

But when I turned the key in the door to apartment 6E and stepped inside, it was still a shock to see Rod. He was stretched out in my dad's recliner with one of my tattered bath towels wrapped around his waist.

"Kate!" Millie cried out from the kitchenette. She pushed a skillet off the burner and ran over, flinging her arms around my neck. "Can you believe it? He's out!"

Rod and I exchanged an uneasy glance as Millie squeezed me in a tight embrace.

"Can't believe it," I said.

Millie released her hold on me and darted back into the kitchen. "He actually swam across the East River from Rikers to the Bronx!"

I said, "You're kidding. That's impossible, he did not."

Rod said to Millie, "No, baby. Not that far."

He met my eye. "They'd moved me to the Boat. The Vernon C. Bain Center."

I was vaguely familiar with the Vernon C. Bain Center. It was a floating prison, a barge anchored off the southern shore of the Bronx. The eight-hundred-bed jail was intended to reduce overcrowding at Rikers.

Millie said from the kitchenette, "Why were you on a boat, Rod? That's weird."

I answered. "That's what they call it, Millie. It's another lockup, on a barge." I sat on the sofa and focused on Rod. "I thought the Boat is supposed to be used for medium- and maximum-security prisoners. What the hell were you doing there?"

"Trying to stay alive," he said.

Millie scraped scrambled eggs from the skillet onto a plate and carried them in to Rod. "Here, baby. There's no bread, so I can't make toast. I'll run out and get you a bagel."

I was astounded to see her head for the door, as if the time was ideal for a deli run. I jumped up and grabbed her before she could make her exit. "Millie. We've gotta talk about this."

She searched my face. "Kate. You're not excited. I thought you'd be glad to see that Rod's okay. He's here with us, safe, in one piece."

I wanted to scream, but I held it together. "He's not safe. Every cop in New York is looking for him. They've got his mug shot on their cell phones."

Her expression was stubborn. "We'll figure it out. We're going to make it work. I just want you to be happy for us."

I was too scared to be happy. In my mind's eye, I could envision a SWAT battalion kicking my door in. And the likely next step involved a change of address for Millie and for me, from Claremont Street to Rosie's.

The prospect made my knees weak. I dropped onto the sofa, watching Rod scarf down the eggs. When he met my eye, I had to ask.

"Why the hell did you do this? It's crazy, insane, there's no way you'll avoid being apprehended. Jesus, Rod, we were in court today when I found out. My mom was about to get you released."

He balanced the plate on the arm of the chair. "Nobody told me I was getting out. From what I could see, I was getting in deeper and deeper. When they stick you with the Russian mob, your life expectancy decreases dramatically."

Millie picked up the empty plate and perched on the arm of the chair. "One of the Russians tried to kill him."

Her voice held an accusatory note—like it was my fault. I ignored it.

"What did you do?" I asked.

"I hurt him worse than he hurt me. We kinda bonded in the infirmary. Not like I trusted him. I couldn't rely on anyone at Rikers, it was dog eat dog. But the Russian dude said we had a shot at getting out of there. His boss had a connection inside and knew how to pay off a guard, to give us a chance for a head start before they blew the whistle."

"No one escapes from Rikers," I repeated. It's common knowledge.

Rod cracked a smile. "It's all a matter of perspective, apparently. The dude said this lockup was a cream puff, compared to Russia's 'corrective colonies.' He did time in Black Dolphin Prison. The way he described it, the prison sounded like that old Paul Newman movie. Hard labor. Nothing to eat but soup."

I shrugged. I don't watch old movies.

Millie picked up the plate. As she carried it to the kitchen, she said, "Come on, Kate, you know. *Cool Hand Luke*. 'What we got here is a failure to communicate.'"

I was curious, despite my apprehensions. "So how did you break out?"

"When we got out of the infirmary, they sent me and Korobov to The Boat, the prison barge. Because we were badasses, they said they'd upped our security level."

"I didn't know that." I felt a lump of shame lodge in my chest. I was Rod's defense lawyer. I should've known, it was my job.

"Our cell was on the fifth floor. Korobov scored the rope; he got it from a guard. The cell windows aren't supposed to open, but this Russian dude, he's like Houdini. And the window's small. I didn't think we could get through it. Amazing what your body can do when you're desperate."

I was trying to get my head around it. "You climbed five stories down a rope?"

"Yeah. It was knotted, that made it easier to hang on. The climb was the easy part, honestly."

"You're kidding." I was glued to the story, despite my reservations. Maybe I should check out the old Paul Newman movie. "What was the hard part?"

"That swim from the barge to the Bronx was no picnic. We scaled a fence and dove off the barge. The currents were brutal, sucked me under more than once. Not gonna lie, there was one point when I thought I was going to die."

Millie ran to his chair, curled up in his lap, and buried

her head in the space between his neck and shoulder. I could barely make out the words she mumbled.

"Don't even say it, Rod. I can't stand to think about it."

I turned away from them to give them a moment of privacy. Staring into the bathroom, I caught a glimpse of a bundle on the tile floor that looked like gray sweatpants.

"Are these your sweats?"

"They are now, I guess," Rod said.

Millie lifted her head. "Rod and the Russian mugged a couple of guys in the Bronx when they made it to shore."

"I just took his pants. Korobov scored a phone, some cash. He said he had a car picking him up, offered me a ride. I got a bad vibe, figured it was time to part ways with him. I opted for the subway."

"Nobody stopped you?"

Rod grinned. "Once I made it onto the 1 train, no one gave me a second look. I wasn't the sketchiest dude in the crowd."

Millie laughed. "After I give you your makeover, you'll get looks. But they'll be admiring looks. You'll be so beautiful."

She hopped off his lap and started digging through the closet that contained our combined wardrobe. After a minute, she pulled out a filmy tie-dyed caftan in shades of turquoise and green.

"I wore this when the conservatory performed a Puccini opera. Rod, the hem's going to hit you at the knee. You need to get back in the tub, shave your legs."

I was amazed to see him rise from the chair without argument. She handed him a razor as he stepped back into the bathroom.

When he shut the door behind him and I heard the water running, I pulled Millie over to the couch and sat her down.

"Millie, this is serious. You've got to know, it's gonna end badly."

"No it's not. Rod's back, it's going to work out."

I took her hand and squeezed it. "Every cop is looking for him. They have his picture. The cameras in the city have facial recognition."

I searched her face, hoping to see that my message was registering. She looked away. I pressed on. "Our neighbor Edie saw Rod outside the apartment. She didn't make the connection, but she's bound to. He's going to be all over the news. She'll probably call the cops; they're going to be banging on the door any minute."

She lifted her shoulders in a shrug. "No problem. We're leaving."

"But Millie, there's going to be a manhunt. You can't stay here, but there's nowhere in the city you can go."

I was about to say it. That he should turn himself in. I couldn't see any other way out of the situation—not for Rod, or Millie. Or me.

"We're leaving the city. We've already decided. It's not safe here anymore."

The bathroom door opened. Rod emerged, still holding the towel. Millie tossed the caftan at him. He caught it with his free hand.

"Try that on, baby."

He disappeared back into the bathroom. Millie turned to me and said, "Rod thinks it's all about the support group.

They're picking us off, one by one. We're going to Jersey. If we can't hitch a ride, we'll get on a Greyhound."

"A Greyhound to where?"

"Missouri. I'm going home."

Rod stepped out of the bathroom, clad in the blue-green caftan. Despite myself, I snorted at the sight of him. He looked like an action figure scantily wrapped in a handkerchief.

Apparently, Rod had reservations about his garb. "Millie, I don't know about this."

"Oh, honey, you're gonna be gorgeous. Just look at those cheekbones." She picked up her makeup box and pushed him back to the chair. "I'll paint your face, make a turban for your head, put my best shades on you—the big ones, like Jackie O wore. You'll be positively elegant."

He tugged at the caftan. "It's too tight."

She rubbed blush onto one cheek. "I'll give it a snip here and there with the scissors. Sit still, you're making me smear it."

Frowning, I watched Millie work. There was no way she could make Rod look like a woman. But she was making him look significantly less like Rod.

"What about money? And IDs? Rod, your license is still locked up at Rikers, but you couldn't use it if you had it."

Millie pulled out a red lipstick. "Oh, we have alternate identification. Gatsby set us up with that ages ago, when we joined up with the vigilantes. We needed it for one of our heists."

She lifted Rod's chin, brushed his face with toner. I sat cross-legged on the couch as I watched them. My muscles were so tight, they might snap. I started rubbing my skin by my thumb, but it had no calming effect.

Millie started crooning an old blues song. "I'm going to Kansas City. Kansas City, here I come."

She sounded happy, like she was going on an adventure. A pleasure trip.

More likely, they were going to jail.

I didn't want to be along for the ride.

CHAPTER 48

I WANTED TO confide in someone. Explain my Rod and Millie dilemma. Seek out advice.

But I was kinda conflicted about what to do with the information.

I stepped into the kitchen and tapped out a quick text to my mother. I intentionally kept it vague.

Hey, Mom. Need some legal advice.

The phone pinged with an answer almost immediately.

What is it? I'm busy.

Staring at the cell phone screen, I reconsidered. I could predict with certainty that she'd react badly to the news. I could already see her eyes widen, hear her voice rising. Mom was going to be angry, and someone would have to bear the brunt of her displeasure.

Pretty sure the person who'd carry the blame would be me.

So I didn't respond to her text. I turned to Steven next.

To stress the importance of the message, I used all capital letters.

NEED TO TALK.

In contrast to Mom, Steven didn't respond immediately. I was pondering a possible follow-up message, something that could convey urgency without leaving an information trail that could be used against me in a court of law. I'd never encountered a case like this one, hadn't been involved in an escape from custody prosecution. I liked Rodney, always had, and appreciated that he'd been a friend to me in the past year. But I didn't want to be caught up in his escape and had no interest in abetting his flight.

Mostly, I didn't want to be incarcerated for the crime of being an excessively loyal friend. I had just googled "accessory after the fact New York" when someone knocked on the apartment door. The sound made my body jerk. My phone fell to the kitchen floor.

Millie had stopped singing. She was staring at the door, wide-eyed, a makeup brush poised in midair.

I grabbed the phone off the floor and tiptoed to the door. When I looked through the peephole, I didn't see anyone standing outside.

Millie tiptoed up behind me. In a loud whisper, she said, "Tell them to go away?"

I turned my head to say, "There's no one out there."

And then the knock sounded a second time. I peeked again. It was Steven. Holding a cat—Edie's cat.

Relief washed over me in a wave. I called through the door, "Just a second!"

And then I grabbed my bag and said to Millie, "It's Steven. I'll tell him I need to go out, okay? So he won't see Rod."

She nodded emphatically. "We'll be headed out pretty soon."

I grabbed her in an impulsive hug. "Be careful."

Rod sat in his caftan, with a silk scarf tied around his head. He didn't speak. I crossed my fingers for luck, held them up for him to see. He gave me a nod. Didn't ask me for any promises or assurance, and I didn't offer any.

As I unlocked the door, Millie said, "We'll be in touch."

Oh God no, I thought. I gave her a warning look. "Nothing by phone."

She looked confused, somewhat hurt. I figured Rod could explain it to her. He had a better understanding of the risk.

I opened the door just wide enough to slip out and step into the hall. Steven was stroking the cat. He gave me a curious look.

"What's up? I was coming by, just saw your text."

"Millie's upset. She doesn't want company."

I lifted my hand to pet the cat. He swiped at me with his claws extended. I took a step back.

"What are you doing with Pierre?" I asked.

"He was roaming the hallway, so I picked him up. Should we take him home?"

Down the hall, Edie's door opened. "Pierre!" she howled. "Fancy Feast!"

Steven laughed. To me, he said, "A cat lady should know that cats don't come when you call them. They're not like dogs."

But Pierre was contrary enough to be an exception to the general rule. He leaped out of Steven's arms and strutted up to Edie. She beamed, holding out an open can of cat food.

As we passed her, she said, "More movie stars? Kate, you're

the luckiest girl in New York." She winked at me before she shut the door.

Steven laughed. "What was that about?"

I wanted to tell him. I hoped he could offer reassurance, tell me I hadn't done anything wrong. But I didn't want to discuss it in the building, with Rod and Millie only a few yards away.

"I need to talk. Let's go somewhere, maybe the park."

He pushed the elevator button. "We're going to Craftsman."

"Really? Okay." I was meeting Bill there at eight, anyway. "That should work. Nobody will be listening to us. It's always loud at Craftsman."

"That's why I picked it."

We were riding down in the elevator before it struck me. "Why'd you come over? Do you have any news?"

He didn't answer, just gave me a cryptic smile. This was a new side to Steven, and it made me uncomfortable. I didn't want to play games. I was absolutely not up for that.

The elevator landed with a thud. As the door opened, I said, "So tell me. Have you heard something?"

"I have."

But he didn't elaborate. Had he heard from Devon? Or was this about Rod?

I stood staring at him so long that the elevator door started to close. Steven caught it in time and pushed it back open.

"We got the information. The evidence of fraud and theft from the Zagcoin scheme."

There should have been an explosion of triumph when I heard that announcement. I waited for the feeling of elation, but it didn't come. Maybe I needed to hear the words again.

"You're certain?" I said.

"Absolutely certain. We're meeting Devon at Craftsman. He's going to lay it all out for us."

I stepped out of the elevator and walked through the lobby, thinking that the gods must be laughing at me. Cracking up.

I got what I wanted. And the timing couldn't possibly be worse.

CHAPTER 49

WHEN STEVEN AND I turned the corner onto Broadway, the string of bulbs that lit up the Craftsman came into view. The sight usually gave me a lift.

But the happy lighting didn't prop me up on that occasion. I was too flipped out over Rod's escape, his presence inside my apartment, and the impending flight. Though I wanted to share my fears, I decided that it wouldn't be fair to pull Steven into the situation. For his own protection, it was best to keep him in the dark.

I shot a glance at Steven as we neared the entrance. He was quieter than usual. When we reached the bar, he paused as he grabbed the handle of the wooden door.

He gave me an inquiring look. "You okay? I thought you'd be more excited."

I tried to project some enthusiasm. "Yeah, I'm excited. Can't wait to hear what Devon found on Zagcoin. Did he send you anything?"

"No." Steven pulled the door open and peered inside. The bar was already crowded, with a customary level of rowdy volume. "He's already here. I see him sitting in the back."

We joined Devon at the far table, a wooden booth that offered relative seclusion. I slid across the bench to face him. As usual, he was bent over his cell phone.

Devon didn't look up until a waitress set a craft beer in front of him.

I figured I'd join him. It had been quite a day. "I think I'll have a Guinness," I said.

Steven didn't order, just shook his head with a slight smile.

As the server walked away, Devon set his phone down on the table, where we could see it. "What the absolute fuck," he said.

His screen displayed the red banner of the *New York Post*. The story had been updated, with a new headline. "Inmates' Daring Escape from NYC's Floating Jail!"

He gave his head a shake, like he was trying to make sense of it. "That's Rod, right?"

Steven's face registered shock as he stared at the screen. "Jesus. Kate's representing him."

"No! Really?" Devon said. His dark eyes fixed me with a dubious look. "Did you know Rod was planning to do this?"

"God, no, Devon." The suggestion sent a wave of panic through me. Was that what the police would think? "I was at the courthouse when I heard about it."

He shrugged as he picked up his phone. "I'm obviously out of the loop. Shit, I didn't know Rod had hooked up with the Russian mob."

Steven sat back against the hard wooden booth. To me, he said, "Is that right?"

"No! Absolutely not. Rod would never do that."

Devon said, "Really? I think that's actually kind of cool. I know everyone's anti-Russia, but you gotta admit that they're totally badass."

Steven ignored Devon's defense of the mob. Turning to me with a curious expression, he said, "You went to see him at Rikers a couple of times. Did Rod ever mention the mob to you? What did he say?"

They were both waiting for me to answer, hanging upon my next words. It made me skittish. "I can't reveal anything Rod communicated to me. Attorney-client privilege. You understand."

They nodded, backing off. My Guinness arrived, and I took a grateful swallow of the foaming brew.

Steven said, "Devon, thanks for coming up here. I told Kate that you had managed to find something from Templeton's phone."

"Found a lot." He sipped his beer. "Got access to his OneDrive. Went through his files. The dude may be a crook, but this Zagcoin thing is brilliant."

The admiration in his voice bugged me. "But it's a scam, right? He's ripping people off."

"Oh, yeah. Absolutely," Devon said.

"Lay it out for me. The big picture," I cautioned, to discourage him from losing me with unnecessary detail.

"There's several moving parts. But I figured out that he's getting rich on Tempcoin by using insider trading information."

"Insider trading?" I said.

I was already confused. I knew the old cliché about buying low and selling high. And I was aware that a trader who knows about highs and lows in advance and uses the information for profit is breaking the law. But I didn't see how it applied to cryptocurrency. "But the new ICO he's touting isn't Tempcoin. People are buying Zagcoin."

"Right—to participate in the Zagcoin ICO, you have to fund it with transfers from Tempcoin. You gotta buy Tempcoin to get Zagcoin."

"Is that a crime?" I asked.

Devon said, "No. Almost all crypto investments require crypto to fund crypto."

He was losing me. "Then what's illegal about it?"

"That's where it gets crazy-smart. When people buy Tempcoin to fund the new ICO, Templeton skims the top off the value of the coins."

There was silence at the table until Steven said, "I don't understand."

"The value of Tempcoin is fluid. It changes every few seconds. So he finds the lowest value and uses that to open the investor's digital ledger."

"Huh?"

Devon rolled his eyes at me. "He's taking coins from every investor. Stealing money on every purchase. Skimming profits that way. I found charts on his phone that lay it all out."

Steven said, "How much money are you talking about?"

"In one of the reports, he shows $30.5 million in skimming profits, from just one of the funding dates."

Steven's brow was furrowed. "So he stole $30.5 million from investor proceeds?"

"At least. But it gets even better."

"Jesus," I said. My head was spinning.

"Cryptocurrencies require a lot of technology to track digital ledgers and every transaction. It's the transactions that drive value. The algorithms involve thousands of computers to track and manage all the accounts and transactions across the world."

"Yeah?" I tried to envision a sea of computers to get a clear picture of crypto mining in my head.

He said, "I scanned several of his emails and texts that show Zagcoin doesn't have a single employee. Or computer network."

That got my attention. "How can he know the value of the cryptocurrency without that?"

"His only basis for the investor's digital ledger value is his imagination. That's a quote, by the way."

I was starting to get it. "So it's all a con, just another Ponzi scheme. With crypto."

Devon laughed. "Yeah, but with Templeton, there's no crypto in the crypto. It's all in his imagination. It's bullshit."

"How much money? Thirty million?"

"No! That's just part of it. His own records show profits of five hundred million between Tempcoin and Zagcoin. And it's still going up."

Steven said, "That white paper he gave Millie, they talk about his vast computer network he's created for Zagcoin, all those computers that are ready to be turned on when the funding is complete."

"Totally false. There's no network. And another thing—that 'core product,' the cool crypto debit card he's promising? It's phony. No credit card company is backing it."

Templeton's swindle involved bald-faced lies, something I could get my head around. "Fraud. Misrepresentation. We've got him. Devon, I'm so grateful to you. You're a genius."

He nodded briefly like he couldn't disagree.

I sighed. It would be a challenge to process and digest the evidence, but I'd have to do it before I presented it to Rubenstein. Maybe Bill Parker could help me make sense of it.

"When can you forward it to me?" I asked.

Devon gave me a suspicious look. "What?"

"The stuff you accessed from Templeton's phone, all that smoking-gun information. I need it."

He raised his glass, finishing off the beer. "Not sure I'm comfortable with that."

"What?" My voice was pitched too loud, and heads turned nearby. I toned it down. "You said there's insider trading. Theft. Fraud. Federal and state crimes. I need to take it to Rubenstein. But I have to have something to show him."

"This has my fingerprints all over it. I'm the one who accessed the phone without Templeton's knowledge or consent. I'm not sharing it unless someone guarantees that there's no fallout for me. Personally."

With a huge effort, I kept my voice steady. "Why did you agree to do it if you don't want to see this through?"

Across the table, Devon glared at me. "Because you scared me into it. How are you going to insulate me? I don't want to go to jail."

I cleared my throat, and tried to sound reassuring. "It's

going to be okay. My friend Bill? He's in the white-collar crime division, and he'll help me figure it out. I'm meeting him here tonight."

Devon looked skeptical so I played my trump card.

"I promise you, Rubenstein will back us up. He wants to see it, he told me to bring it to him. I talked to him about it last Friday. I'll cut a deal."

Devon said, "For me? You're cutting a deal for me? *After* you hand off what I found?"

It sounded iffy when he put it that way. But I said, "Yeah."

"Nope. Fuck that shit." He snickered, glancing away. "You couldn't get Rod out of jail on a misdemeanor. I'm not turning anything over to you until you get a commitment up front that protects me from liability. When you figure out how to do this without messing up my life, let me know. That's when you can have it."

He picked up his tab and scooted out of the booth. "I'm out of here."

As Devon walked through the crowded bar, Steven turned to me with an inquiring look. "Want me to follow him? Try to talk to him, see if he'll reconsider?"

"Hell, I don't know." I slumped on the bench and drank down the Guinness. "Devon is such an arrogant little shit."

"Okay, maybe there's another way," Steven said. "You've got the recording on your phone. We can take that to Rubenstein and try to explain what we know about Zagcoin and Tempcoin."

My shoulders sagged. "Oh, hell. We can't even show that it's fraudulent without the documentary evidence from Templeton's phone. Yeah, try to catch up with Devon, see if you can get him back on board. You mind? I know he won't listen to me."

Steven gave me a quick kiss before he left the booth. "I'll see what I can do."

It didn't sound encouraging. I wanted to think it through, to examine all the angles, but my powers of concentration were shot. Between the bank, the chambers conference, the escapee in my apartment, and the conversation with Devon, I was all wound up.

I checked the time and then called out to the waitress. "Heather! Bring me a Tanqueray and tonic!"

I pulled out my mother's credit card once again. It was getting easier. I promised myself that I wouldn't get too boozed up. I wanted to be relatively sharp when I met Bill at eight o'clock.

Heather delivered the cocktail. I'd just propped my feet up on the bench Devon vacated and taken a sip from the glass. The barroom door opened, letting in a burst of evening light.

When the door shut behind him, I glanced over. I didn't expect to see a familiar face. But it was a neighborhood pub, you never know.

Damn. Couldn't believe it.

My brother walked up to the bar and shouted out a greeting to the bartender.

CHAPTER **50**

I GRABBED MY drink, my phone, my wallet and charged over to the bar. He'd just settled onto a stool, facing the array of assorted liquor bottles.

"Why didn't you answer my texts?" I demanded.

My abrupt greeting startled him. He almost fell off his seat, had to grab on to the bar to keep from falling.

"Jesus, Kate! Don't sneak up on me. You've always done that, since we were kids. I hate it, it's nerve-racking."

I pulled my phone out, hit the tracking app he'd begged me to install. "Look. You're the one who made me get this location app. Now it says you cut me off."

I hit the app, swiped his name, then held it up to Leo's face. "No location found? What's up with that? Maybe I'll delete the damn thing."

"Whatever," he said.

That surprised me. I expected him to plead with me to keep it.

Leo wasn't even looking at me. He was waving the

bartender down. "Tito's on the rocks, Liam!" When the bartender acknowledged the order with a nod, Leo turned his attention back to me. "I'm over that tracking app. Sometimes a person has to protect his privacy."

It felt like a body snatcher had taken possession of my brother, because I was talking to someone new. "Did you come down here to find me?"

"No! I didn't expect to see you. I'm meeting a friend."

"A friend? Here at Craftsman? In Morningside Heights. Leo, you live and work in New Jersey."

Unruffled, he said, "Well, my support group meets in Manhattan. And we've been coming here on jazz nights. It's worth the commute."

I slid onto the barstool beside him. "Hey, I ran into Bill. We're meeting up later. He said some of the people in that support group are really bad news. He's backed away from it, and he thinks you should, too."

"Yeah, that's not going to happen."

I was about to ask him why when the rumble of the train gave out a warning. I covered my ears just as it rushed overhead, making the bottles shake in the bar. The Craftsman was located right where the subway rose out of the ground and became an elevated train that ran right over Broadway.

When the train passed, I doubled down on the sisterly advice. "Some groups can be toxic, depends on the personalities. Remember what I got myself into? We both landed in the hospital because of those crazed vigilantes. Jeez, Leo, I'm still not rid of them. I think you should listen to Bill."

Leo sighed with regret. "Kate, this isn't anything like your experience. Sorry the group didn't work out for Bill but I'm sticking with it. The talk therapy is really valuable. They're helping me with my social anxiety. Even my test anxiety. That's going to be incredibly helpful with the bar exam coming up."

My phone pinged. I looked at the screen. Mom was calling. It was uncanny, like she was a mind reader.

As I swiped the screen, Leo grabbed my hand and whispered, "Don't!"

Too late.

Even without speaker, my Mom's voice blared into the bar. "Kate! Do you have any idea where Leo could be? He didn't come home after work."

He cringed, squeezing his eyes shut. My heart tugged at the sight, and I considered lying to her.

Changed my mind. Leo needed to get out of Craftsman and return to New Jersey. "He's sitting right here with me, Mom. We're at a bar in my neighborhood."

Leo shook his head in a desperate plea, whispering the word, "Nooooo!"

"What the hell is he doing there? He's supposed to be studying for the bar!"

"He knows that. He's getting on it, he told me."

She almost blew up the cell phone with righteous indignation. "He's not going to pass the bar if he spends his evenings drinking cocktails. Leo? Do you hear me?"

I held the phone to my ear. People were looking at us. And it was New York. "He can't hear you, Mom."

"Put him on. I want to talk to him."

He stumbled off the stool and backed away, like he was going to make a run for it. I waved him back.

"He can't talk right now. He's in the restroom."

He sat back down, slumping over the bar with relief. He picked up the vodka and downed it.

"Mom, I'll keep an eye out for him. He knows he needs to work on the bar exam. I'll send him your way."

"You better. I don't want to drive to Morningside Heights and drag him out of there."

Good God, not that. I pumped a measure of reassurance into my voice. "Not necessary, Mom, I promise. I'll take care of it. He'll be home soon."

When I ended the call, he was defeated, all the upbeat confidence sucked out of him.

"I'm just gonna fail it again," he said. "I don't know why she expects a different result. It's the same old thing over and over again."

He hunched over his glass, with his elbows on the bar. Tipped up his cocktail glass and crunched an ice cube.

The sight sent a jolt of remorse through me. Hell, I'd passed the New York bar without difficulty. I needed to exert myself to help Leo; I'd never even offered to assist him. By the time he was studying, I was already in the DA's office, too busy to lend a hand.

I wasn't so busy now. My only client had opted for a self-help method to get out of jail. It seemed like I could take some time to tutor my only sibling.

"Hey, Leo. Let's start reviewing the New Jersey bar materials together."

He shrugged. "You don't need to bother. It won't help. Just a waste of time."

"Not a waste of my time. Maybe I want to prep for the New

Jersey exam. If I start now, I'll be ahead of the game when the next exam comes around."

He looked up, with puppy dog eyes. "You serious? You want to do that?"

"Hell yes. We'll start tomorrow. I promise."

He nodded, looking less wretched. "Mom doesn't believe in my competence. At all. The thing about this friend of mine in group? She believes in me."

She? That sparked my curiosity. "Is she someone you're interested in? Romantically, I mean?"

He pulled a face. "God, no. She's older. More like a much older sister. Or a youngish aunt."

The bartender stepped over. "Another round?"

Leo glanced at me, like he was asking permission. Suddenly I felt like the youngish aunt. "Sure, one more. Then you're heading out, okay? Promise?"

He nodded, restored to good humor. As I paid the tab, I thought about Leo's new friendship. Any normal person would encourage it. He needed all the support he could get.

But the idea of a substitute sister rubbed me wrong. Leo already had a big sister.

Who was trying to replace me?

CHAPTER 51

BY EIGHT O'CLOCK, it felt like the longest day of my life. A day that had stretched far beyond twenty-four hours, into infinity.

And I was sick of the Craftsman, weary of killing time while everyone around me was having fun. After I persuaded Leo to leave, it was barely six o'clock. I still had to wait around for my eight o'clock meeting with Bill. While I nursed a single warm beer for two hours, I texted him repeatedly, asking whether we could push up our meeting time. He didn't answer.

I watched the crowd for a while, trying to pick out the woman Leo had come to meet up with. But there were no women sitting alone, other than me. Women arrived in groups of two or three, and the ones who walked through the door alone joined other parties who were already seated. After a while, I gave up and played with my phone, reading the social media posts touting Zagcoin. Someone had made a rap about the Zagcoin crypto credit card on YouTube. It was pretty entertaining, frankly. If I didn't know better, it would pique my interest in the investment.

But I had the hot skinny, the inside dope. And if it was up to Devon, it might never see the light of day.

By eight o'clock, the jazz band had set up and was starting to play. Edgy and impatient, I decided to step outside for a minute. The bartender was a smoker; he regularly stood by the street with a cigarette when he was on break. I swapped a dollar bill for one of his smokes, borrowed his lighter.

"If you don't return my lighter, I'll come looking for you, Kate."

He wasn't kidding. I'd had to beg for the use of it.

"I'll have it back in five minutes. Cross my heart."

"You better," he said, giving me a stern look of warning.

I stepped outside the door and lit up. The area outside Craftsman was crowded with outdoor seating they'd set up during the pandemic and kept going ever since. When I blew out a cloud of smoke, the people seated nearby gave me the stink eye.

A woman said, "Can you move along? There's a smoking ordinance."

She was right. When I wasn't personally partaking of the vice, I'd been known to bitch at smokers who got too close. To put distance between us, I walked down the sidewalk and stood right on the curb, by the roadway.

It didn't satisfy her. She stood up at the table and raised her voice. "Smoking is not allowed in outdoor dining areas. It's the law!"

Jesus. She was taking all the joy out of the tobacco experience.

The outdoor seating extended into the roadway, across from the elevated train. I skirted it, taking refuge at the far corner of the designated space. I didn't want to subject anyone to secondhand smoke. But if I stepped any farther into the street, I'd be standing in the midst of traffic, a target for a passing car.

When I took another hit, the woman appeared beside me. "You're violating city law! Put it out!"

At that point, it would have been the safest course to toss the damned thing onto the pavement and go back inside. But she was making me angry. Not so mad that I wanted to throw down; a smoke wasn't worth fighting over. But I couldn't let her win, I was too stubborn for that. She didn't have the right to order me around.

I watched for a lull in the street traffic—and darted across two lanes, to stand under the steel railway of the elevated train. Drivers had parked their cars under the structure. I leaned against the back end of a silver Subaru sedan and sucked on the filter. The cigarette had gone out, so I fired up the borrowed lighter and relit it. While I took a hit, I kept my eyes on the sidewalk by Craftsman, hoping to see Bill walk by.

I checked my phone: 8:13. That was out of character. Bill was a stickler for punctuality—even in the city, where people habitually run late. And he hadn't called, hadn't texted. For a moment, I wondered whether he was ghosting me—but disregarded the notion. That wasn't possible. Not Bill.

From a distance, I heard the rumble of the approaching train. It would be passing directly overhead in a minute. I dropped the cigarette onto the pavement, so that I could cover my ears. I hate the noise of the train, especially in the weeks since one literally ran right over me.

As it rushed over, sending vibrations down my spine, I gritted my teeth and waited for it to pass. When it ran on down the tracks, the pounding noise eased up, but I kept my ears covered until it was gone.

Right after I dropped my hands, the screaming started. The sound came from a man standing under the railway, about three parked car-lengths away from me. His mouth was wide open as he shrieked, waving his arms and pointing to the ground.

Most of the diners across the way didn't react. They continued to drink, to talk. A couple of people shot suspicious glances in his direction.

I stepped closer to Broadway, with an eye on the traffic. If some guy was losing it under the elevated railway, I preferred to be back safely on the sidewalk. But he caught sight of me, pointed his key fob in my direction.

He screamed at me. "Police! Call the police!"

That made me pause. If he genuinely needed assistance, I didn't want to run the other way. My dad taught me that I needed to be street savvy, but that I shouldn't turn a blind eye to another person's plight.

So I edged close, to see if I could discern what the emergency was. When he saw me approach, he waved his hand at the railway over his head.

He wailed, "It fell off! Rolled right by my car!"

He tried to say more, but hysteria garbled his speech. Still cautious, I came closer—though I was prepared to turn and run, if the situation required it.

I called out, "Are you hurt?"

He shook his hand wildly, grimacing. "It fell down. He's dead!"

When I saw it, I couldn't understand, not at first. My brain refused to make sense of it. And once I realized what I was seeing, the horror made me back away, until I stumbled onto Broadway.

A car veered by, narrowly missing me. I felt the brush of the metal fender swiping my thigh. I ran back under the railway, to the screaming man. He clutched my arm as we stood together by the grisly sight.

It was a head. A human head.

And I was pretty sure it used to belong to Bill.

CHAPTER 52

I SAT ON the pavement under the railway, with my back against the steel column supporting the elevated subway lines over my head. It was a perilous resting place—or it would have been, anyway, had all traffic not been cut off by the cluster of emergency vehicles.

The rotating lights from the beacons and light bars of the emergency vehicles assaulted my vision, but I refused to close my eyes or cover them. I preferred the blinding glare of red and white and blue to the image that was stuck in my mind's eye, waiting to pop up into memory like a scene from a slasher film.

Because it had been Bill's head that dropped from the tracks to the pavement, rolling like a cue ball when it hit the ground. I'd been the one to make the 911 call. The shrieking man who first encountered Bill had fainted after losing his shit—and I couldn't fault him for it. It felt like it took forever for the police to respond, but that was probably because time was suspended for me.

NYPD arrived first; when they saw Bill's severed head, the sirens cried out a symphony as vehicles rolled in from all directions. New York Fire Department, more police, two ambulances. When the second ambulance arrived on the scene, I tried to make sense of it. Were they planning to convey the head in one vehicle? And the body in another?

Because the police found Bill's body on the tracks of the elevated line. They concluded that his body had been resting on the tracks. He was decapitated when the train hit him, and the momentum sent Bill's head rolling off the tracks, where it fell to the pavement below.

His body was recovered on the tracks almost directly across from the entrance of Craftsman. None of the outside diners provided any assistance to law enforcement. By contrast, I was a gold mine of information for the cops who responded. Not only could I confirm the identity of the deceased, but I was also the person he'd agreed to meet at the bar at eight o'clock.

When the cop took my statement, he didn't volunteer any information about the condition of the body. He asked me to explain why Bill had been sitting like that, right by the tracks. He wanted to know whether he was depressed, whether he'd experienced a tragedy or disappointment.

I insisted that foul play was involved, that he wasn't suicidal. But when he doubled down, I had to admit he'd been troubled. That he suffered from anxiety and took medication to control it. I told the officer he'd felt like he'd made some bad associations, that he was being followed.

The cop's forehead furrowed. "Who was following him?"

"He didn't say who it was."

I was debating. Should I tell the cop that he got involved

with a crazy support group? He'd probably think I was nuts. I was pondering the right way to broach it when the cop asked, "Did he tend to be paranoid? See things that weren't there?"

The question hit me wrong. I flipped out, lit into the cop with an angry outburst fueled by fury and grief. Another officer dragged me back, sat me down by the steel column and told me to shut up and stay put.

So I did. I'm a law-abiding citizen. Basically.

I reclined against the column and tipped my head back, staring at the structure above. The change of focus gave my eyes a rest from the LED lights.

Someone squatted down beside me. I didn't look his way. If he had a question, he'd let me know.

"Hey, Kate Stone," he said.

Wearily, I pulled my head away from the steel resting place and met his eye. He wasn't in uniform, wasn't one of the cops who'd been interrogating me. But his face was familiar.

He was the cop from the graveyard at St. Paul's. The one who had carried me back to Rubenstein's press conference. Jankovich.

I said the first thing that came to mind. "This isn't your precinct."

"No," he said. "It's my neighborhood. I live a couple blocks from here, on Broadway."

I tried to process the information, but my head wasn't working. So I didn't say anything.

He cleared his throat. "I was out for a drink, one of my friends got word about the suicide."

"It wasn't a suicide," I said automatically. I'd spoken those words dozens of times in the years since my dad's death, denying the purported cause of death.

"You think? Anyway, I was talking to one of the guys who responded, heard your name. At first, I thought it must be a coincidence. Not the same Kate Stone. But it's really you."

The statement made me sad. It sounded tragic. I repeated it. "It's really me."

"I thought I'd come over here, make sure you're okay. See what you've gotten yourself into this time."

The EMT workers passed us, right then. I saw two stretchers roll by. One had a large black bag strapped onto the cot. The second ambulance stretcher carried a smaller burden.

My chest tightened; I couldn't breathe. The cop from the graveyard grabbed my hands.

"God, your hands are freezing. Do you need to be checked out? Want me to get an EMT over here, to examine you?"

I shook my head vigorously as I tried to catch my breath.

He pressed me. "You could be going into shock. I'll be right back."

When he stood and walked away, I scrambled to my feet. Clutching the steel support, I lingered just long enough to catch my breath.

And then I stumbled off, past the flashing lights of the vehicles. Bill was gone. No reason for me to hang around.

CHAPTER 53

MOVING LIKE A sleepwalker, I crossed the street and walked down Broadway, turned the corner, climbed the hill to Claremont. My apartment building was half a block away. I trudged toward it, too numb and weary to worry whether Rod and Millie were still inside. If they hadn't departed, I'd let them have the bed. I just wanted to collapse in the old recliner. I hoped I would sleep. A deep, dreamless sleep, undisturbed by the nightmarish images I'd stored up in my head.

When I reached the stone steps leading to the building, I almost tripped over Edie's feet. She reached up and caught my arm before I fell.

When she pulled me down beside her, I didn't protest. My knees were weak. I needed to catch my breath.

She was breathless with excitement. "I'm so glad I ran into you! I wanted to knock at your door, but I'm a coward. I was too scared."

I didn't follow the thread of her remarks. My head was spinning, like I'd been running a marathon in the heat of summer. Squeezing my eyes shut, I rubbed my forehead, trying to get my brain to work.

She prattled on, the noise drilling in my ear. "I saw you coming up the hill. Did you see all the lights? A man was decapitated on the tracks. The train chopped his head right off. It fell off the elevated and rolled across the street. Can you believe that?"

She didn't have the story quite right. Bill's head didn't make it across the street, it rolled on the pavement under the tracks and stopped. But I didn't enlighten her.

"When I heard about it, I looked for it on the *Post*, and I saw the other story—that's why I'm out here. Kate, I gotta show you."

She pulled out her phone and fumbled with it in the dim glow of the distant streetlight. After minutes of tapping, she found what she was seeking.

She leaned in next to me and held up the cell phone. "See? It's the guy!"

With heavy eyes, I focused on the screen. It was the story of the Rikers escape, with Rod's mug shot. She pecked at his likeness with her index finger.

"Kate, he's the guy! The guy I was telling you about earlier. He was on our floor today, half naked. Looked like he was trying to break into your apartment."

She slipped the phone into her pocket and gave my arm a pat. "Don't you worry, hon. I already called the police. They're on their way. We'll wait right here for them, together. No one's gonna get you."

I couldn't speak. My mind was frozen. Edie knew that Rod had been to my place that day, and she was making a police report. I was screwed. Totally fucked.

I had to run.

I stood so suddenly that I rocked on my feet and had to grab on to the metal handrail by the stairs to keep from falling. Edie struggled to her feet. Concern was etched in her face as she studied me.

"You okay, sweetie? You look like you're going to faint. Sit back down, put your head between your knees."

It was a valid suggestion, and not only because I was light-headed. I was suddenly nauseous. Bile rushed up into my throat.

I gagged first, then stumbled to the curb and vomited into the street. After I heaved up the contents of my stomach, I leaned against a car.

Edie remained on the stoop, keeping her distance. I couldn't blame her. Her voice was kind, though, when she called to me.

"Did the news give you a nervous stomach? Or do you think you're coming down with something?"

I cleared my throat and spat before I answered. "I'm not feeling so good. Better run down to the pharmacy for some Pepto-Bismol."

Leaning on a parked vehicle for balance, I waited for my head to clear. When I was able to move, I walked down the sidewalk, leaving Edie behind. She cried out as I staggered down the street. "Don't you think you should wait? The police will want to talk to you!"

Yeah. I knew they would. That's what I was afraid of.

I struggled to devise a plan for my next few hours. I needed a place to crash, somewhere that I could find refuge. My prospects were winnowing away.

Mom's house was the reasonable option, but I knew I didn't have the stamina to get to New Jersey and face her cross-examination.

As soon as I turned the corner, Edie's voice quit calling my name.

I pulled out my phone, hit Steven in my contacts.

Sent a text, got an answer.

Like a miracle, an unoccupied yellow cab happened by. I hailed it, dropped into the seat and gave him the address for the BoHo.

I'd be spending the night in a homeless shelter.

That was a first for me.

CHAPTER 54

THE NEXT MORNING, I huddled at a tiny table in the far corner of a Morningside Heights bodega, nursing a cup of coffee. The proprietor kept casting disgruntled looks in my direction. There were only two tables in the crowded store, reserved for people who ordered food. My coffee purchase didn't entitle me to seating.

I ignored him. Behind the counter, a small old-fashioned television with a humpback was tuned to a news channel. My heart started to race when the video cut to a dark street scene, lit by flashing lights of emergency vehicles. The sound was muted; and the subtitles appearing on the screen were in Spanish. If the news story was about Bill, I needed to hear it.

"Hey! Can you turn up the volume? Please?"

He'd been giving me fishy looks since I arrived, but that time, he ignored me. I was too weary to fight. I slumped in my small metal seat, trying to read the announcer's lips.

When I felt a hand on my shoulder, I almost jumped out of my skin. I scooted around, ready to bolt. And then I sighed with relief.

My mom pulled out the other chair. After a glance at the grimy floor, she set her handbag in her lap.

She gave me a swift appraisal. "You look like you're living on the streets, Kate."

She wasn't far off. I'd shared Steven's narrow bed the night before, but lay awake, listening to sirens while he slept. I couldn't use the communal shower in the shelter, so I tried to wash up in the sink in his room. Borrowed Steven's comb and toothbrush, but I was dressed in yesterday's clothing, with lank hair and sallow skin, dark circles under my eyes. When I glimpsed my reflection in a store front window on the street, I barely recognized myself.

"Honey, I know you're shook up by the death of your friend. But you can't fall to pieces, Kate."

I was too tired to argue. "Right."

"Is that what you want to talk about? That you couldn't discuss over the phone?"

She reached out and patted my hand. The gesture felt forced, unnatural. My mother had never been comfortable with physical displays of affection. But she was trying. I had to give her props for that.

I glanced around, fearful of being overheard. "I have to consult with you about a legal problem. I need your advice."

She raised a brow. Her forehead wrinkled. She'd definitely laid off the Botox injections. "Is it about a particular case?"

"Yeah. Our case. Rodney Bryant."

She sighed, shaking her head. "There's nothing we can do

for him now. You can surely see that. When they pick him up, we'll withdraw. The public defender can take over."

"Mom." My voice was too loud; I softened it to a whisper. "I saw him yesterday. After court."

Her eyes widened with alarm. "What do you mean?"

"He was at my apartment when I got home. With Millie. They were getting ready to take off."

She rolled her head back on her neck. "Shit."

"They were heading out of town. Going to Missouri."

"Hush." She glared at me over her glasses. "You don't know that. You don't know anything."

I nodded, desperate to grasp a narrative, so that I could fix it in my head, and stick to it. "That's true, I don't know anything for certain."

"And you won't tell anyone that you saw him. Understand? No one can know that he came to you."

I stopped nodding my head. Because that was a problem. "What if someone already knows? Someone saw him?"

"Shit!" That time, she barked the word. The guy behind the counter looked at us with apprehension.

"That's why I can't go back to the apartment. An old lady on my floor saw him. She called the police and ratted me out."

Mom clutched my hand. This was no comforting squeeze. I thought the bones of my knuckles might break. Her voice was terse. "The neighbor saw him going inside your apartment? Or coming out?"

"No, she saw him in the hall, heading up to my door. Knocking on it, maybe." I couldn't remember exactly what Edie had said. My brain wasn't functioning at a normal level.

She released my hand and sat back in the chair. "That's not

so bad, then. I'm sure they'll be looking for you, though. You should avoid the apartment for a while. The office, too. When they don't reach you, they may try to contact you at work."

I wanted her to fix it somehow, though I knew it was impossible. A lump formed in my throat. I was in danger of bawling like a kid. It embarrassed me. "Where am I gonna go?"

Her face softened with an expression of regret. "You want to stay at my house? It's going to take some time to iron out your dilemma. But you'll be safe there, and you can avoid talking to the police."

I appreciated her offer of refuge. I'd spent a lifetime in a battle of wills with my mother, but it was a comfort to know she'd be there in a pinch, if I needed it.

But hiding under the bed in New Jersey wasn't the answer, not in my current situation. Time to grow up. "Thanks, Mom. I need to stick around town for a while."

"Where will you go?"

I didn't have an answer for that. Mom lowered her voice and said, "I don't think they're going on some kind of manhunt for you, Kate. You had no part in Rod's escape. We were at the courthouse when we found out. Saul knows that, he can vouch for us."

"I don't want to be questioned. I want to avoid it for right now."

"Then you'll want to be difficult to locate. Stay in hotels, ones where you can pay in cash. These neighborhoods should provide accommodations of that variety. Do you have cash?"

I shook my head. She made a clicking noise with her tongue as she opened her handbag and pulled out a stack of hundred dollar bills, sealed with a brown bill wrapper.

She handed the money to me under the table—literally. I took it. But I had to ask.

"Mom, is this Victor's money? You're a fiduciary. Are you going to replace it?"

Her tone was impatient. "Of course I'll replace it. Funny to hear that from you, though, considering your current situation."

She snapped the purse shut. I didn't speak. Maybe she read something in my face.

"What? Don't worry, I'm going to take care of it. It's not like I don't know how to handle an estate. And I'm a primary beneficiary, anyway."

I almost choked. "You? You're the beneficiary of Victor Odom's will? Dad's partner? Why?"

She looked sheepish. "Who knows? It came as a shock. But he didn't have any children. He divided his property between me and the police offers' association." Her eyes narrowed. "Maybe he felt guilty. He viewed it as payback."

Her words sparked a recollection. "I visited him in the nursing home a while back when I was trying to find out about Dad's death. Victor talked about you. Did I ever tell you? Maybe I forgot."

She pursed her lips. I saw her flush.

I said, "Victor said 'remember the good times,' or something like that. What good times was he talking about?"

She was definitely blushing. But her voice was defiant. "I've been single for over twenty years. Don't preach to me. If I had some fun along the way, I was entitled to it."

Now I was uncomfortable. There's something unsettling about hearing that your middle-aged mother had a sex life.

Curious, I thought to ask, "What was the cause of death?"

"Died in his sleep. He was in a coma, Kate. No one requested an autopsy."

We sat quietly for a moment before I said, "Victor was a crooked cop. Wasn't he?"

She sighed. "Your dad thought so, toward the end. He thought he was taking payoffs. It ate at him. He loved Victor. They'd been through a lot together."

We fell into an uneasy silence. Dad was always a tricky subject between us.

After a minute, she opened the purse again. Pulling out a compact, she checked her reflection, reapplied lipstick. As she dropped the tube back into her purse, she said, "So you'll take it easy for a few days, okay? I'll call you, let you know what's up."

I wanted more from her. Though she was true to form, I felt dejected, vulnerable. "This is flipping me out. I'm scared."

Her gaze was sharp. "Scared? Of what?"

"Of people coming after me. Because of that group I got involved with. I've had more than one close call, my friends are threatened, Bill is dead."

My voice cracked when I said, "I'm afraid I'm going to be next."

She gave me a sad smile. "Oh, honey. You're going to be fine. We'll get through this. You're tough, just like me."

Just like her? That was a disturbing thought. Fortunately, I was distracted when my phone pinged.

I pulled it out. It was a message from Steven.

Devon says yes.

Meet us @6:00

I had to read the text twice before it made sense. I'd already forgotten about Devon and his lukewarm reception to my proposal. Bill's death had wiped Templeton's crypto scheme completely out of my head.

When I made the connection, I hesitated. Maybe I needed to concentrate on my immediate problems, put off the pursuit of Templeton.

But I knew I couldn't accomplish it without Devon's help. He'd been ambivalent the night before. If he'd overcome his reservations and was ready to assist, I needed to move on it immediately. So I answered.

meet where?

Steven responded.

same spot you slept last night

My shoulders tensed as I tucked the phone away. When I looked up, my mother's eyes burned a hole in me.

"What?" she said.

"It's Steven. We're meeting up tonight with another guy from the group. Gonna talk."

I didn't elaborate because I thought she'd disapprove. And I was right.

"Damn it, Kate! What did you just tell me? How many times have I warned you away from this?"

I shrugged. Because I'd lost count.

In a harsh whisper, she said, "Block those people, now. I should never have permitted them to stay in my house. They're nothing but trouble."

I stood up and pulled my bag onto my shoulder. I held tightly to the strap because I was carrying serious cash. "Love you, Mom. Talk to you in a week."

I heard her whisper as I walked away—something like "Why won't you listen to me? This won't end well."

But I couldn't stop, not yet. I had loose ends to tie up before I could move on. I wanted to cause Ian Templeton some grief. He'd done it to me. Time to return the favor.

Besides that, I had all the time in the world.

As I left the bodega, I turned in the direction of T.J.Maxx. I needed to buy some new underwear.

And I was paying for it in cash.

CHAPTER 55

FYI, A PERSON can find a room in Manhattan for eighty bucks a night. Cash accepted, no credit card required.

It was a building off Malcolm X Boulevard, just a brisk walk from the BoHo. I got the lead from Booking.com. When I arrived in my wrinkled pink dress, carrying a bag from Duane Reade inside my T.J.Maxx sack, the check-in host didn't give me a second glance. Just took my money and handed me a key.

My expectations of the accommodation weren't high. When I unlocked the door and stepped inside, I had a happy surprise. The space I'd rented wasn't a hotel room, it was a studio apartment. And it was considerably nicer than my place.

I dug supplies from my shopping bag and headed directly for the bathroom. After I brushed my teeth and showered, I felt human again. Dressed in new underwear and a Fruit of the Loom men's T-shirt, I flopped down on the bed with a Pringles can and a plastic bottle of Diet Coke. I'd done my grocery shopping at Duane Reade, too.

I shot off a couple of texts to Steven, but he didn't answer. I wasn't worried. When he was working, he didn't keep his phone at hand. I thought about texting my brother, to repeat the warning I'd passed along the day before. After the fate Bill had suffered, it was imperative that Leo steer clear from Bill's associates in the support group.

I started tapping out the text, explaining how serious the circumstances had become. I was almost done when it occurred to me. Mom had instructed me to avoid contact. If I couldn't get in touch with her, the prohibition would also apply to Leo. I didn't want to pull my brother into my current shitstorm.

So I couldn't communicate with anyone I knew other than Steven, and he was out of pocket. I plugged my phone into a charger I'd picked up on my shopping spree and pulled up the headlines. When I didn't see any updates on Rod, it was a relief. If they'd apprehended him, it would make headlines.

But the story on Bill had the lead. They'd just released his identity to the media, and the headline jumped out, assaulting me. "ADA Loses His Head on Subway!"

The headline was such callous clickbait that it infuriated me. Did they think they were being witty? Making a play on words when they were reporting my friend's tragic death? My chest started heaving. "Assholes. Insensitive assholes."

I threw the phone across the room. When it landed on the wooden floor, the phone case and screen protector fell off and slid under a dresser.

I lay on the bed, overcome with grief. The image of Bill returned to me, his head rolling on the pavement. When I shut my eyes, the picture reemerged. I began to struggle for air, couldn't catch my breath. The weight on my chest felt like I'd been buried alive.

When my sobbing commenced, it was physically painful. Noises wrenched from my throat involuntarily, cries I couldn't control. Tears came, snot rolled over my lips and down my chin. The horrific death of my friend played out in my mind, over and over again.

I cried until I was exhausted, and the tears had given out. I rose from the bed, blew my nose on toilet paper and splashed water on my face.

And then I returned to the bed and flopped down onto the mattress. Though it was early afternoon, I fell into a heavy sleep.

CHAPTER 56

I WOKE UP in the rented room feeling better, refreshed, and more composed. Snatching up the phone, I checked the time. I should've set an alarm. I was running late.

Steven had sent two texts with the same message: RU coming over?

I answered, briefly stating that I was on my way. I hastily removed the T-shirt and pulled a new garment from the bag, a loose mini dress in a yellow floral print. It had flutter sleeves and a ruffle at the neck. I hadn't worn a frock of that kind since pre-K, and maybe not then, who knows? That's why I'd chosen it. No one hunting for the real Kate Stone would take a second look at the woman in the short, ruffled yellow dress.

On the sidewalk, I didn't break into a run because that might attract undue attention. I strolled the blocks to the BoHo, trying to affect a breezy attitude, to carry off a yellow dress. If I hadn't been so wound up, it would've been fun, like I was filming a TV ad for feminine hygiene products. I could imagine running down the stairs of a stoop and twirling around in the loose dress, saying, "I feel so fresh!"

The vision of my commercial television debut made me smirk as I crossed the intersection and stepped onto the block where the BoHo was located. The expression faded when I saw a man near the entrance: the panhandler I'd encountered before. He had his foam cup in hand, was holding it out to passersby, making a request for loose change. My step faltered as I approached. Though I wasn't cash poor, I'd left my wad of bills in the rented room, tucked inside the Pringles can.

And I didn't want to interact with him. The last time I'd encountered the guy, he made me uncomfortable.

He extended the cup to everyone who passed. But I was determined to ignore him. When I neared the BoHo, I didn't slacken my pace, because I had no intention of pausing to hear his pitch.

I need not have bothered. When I came within earshot, he rattled the cup, opened his mouth to solicit me. But when we exchanged a glance, his eyes widened in alarm.

The man backed off, cutting short his request for money. Before I reached him, he turned his back to me, ducked his head and made a hasty departure. As he hurried down the street away from me, I saw the hand he tucked behind his back.

He was making the sign of the horns. As if my presence constituted a threat he needed to ward off.

After the events of the past twenty-four hours, the man's reaction struck an uneasy chord. But I pulled myself together, shook it off. I refused to be affected by the random action of a man I didn't even know. As superstition whispered in my ear, I suppressed the voices. I wouldn't give into those childish tendencies.

When I walked inside the BoHo, I expected to see Rueben manning the desk. When he was nowhere to be found, I paused to take a look around. The lobby was surprisingly empty. No residents rested in the rickety chairs under the windows, passing time and shooting the breeze. The typical buzz of voices was missing. The lobby was eerily quiet.

I brushed it off. I'd spent little time inside the place, had no knowledge of their schedule. Maybe the residents had activities that occupied them in the afternoon. Job training, or therapy, or classes, offered in a different setting.

I headed to the elevator, grateful that it was in far better service than the one in my apartment building. Steven had told me that it functioned reliably, though the BoHo was older than my place. The elevator opened up immediately. I took it to the top, the twelfth floor.

I knew that the top floor was reserved for staff. Both Steven and Rueben lived up there, so they could be on call 24/7. When I stepped out of the elevator, I looked around. I'd been there just the night before when Steven let me stay with him. Funny how different it looked in the daytime. Most of the rooms had the doors propped open. Walking down the hall, I peeked inside them. They were unoccupied—abandoned, undergoing renovation, from the look of it. I saw black mold growing up the wall of one room. That was the likely reason for the ladders and tools I saw in those old hotel rooms. Black mold renders a space uninhabitable.

Steven's room was in the middle of the hallway. I walked

up to the door. As I lifted my hand to knock, I heard voices inside. Devon must have already arrived. It made sense that he'd be there ahead of me, since I was late.

I rapped on the door. The conversation inside the room halted. Steven called out. "Yeah? Who's there?"

I stepped right up to the old paneled door and spoke into the crack. "It's me, Steven."

He pulled the door open. Looking inside, I could see Devon, sitting at an old metal desk where Steven kept his computer.

Steven was blocking the entrance, as if he didn't want me to come in. Perplexed, I studied his face. He looked like he was distraught, miserable.

Something was obviously wrong. I put a hand to his cheek. "Are you all right, Steven?"

He nodded, without speaking. And he stepped aside to permit me to enter the room.

I walked in, looked around. The bed was unmade, and his medical supplies were spread across the sheets, as if he hadn't had a chance to reorganize them after the clinic.

Devon sat with his back to me, tapping furiously on the keyboard. I said, "Devon, what are you working on?"

He didn't respond.

There was definitely a weird vibe in the room, one that set my senses on alert. My gut was telling me to turn and run.

Just as I was ready to bolt, Steven pulled me into an embrace, bent his head down and kissed my cheek. His face was wet.

I leaned back. "Are you crying?"

He was. I could see the tears well up in his eyes. I wanted

to ask him what was wrong, to offer the kind of comfort and support he'd provided to me before.

He pulled me to him with his left arm and held me in a tight grip. I realized with a shock that he was pulling up the back of my dress. I registered one thought: *What the hell?*

I felt a sensation in my hip, like a beesting.

CHAPTER **57**

VOICES IN THE room gradually roused me. I tried to ignore them. I just wanted to sleep. But my position was uncomfortable. My head was hanging down, my chin almost resting on my chest. And my shoulders were tight. When I tried to flex them, my arms wouldn't move.

I struggled to recall where I was, what was happening, but a fog in my head prevented any clarity of thought.

Someone pulled on my wrist, jiggling it. "Is she secure? Do you think you have her restrained?"

It was Devon's voice. I heard Steven answer. "She's tied to the chair. What else am I supposed to do? I'm not a guerrilla soldier, for God's sake. I'm a doctor."

I was sitting in a chair, a hard wooden seat. My brain struggled to piece it together. Last thing I remembered, Steve had held me in an embrace. There was a sting.

I cracked my eyes open. My hair hung down over my face. I wanted to push it away from my eyes, but my arms didn't work.

The terror that seized me lifted the grogginess. I raised my head, shook it in an attempt to clear it. Huddled in the chair, I struggled in a fruitless attempt to move my arms and legs. My ankles were tied to the legs of the chair; my wrists were bound behind me, to spindles.

As I realized I was held captive, I fought the restraints, jerking against them. He'd used nylon zip ties. I couldn't break the bonds.

Writhing in the chair got their attention. Through the curtain of hair, I saw Steven watching with a mournful expression. I wanted to confront him, to demand what the fuck was going on. The only sound I made was a gurgle.

They'd gagged me. My mouth was covered with a strip of duct tape.

Steven's hand swiped over his face. "I can't stand this. I've got to get out."

He stepped over to the door. Devon followed. He said, "You better stick around until Gatsby gets here."

When the words registered in my head, a wave of fury almost made me black out again. As my vision began to clear, I tried to scream at Steven, to fling curses at my traitorous lover. He must have caught the gist of my garbled speech, because he offered up a bizarre defense for his deceit.

"Kate, I swear, this is breaking my heart. But Gatsby made it a catch twenty-two, he didn't give me any other way out. If I want to get my medical license back, I have to go along."

His medical license? How did I fit into the bizarre puzzle? I made more strangled sounds.

"Only one person has the power to make it happen. I like you, Kate, really. But I can help thousands of people with my license to practice. It wouldn't be right to choose one person's welfare over the common good."

None of it made any sense. The only thing I understood with any clarity was the bitter realization that my mother was right about that asshole. And that made me even angrier. I felt bile rise up in my throat; the vomit choked me. I commenced gagging behind the duct tape.

Devon watched me with a look of alarm. "Is she choking? Or is she faking it?"

Steven stepped up and ripped the tape off my face. I leaned forward as far as I could and heaved the bitter bile on the floor.

With a note of concern in his voice, Steven said, "Are you okay?"

Really? I tried to spit in his face but the phlegm landed on his shirt.

He slapped the tape back on my face. As he jerked the soiled shirt over his head, Devon trailed behind him. He pleaded, "Don't leave me alone with her, man. She's a crazy bitch, no telling what she'll do."

Steven pulled on a fresh shirt and headed out without a backward look. The door clicked shut.

So. That romance was over.

A sense of betrayal swept over me like a toxic wave. My chest felt like it might explode and my head was heavy, like it had been filled with lead. I bowed it, and concentrated on taking deep breaths.

From my peripheral vision, I saw Devon crack the door open and peer out into the hallway. He shut it again and turned the lock. For a few minutes, he nervously paced the floor of the small room. Then he walked to the desk and leaned over to check the computer. He stood, toying with the mouse, his attention on the screen.

I flexed my arms again, shifted my weight in the seat. I couldn't break the zip ties, it was senseless to try. They'd tied me to an old wooden kitchen chair. The spindles were strong, probably made of oak, not some recent plywood construction, but they had loosened with years of use. I used my weight to rock against the back of the chair, trying to figure how much force it would take to crack it. As I put pressure on the spindle that secured my left wrist, I felt it wiggle. A shot of energy zapped me, and I increased the pressure, ignoring the pain as the hard nylon ties cut into my skin. If I could break away from the chair, I had a shot. There was no way Devon could beat me in a fair fight.

The doorknob jiggled, but didn't open. Someone rapped softly on the door.

My breath caught. Had Steven returned? Maybe he'd had a change of heart. Or was it actually the mythical Gatsby?

A moment of suspended anticipation set my heart pounding as Devon went to the door. He paused in front of it and whispered. "Who's there?"

"It's me."

Devon breathed out in relief as he flipped the lock and pulled the door open.

When I saw Gatsby at last, I wasn't shocked, exactly. Just really, really pissed.

Rubenstein.

CHAPTER 58

MY VISION WAVERED at the sight of Rubenstein, standing before me in one of his beautifully tailored business suits. I squeezed my eyes shut and breathed in through my nose as I struggled to hang on to my wits.

He walked over to the window and tried the latch. It was a casement window with a metal frame, which opened outward onto the air shaft that rose from the interior courtyard of the old hotel building. Steven and I had stood together in front of the window that morning, when he'd opened it after I'd mentioned the room was stuffy. I had glanced down the twelve-story drop to the square of pavement before stepping back. I don't linger by open windows.

Rubenstein turned away from the window and addressed Devon. "Where's Steven?"

Devon lifted his shoulders in a shrug. "He took off."

A look of irritation crossed Rubenstein's face. "Predictable. Well, I guess he did his part. Got Kate up here and administered the sedative."

The reminder of his betrayal made me throw my head back and holler. When I roared, the duct tape shifted; my stomach bile had loosened the adhesive. I popped my jaw as hard as I could, opening my mouth wide. The tape pulled away from my upper lip.

I let out a scream, as long and loud as I could make it. When the sound ran out, I took a quick breath and cried, "Help me!"

Rubenstein said something to Devon, who scrambled over to the desk to cut off a fresh strip of tape. I twisted my head when he tried to silence me again. Rubenstein had to intervene. He grabbed my hair and held my head, so I couldn't move.

With the tape back in place, Rubenstein walked back in front of the chair and studied me as my chest heaved. His tone was solemn when he said, "No one is going to run up here to save you, Kate, no matter how much you scream. This is a shelter where a fair portion of the occupants suffer mental illness. *Untreated* mental illness. People scream all the time, no one pays much attention."

With a sinking feeling in my gut, I realized he was right. In the night, I'd heard cries from some of the residents. Steven had shrugged it off, and told me that it was a fact of life at the BoHo.

"Kate," Rubenstein said. I looked up, met his eye. He gave me a wry smile. "I need some information from you. If we remove that tape, will you refrain from screaming?" When I didn't give him a nod, he said, "You understand that I can utilize tactics to force compliance. Strong-arm tactics, which I'm not really comfortable with. Like breaking your fingers."

The suggestion made me clench my hands into fists. I

decided that screaming was futile. I needed to conserve my strength, to put it to better use.

I nodded my head, maintaining eye contact.

"Good, glad to see that." To Devon, he said, "Pull it off. Do it carefully, don't pull the skin."

That surprised me, until it struck me that he might not want me to bear the marks of a kidnap victim. He wasn't being considerate.

When Devon removed it, I fought the urge to sink my teeth into his hand.

With the tape removed, Devon stepped quickly away. Rubenstein leaned against the door, almost as if he intended to prevent escape. Possibly Devon's, I wondered.

"I'm curious. Who have you told about the group, about your band of justice fighters?"

I honestly didn't understand the question. "You mean the original group? The nine of us?"

"Yes. Who knows?"

"I told the police."

He blinked. Maybe it was a tell, I couldn't say. "When?"

"When I was in the hospital. After Edger pushed me onto the tracks and Whitney came to my hospital room."

He nodded, looking satisfied. Did he think I'd revealed something else? I wished I knew.

"Where's your roommate?"

I should've seen that coming. Frantic, I tried to remember what I'd let slip the night before.

I tried to dodge the question. "What roommate? You mean Steven? We've been staying together."

"Don't be coy, Kate. I'm talking about Millie. We sent

someone to your apartment. It appears she had absconded. Where did Rod and Millie go?"

I could hear Mom's voice in my head: *You don't know anything.* "I don't have any idea. Have you looked in Rod's apartment?"

He huffed an impatient breath. "Steven tells me you went to the bank to empty out Victor Odom's safe-deposit box. What was inside?"

My head buzzed with indecision. Should I tell him it was empty? If he knew about the money, would he go after my mother?

He must have read my face. "You're a bad liar, Kate. Did he leave anything incriminating?"

I blurted out, "Just money. Cash."

His brow furrowed. "Nothing in writing? No envelope, 'To Whom It May Concern'?"

I shook my head, kept my eyes on his. "Nothing like that. Just packets of bills. A lot of money."

From the corner, Devon said, "How much?"

"Probably a million."

Rubenstein shot him a quelling look. Devon shriveled under the scrutiny.

Rubenstein continued. "About the cryptocurrency, Zagcoin and Tempcoin. Who have you talked to?"

"I confided in Bill about it."

"Of course you did. Bill's knowledge of the scam got him killed."

Those words sent a wrench of pain through me. It was hard to recover. Impatiently, Rubenstein prompted me, saying, "Aside from Bill?"

I took a deep breath. "Just the four of us, that's all. When we planned the meeting at Hudson Yards, I never got the chance to share the stuff Devon said he found on the phone." The irony almost made me snarl as I added, "I had planned to tell you, Frank."

The ghost of a smile flickered again. "Your obsession with Ian Templeton's financial success has become problematic."

"Right," I said. That confirmed it. "Because you're working for him. You're on his payroll."

Studying me, he shook his head. "I'm sorry it had to come to this, Kate. But it's entirely your own fault. I felt responsible for you, so I decided to take you into the fold."

He was speaking in riddles, but I kept my mouth shut. As long as he kept talking, I might have an opening.

"I took you into my office because I thought you had promise. When I realized that you were too temperamental, I incorporated you into my group of specialists. You fouled that nest, essentially destroyed it."

While he talked, I assessed the room. It was a spartan living space, almost bare, offering little in the way of a makeshift weapon. It was furnished with a bed, one dresser, the computer table, and the chair I sat on. No way out, aside from the door he blocked and the window that led to a twelve-floor drop.

And I was pretty sure Rubenstein was armed. I recognized the outline of a shoulder holster under his jacket, like the one my dad used to wear when he carried a gun in plainclothes.

"When you survived the subway, I was impressed, actually, by your persistence. So I decided to give you one last chance. I thought I'd personally oversee your development, put you on the committee with some other special cases. But you just can't stop. You're too thick-headed. You ignored every warning I sent. The ride from LaGuardia was supposed to be a minor incident, like the welcome gift in your bed."

I couldn't keep my mouth shut. "Don't pretend Templeton wasn't involved with the LaGuardia guy. It was Templeton's car that picked me up."

He sighed. "God, Kate—your obsession with Ian makes you unhinged. Even now, in this situation, you can't stop yourself. Ian is just a financial resource, one of many. He's a backer, a donor. We have to protect the people who support us. He wants to be left alone, but you keep on attacking him."

Devon volunteered, "Now she wants to ruin his cryptocurrency offering. She wouldn't back off."

Rubenstein didn't acknowledge Devon's comment. He opened his jacket and said, "I need you gone before I announce my candidacy."

He pulled out a semiautomatic pistol. My attention was so focused on the gun that I almost missed his next statement.

"You're as much trouble as your old man."

CHAPTER 59

THE MENTION OF my father made my throat close up. I wanted to tell him to shut up, that he wasn't worthy of speaking about my father. But for the moment, I was struck dumb.

He held the gun in his right hand. I stared at it—a Glock 19 semiautomatic, just like my dad used to carry.

Rubenstein said, "You remind me of him, it's in the eyes. He was a state's witness in the first case I ever tried, at about your age. He wouldn't fudge on anything. Straight arrow."

Tears stung my eyes. I blinked them back, didn't want Rubenstein to know I was affected by his words.

"Most honest cop I ever ran across, truly. That was his flaw. You just can't be that inflexible, unmovable. It's what led him to jump out the window."

My response was automatic, like a reflex. "He didn't jump. He was murdered."

He looked away, shaking his head ruefully. "That's where you're wrong. He jumped. It was his own choice."

My voice was gravelly when I said, "No."

Thoughtfully, he rubbed a knuckle across his chin. "You're young, immature, inexperienced. It takes time to develop an understanding of what motivates people. Your boyfriend Steven, for example. He wants to be restored to the status he worked hard to attain, rising up from the class he was born into. Your friend Devon? He's mostly into money. Isn't that right, Devon?"

Devon was hunched in a corner. He looked edgy. "How long are we going to be here?"

Rubenstein ignored the question. "Whitney actually likes to create chaos. I'm no doctor, but I think she'd make a colorful diagnosis. She lured your friend onto the tracks last night. How many people could pull that off?"

Bill. My head dropped. I couldn't stand the sight of Rubenstein; if my hands were free, I would have covered my ears to block out the sound of his voice.

"But with your father, the weakness was his kids. Victor and I gave him an option. He could jump, or we'd kill his daughter and son."

I grimaced, squeezing my eyes so tightly shut that it made my head hurt.

I said, "Victor worked for you. You used the DA's office to make money. Extortion, I'd bet. Blackmail."

"Nothing that primitive. Not any longer. There's a global financial network. It has to be protected. It's what makes the world go round. Your father caught on. He refused to be reasonable."

I lifted my head as the realization hit. "You're supported by it. All those big money interests. So you use the office to protect them when they break the law. Your white-collar division and the cybercrimes unit."

"Your friend Bill didn't have the stomach for it. He might have come around, but you just couldn't leave him alone. But his death wasn't in vain. We intended it as a message to you and anyone you had sucked into your enterprise."

He squatted on his haunches right in front of the chair, so he was directly at eye level.

"If I let you continue, how many people will have to die? So that you can carry that pious torch of yours?"

The gun was still aimed at me. With his free hand, he pulled his cell phone from his pocket and handed it to Devon. "Make the call."

Devon said, "Want me to FaceTime?"

"Yeah! Let's see who's at the party."

Devon tapped the screen. He only had to wait for a second before I heard a voice. "Hi."

"Hi, Whitney," Devon said. "I'm here with Gatsby."

He handed the phone back to Rubenstein. Rubenstein smiled at the screen. "There you are! I'm going to mute the phone, Whitney. But I want to see your friend."

He walked behind my chair, held the phone out, and reversed the camera so that our faces weren't shown.

I saw Whitney on the screen, standing shoulder to shoulder with my brother. Leo smiled into the phone, held his hand up in a wave. Then Whitney reversed her camera, swept it to make a panoramic video.

They were standing outside the entrance of the BoHo.

I struggled to escape the chair as I screamed, "Leo! Get away—now!"

Rubenstein smacked the side of my head. It made me see stars.

"You promised not to scream."

He ended the call and slipped the phone back into his pocket. "Devon, send her a text. Tell her they should wait in the lobby for further instructions."

My body was shaking, my heart pounding. Rubenstein looked at my trembling knees. "What should I report to Whitney? Will she need to take him into an alley? Because you can guess how that will go down. Or will you make the jump that saves your brother's life? Like your father did."

Panic overwhelmed me. It kept my brain from functioning properly, I couldn't think.

Rubenstein said, "There's a symmetry to this, isn't there? Your father jumped, and you'll follow in his steps. That holds a certain appeal, doesn't it? You always purported to admire him, to want to be like him. There's a rightness to it, a balance."

Desperate ideas bounced in my brain. I could plead for mercy, make a vow of silence, promise to leave the city. The words died without being spoken. I couldn't negotiate with a man who lacked all moral integrity. He couldn't be trusted.

I had to get out of that chair. It was my only chance.

When I spoke, I chose two words.

"I'll jump."

He looked surprised. A shade of disappointment crossed his face, as if he'd wanted to prolong the drama.

"Okay. Good. Devon, cut her loose."

Rubenstein backed away from me, grasping the pistol with both hands.

Devon advanced gingerly, as if approaching a mad dog. He

stepped behind the chair and cut the zip ties that bound my hands. My joints ached as I shook my arms and rubbed my wrists. The nylon ties had cut into my skin. I wiped the blood onto my yellow dress.

After he snipped the restraints that bound me to the legs of the chair, Devon scurried away, out of my reach.

Still seated, I stretched out my legs and massaged my thigh muscles. After the confinement, it felt like needles and pins were jabbing me. I needed my limbs in working order.

"How do I know you'll leave Leo alone? What's the guarantee?"

"You're living proof. Right? I left you alone for three years after your father made his sacrifice. If you hadn't made trouble for Templeton, you wouldn't be here now."

I thought of Victor and Rubenstein in my dad's apartment, sending him out the window to land headfirst on the sidewalk.

The rage had started to boil. I could feel it churning, charging my energy. I tried to school my features, wear a poker face, so that I wouldn't give myself away.

Maybe he sensed the change. He broadened his feet in a shooter's stance, holding the gun out with both hands. He placed his finger on the trigger. Devon cowered in the corner, beside the desk.

I said, "Too bad for you that Victor's dead."

He frowned. He didn't get it.

I said, "The odds are different this time."

And then I sprang, grabbing the wooden chair and flinging it at him. He fired as the chair hit him; the shot went wild. As he recovered and tried to take aim again, I lunged, seizing his right wrist and twisting his arm to the side. When he fired again, I grabbed the gun with both hands, and twisted it down and to the right. Rubenstein screamed as it broke the finger he'd held on the trigger.

When I jerked the gun away from his broken finger, it slipped from my bloody hands and slid across the floor.

While we fought, Devon had jumped across the bed and was trying to flee. I saw him fighting to flip the lock that secured the door.

Rubenstein and I both dove to the floor to get the gun. He was taller, had barely reached it and was fumbling to get his hand around the grip. I got an arm around his neck, managed to pull him back. When he shook me off, he got on his knees to lunge for it again. I bent my arm, twisted my torso and swung back, hitting him with an elbow strike to the eye socket. When my blow connected, I heard the bone crunch.

He howled, clutching his face. I scrambled for the gun. When I had it in hand, I jumped to my feet and backed away, keeping my focus on Rubenstein as he wailed.

Devon was out the door. He had run for the stairway. I heard the echo of his footsteps as he descended the stairs. He had twelve flights to run down. The clock was ticking, I had to act before he reached the lobby.

Taking aim, I watched as Rubenstein looked up at me with his one good eye. He tried to drag himself to the open door.

I straddled him and put the muzzle of the gun to the back of his head as I fumbled in his pocket for the phone. When I had it in hand, I pulled up the last phone contact. I sent a text.

Let him go

Got a quick reply.

OK

I tossed the phone across the room and stepped over to the door. No noise out in the hallway. No sirens, nothing. I flipped the lock, shutting us inside.

Rubenstein got onto his hands and knees. "What do you want?"

He pulled to a stand, covering his eye with one hand. I checked the safety on the Glock, moving closer and backing him up to the window. He glanced over his shoulder and started shaking his head.

"Your choice," I said.

I backed him all the way to the windowsill. He glanced out, looked down. When he turned back to me, he spoke in a trembling voice. "You won't escape liability for this. I'm a public figure, you'll be indicted for murder. You can't get away from it."

"You did."

He started babbling. "I'll give you whatever you want. Tell my people you're untouchable. There's so much money, so many directions to go, you can have anything you dream of. Want to be DA of one of the boroughs? My people can make that happen, put the machinery in place. You want to be a judge someday? You'd like that, wouldn't you? Tell me what you want. It's yours."

The thing about having an anger management problem: It's really tough to control. My rage had taken over. There was only one outcome I desired.

"I want you to die just like my dad did."

He was unsteady on his feet, rocking back and forth. And the blow I'd struck probably interfered with his vision. With the gun in my hand, I had all the power in the situation. I could shoot him, right where he stood. Or back him all the way out that window.

With a pang of regret, I realized I couldn't do it. Too much law and order was still in my blood. I needed to call 911. Do it the right way, like my father would have wanted.

I took one hand off the gun to reach for the phone. Maybe my expression changed. Maybe he read the hesitation in my face and thought I was weak.

Because he lunged for the gun, trying to take it from my hand.

I'd been kickboxing for years. All that training had prepared me for that ultimate strike. I felt the power surge as my foot left the floor.

It only took one well-placed kick to send him out that window.

He screamed on the way down. It was a noise that seemed to cut through the air for a long time, though in reality, the sound only lasted seconds. I tensed before I heard the thud as Rubenstein landed on the pavement twelve floors down.

I stepped up to the window and peered out to take a look. I had to be certain that it was over.

It was done.

He landed headfirst. Just like Dad.

CHAPTER 60

WHEN I LEFT the grand jury room following my testimony, my mother was waiting for me in the hallway. As the door shut behind me, she rose and linked her arm through mine.

Mom spoke in a hushed voice as she propelled me toward the elevator. "How did it go?"

"It was fine. Good, in fact. Everything went down pretty much as you predicted."

Over the past months, I'd learned the value of an effective defense attorney, through personal experience. Since the day Rubenstein landed at the bottom of the air shaft in the Bohemian Hotel, my mother had my back.

After I'd run away from the BoHo, she was my first contact. It was Mom who communicated with the police, who demanded that they preserve and test the evidence from the scene that supported my story. Thank God for DNA testing. It confirmed that my blood was on the zip ties, my spit and bile was on the duct tape. They even found my DNA in the sink in Steven's room, where I'd brushed my teeth, and my hair in his bed.

The police found that the gun was registered to Rubenstein. It bore both our prints—also consistent with my version of the events. And his cell phone demonstrated the threat to my brother, and provided contacts to Whitney, Devon, Steven, and Nick, the elusive LaGuardia driver.

So though they initially viewed me as a suspect rather than a victim, the evidence supported my veracity. And my mother kept the pressure on, insisting that they hunt down the perpetrators.

When they apprehended Whitney and Nick, they refused to answer any questions—no surprise there.

But Devon cut a deal, and he sang like a bird. That's when things really started to turn around. He told them he'd been coerced into working underground with a few handpicked attorneys in the white-collar and cybercrime divisions of the DA's office, to shield Templeton and others from liability for their wrongdoing. Devon's testimony was so explosive, the feds had placed Devon in the witness protection program.

By contrast, Steven was languishing in Rikers. By the time he tried to cut a deal, he was late to the party. Sometimes, I would recall tender moments we'd shared. Then I'd get mad all over again.

Ian Templeton had been hauled out of Rikers in a body bag. Just forty-eight hours after he was taken into custody, he was found hanging from a bedsheet in his cell. We'd heard that his attorneys were demanding an investigation into his death. No one believed that Templeton would actually hang himself in jail.

Mom and I got off the elevator and walked through the lobby. She still held tightly to my arm. "More indictments should be coming down soon. When it happens, the press will realize you're a star witness. If anyone contacts you, refer them to me."

"Right."

"I'm serious." She turned to me with a severe look. "Don't get a big head and decide you want your fifteen minutes of fame. I'm your mouthpiece. Got it?"

"Got it," I said—and it was no lie. My mother had handled the matter like an Amazon warrior from the very start. Now that I'd seen advocacy from the client's side, I had come to understand why she was so successful. She was worth every penny she charged.

It was an eye-opening experience. I decided that I had a lot to learn, as a defense attorney. And she could teach me what I needed to know.

As we left the courthouse and walked together to her car, she said, "Leo gets his results today. I'm nervous as a cat. First, the grand jury testimony. Now, I'm counting down to the bar results."

"He's going to make it this time, Mom. Guaranteed."

My confidence was sincere. I'd prepped Leo for the bar for weeks before the test. We took it together, and the practice paid off. He didn't exhibit any panic, didn't pull a blank on the information we'd toiled over. I honestly believed that the New Jersey Bar Association would soon count two more family members among its ranks.

Mom gave me a lift to my apartment. As we drove through the city, we passed through Dad's old precinct. A neglected playground was occupied by a handful of kids swinging on the battered equipment. The sight of it stirred a recollection.

"Leo and I used to hang out there when we were kids, remember?"

She glanced over at the property. "I do."

I sighed. "I don't recall it looking so dingy. Seems like we had a lot of fun there."

She adjusted her sunglasses and trained her eyes on the road. "It's going to get some improvements. Soon."

I twisted in my seat to take another look. "Really? How do you know?"

There was a moment of silence before she answered. "Because I'm donating a chunk of Victor's money, designating it for the improvement of the playground. The purchase of new equipment."

I gaped at her. She looked at me and said, "What?"

"Mom. That's great."

"Oh, hush. What did you think I'd do with the money? Stuff it in a mattress?" After a pause, she said, "It's a good tax deduction."

I didn't say anything. But I found myself grinning as we drove uptown.

When she pulled up to the curb by my building, she said, "Why don't you come home tonight? I'll wait while you change. We'll have dinner at the house, wait for the results with your brother."

"No—can't come right now. I'm meeting someone. Maybe later."

She wheeled around and pinned me with a suspicious glare.

"Please. Don't tell me you're seeing that young man," she said.

I had my eye on the street, keeping a lookout. When I saw him turn the corner and head our way, I rolled down the window to wave.

My mother groaned. "A cop? After all you've been through, everything I've tried to tell you. And you're dating a damned cop?"

Adam Jankovich strutted down the sidewalk toward us, looking like sex on a stick. He wore the blue NYPD uniform.

"Best looking thing in pants."

I wasn't aware I'd said it aloud until my mother snorted. "Kate, you've got a lot to learn."

That was undoubtedly true. But I intended to enjoy myself along the way. I started down the sidewalk, meeting him halfway.

"Everything go okay in court?" he said.

"Yeah. I'm in the mood to celebrate."

I turned to give my mother a parting wave, calling out, "See you later!"

I wasn't sure how much later. It was hard to predict. I might want to pull the Murphy bed down.

As we walked into the building, Adam said, "Are you starting to feel like things are back to normal? Like you can walk down the street without looking over your shoulder?"

That was hard to answer. When all of the grand jury indictments were finally handed down, it would create a furor—in the DA's office, financial circles, and law enforcement. But New York was a big place. I could handle a handful of enemies. My mother said that an attorney who didn't generate a fair amount of ill will wasn't doing her job. Adversaries were part of the profession. And she would know.

So I said, "I keep my eyes open. But I always have. My old man taught me that, long ago."

I stopped in the lobby to check my mail. When I turned the key and opened the mail slot, there was a single item inside. I pulled it out and studied it. It was a picture postcard. The front of the card was printed with large letters that read "Greetings from the Lake of the Ozarks!"

I turned it over. The back bore no message, just two smiley faces and the letters "BFF."

It was stamped with a postmark from Osage Beach, Missouri.

Adam was looking over my shoulder. "Who do you know in Missouri?" he asked.

I tucked the card in my bag. "Nobody. Somebody sent it as a joke."

A person is entitled to her secrets. Especially when she's romancing a cop.

I didn't learn that lesson from my dad.

I learned it from my mother.

ACKNOWLEDGMENTS

Bringing *Payback* to the page was great fun, and some people provided excellent assistance along the way. Many thanks to the team at Assemble Media, including Jack Heller, Caitlin de Lisser-Ellen, Madison Wolk, and Steven Salpeter. I'm grateful to my agent, Jill Marr of the Sandra Dijkstra Literary Agency, for her friendship and support. I owe a huge debt of thanks to Alex Logan, my editor at Grand Central Publishing, for the inspiration, motivation, and guidance she provided through each draft of the manuscript.

This book opens with a dedication to my marvelous husband and closes with his name in the acknowledgments. Randy Allen, thanks for everything! I couldn't have done it without you!

ABOUT THE AUTHOR

Bestselling author Nancy Allen practiced law for fifteen years as Assistant Missouri Attorney General and Assistant Prosecutor in her native Ozarks, trying over thirty jury cases. She served on the faculty of Missouri State University for fifteen years, teaching law classes. She is the author of the Ozarks Mystery series. With James Patterson, Nancy is coauthor of *New York Times* Bestseller *Juror #3* (2018) and *The Jailhouse Lawyer* (2021). *Payback* is the second book in her *Anonymous Justice* series.